THRAWN
ASCENDANCY
CHAOS RISING

STAR WARS

THRAWN
ASCENDANCY
CHAOS RISING

TIMOTHY ZAHN

3 5 7 9 10 8 6 4 2

Del Rey
20 Vauxhall Bridge Road
London SW1V 2SA

Del Rey is part of the Penguin Random House group of companies
whose addresses can be found at global.penguinrandomhouse.com.

First published in Great Britain by Del Rey in 2020

www.penguin.co.uk

A CIP catalogue record for this book is available from the British Library.

Hardback ISBN 9781529124583
Trade Paperback ISBN 9781529124590

Book design by Elizabeth A. D. Eno

Printed and bound in Great Britain by Clays Ltd, Eclograf S.p.A.

Penguin Random House is committed to a sustainable
future for our business, our readers and our planet. This book
is made from Forest Stewardship Council® certified paper.

For all those who stand on the edge of chaos

THE DEL REY

STAR WARS™

TIMELINE

DOOKU: JEDI LOST
MASTER & APPRENTICE

I THE PHANTOM MENACE

II ATTACK OF THE CLONES
THE CLONE WARS (TV SERIES)
DARK DISCIPLE

III REVENGE OF THE SITH
CATALYST: A ROGUE ONE NOVEL
LORDS OF THE SITH
TARKIN

SOLO
THRAWN
A NEW DAWN
THRAWN: ALLIANCES
THRAWN: TREASON
REBELS (TV SERIES)

ROGUE ONE

THE DEL REY

STAR WARS

TIMELINE

DRAMATIS PERSONAE

THRAWN | Mitth'raw'nuruodo—Mitth family merit adoptive

ZIARA | Irizi'ar'alani—Irizi family blood

THALIAS | Mitth'ali'astov—Mitth family merit adoptive

THURFIAN | Mitth'urf'ianico—Mitth family syndic

SAMAKRO | Ufsa'mak'ro—Ufsa family merit adoptive

GENERAL BA'KIF

CHE'RI—sky-walker

QILORI OF UANDUALON—Pathfinder navigator (non-Chiss)

GENERAL YIV THE BENEVOLENT—Nikardun commander

THE CHISS ASCENDANCY

Nine Ruling Families

UFSA	PLIKH
IRIZI	BOADIL
DASKLO	MITTH
CLARR	OBBIC
CHAF	

Chiss Family Ranks

BLOOD	TRIAL-BORN
COUSIN	MERIT ADOPTIVE
RANKING DISTANT	

Political Hierarchy

PATRIARCH—head of family

SPEAKER—chief syndic of the family

SYNDIC—member of the Syndicure, main governmental body

PATRIEL—handles family affairs on a planetary scale

COUNCILOR—handles family affairs at the local level

ARISTOCRA—mid-level member of one of the Nine Ruling Families

A long time ago, *beyond* a galaxy far, far away. . . .

STAR WARS

THRAWN
ASCENDANCY
CHAOS RISING

For thousands of years it has been an island of calm within the Chaos. It is a center of power, a model of stability, and a beacon of integrity. The Nine Ruling Families guard it from within; the Expansionary Defense Fleet guards it from without. Its neighbors are left in peace, its enemies are left in ruin. It is light and culture and glory.

It is the Chiss Ascendancy.

PROLOGUE

The attack on the Chiss Ascendancy homeworld of Csilla was sudden, unexpected, and—despite its limited scope—impressively efficient.

The three large warships came out of hyperspace on widely spaced vectors, driving inward toward the planet with spectrum lasers blazing at full power toward the defense platforms and the orbiting Chiss Defense Force warships. The platforms and ships, caught by surprise, nevertheless took less than a minute to begin returning fire. By then the attackers had altered their directions, angling in toward the cluster of lights spread across the icy planetary surface that marked the capital city of Csaplar. Their lasers continued to fire, and as they came within range they added salvos of missiles to their attack.

But ultimately it was all for nothing. The defense platforms easily picked off the incoming missiles while the warships targeted the attacking ships themselves, blasting them into rubble and making sure that any fragments entering the atmosphere were too small to survive the journey. Within fifteen minutes of the attack force's arrival, it was over.

The threat had ended, Supreme General Ba'kif thought grimly as he strode down the central corridor toward the Cupola where the syndics and other Aristocra were assembling after making their way back from the shelters.

Now came the *real* sound and fury.

And there would be plenty of both. As the supreme ruling body of the Ascendancy, the Syndicure liked to project an image of thoughtfulness, nobility, and unflappable dignity. Most of the time, aside from the inevitable political wrangling, that was close enough to the truth.

But not today. The Syndicure had been in full session, and the Speakers had had their own private meeting scheduled for later in the afternoon, which meant nearly all of the Ascendancy's top-level Aristocra had been in the offices, corridors, and meeting rooms when the alarm sounded. The shelters deep beneath the Cupola were reasonably roomy and marginally comfortable, but it had been decades since the last direct attack on Csilla and Ba'kif doubted any of the current government officials had ever even been down there.

Two hours of forced idleness while the Defense Force waited to see if there would be a follow-up attack hadn't gone over well with them, and Ba'kif had no illusions that the coming storm would be thoughtful, noble, or unflappable.

He was right.

"What *I* want to know," the Speaker for the Ufsa family spoke up after Ba'kif had finished his report, "is who the aliens are who dared think they could get away with an attack against us. A name, General—we want a *name*."

"I'm afraid I can't give you one, Speaker," Ba'kif said.

"Why not?" the Speaker demanded. "You have debris, don't you? You have data records and bodies and weapons profiles. Surely a name can be gleaned from all that."

"The Ascendancy has been attacked," the Speaker for the Mitth family cut in gravely, as if the others might somehow have missed that fact. "We need to know who to punish for such arrogance."

"Yes," the Usfa said, throwing a brief glare down the table.

Ba'kif suppressed a sigh. In times gone by, major threats to the Ascendancy had usually drawn the Ruling Families into a unity that superseded the usual political maneuvering. He'd held a small hope that today's attack might spark such a response.

Clearly, that wasn't going to happen. In the case of the Usfa and Mitth, in particular, those families were in the midst of a particularly tangled campaign with a newly opened mining field on Thearterra as the prize, and the Usfa was clearly annoyed at having had some of his spotlight stolen by his family's current chief rival. "More than that," he added, his glare daring the Mitth to interrupt again, "we need assurance that the Defense Force has the resources to defend the Chiss against further action by these unidentified enemies."

The questis data-link reader lying on the table in front of Ba'kif lit up as a fresh report came in. He picked it up, propping it at an angle on his left palm while he slid his finger along the edge to scroll the screen. "The Syndicure need not be concerned about their safety," he said. "I've just received word that four additional warships from the Expansionary Fleet have been rushed in from Naporar and are moving to support the Defense Force ships already in place."

He winced to himself. Young men and women, ready to give their lives to protect their homeworld. Noble and honorable . . . and a sacrifice, if it was ever required, that he and everyone else currently in the Cupola knew would be a complete and utter waste.

Fortunately, it didn't look like any such sacrifice would be needed today.

"And if they attack other worlds within the Ascendancy?" the Usfa pressed.

"Other ships have already been sent to bolster the patrol forces of the neighboring systems in case they're the targets of subsequent attacks," Ba'kif said.

"Has anyone else reported attacks or enemy sightings?" the Speaker for the Clarr asked.

"Not as yet, Speaker," Ba'kif told him. "As far as we can tell, this was an isolated incident."

The Speaker for the Obbic family gave a theatrical little snort. "I seriously doubt that, General," she said. "No one sends warships against the Ascendancy on a lark and then goes home. Someone out there is plotting against us. That someone needs to be found and taught a serious lesson."

It went on that way for another hour, with each of the Nine Ruling Families—and many of the Great Families who had aspirations of joining that elite group—making sure to get their outrage and determination on record.

It was, for the most part, a waste of Ba'kif's time. Fortunately, extensive experience in the military had taught him how to listen to politicians with half his mind while focusing the other half on more urgent matters.

The Speakers and syndics wanted to know who had attacked the Ascendancy. They were looking in the wrong direction.

The more interesting question was not *who*, but *why*.

Because the Obbic had been right. No one attacked Csilla for the fun of it. That went double for an attack that cost three major warships without providing any obvious gain. Either the attacker had misjudged badly, or else he'd achieved a more subtle goal.

What could such a goal look like?

The majority of the Syndicure clearly assumed the attack had been a prelude to a more sustained campaign, and once they finished their posturing they would undoubtedly start urging the Defense Force to pull its ships inward for the protection of the major systems. More than that, they would probably insist the Expansionary Defense Fleet likewise withdraw from the borders to augment them.

Was that the goal? To keep the Chiss looking inward and not outward? In which case, bowing to the Syndicure's demand for security would play directly into the enemy's plans. On the other hand, if the syndics were right about this being the start of a full-fledged campaign, leaving the Espansionary Fleet out in the Chaos could be an equally fatal move. Either way, if they guessed wrong, it would be too late to correct the error by the time they knew the truth.

But as Ba'kif weighed the possibilities, it occurred to him that there was one other possibility. Perhaps the attack wasn't meant to draw the Ascendancy's attention from something that was about to happen, but to distract it from something that had *already* happened.

And *that* possibility, at least, he could look into right now. Surreptitiously, he keyed a search order into his questis.

Midway through the Cupola session, as he continued to make his soothing noises to the Aristocra, he had the answer.

Maybe.

One of Ba'kif's aides was waiting when the general finally made it back to his office. "Were you able to locate him?" Ba'kif asked.

"Yes, sir," the aide said. "He's on Naporar undergoing his final round of physical therapy for the injuries sustained during the Vagaari pirate operations."

Ba'kif scowled. Operations that, while successful in a military sense, had been a complete disaster on the political front. Months later, many of the Aristocra were still brooding over that whole mess. "When will he be free?"

"Whenever you wish, sir," the aide said. "He said he would be at your disposal whenever you wanted him."

"Good," Ba'kif said, checking the time. Half an hour to bring the *Whirlwind* to flight status, four hours to get to Naporar, another half hour to get a shuttle down to the Chiss Expansionary Fleet medcenter. "Inform him that I want him ready in five hours."

"Yes, sir." The aide hesitated. "Do you want the order logged, or does this qualify as a private trip?"

"Log it," Ba'kif said. The Aristocra might be unhappy when they found out about this—the Syndicure might even assemble a tribunal somewhere down the line to waste more of his time with useless questions—but Ba'kif was going to do things strictly by the book. "Order from Supreme General Ba'kif," he continued, hearing his voice drop into the tone he always used for formal orders and reports. "Preparing transport for myself and Senior Captain Mitth'raw'nuruodo. Destination: Dioya. Purpose: investigation of a derelict ship found two days ago in the outer system."

"Yes, sir," the aide said briskly. His voice was studiously neutral, giving away nothing of his own personal feelings on the matter. Not all those who thought poorly of Captain Thrawn, after all, were members of the Aristocra.

At the moment, Ba'kif didn't care about any of them. He'd found the first half of the *why*.

Now there was only one person he trusted to come up with the other half.

MEMORIES I

Of all the duties foisted on mid-ranking family members, Aristocra Mitth'urf'ianico thought sourly as he strode down the senior school hallway, recruitment was one of the worst. It was boring, involved way too much travel, and more often than not was a waste of time. Here on Rentor—physically close to Csilla yet paradoxically in the back-water of the Chiss Ascendancy—he had no doubt what the outcome of the trip would be.

Still, when a general—even a newly minted one—said he had a promising recruit, it was incumbent on the family to at least check it out.

General Ba'kif was waiting in the assembly overlook balcony when the Aristocra arrived. The expression on the general's face was one of controlled eagerness; the face itself was far too young to be attached to a field-grade officer. But then, that was what family connections were for.

Ba'kif's eyes lit up as he spotted his visitor. "Aristocra Mitth'urf'ianico?" he asked.

"I am he. General Ba'kif?"

"I am he."

And with that formality over, they could move on to the far less awkward use of titles and core names. "So where is this student you thought was worth my flying halfway across the planet for?" Thurfian asked.

"Down there," Ba'kif said, pointing at the lines of students reciting the morning vows. "Third row back on the right."

So he was a line leader? Impressive, but only mildly so. "Name?"

"Kivu'raw'nuru."

Kivu. Not a family Thurfian was familiar with. "And?" he prompted as he pulled out his questis and keyed in the family name.

"And his grades, aptitude, and logic matrix are off the boards," Ba'kif said. "Makes him a prime candidate for the Taharim Academy on Naporar."

"Mm," Thurfian said, peering at the record. Kivu was about as obscure a family as the Chiss Ascendancy had ever spawned. No wonder he'd never heard of them. "And you contacted us why?"

"Because the Mitth still have two appointment slots left for this year," Ba'kif said. "If you don't bring Vurawn in, he won't have another chance until next year."

"Would that be such a catastrophe?"

Ba'kif's face hardened. "Yes, I believe it would," he said, offering his own questis. "Here's his school record."

Thurfian pursed his lips as he scrolled down the screen. He'd seen better, but not very often. "I don't see any indication that his family has prepped him for military service."

"No, they haven't," Ba'kif confirmed. "It's a smaller family, without the resources or access the Mitth have for such things."

"If they thought he was so exceptional, they should have found or made the resources," Thurfian said tartly. "So you think the Mitth should step to the front and just welcome him in with no questions asked?"

"Ask all the questions you like," Ba'kif said. "I've arranged for him to be pulled out of first class for an interview."

Thurfian smiled tightly. "Are the Aristocra that predictable?"

"The Aristocra? No." Ba'kif matched Thurfian's smile. "But their rivalries are."

"I imagine so," Thurfian conceded, lowering his eyes again to Vurawn's records. If the boy lived up to even half of his potential, he would be a worthy addition to the Mitth family.

Once, thousands of years ago, families had been just that: groups of people bound by blood and marriage and closed to everyone else. But the inherent limitations of such a system had led to decline and stratification, and some of the patriarchs had begun experimenting with methods for absorbing outsiders that didn't involve marriage. The result had been the current system, where likely prospects could be brought in as merit adoptives, with those who proved themselves especially worthy rising to Trial-born and possibly even ranking distant.

Vurawn certainly fit the criteria for becoming a merit adoptive. More important, if the Mitth took him the Irizi wouldn't be able to snatch him up. One of the many family rivalries Ba'kif was no doubt thinking of when he spoke of predictability.

But even that was beside the point. The Syndicure had finally agreed to the Defense Force's long-standing pleas to expand its capabilities and mandate, and the newly formed Expansionary Defense Fleet was the result. Its mission was to watch over Chiss interests in the parts of the Chaos extending beyond the Ascendancy's borders, to learn who was out there and assess their level of threat.

And for once, the Aristocra had actually been generous with their military funding. The Expansionary Fleet's new ships, bases, and support facilities were already under construction, and they were going to need all the competent officers and warriors they could get.

This Vurawn looked like someone who would fit into such a role. A man who might make a name there, both for himself and for his family.

"Fine," he said. "Let's go talk to him. See how he stands up to a proper interrogation."

"I trust the compound isn't too far away," Vurawn said as Thurfian's car flew swiftly across the Rentor landscape. "I'm already missing all of today's classes. My instructors would be displeased if I missed tomorrow's, as well."

"You'll be all right," Thurfian said, hearing the strained patience in his voice. Did the boy really not understand the depth of the honor that had been bestowed upon him?

Apparently not. Attending his classes was important. Adoption into one of the Nine Ruling Families wasn't.

Rentor wasn't exactly a political and cultural hub, and Thurfian knew he had to make allowances for a certain degree of ignorance. Even so, such a lack of awareness set Vurawn apart from even the unsophisticated commoners around him.

Still, if Ba'kif's assessment was correct, the boy would be heading for a military career. Politics weren't nearly so important there.

If Vurawn was rematched to the Mitth, which was hardly yet guaranteed. Thurfian had sent in his own report, but there was still an interview to be conducted by the Councilors who oversaw Mitth interests on Rentor, followed possibly by a short meeting with the local Patriel herself if the Councilors were suitably impressed. Once all that was over, the results would be forwarded to the homestead on Csilla for final review, and only then would Vurawn learn whether or not he'd been selected to be a Mitth merit adoptive. The whole process typically took two to three months; Thurfian had seen it take as many as six—

His questis signaled. Pulling it from his pocket, he keyed it.

It was a script message. A very brief script message.

Vurawn accepted as merit adoptive.

Thurfian stared. *Accepted?*

Impossible. The interviews—the Patriel evaluation—the homestead review—

But there it was, staring him in the face. The process had been short-circuited by someone, and none of the usual procedures were going to matter.

In fact, none of them were now even necessary. Presumably the Patriel had received the same message, and the only thing that would happen when they reached the compound would be the brief ceremony detaching Vurawn from the Kivu family and rematching him to the Mitth.

"Is there trouble?" Vurawn asked.

"No, nothing," Thurfian said, putting the questis back in his pocket. So on the strength of Thurfian's own interrogation, plus perhaps the boy's school records and evaluations, he was accepted?

That made no sense. Impressive though the boy might be, there still had to be more to it. Clearly, someone high up in the family had been keeping watch on Thurfian's mission today. That same someone had apparently also been following Vurawn's life and had already decided that taking him was in the Mitth's best interests.

So if the decision had already been made, why had Thurfian been sent to do an interview in the first place? Surely his recommendation didn't hold that much weight with the homestead.

Of course it didn't. Thurfian had been sent here to help

cover the fact that Vurawn had already been selected for rematching. Pure politics, because with the Nine Families, it was always about politics.

He frowned, his thoughts belatedly catching up with him. He hadn't reacted in any way when he received the message—he'd been an Aristocra and political creature long enough to know how to keep emotions like surprise out of his face and voice. Yet somehow Vurawn had recognized that the message had been disturbing enough to inquire about it.

He eyed the boy again. That kind of observational skill wasn't common. Maybe there was more there than he'd realized. Some spark that would someday bring honor and glory to himself and his family.

Apparently someone at the homestead thought so, too, and that someone had determined that the family on the receiving end of that glory would be the Mitth.

There was still the question of whether or not the boy would be sent to the Taharim Academy. But with Vurawn's unidentified benefactor pulling the strings, Thurfian expected that would also be a foregone conclusion.

He scowled at the landscape racing past beneath them. He didn't like being manipulated. He very much didn't like proper and time-honored procedures being thrown out the window on someone's whim.

But he was an Aristocra of the Mitth, and it wasn't his job to approve or disapprove of his family's decisions. His job was merely to do the tasks he was given.

Perhaps someday that would change.

"No, no trouble," he said. "I just received word that you've been accepted."

Vurawn turned widened eyes on him. "Already?"

"Yes," Thurfian confirmed, secretly enjoying the other's confusion. So he *could* be surprised. And at least he knew enough politics to recognize the unusual nature of the situation. "We'll presumably go through the ceremony when we reach the compound."

"As a merit adoptive, I assume?"

So the kid also knew something about the Ruling Families. "That's where everyone starts," Thurfian told him. "If and when you go through the Trials, you'll move up to Trial-born."

"And then ranking distant," Vurawn said thoughtfully.

Thurfian huffed out a silent breath. That, at least, would never happen. Not to someone from such an insignificant family. "Perhaps. For now, just start getting used to the name Mitth'raw'nuru."

"Yes," the boy murmured.

Thurfian studied him out of the corner of his eye. The boy might bring glory to the Mitth, the way Ba'kif thought. He might just as easily bring shame and regret. That was how the universe operated.

But either way, it was done.

Vurawn was no more. In his place now stood *Thrawn*.

CHAPTER ONE

There were times, Ba'kif thought distantly, when it was good for a man to stare out of the relative stability of the Chiss Ascendancy into the Chaos. It was a chance to appreciate all that the Ascendancy was, and all that it meant: order and steadfastness, security and power, light and culture and glory. It was an island of calm amid the twisted hyperspace lanes and the ever-changing pathways that slowed travel and stunted trade for all those who lived out there.

The Chaos hadn't always been that way, or so the legends went. Once, at the dawn of space travel, it had been no more difficult to move between any of the stars than it was now to travel in the Ascendancy. But then, millennia ago, a series of chained supernova explosions throughout the region had sent huge masses tumbling at high speeds between the stars, some of them demolishing asteroids or whole worlds, others sparking more supernovas with their near-lightspeed impacts. The movement of all those masses, coupled with regions of heavy electromagnetic flux, resulted in the constantly changing hyperlanes that made any voyage longer than a couple of star systems difficult and dangerous.

But that instability was a two-bladed knife. The limitations that stifled travel and thus helped protect the Chiss from invasion also slowed recon and intelligence gathering. There were dangers out there in the darkness, hidden worlds and tyrants who sought conquest and destruction.

One of those tyrants had apparently now set his sights on the Ascendancy.

"Are you certain this is the way?" he asked the young woman at the helm of their shuttle.

"Yes, General, I am," she said. A flicker of controlled pain crossed her face. "I was part of the team that found it."

Ba'kif nodded. "Of course." There was another short silence, another moment of gazing out at the distant stars—

"There," the woman said suddenly. "Ten degrees to starboard."

"I see it," Ba'kif said. "Take us alongside."

"Yes, sir."

Their ship moved forward, steadily closing the distance. Ba'kif gazed out the viewport, his stomach tight. It was one thing to see holos and recordings of a destroyed refugee ship. It was something else entirely to look personally upon the stark reality of slaughter.

Beside him, Senior Captain Thrawn stirred. "This wasn't pirates," he said.

"Your reasoning?" Ba'kif asked.

"The damage pattern is designed to destroy, not immobilize."

"Perhaps the majority of the destruction was inflicted after they plundered it."

"Unlikely," Thrawn said. "The angle of the majority of the shots indicates an attack from the rear."

Ba'kif nodded. That was the same analysis and logic he'd followed, and it had taken him to the same conclusion.

That logic plus one more crucial, terrible fact.

"Let's get the obvious question out of the way," he said. "Is this ship at all related to the ones that attacked Csilla two days ago?"

"No," Thrawn said promptly. "I can see no artistic or architectural connection between them at all."

Ba'kif nodded again. That, too, had been his conclusion. "So it's possible the two incidents are unrelated."

"If so, it would be an interesting coincidence," Thrawn said. "I consider it more likely that the attack on Csilla was a diversion to draw our attention inward and away from this event."

"Indeed," Ba'kif agreed. "And given the cost of the diversion, it further suggests someone *really* doesn't want us taking a good look at this ship."

"Indeed," Thrawn said thoughtfully. "I wonder why they left the wreckage instead of destroying it completely."

"I can tell you that, sir," the pilot put in. "I was on the patrol ship that spotted the attack. We were too far away to intervene or to get any real sensor data, but the attacker apparently spotted our approach and decided not to risk a confrontation. By the time we arrived and began our investigation, it had escaped back into hyperspace."

"So we already knew about the attack," Ba'kif added. "The diversion was then presumably an attempt to push it out of our attention."

"At least until more time had passed," Thrawn said. "How much time, sir, do you estimate?"

Ba'kif shook his head. "Impossible to say for certain. But given the Syndicure's outrage at the Csilla attack, I'm guessing they'll keep up the pressure on the fleet to find the culprits for at least the next three or four months. Assuming, of course, that we don't identify them before then."

"We won't," Thrawn said. "From the recordings I saw of the attack, the ships looked old, even marginally obsolete. Whoever their master was, he chose ships that'll most likely bear little resemblance to what he's using now."

Ba'kif smiled grimly. "But then, a little resemblance may be all we need."

"Perhaps." Thrawn gestured toward the wrecked ship. "I assume we'll be going aboard?"

Ba'kif looked at the pilot. Her cheeks were tight, the skin around her eyes pinched. She'd been aboard once, and clearly had no desire to go back. "Yes," he said. "Just the two of us. The shuttle crew will stay here on watch."

"Understood," Thrawn said. "With your permission, I'll prepare the boarding suits."

"Go ahead," Ba'kif said. "I'll join you in a moment."

He waited until Thrawn had left. "I presume you left everything as you found it?" he asked the pilot.

"Yes, sir," she said. "But . . ."

"But?" Ba'kif prompted.

"I don't understand why you wanted it left intact instead of bringing it in for a more thorough investigation," she said. "I can't see how anything in there will do you any good."

"You may be surprised," Ba'kif said. "We may both be."

He looked toward the hatch where Thrawn had gone. "In fact, I'm counting on it."

Ba'kif had seen the holos the patrol had sent to the Syndicure on Csilla and the Expansionary Defense Fleet headquarters on Naporar.

Like the ship itself, the reality was far worse.

Wrecked consoles. Fried data storage banks and modules. Destroyed sensor clusters and analysis pods.

And bodies. Lots of bodies.

Or rather, the remains of bodies.

"This wasn't a freighter." Thrawn's voice came softly through Ba'kif's helmet speaker. "It was a refugee ship."

Ba'kif nodded silently. Adults, midagers, children—the whole range of life experience had been represented.

All of them slaughtered with the same brutal efficiency.

"What did the fleet's analysis give us?" Thrawn asked.

"Precious little," Ba'kif admitted. "As you already noted, the ship's design isn't one we've seen before. The victims' nucleic code isn't in our data listings. The size of the ship suggests it didn't travel overly far, but there are a lot of planetary systems and small nation clusters in the Chaos that we've never visited."

"And their physical characteristics . . ." Thrawn waved a hand.

"Not easy to read," Ba'kif said grimly, shivering in spite of himself. Explosive rounds had left very little for even the best reconstruction team to work with. "I was hoping there might be something you could glean from what they left behind."

"There are a few things," Thrawn said. "The basic ship design has certain characteristics that likely translate to other aspects of their culture. Their clothing, too, is distinctive."

"In what way?" Ba'kif asked. "Material? Design? Patterning?"

"All that, and more," Thrawn said. "There's a certain air about such things, an overall feeling that forms in my mind."

"Nothing you can codify for us?"

Thrawn turned to him, and through his faceplate Ba'kif saw the other's wry smile. "Really, General," he said. "If I could write all this down, I certainly would."

"I know," Ba'kif said. "It would be a lot easier for all of us if you could."

"Agreed," Thrawn said. "But rest assured I'll be able to recognize these beings when I see them again. I presume your plan is to search for the ship's point of origin?"

"Under normal circumstances, I would definitely do so," Ba'kif said. "But with the Syndicure in its current state of uproar and outrage, it might be difficult to detach a task force from Ascendancy defense."

"I'm prepared to go alone if necessary."

Ba'kif nodded. He'd expected Thrawn to volunteer, of course. If there was one thing the man enjoyed, it was chasing down enigmas and working through puzzles. Add in his unique ability to see connections others couldn't—and the fact that a large percentage of the Aristocra would be happy to have him out of their sight for a while—and he was the perfect person for the job.

Unfortunately, it wasn't that easy.

"I'll need something reasonably well equipped for a mission of this sort," Thrawn continued, looking around at the wreckage. "The *Springhawk* would do quite well."

"I thought that would be next," Ba'kif said sourly. "You *do* know it was taken away from you for a reason, right?"

"Of course," Thrawn said. "Supreme Admiral Ja'fosk and the Council were displeased by my actions against the Vagaari pirates. But surely that anger has dissipated by now."

"Perhaps," Ba'kif said evasively. "However . . . well. Let's just say that your reputation among the other Council members continues to be tenuous." Certainly the Defense Hierarchy Council's annoyance at Thrawn's actions had been the official reason for him being removed as the *Springhawk*'s commander. Not just his unauthorized action against the pirates, but also the subsequent death of Syndic Mitth'ras'safis and the loss of valuable alien technology.

But behind the scenes, there'd been other factors in play. Thrawn's successful campaign, whether the Aristocra approved of it or not, had elevated the *Springhawk*'s name and prestige, and the Ufsa family had decided they wanted the ship to be commanded by one of their own. A quiet petition to the Council, probably an even quieter exchange of favors or future owings, and Thrawn was out.

All strictly against protocol, of course. The Aristocra weren't supposed to have any influence over military assignments. But that didn't mean it never happened.

The point was that, as usual, Thrawn had seen only the surface situation and completely missed the political subtleties.

Still, this might be a good opportunity to remind the Ascendancy's civilian leaders that the Council, not the Syndicure, was in charge of the military. The syndics had taken away the *Springhawk*; it was time for the Council to take it back. "Let me see what I can do," he said. "The *Springhawk*'s scheduled to join Admiral Ar'alani's punitive attack on the Paataasus in a few days, but we should be able to get you back in command after that."

"Do you really think the Paataasus are responsible for the Csilla attack?"

"*I* don't, no," Ba'kif admitted. "Nor does most of the Council. But one of the syndics trotted out that theory, and the rest are warming to it. Regardless, the Paataasus have been poking at the edge of the Ascendancy again, so a quick punitive slap was in order anyway."

"I suppose that's reasonable," Thrawn said. "Instead of waiting until after the operation, though, I'd like to join the ship before the attack. Not necessarily as commander, but to observe and evaluate the officers and warriors."

"That might be possible," Ba'kif said. "On the other hand, why not as commander? I'll run it past Ar'alani and see if she approves."

"I'm sure she will," Thrawn said. "I assume I'll also be assigned a sky-walker for my investigation?"

"Most likely," Ba'kif said. The sky-walker corps was stretched thin these days, but without knowing how far Thrawn's investigation would take him it would be inefficient to make him travel at the much slower jump-by-jump speed. "I'll see who's available when we get back to Naporar."

"Thank you." Thrawn gestured aft. "I presume the attackers here left little to find in the engine compartment or the supply rooms?"

"Little to nothing," Ba'kif said grimly. "Mostly just a few more exploded bodies."

"Regardless, I'd like to see those areas."

"Of course," Ba'kif said. "This way."

For a long moment, Mid Captain Ufsa'mak'ro gazed at the fresh orders on the questis his first officer had handed him.

No. Not *his* officer. Senior Commander Plikh'ar'illmorf was now Senior Commander Mitth'raw'nuruodo's officer. And no longer first, but second.

Samakro himself had become Thrawn's first officer.

He looked up from the questis at the man standing stiffly in front of him. Kharill was seething, though he probably thought he was hiding it. "You have a question, Senior Commander?" Samakro asked mildly.

Kharill's eyebrows twitched, just a bit. Apparently, he'd expected the *Springhawk*'s captain to be as angry at the unexpected orders as he was. "Not so much a question, sir, as a comment," he said, his voice tight.

"Let me guess," Samakro said, lifting the questis slightly. "You're outraged that my ship's been taken away from me and given to Senior Captain Thrawn. You're wondering if we should lodge our complaints individually or jointly, and if jointly which of our families should be contacted first. You think we should also protest to Admiral Ar'alani, Supreme Admiral Ja'fosk, and the Defense Hierarchy Council, probably in that order, arguing that changing a ship's command structure on the eve of battle is both foolish and dangerous. And you absolutely think we should show our displeasure by obeying Thrawn's orders as unenthusiastically as possible. Does that about cover it?"

Kharill's mouth had started dropping open somewhere around Samakro's second sentence, and was now as far open as Samakro had ever seen it. "Ah . . . yes, sir, it does," Kharill managed.

"Well, then," Samakro said, handing him back the questis. "Since I've now said all of it, there's no reason for you to do so. Return to your duties, and prepare for the change in command."

Kharill's throat worked, but he gave a brief nod. "Yes, sir," he said, and turned to go.

"One more thing," Samakro called after him.

"Sir?"

Samakro let his eyes narrow. "If I ever catch you disobeying an order—*anyone's* order—or obeying a legal order slowly or improperly, I'll personally have you brought up on charges. Clear?"

"Very clear, sir," Kharill said between stiff lips.

"Good," Samakro said. "Carry on."

He watched Kharill's rigid back as the other strode down the corridor toward the *Springhawk*'s bridge. Hopefully, Samakro had convinced the younger man to at least pretend enthusiasm for the ship's new commander, even if he didn't actually feel any.

Which was a façade that Samakro himself had better make sure was nailed up in front of his own feelings.

Because he was furious. Furious, outraged, betrayed—all of it. How *dare* the Council and Supreme Admiral Ja'fosk do this to him and the *Springhawk*? Supreme General Ba'kif's starry-eyed attitude toward everything Thrawn touched was well known, but surely Ja'fosk had more sense.

Still, the orders had been cut, and protesting the way Kharill wanted would do nothing except add fuel to an already simmering fire. So Samakro would do his job, and he would make sure the rest of the ship's officers and warriors did the same.

And he would hope very hard that whatever political mess Thrawn made this time wouldn't blow up in all of their faces.

MEMORIES II

The journey ended, and Al'iastov brought herself out of Third Sight into the muted light of the Chiss Defense Force Transport *Tomra*'s bridge. She lifted her hands away from the navigational controls, a hollow feeling in both stomach and heart. "Senior Commander?" she asked tentatively, looking at the helm officer seated beside her.

"We've arrived," he confirmed. "Thank you. I'll take it from here."

"Okay," Al'iastov murmured. Unstrapping, she stood up and walked across the quiet bridge to the hatch.

She walked through the opening and continued down the empty corridor toward the captain's quarters, where she and her caregiver had been given space. The *Tomra* never went outside the Ascendancy, so it didn't have a proper sky-walker suite. Mafole, Al'iastov's caregiver, had complained about that, very loudly, which had made Junior Captain Vorlip mad right back at her.

On Al'iastov's other ships, her caregiver usually met her outside the bridge and walked her back to the sky-walker suite. But after Mafole's fight with Vorlip, she'd declared she wouldn't leave their room until they reached Naporar, and had told Al'iastov she'd be walking back and forth alone.

And as Al'iastov walked the long corridor, her eyes blurred with tears.

There was no reason to have a sky-walker on this trip. She knew that. The routes within the Ascendancy weren't like the ones out in the Chaos. Here, the pathways were clear, and the pilots knew how to get where they were going.

That was why the fleet had put Al'iastov's test here. Trips like this were a safe way to see if a sky-walker could still do her job.

The pilot hadn't said anything. Neither had Junior Captain Vorlip.

But Al'iastov knew.

She hadn't been able to keep the *Tomra* on the right path. The pilot had had to correct the course as they traveled.

Her Third Sight was mostly gone. Her job was ended. The only life she'd ever known was over. A full year ahead of the usual schedule, her life was over.

At age thirteen.

"Are you all right?"

Al'iastov stopped short, rubbing away the tears that had kept her from seeing the other person's approach. A young man in a black uniform stood facing her a few steps away. There weren't any insignia pins on his collar, which marked him as a cadet, and his shoulder patch had a sunrise on it. That was one of the Nine Families, she knew, but she couldn't remember which one. "I'm fine," she said. One of her other caregivers had told her once that she should never complain about how she was feeling. "Who are you?"

"Cadet Mitth'raw'nuru," he said. "Journeying to the Taharim Academy. Who are you?"

"Al'iastov." She winced, remembering too late that her identity was supposed to be kept a secret from everyone except the highest-ranking officers. "I'm the captain's daughter," she added, repeating the lie she was always supposed to give if anyone outside the bridge crew asked.

Thrawn's eyebrow rose, just a bit, and Al'iastov's sinking heart sank a little deeper. He didn't believe her. Not only was her life over, but she was probably in trouble now, too. "I mean—"

"It's all right," Thrawn said. "What's wrong, Al'iastov? Can I help?"

Al'iastov sighed. She wasn't supposed to complain. But for once she didn't really care what she was supposed to do. "I don't think so," she said. "I'm . . . just worried. About . . . I don't know. About what I'm going to do."

"I understand," Thrawn said.

Al'iastov caught her breath. Had he figured out what she was? Her brief moment of uncaring rebellion vanished, leaving her once again fully aware that she was going to be in trouble. "You do?" she asked carefully.

"Of course," Thrawn said. "All of us feel uncertainty as we travel through life. I don't know specifically what concerns you, but I assure you that all the cadets aboard this ship are also facing changes in their futures."

She felt a bit of relief. So he *didn't* know she was a skywalker. "But you all know where you're going," she said. "You're a cadet, and you're going to be in the Defense Force. I don't know what I'm going to do."

"You're a ship captain's daughter," Thrawn said. "That will surely open many opportunities. But just because I know I'm going to the academy doesn't mean there aren't a great many unknowns. And uncertainty can be the most frightening of mental states."

And then, to Al'iastov's surprise, Thrawn got down on one knee in front of her, putting his face a little lower than hers. Grown-ups almost never did that. Even most of Al'iastov's other caregivers had usually stood straight up looking down at her. "But while all of us face a variety of paths, we all have the power to choose among them," he continued. "You have that power as well, the power to choose which of those paths is the right one for you."

"I don't know," Al'iastov said, feeling the tears start up again. What kind of choices did a thirteen-year-old failed sky-walker even have? No one had talked much to her about that. "But thank you for—"

"What's going on here?" The harsh voice of Junior Captain Vorlip came from behind her. "Who are you, and what are you doing here?"

"Cadet Mitth'raw'nuru," Thrawn said as he quickly stood up. "I was exploring the ship when I came upon your daughter. She seemed distressed, and I stopped to offer assistance."

"You're not supposed to be in this corridor," Vorlip said sternly. She walked past Al'iastov and stopped in front of Thrawn. "Didn't you see the AUTHORIZED PERSONNEL ONLY signs?"

"I assumed they were intended to stop nonmilitary personnel," Thrawn said. "As a cadet, I thought I would be exempt."

"Well, you aren't," Vorlip said. "You're supposed to be back with the other cadets."

"My apologies," Thrawn said. "I merely wished to get the feel of the ship." He bowed his head and started to turn away.

Vorlip put out her arm to block his path. "What do you mean, the feel of the ship?"

"I wanted to study its rhythms," Thrawn said. "The deck has subtle vibrations that reflect the ebb and flow of the thrusters. Our movement through hyperspace was punctuated by slight hesitations and swells. The airflow indicates small variations as we change direction. The compensators occasionally lag slightly behind course changes, with effects that are again transmitted through the deck."

"Really," Vorlip said. She didn't seem as angry now. "How many spaceflights have you had before this one?"

"None," Thrawn said. "This is my first voyage away from my home."

"Is it." Vorlip stepped close to him. "Close your eyes. Keep them closed until I tell you otherwise."

Thrawn closed his eyes. Vorlip took him by the upper arms, and without warning, began spinning him around.

Thrawn's arms flailed outward with surprise. His feet stumbled, trying to keep up with his body's movements. Vorlip kept him spinning, and also slowly moved around with him. When she was a third of the way from where she'd started, she caught his upper arms and brought him to a stop.

"Eyes still closed," she said, holding him steady. "Which way is forward?"

Thrawn was silent a moment. Then, he raised a hand and pointed toward the *Tomra*'s bow. "There," he said.

Vorlip kept holding him for a second. Then she let go and moved a step back. "You can open your eyes," she said. "Return to your quarters. And don't ever pass that kind of sign until you're damn sure you're allowed."

"Yes, Captain," Thrawn said. He blinked a couple of times as he finished getting his balance. He nodded to Vorlip, nodded and smiled at Al'iastov, then turned and left.

"I'm sorry," Al'iastov said quietly.

"It's all right," Vorlip said. She was still looking at Thrawn.

"Are you mad at him?" Al'iastov asked. "He was only trying to help me."

"I know."

"Are you mad at *me*?"

Vorlip turned and gave her a small smile. "No, of course not," she said. "You've done nothing wrong."

"But . . ." Al'iastov stopped, feeling confused.

"I'm not mad at anyone," Vorlip said. "It's just . . . it took me fifteen voyages, in four different ships, before I developed that kind of awareness. This Mitth'raw'nuru did it in one."

"Is that strange?"

"Very," Vorlip assured her.

"He seems nice," Al'iastov said. She paused, thinking about what he'd said about paths. "What happens to me when I leave here?"

"You'll be adopted," Vorlip said. "Probably into one of the Nine Ruling Families—they like to have former skywalkers."

"Why?"

"It's a prestige thing," Vorlip said. "I'm sure you realize that girls with your ability are very rare. It's an honor for one of you to be made a merit adoptive."

Al'iastov felt her throat tighten. "Even when we're no use to anyone?"

"Don't say things like that," Vorlip said sternly. "Every person is valuable. My point is that you'll be welcomed into whatever family adopts you. They'll take care of you, send you on to further education, and eventually find a career that you're best suited for."

"Unless they throw me out."

"I told you to stop talking like that," Vorlip said. "They're not going to throw you out. You're prestige for the family, remember?"

"Yes," Al'iastov said. She still didn't completely believe it, but there was no use talking any more about it now.

But there *was* one more point. "Do I get to choose which family I want?"

Vorlip frowned. "I don't know. To be honest, I don't know any of the details about how these things are done. Why, are you looking at a specific family?"

"Yes," Al'iastov said. "The Mitth."

"Really." Vorlip glanced over her shoulder. "Like Cadet Thrawn?"

"Yes."

Vorlip huffed out a thoughtful breath. "As I say, I don't know how it works. But there's certainly no reason you can't ask. Actually, now that I think about it, a former sky-walker with your record should be able to ask for whatever you want."

And there it was. Vorlip had said it. *Former sky-walker.*

Al'iastov's navigational career was officially over.

But strangely, it suddenly didn't seem to matter so much now. "That's what he said," she told Vorlip. "He said I'd be able to choose my path."

"Well, cadets say all sorts of things," Vorlip said, dismissing both Thrawn and the conversation with a wave of her hand. "Come—I need you and your caregiver in my office. There are forms we need to fill out."

Mitth'raw'nuru, he'd named himself, Al'iastov reminded herself as she and the captain walked. *Mitth'raw'nuru*. She would remember that.

And when the time came, the Mitth family would definitely be getting a request.

CHAPTER TWO

The personnel officer shook his head. "Request denied," he said briskly. "Good day."

Mitth'ali'astov blinked. Had she just heard him right? "What do you mean, denied?" she asked. "I have all the datawork right there."

"Yes, you do," he said. "Unfortunately, it needed to be filed four days ago."

Thalias clenched her teeth. She'd had to fight the Mitth family bureaucracy the whole way, tooth and tongue, to get them to agree to this. Now, too late, she understood why they'd suddenly backed off the fight and given in to her request. "I'm afraid I don't understand," she said, forcing back her anger at the family. The man sitting in front of her was the key to getting her aboard the *Springhawk*, and she needed him on her side. "I'm a member of the Mitth family, the *Springhawk* is being commanded by a member of the Mitth family, and I was told the fleet offers the right of observation."

"Yes, it does," the officer confirmed. "But there are limits to that right." He tapped his questis. "Proper timing is one of them."

"I understand that now," Thalias said. "Unfortunately, the family didn't make that clear to me. Typical. Isn't there anything you can do?"

"I'm afraid not," he said, a little less truculently. Putting the mess onto the Mitth family instead of him had edged him at least a little closer to sympathy for her current situation. "There's processing time to consider, especially since the other senior officers' families have a right to challenge."

"I see," Thalias said. "Always comes down to the families, doesn't it?"

"It *does* seem to go that way a lot," the officer said, his stiffness bending a little more.

"Well, if I can't get aboard as an observer, is there any other way I can join the ship?" Thalias asked. "Some other job I could do? I'm proficient in computers, data analysis—"

"Sorry," he cut in, stopping her with an upraised hand. "You're a civilian, and the *Springhawk* doesn't have any positions for civilians." He frowned suddenly. "Unless . . . just a moment."

He keyed his questis, paused, keyed it again, scrolled slowly down the pages. Thalias tried to read along from her side of the desk, but the text was upside down and he was using one of the scripts specifically designed to be hard to read that way.

"Here we go," he said, looking up again. "Maybe. There's one job you *might* be able to take. The *Springhawk*'s just been assigned a sky-walker, but a caregiver hasn't been appointed yet. You have any experience or qualifications in handling children?"

"Not really," Thalias said. "But I was once a sky-walker myself. Does that count?"

His eyes widened. "You were a *sky-walker*? Really?"

"Really," she assured him.

"Interesting," he muttered, his eyes shrinking back to normal, and maybe just a little in the other direction. "A hundred years ago all caregivers were former sky-walkers. Or so I've heard."

"Interesting," Thalias said. There was her opening.

If she wanted to go for it.

It wasn't an easy or obvious answer. That part of her life was far behind her. More than that, it was filled with some memories she'd just as soon leave there.

Of course, many of those unpleasant memories were wrapped around the women who'd been assigned to look after her aboard her ships. Some of them had been reasonable; others hadn't understood her at all. She would be on the other side of the relationship this time, which should help a lot.

Maybe. If she was being honest, she would have to admit that she probably hadn't been the easiest of caregiver assignments, either. A lot of that time blurred together, but she distinctly remembered several long-term sulks and more than a few full-rage screaming fits.

To take that job onto herself—to face a sky-walker with all that entailed—to try to make a little girl's life less stressful—

She squared her shoulders. Visiting those dark parts of her past would be hard. But it might be her only chance to once again see Thrawn. It would certainly be her best chance for real observation of him. "All right," she said. "Yes. I'll take it."

"Whoa," the officer warned. "It's not that easy. You'd still need—"

He broke off as the door behind her opened. Thalias turned to see a middle-aged man stride into the office. Pinned high on his yellow outerwrap robe was the sunrise crest of a Mitth family syndic. "I see I'm not too late," he commented. "Mitth'ali'astov, I presume?"

"Yes," Thalias said, frowning. "And you?"

"Syndic Mitth'urf'ianico," the man identified himself, his eyes shifting to the officer. "I understand the young lady is trying to secure a place aboard the *Springhawk*?"

"She is, Syndic," the officer said, his eyes narrowing a bit more. "You'll excuse me, but this is a matter for the fleet, not the Aristocra."

"Not if she's going aboard as a Mitth family observer," Thurfian countered.

The officer shook his head. "Her datawork isn't in order for that."

"Someone in the family delayed the processing," Thalias added.

"I see," Thurfian said. "And there's nothing that can be done?"

"There's an opening for the sky-walker's caregiver," Thalias said. "We were just starting to talk about that."

"Perfect," Thurfian said, brightening. "What still needs to be done to make that happen?"

"It's not that easy," the officer said.

"Of course it is," Thurfian said. "The position's open, and the Mitth family still has the right of observation."

"The approvals haven't been completed."

"I'm completing them now," Thurfian said.

The officer shook his head. "With all due respect, Syndic—"

"With all due respect to *you*," Thurfian interrupted. He drew himself up—

And suddenly Thalias had a sense of the true power the Syndicure wielded. It stretched far past their political authority, carrying the full weight of Chiss history. "The Ascendancy lies under threat of attack," Thurfian said, his voice low and dark. "The Defense Force and Expansionary Fleet need to stand at full readiness. Every ship that requires a sky-walker needs to have one, and a sky-walker cannot go aboard without a caregiver. The *Springhawk* leaves Naporar in four hours for combat. We don't have time—*you* don't have time—to dither around."

He took a deep breath, and it seemed to Thalias that his stance and manner softened a bit. "Now. You have here a caregiver who's ready, willing, and able to serve. You have her family's authorization to be aboard. Surely you can find a way to provide the *Springhawk* the resources it needs for the task that lies ahead."

For a moment he and the officer remained silent, their eyes locked. The rivalry between the fleet and the Aristocra . . .

But there were reason and urgency in Thurfian's argument, and the officer clearly knew it. "Very well," he said. He lowered his eyes and worked his questis a moment. "All right," he said, looking up at Thalias. "Your orders, instructions, and authorizations are on your questis. Read them, and be where you're supposed to be when you're supposed to be there." His eyes flicked to Thurfian. "As Syndic Thurfian said, the *Springhawk* leaves in four hours."

"Thank you," Thalias said.

"You're welcome." He gave her a small smile. "Welcome to the Expansionary Fleet, Caregiver Thalias. And best of luck with that sky-walker."

A moment later, Thalias and Thurfian were back out in the corridor. "Thank you," Thalias said. "You were just in time."

"I'm glad I could help," Thurfian said, smiling. "You really are a remarkable person, Thalias."

She felt her face warm. "Thank you," she said again.

"And as I helped you," Thurfian continued, "there's something you can do to help me."

Thalias felt herself draw back from him. "Excuse me?" she asked carefully, coming to a halt.

"Time is short," Thurfian said, taking her arm and starting them moving again. "Come. I'll tell you on the way to your ship."

It had been two decades since Thalias had had to even read a military timetable, let alone follow one. Fortunately, once the initial shock wore off, old habits and reflexes took over and she made it to the *Springhawk* shuttle in plenty of time.

The young girl was waiting in the sky-walker suite's dayroom when she arrived, sprawled across a massive chair and playing a tap-click game on her questis. She looked to be nine or ten, but sky-walkers tended to be on the short side, so that was only a guess. She looked up as Thalias came through the hatchway, gave the woman a rather suspicious-looking appraisal, then returned her attention to the game. Thalias started to introduce herself, remembered how touchy she'd usually been whenever a new caregiver came to call, and instead took her luggage to her part of the suite.

She took her time getting settled. By the time she once again stepped into the dayroom, the girl had set her questis on the chair beside her and was gazing moodily at the line of repeater displays set into the bulkhead beneath the snack bar. "Have we left yet?" Thalias asked.

The girl nodded. "A little while ago," she said. She hesitated, then furtively looked over at Thalias. "Are you my new momish?"

"I'm your new caregiver," Thalias said, frowning slightly. *Momish?* Was that a new official term for her position, or was it something this girl had come up with on her own? "I'll be taking care of you while we're aboard the *Springhawk*," she continued as she walked over to one of the other chairs and sat down. "My name's Thalias. What's yours?"

"Aren't you supposed to know already?"

"This was kind of a last-minute assignment," Thalias admitted. "I spent all my time making sure I got to the spaceport before the shuttle left."

"Oh," the girl said, sounding a little confused. She was probably used to caregivers with more discipline. And competence. "I'm Che'ri."

"Nice to meet you, Che'ri," Thalias said, smiling. "What game were you playing?"

"What? Oh." Che'ri touched her questis. "I wasn't playing anything. I was drawing."

"Really," Thalias said, wincing a little. Che'ri liked to draw, and Thalias barely knew one end of a stylus from the other. No common ground there. "I didn't know tap-click could be adapted to artwork."

"It isn't really art," Che'ri said, sounding embarrassed. "I just take pieces already in the questis and put them together."

"Sounds interesting," Thalias said. "Like a collage. May I see it?"

"No," Che'ri said, jerking back a little as she grabbed the questis and pressed it close to her chest. "I don't let anyone look at it."

"Okay, that's fine," Thalias hastened to assure her. "But if you ever change your mind, I'd love to see what you do."

"Do you like to draw?" Che'ri asked.

"I'm not very good at that sort of thing," Thalias said. "But I like looking at art."

"You don't think drawing is silly?"

"No, of course not," Thalias assured her. "Having that kind of talent is a good thing."

"I don't really draw," Che'ri said. "I already told you I just put things together."

"Well, it's still a talent," Thalias said doggedly. "And talents are never silly."

Che'ri lowered her eyes. "My last momish said it was."

"Your last momish was wrong," Thalias said.

Che'ri gave out a little snort. "She always thought she was right."

"Trust me," Thalias said. "I've seen momishes come and go, and I can tell you straight up that one was wrong."

"Okay." Che'ri peered at her. "You're not like the others."

"The other momishes?" Thalias tried a small smile. "Probably not. How many of them have you had?"

Che'ri lowered her gaze again. "Eight," she said, her voice barely audible.

Thalias winced at the pain in the girl's voice. "Wow," she said gently. "Must have been hard."

Che'ri snorted again. "How would you know?"

"Because I had four," Thalias said.

Che'ri looked up, her eyes wide. "You're a *sky-walker*?"

"I was," Thalias said. "And I remember how it hurt each time they took one caregiver away and gave me a new one."

Che'ri looked down again and hunched her shoulders. "I don't even know what I did wrong."

"Probably nothing," Thalias said. "I worried about that a lot, too, and I could never come up with anything. Except sometimes she and I didn't get along very well, so that might have been one reason."

"They didn't understand." Che'ri's throat worked. "None of them understood."

"Because none of them had ever been a sky-walker," Thalias said. Though that hadn't always been the case, if that personnel officer had been right. Fleetingly, she wondered why that policy had been changed. "Once we leave the program, most of us don't come back."

"So how come *you* did?"

Thalias shrugged. This wasn't the time to tell the girl she was here to reconnect with someone she'd only met once. "I remember how hard it was being a sky-walker. I thought someone who'd been one herself might make a better caregiver."

"Until you leave," Che'ri muttered. "They all do."

"But not necessarily because they want to," Thalias said. "There are all sorts of reasons for caregiver transfers. Sometimes the sky-walker and caregiver just don't get along, like you and your last one, and me and that one I just mentioned. But sometimes there are other reasons. Sometimes they need a special caregiver to watch over a new sky-walker. Sometimes there are family disputes—I mean between the various families—that get in the way." She felt her lips pucker. "And sometimes it's because there are shortsighted idiots in charge of the process."

"You mean shortsighted, like they don't see very good?"

"I mean shortsighted like they have the brains of a hop-toad," Thalias said. "I'm sure you've met people like that."

Che'ri gave her an uncertain smile. "I'm not supposed to talk like that about people."

"You're right, you probably shouldn't," Thalias said. "Neither should I. Doesn't change the fact they've got the brains of hop-toads."

"I guess." Che'ri squinted at her. "How long were you a sky-walker?"

"I was seven when I navigated my first ship. I was thirteen when I navigated my last."

"They told me I'd be a sky-walker until I was fourteen."

"That's the usual age," Thalias said. "My Third Sight apparently decided to quit early. You're—what?" She made a show of squinting at Che'ri's face. "About eight?"

"Nine and a half." The girl considered. "Nine and three-quarters."

"Ah," Thalias said. "So you've had lots of experience. That's good."

"I suppose," Che'ri said. "Are we going into a battle?"

Thalias hesitated. There were things adults weren't supposed to tell sky-walkers, things the Council in its odd wisdom had decided might upset them. "I don't know, but it's nothing to worry about," she said. "Especially not aboard the *Springhawk*. Senior Captain Thrawn is our captain, and he's one of the best warriors in the Ascendancy."

"Because they wouldn't tell me why I'm here," Che'ri persisted. "There's nobody very far away we have to fight, is there? They say we don't go outside the Ascendancy to fight anyone. And if the people they're fighting are close, the ship doesn't need a sky-walker."

"Good points," Thalias said, an unpleasant feeling stirring in her stomach. Even if the task force was heading off for some punitive action, traveling jump-by-jump would get them any reasonable distance without having to risk taking a sky-walker into combat. So why were she and Che'ri aboard? "Well, whatever we're doing, Senior Captain Thrawn will get us through."

"How do you know?"

"I've read a lot about him." Thalias pulled out her questis. "Do you read? Would you like to read about his career?"

"That's okay," Che'ri said, wrinkling her nose a little. "I'd rather draw."

"Drawing's good, too," Thalias said, sending Thrawn's files to Che'ri's questis. "This is just here if you want to read some later."

"Okay," Che'ri said uncertainly as she peered at her questis. "There's an awful lot there."

"So there is," Thalias conceded, feeling a pang of embarrassment. She'd loved reading when she was a sky-walker. Naturally, she'd assumed Che'ri would be the same. "Tell you what. I'll go through it later and make up a shorter version for you. Some of the more exciting stories of things he's done."

"Okay," Che'ri said, sounding marginally less unenthusiastic.

"Good." For a moment, Thalias tried to think of something else to say. But she could see the wall still standing between them, and she remembered how moody she'd sometimes been when she was Che'ri's age. Best not to push it. "I have to check in with the first officer," she said, standing up. "I'll let you get back to your drawing."

"Okay," Che'ri said. "Am I supposed to get my own lunch?"

"No, no, I'll make it for you," Thalias assured her. "Are you hungry?"

Che'ri shrugged. "I can wait."

Which wasn't exactly an answer. "Do you want me to make you something now?"

"I can wait," Che'ri repeated.

Thalias clenched her teeth. "Okay, then. I'll go check in, and then come back. While I'm gone, you think of what you'd like to eat."

Another shrug. "I don't care."

"Well, think about it anyway," Thalias said. "I'll be back soon."

She headed out, glowering to herself as she strode down the corridor. Maybe taking this job had been a mistake.

Still, she and Che'ri had barely met. It wasn't surprising the girl was holding back, especially given that she was still hurting from what she saw as desertion by her previous caregivers.

So Thalias would give the girl time, and space, and probably more time. Eventually, hopefully, she would come around.

And if she still didn't know what she wanted for lunch by the time Thalias returned, it would be nut-paste sandwiches. Even if Che'ri didn't read, surely she at least liked nut-paste sandwiches.

Thrawn was taller than Samakro had expected, and carried himself with grace and a certain air of confidence. He was also courteous to the officers and warriors, and knew his way around the *Springhawk*. Aside from that, he really wasn't that big a deal.

Right now, he was also late.

"Approaching target system," Kharill reported. "Breakout in thirty seconds."

"Acknowledged," Samakro said, looking around the bridge. All weapons systems showed green, including the balky plasma sphere targeting computer that had been giving them trouble for the past few days. All air lock doors were sealed against possible breach, the electrostatic barrier that hugged the *Springhawk*'s hull was at power, and all warriors were at their stations.

Impressive, but hardly really necessary. As far as Samakro could tell, this whole mission was only a small step above a wargame exercise. The *Vigilant* was a full-class Nightdragon man-of-war, and Admiral Ar'alani's current force also included five other cruisers besides the *Springhawk*. With that much firepower, appearing without warning over the Paataatus homeworld, they weren't likely to face any effective resistance.

None of which meant that *Springhawk* and its crew should be anything less than fully professional here, of course. And that professionalism included its captain. If Thrawn wasn't here by the time they left hyperspace, Samakro would just have to take over—

"Stand ready," Thrawn's calm voice came from behind him.

Samakro turned, fighting back a reflexive twitch. How in *hell* had Thrawn sneaked onto the bridge without him hearing the hatch open? "Captain," he greeted his superior. "I was starting to think you'd missed the alert."

"I've been here for the past hour," Thrawn said, sounding mildly surprised that Samakro hadn't noticed. "I was overseeing the work on the sphere targeting computer."

Samakro looked over at the plasma sphere console as two techs emerged into sight from behind it. "Ah. I see it shows green now."

"Indeed," Thrawn said. "The quality of the *Springhawk*'s repair and maintenance crews has improved considerably since you were placed in command."

Samakro felt his eyes narrow. A compliment? Or a subtle reminder that Thrawn was the ship's captain now?

"Any last-minute instructions from the *Vigilant*?" Thrawn continued.

"Nothing since the last jump," Samakro said. Probably a compliment, he decided. Thrawn didn't strike him as the gloating sort. "Just Ar'alani's usual warning to be ready for anything."

"I believe we are," Thrawn said. "Breakout . . . now."

Through the viewport, Samakro saw the star-flares flash and shrink, bringing the *Springhawk* out of hyperspace.

Into a storm of laserfire.

"Enemy fighters!" Kharill snapped. "Bearing . . . all around us, Captain. Swarming us. Swarming *everyone*."

Samakro hissed out a minor curse. Kharill was right. There were at least fifty Paataatus fighter craft out there, buzzing around the Chiss attack force like angry weltflies, their lasers creating flashes of pale green as they cut through the rarefied interplanetary dust.

And as with weltflies, even though each individual sting was too weak to damage the *Springhawk*'s electrostatic barrier, a sufficiently massive barrage of such fire could conceivably take down the defenses and start eating into the hull.

"Acknowledged," Thrawn said calmly. "Sphere One: Fire at nearest attacker on my vector."

"Sphere One firing." The plasma sphere blazed away from the *Springhawk*'s portside launcher.

And missed its target completely.

"Sphere control!" Samakro snapped. "Retune and fire again."

"Belay that," Thrawn said. "Helm: Yaw ninety degrees to port and bring Sphere Two to bear. Fire when ready."

"No, wait!" Samakro snapped.

Too late. The *Springhawk* was already turning, angling toward the enemy ships on that side.

Turning *away* from the *Vigilant*.

And before even the plasma sphere launcher was in position to fire, the enemy fighters were repositioning to take advantage of Thrawn's mistake, sweeping in to surround the *Springhawk* as it pulled away from the other Chiss ships.

"*Springhawk*, get back in formation," Ar'alani's voice boomed from the bridge speaker. "Thrawn?"

"No reply," Thrawn said. "Fire Sphere Two."

This time the plasma sphere flew true, bursting into its target fighter and unleashing a multicolored flash of ionic energy across the enemy's hull as it took down the fighter's electrostatic barrier and scrambled all the electronics within its reach. "Reload and prepare to fire," Thrawn said.

"Shouldn't we get back to the main force?" Samakro pressed. "Admiral Ar'alani—"

"Hold course," Thrawn said. "Sphere Two, fire when ready. Lower barrier strength twenty percent."

Samakro mouthed another curse, a major one this time. "May I suggest we deploy decoys?" he pressed. "It would at least divert some of the focus away from us."

"It would indeed," Thrawn agreed. "Negative on decoys. Yaw another five degrees to portside, then three degrees starboard."

The *Springhawk* turned, then turned again. The Paataatus lasers continued to beat against the weakened electrostatic barrier, and through the viewport Samakro could see the Paataatus fighters again re-forming their attack cluster to bring more of their force to bear.

"Captain, if we don't get back to the others, we're not going to last long," he warned quietly, wondering distantly what had happened to the Thrawn who'd once brought renown to the *Springhawk*.

"We'll last long enough, Mid Captain," Thrawn said. "Don't you see it?"

Samakro lifted a hand in a gesture of confusion and futility.

The hand froze in midair as he suddenly understood. More ships attacking the *Springhawk* meant fewer attacking the other ships. Fewer attackers meant less confusion for the Chiss gunners, targeting computers, and triangulation observers, allowing for an organized, systematic destruction of the attackers who weren't focused on the *Springhawk*.

And that systematic destruction meant . . .

From the *Springhawk*'s starboard side came a sudden barrage of laserfire, breaching missiles, and plasma spheres, ripping into the swarm of enemy fighters. Samakro looked at the display to see the *Vigilant* and the other Chiss ships charging toward them in full battle-wedge formation.

"Raise the barrier to full power; all weapons: Fire," Thrawn ordered. "Focus on the enemies outside our other ships' firing arcs."

The *Springhawk*'s lasers and plasma sphere launchers opened up, and the number of attackers dropped precipitously as the Chiss force continued to blast the enemy ships to dust. Samakro watched until the Paataatus force was down to a few fleeing ships being pursued by two of Ar'alani's other cruisers, then stepped close to Thrawn's side. "So we play the wounded animal and draw the enemy to us," he said. "Giving the rest of the force time to regroup and counterattack."

"Yes," Thrawn said, sounding pleased that Samakro had figured it out. Even if he'd figured it out a little late in the day. "The Paataatus have a swarm mentality. That thought pattern predisposes them to concentrate their attention on wounded opponents."

"They start by finishing off the weakest, then work their way up," Samakro said, nodding.

"Exactly," Thrawn said. "When I saw the size of the attacking force, I realized the best strategy would be to draw as many of them as possible away from the rest of our ships before they were able to inflict significant damage."

"As well as drawing them into a tighter cluster that our gunners and targeting computers would have less trouble with."

"Correct." Thrawn smiled wryly. "That multi-targeting difficulty is *our* weakness. I trust the fleet's technicians and instructors are working to resolve it."

"Senior Captain Thrawn?" Ar'alani's voice came over the speaker.

"Yes, Admiral?" Thrawn called.

"Well done, Captain," Ar'alani said, an edge of annoyance in her tone. "Next time you have a clever plan, kindly share it with me before executing it."

"I'll endeavor to do so," Thrawn promised. "Provided there's time."

"And provided you don't mind tipping off the enemy if they're eavesdropping," Samakro added under his breath.

Apparently not under his breath enough. "If you think that's a legitimate excuse, Mid Captain Samakro, let me suggest otherwise," Ar'alani said. "I'm sure that in the future Captain Thrawn will find a way to communicate the necessary information without the enemy listening in."

"Yes, ma'am," Samakro said, wincing. There was a rumor that flag officers had a special comm setting that enabled them to hear more from their escort ships than was normally possible.

"Captain Thrawn?"

"Admiral?"

"I think we have the situation under control," Ar'alani said. "You may continue on to your next mission whenever you're ready."

Samakro frowned. There hadn't been anything about an extra mission in the *Springhawk*'s orders.

"Thank you, Admiral," Thrawn said. "With your permission, I'd like to take an hour first to run a check on the ship and begin repairs on any damage we may have sustained."

"Take all the time you want," Ar'alani said. "We're heading insystem to talk to the Paataatus commanders. Hopefully, they've learned the folly of attacking the Chiss Ascendancy."

"They have," Thrawn said. "A defeat of this magnitude will stifle their expansionary desires. They should stay within their own borders until the current generation has passed."

"Except possibly for a swipe or two at Csilla?" Ar'alani suggested.

Thrawn shook his head. "I don't believe they were responsible for that attack."

Samakro winced. Personally, he didn't believe it, either, but that didn't mean it was something a senior officer should be saying out loud. Especially when a large percentage of the Syndicure *did* believe it.

"Perhaps," Ar'alani said, her words and tone a much more politically acceptable neutral. "That's for others to investigate. Get to your repairs, and let me know when you're ready to leave. Admiral out."

There was the sound of the comm disconnecting. "Mid Captain, please initiate a full status check," Thrawn said. "Pay particular attention to weapons and defense systems."

"Yes, sir," Samakro said, feeling a trickle of relief. And with that, they were done with politics. At least for now. "All personnel: Full examination of the ship. Section chiefs report status when completed."

There was a chorus of acknowledgments, and the bridge descended into a studious silence as the personnel began their scans. "I hope you're right about the Paataatus," Samakro said. "Just because the Csilla attackers used different ships doesn't mean they hadn't scavenged something that would hide their identity."

"No," Thrawn said. "You saw their tactics here—swarming with overwhelming numbers. Their tactics don't allow for what we saw at Csilla, particularly not a halfhearted attack that costs three ships. No, the Csilla attack was launched by someone else."

"Why couldn't they have talked someone else into doing it for them?" Samakro suggested, perversely unwilling to let it go. He'd never been comfortable with gut-level conclusions, and as far as he could tell that was all Thrawn had here. "There are pirate gangs out there that could be hired to launch a feint."

"The purpose of the attack was certainly to draw our attention,"

Thrawn said. "But not from this part of the border." His lips compressed briefly. "Once we've left the rest of the task force, I'll be able to tell you and the other senior officers about the mission Admiral Ar'alani mentioned."

"Yes, sir," Samakro said, eyeing him closely. He'd never been comfortable with top-secret missions, either. "Any chance of a preview?"

Thrawn gave him a small smile. "Yes, I always hated sealed orders, too," he said. "What I can tell you is that there may be a new threat on the other side of the Ascendancy. Our task is to locate, identify, and evaluate this threat before they turn their attention to our worlds."

"Ah," Samakro said. So that was why they'd suddenly had a sky-walker assigned to them. Jump-by-jump was an inefficient way to travel any real distance into the Chaos, and with this kind of investigation there was no telling how far out the search would take them. "May I ask if you're expecting this search to end in combat?" he added, his mind flicking back to Thrawn's specific instructions to check the *Springhawk*'s weapons and defenses.

"There's always that possibility," Thrawn said. He saw the look on Samakro's face and smiled again. "Don't worry, Captain. I've had the protocols concerning preemptive attacks carefully and specifically laid out for me."

"Yes, sir," Samakro said. "With your permission, I'd like to personally supervise the checks on the barrier."

"Very good, Captain," Thrawn said. "Carry on."

Samakro headed toward the defense station, his stomach tight. The electrostatic barrier was the *Springhawk*'s first line of defense against any attacker and, as such, needed to be in perfect working order.

Because he'd heard some of the stories about Thrawn. And just because the protocols had been laid out for him didn't necessarily mean he'd listened.

MEMORIES III

In nearly four years at Taharim Academy, Senior Cadet Irizi'ar'alani had built up a spotless record. She'd distinguished herself, she was well on the way to command rank and position, and not the slightest hint of scandal had ever touched her name.

Until now.

"Senior Cadet Ziara," Colonel Wevary intoned in the voice he saved for the most heinous of offenders against Taharim's traditions, "a cadet under your tutelage has been accused of cheating. Have you anything to say in your or his defense?"

Under your tutelage. All Ziara had done was to proctor the damn simulation exercise Cadet Thrawn had been taking.

But her name was attached to the charge, and so here she sat.

Not that there was much chance of serious consequences. Certainly the Irizi representative seated at one end of the three-officer panel didn't look worried. At the other end of the table—

She felt a flicker of sympathetic pain. Thrawn was the one standing on the brink here, and yet the Mitth family representative hadn't even shown up. Either he'd forgotten about the hearing or else he just didn't care. Either way, it didn't bode well for Thrawn's future.

The strangest part was that none of this made any sense. Ziara had looked up Thrawn's records, and he was already far ahead of his classmates. The last thing he needed to do was cheat on a simulator exercise.

Still, while his normal simulator scores were consistently high, most of them were within or only slightly above the academy's high-water marks. On this particular exercise, no one in Taharim's history had ever gotten even close to Thrawn's score of ninety-five. There had been only one logical explanation for such a high score, and Colonel Wevary had come to it.

Ziara shifted her attention to the accused. Thrawn was sitting stiffly in his chair, his face a rigid mask. He'd already pled not guilty to the charges, insisting that he hadn't cheated but merely taken advantage of the parameters the exercise had set up for him.

But as one of the other panel members had already said, that was exactly what a guilty person would also say. Unfortunately, too many cadets in the past had gamed the system by secretly running practice sessions with their upcoming test parameters, a cheat the instructors had countered by making sure no simulations could ever be exactly rerun. That built-in limitation meant that Thrawn couldn't repeat his technique and prove his innocence.

Presumably, the instructors could dig into the programming and change that. But it would take a lot of time, and apparently no one thought a single cadet was worth that much effort.

Mentally, Ziara shook her head. The other part of the problem was that the records of the exercise were limited to the points of view of the three attacking patrol ships. One of the records had gone blank at the wrong moment, showing nothing of the climactic encounter, while the other two simply showed Thrawn's patrol ship vanishing for several crucial seconds.

A practical cloaking device had been a dream of Defense Force scientists for generations. It was unlikely that a cadet simulation would have made that elusive breakthrough. At least, not without an illegal tweaking of the programming.

And yet . . .

Ziara studied Thrawn's face. He'd explained his tactics to the board at least twice, and they still didn't believe him. Now, with nothing left for him to say, he'd taken refuge in silence. Ziara might have expected to find defiance or anger there, but she could see neither. He stood alone, without even his family to support him.

In the meantime, Colonel Wevary had asked Ziara a question.

"I have nothing to say," she said. She looked at Thrawn again.

And suddenly an odd thought occurred to her. Something she'd glimpsed in Thrawn's record, the story about how he'd risen from an obscure family to gain an appointment to Taharim . . .

"For the moment," she added quickly. "If I may beg the board's indulgence, I would like to take the luncheon break to again consider the situation and the evidence."

"Nonsense," one of the other board members scoffed. "You've seen the evidence—"

"Given the lateness of the morning," Wevary interrupted calmly, "I see no reason why we can't postpone a decision until after midday. We'll meet again in one and a half hours."

He tapped the polished stone with his fingertips and stood up. The others followed suit, and they filed silently from the room. None of them, Ziara noted, gave either her or Thrawn a second look.

Except Colonel Wevary. The last one out, he paused beside Ziara's chair—

"I don't appreciate stalling tactics, Ziara," he murmured, a hard look in his eyes. "You'd damn well better have something when we reconvene."

"Understood, sir," Ziara murmured back.

He gave her a microscopic nod and followed the others from the room.

Leaving Ziara and Thrawn alone.

"I appreciate your efforts," Thrawn said quietly, his eyes still on the colonel's empty place at the table. "But you can see they've already made up their minds. Your action does nothing but risk their displeasure, and possibly alienate you from your family."

"If I were you, I'd worry more about your family than mine," Ziara said tartly. "Speaking of whom, why isn't your rep here?"

Thrawn gave a small shrug. "I don't know. I suspect they don't like one of their merit adoptives being attached to a scandal."

"No family does," Ziara said, frowning. He was right about that, of course.

But even merit adoptives counted as part of the family and, as such, were to be guarded and defended. If the Mitth were standing back from Thrawn at such a crucial moment, there had to be something else going on. "Meanwhile, Colonel Wevary called luncheon," she reminded him as she stood up. "I'm going to get something to eat. You should do the same."

"I'm not hungry."

"Eat something anyway." Ziara hesitated, but it was too good a chance to pass up. "That way, if they kick you out, you'll at least have had one more free meal."

He looked at her, and for a moment she thought he was going to lash out at her insensitivity. Then, to her relief, he smiled. "Indeed," he said. "You have an eminently tactical mind, Senior Cadet."

"I try," Ziara said. "Make it a good meal, and don't be late getting back." She gave him a nod and headed out.

But she didn't go to the mess hall. Instead, she found an empty classroom a few doors down and slipped inside.

An eminently tactical mind, Thrawn had said. Others had told her the same thing, and Ziara had never found a reason to disagree with them.

Time to find out if all of them were right.

The receptionist answered on the third buzz. "General Ba'kif's office," he announced.

"My name is Senior Cadet Irizi'ar'alani," Ziara said. "Please ask the general if he can spare a few minutes of his time.

"Tell him it concerns Cadet Mitth'raw'nuru."

Colonel Wevary and the others filed into the hearing room precisely one and a half hours after they left it. Neither the officers nor the Irizi rep looked at the two cadets as they seated themselves.

Which made the suddenly stunned expressions on all four faces all the more amusing when they belatedly spotted the newcomer sitting beside Ziara. "General *Ba'kif*?" Colonel Wevary said with a sort of explosive gulp. "I—excuse me, sir. I wasn't informed of your arrival."

"That's all right, Colonel," Ba'kif said, giving each of the men at the table a quick look. The other two officers were as unprepared as Wevary to find a field-rank officer in their midst, but their surprise was rapidly turning to proper respect.

The Irizi's surprise, in contrast, was quickly turning to suspicion. Clearly, he'd had his own look at Thrawn's history and suspected Ba'kif was here for a cover-up.

"I understand Cadet Mitth'raw'nuru is under suspicion of cheating," Ba'kif continued, turning back to Wevary. "I think Cadet Ziara and I may have a way to resolve the issue."

"With all due respect, General, we've examined all the evidence," Wevary said, some stiffness creeping into his deference. "The exercise cannot be repeated with the same parameters as were in place when he took it, and he claims that without those parameters he cannot duplicate his success."

"I understand," Ba'kif said. "But there are other ways."

"I hope you're not going to suggest we reprogram the simulator," one of the other officers put in. "The safeguards that were put in to prevent cadets from doing that very thing would take weeks to unravel."

"No, I'm not suggesting that," Ba'kif assured him. "I presume, Colonel, that you have all the relevant exercise parameters?"

"Yes, sir," Wevary said. "But as I said—"

"A moment," Ba'kif said, turning to Thrawn. "Cadet Thrawn, you've logged two hundred hours on the patrol craft simulator. Are you ready to try the real thing?"

Thrawn's eyes darted to Ziara, back to Ba'kif. "Yes, sir, I am."

"Just a minute," the Irizi cut in. "What exactly are you proposing?"

"I should think that was obvious," Ba'kif said. "The danger inherent in teaching via simulator is that if the simulation diverges from reality, we may not notice until too late." He waved a hand at Thrawn. "We have here an opportunity to compare the simulation with reality, and we're going to take advantage of it."

"Taharim Academy is under Colonel Wevary's authority," the Irizi insisted.

"Indeed it is." Ba'kif turned to Wevary. "Colonel?"

"I concur, General," Wevary said without hesitation. "I'm looking forward to the exercise."

The Irizi glared at him. But he merely compressed his lips and inclined his head.

"Good." Ba'kif turned back to the board. "Gentlemen, I have four patrol craft prepped and waiting at the platform, plus an observation launch for the six of us to watch from." He stood up and gestured toward the door. "Shall we go?"

The four patrollers were in their starting positions: Thrawn in one, three of General Ba'kif's pilots in the others. The test area had been cordoned off, and the initial points for the exercise mapped out. The observation launch was in position, outside the combat area but close enough to see and record everything.

Ziara sat beside Ba'kif in the second seating tier, staring out the canopy past the heads of the other three officers and the Irizi. She'd pitched this to the general as an unfair charge against Thrawn, wrapping her concerns in the glow of the younger cadet's academic record. And in all honesty, Ba'kif hadn't seemed to need a lot of persuasion.

But that didn't change the fact that Ziara had stuck her neck out, and there was now a fresh target painted on her forehead. Before her call to Ba'kif, she'd been peripheral to the situation, with little danger to her or the Irizi name. Now, if Thrawn failed to prove his case, her name would be right up there with his.

"Patrols One and Three: Go," Ba'kif said into the comm. "Patrol Four: Go. Patrol Two: Go. Make sure your vectors stay precisely on track."

In the distance in front of them, the three patrol ships began to move. Beneath them, Thrawn's Patrol Four headed toward them. "Steady," Ba'kif warned. "Two, increase thrust a couple of degrees. One and Three, running true. Cadet Thrawn?"

"Ready, sir," Thrawn's measured voice came.

Ziara felt her lip twist. *Now,* when her stomach was tied up in knots, was naturally the moment he picked to be cool and calm.

Or maybe it was just that space and combat were a more comfortable environment for him than a courtroom filled with officers, regulations, and family politics.

"Stand by," Ba'kif said. "Exercise begins . . . now."

The four patrol ships leapt toward each other, precisely matching the exercise's original parameters. Thrawn cut to starboard, heading toward Three. One and Two angled toward him, closing the distance. Thrawn opened fire, raking One and Three with low-power, exercise-level spectrum laser shots. The two ships veered apart, moving out of the lines of fire, as Two headed toward Thrawn's flank, all three targeting Thrawn with their own fire. For a few seconds, Thrawn ignored the theoretical destruction hammering at his ship's hull and continued toward One and Three. Then, abruptly, he spun his ship around in a 180-yaw, turning his thrusters toward One and Three as if preparing to escape.

But instead of firing his aft thrusters, he threw full power to the forward ones, continuing his drive toward One and Three.

The maneuver caught all three attackers off guard. One and Three veered even farther apart, reflexively shying away from the threat of being rammed. Two, which had been intent on a flanking close-fire position, instead shot past Thrawn's bow.

And as Two passed in front of him, Thrawn fired his lasers at its stern, simultaneously firing his rear thrusters full-power toward One and Three.

Someone swore softly. Somehow, Thrawn's attack had killed Two's acceleration and sent it into a slow tumble. Thrawn's own thruster burst sent him past Two's stern, once again leaving him a clear path for escape.

But to Ziara's astonishment, instead of running he fired his forward thrusters, killing his speed and dropping beside Two, putting the tumbling ship between him and the more distant One and Three.

And somehow, right in the midst of that maneuver, his ship picked up the exact same tumble that his attack had given Two, precisely matching its speed and rotation as he settled in behind it.

Ziara huffed out a half laugh. "He did it," she said under her breath. "He disappeared."

"What are you talking about?" the Irizi asked, sounding confused. "He's right there."

"Not done," Ba'kif warned.

A second later Thrawn broke his ship out of its wobble, and as Two rotated past him he fired his bow-flank and stern-flank lasers, catching One and Three squarely in their bows.

"Hold!" Ba'kif called. "The exercise is over. Thank you all; please return to the launch platform. Cadet Thrawn, are you comfortable with docking your ship by yourself?"

"Yes, sir."

"I'll see you inside, then. Well done, Cadet." He keyed off.

"What do you mean, well done?" the Irizi demanded. "What did that prove? It was a skillful enough maneuver, I'll grant you, but we all saw it. He hardly disappeared the way he claimed."

"On the contrary," Ba'kif said, a mixture of admiration and amusement in his voice. "We only saw it because we were above the field of combat, and because we were using low-power lasers that skewed the real-world effects.

The simulation, on the other hand, wasn't so limited." He looked at Wevary. "Colonel?"

"Yes," Wevary said. He didn't sound as amused as Ba'kif, but Ziara could hear the same admiration in his voice. "Well done, indeed."

"General–" the Irizi began.

"Patience, Aristocra," Ba'kif said.

And to Ziara's surprise, he turned to her. "Senior Cadet Ziara, perhaps you'd be good enough to explain?"

"Yes, sir," Ziara said, feeling like she'd suddenly been tossed into the deep end. The most junior person in the compartment, and he wanted *her* to give what amounted to a lecture?

Still, having an Irizi explain to another Irizi was probably the politically smart move.

"The first attack against Thrawn would have opened up his aft oxygen reserves and fuel tanks, spewing both gases into space behind him," she said. "When he turned aft to One and Three and fired a thruster burst, those escaping gases would have ignited, temporarily blinding the attackers' sensors."

The Irizi snorted. "Speculation."

"Not at all," Wevary put in. "That's exactly what happened in the simulation, and the reason why it happened. Continue, Senior Cadet."

Ziara nodded. "At the same time Thrawn fired at Two's aft thrusters, damaging them in a precisely specific pattern that not only temporarily knocked them out but also gave the ship a predictable wobble. All he had to do then was duplicate the effect with his own thrusters as he came alongside, matching the pattern and hiding behind the ship. He then waited just long enough for One and Three to turn their attention elsewhere in an attempt to locate him, then came out and fired before they could respond."

The Irizi seemed to ponder that. "Fine," he said reluctantly. "But what of Two's own sensors? The simulation shows no images from that ship while the cadet is hiding."

"The crew would have been using the flank thrusters to dampen the wobble," Ziara said, feeling a sense of relief. The other still wasn't happy, but he clearly realized there was no point in pushing this any further. She and her family would not, it seemed, be caught in scandal after all. "All that firing would have obscured the sensors."

"So," Ba'kif said. "I trust, Colonel, that this will bring an end to your inquiry?"

"It will indeed, General," Wevary said. "Thank you for your assistance. This has been most enlightening."

"Indeed it has," Ba'kif said. "Helm: Return us to dock, if you please."

And as the launch turned and headed toward the platform, Ba'kif gave Ziara a sideways look. "And a lesson for you, Senior Cadet," he said, just loud enough for her to hear. "You have good instincts. Continue to trust them."

"Thank you, sir," Ziara said. "I shall strive to do so."

CHAPTER THREE

T he corridor leading to the Aristocra hearing room was long, a little dark, and more than a little echoey. Ar'alani listened to her footsteps as she walked, hearing a sort of mocking *doom, doom, doom* in the dull thuds. Dramatics, designed to put approaching witnesses and speakers at a psychological disadvantage before they even entered the chamber.

The one they really wanted to rake over the firepit was Thrawn, of course. But he was off on some top-secret mission for Supreme General Ba'kif and out of reach. In his absence, someone had apparently decided that his commander during the battle should be called in front of an official tribunal, presumably in the hope that she would say something derogatory they could use against him at a later date.

A complete waste of time, really. Ar'alani had already said all she was going to say to the Defense Hierarchy Council, and she doubted anyone here truly expected her to change that testimony. And no matter how mad they might get at her, in theory the Aristocra and Nine Families could do nothing to a flag officer of her rank.

In theory.

"This," Senior Captain Kiwu'tro'owmis huffed as she and her shorter legs labored to keep up with Ar'alani's longer stride, "is bogus. Totally bogus. Bogus to the ninth, factorial."

"That's a lot of boguses," Ar'alani said, smiling to herself. Not only was Wutroow an excellent first officer, but she was gifted with a knack for breaking tension and calling out absurdity.

"And I stand by every one of them," Wutroow said. "We blasted the Paataatus into small bits of metal and got as groveling a peace settlement from them as I've ever seen. And the Aristocra *still* aren't happy?"

"No," Ar'alani agreed. "But we're not the ones they're unhappy at. We just happen to be the most convenient targets right now for their annoyance."

Wutroow huffed. "Thrawn."

Ar'alani nodded. "Thrawn."

"In that case, it's bogus to the *tenth* factorial," Wutroow said firmly. "There was a good reason why he disobeyed your order. Plus his plan worked."

Which was precisely why the Council hadn't brought any charges or reprimands down on him, of course. Especially since neither Ar'alani nor any of the other ship commanders had been willing to file a charge.

But Thrawn had enemies among the Aristocra. And Council vindication or not, those enemies were smelling blood.

"So what do we do, ma'am?"

"We answer their questions," Ar'alani told her. "Honestly, of course. Most Aristocra know not to ask a question they don't already know the answer to."

"I assume that doesn't mean we can't spiral our answers a little?"

"That's certainly going to be *my* strategy," Ar'alani said. "Just be careful you don't spiral too far and end up staring into your own laser. Some of the Aristocra have honed that tactic into a fine art, and very much know it when they see it."

Wutroow chuckled. "A fine art. Thrawn should like that."

"Not the kind of art he excels at, unfortunately," Ar'alani said. "Just watch yourself. If they can't have his blood, they may try to get some of ours."

"I don't think we have to worry too much, Admiral," Wutroow said. "Remember the old saying: The sky is always darkest—"

"—just before it goes completely black," Ar'alani finished for her. "Yes, I had that same instructor at the academy."

And then they were there. The door wards pulled on the rings, swinging the heavy panels open—more psychological dramatics—revealing the witness table and two chairs facing the darkened semi-circle where the group of syndics silently sat awaiting them. Putting a note of confidence into her step, Ar'alani walked to the table and stood behind one of the chairs, Wutroow taking up position beside her. "Syndics of the Chiss Ascendancy, I greet you," Ar'alani called, making sure her voice held the same confidence as her step. "I am Admiral Ar'alani, currently in command of the *Vigilant* and Picket Force Six of the Expansionary Defense Fleet. This is my first officer, Senior Captain Kiwu'tro'owmis."

"Greetings, Admiral; Senior Captain," a voice said from the ring.

And suddenly the darkness blazed with light.

Ar'alani blinked a couple of times as her eyes adjusted, a back corner of her mind appreciating this final gambit. The syndics had no need to cower in darkness; they could face anyone in the Ascendancy without fear.

"Please be seated," another voice said. "We have just a few questions for you."

"We stand ready to answer," Ar'alani said, pulling out her chair and sitting down, her eyes flicking across the table. None of the faces were familiar to her, but the family nameplates at the front edge of the table told her everything she needed to know. Six families had been chosen for this particular tribunal, as usual comprising a mix of the Nine and the Great: the Irizi, Ar'alani's old family; the Kiwu, Wutroow's current family; plus the Clarr, Plikh, Ufsa, and Droc.

Conspicuous by its absence was Thrawn's family, the Mitth.

Conspicuous *and* suspicious. The fact that Thrawn himself wasn't here had probably been the others' excuse for keeping the Mitth out of the questioning. But given that he was clearly the focus of the interrogation, the Mitth should have insisted on being present.

Unless they'd already decided among themselves that Thrawn was a liability and were throwing him to the nighthunters. It wouldn't be the first time they'd considered that path.

"Let me get directly to the point," the Clarr said. "Six days ago, your picket force was sent against the Paataatus in reprisal for their probes against our southeast-zenith border. During that battle, one of your ship commanders, Senior Captain Mitth'raw'nuruodo, disobeyed a direct order. Is this true?"

Ar'alani hesitated. Truthful, but spiraled. "He disobeyed a lesser order, yes, Syndic," she said.

The Clarr frowned. "Excuse me?"

"I said he disobeyed a lesser order," Ar'alani said. "At the time, though, he was obeying a greater order."

"Well, this is certainly fascinating," the Irizi put in drily. "The Irizi family has been honored to supply officers and warriors to the Defense Force for generations, and I don't recall ever hearing of greater and lesser orders."

"Perhaps *priorities* would be a better term," Ar'alani amended. "A warrior's first priority is of course to defend the Ascendancy. The second is to win the current battle and war. The third is to protect the ship and crew. The fourth is to obey a specific order."

"Are you suggesting the Expansionary Defense Fleet operates like a free-form melee?" the Droc asked.

"More like a free-form sculpture if Thrawn is involved," the Ufsa added under her breath.

A couple of the others chuckled. The Clarr didn't so much as smile. "I asked you a question, Admiral."

"Certainly the fleet isn't as chaotic as your comment would make it appear," Ar'alani said. "Ideally, the senior commander's orders are perfectly in line with all those priorities." She cocked her head, as if a thought had suddenly occurred to her. "In fact, I would venture to say it's much the same with you."

The Clarr's eyes narrowed. "Explain."

"Your first duty is to the Ascendancy," Ar'alani said. "Your second is to your individual families."

"What's good for the Nine Families is good for the Ascendancy," the Plikh said stiffly.

"No doubt," Ar'alani agreed. "I simply refer to the hierarchy of goals and duties."

"Even within the families," Wutroow put in. "I imagine you treat blood differently from cousins, ranking distants, Trial-borns, and merit adoptives."

"Thank you for your statement of the obvious, Senior Captain," the Clarr said acidly. "But you weren't brought here for a discussion of family relationships. You were brought here to explain why Captain Thrawn was permitted to disobey a direct order from his superior without suffering any consequences for his actions."

"Forgive me, Syndic," Wutroow said before Ar'alani could answer, "but I have a question."

"Admiral Ar'alani, kindly inform your first officer that she's here to answer questions, not ask them," the Clarr snapped.

"Again, forgive me, Syndic," Wutroow said doggedly, "but my question has a direct bearing on Captain Thrawn's actions."

The Clarr started to speak, hesitated, then pursed his lips. "Very well," he said. "But I warn you, Captain, that I'm not in the mood for frivolous deflection."

"Neither am I, Syndic," Wutroow said. "As has been established, the reason Captain Thrawn moved the *Springhawk* away from Admiral Ar'alani's force was to draw the ambush to himself and give the rest of the ships time to adjust and counterattack. My question is this: *Why* was the force ambushed so quickly and completely?"

"Because the Paataatus knew that their actions against the Ascendancy would naturally invite reprisals," the Clarr said. "Especially if they were the ones behind the Csilla attack. I warned you about frivolous questions—"

"But why *there*?" Wutroow persisted. "Why that particular spot? Because they were very clearly expecting us."

"You sound as if you already know the answer," the Kiwu said. "Why don't you tell us?"

"Thank you," Wutroow said, inclining her head to him. "I've obtained a detailed report of the mission the Syndicure sent to the Paataatus shortly after they were identified as the ones pressing against our flank. The conversations were brief—"

"We've all read the report," the Clarr interrupted. "Get on with it."

"Yes, Syndic," Wutroow said. There was no trace of a smile on her face, Ar'alani noted—Wutroow knew better than to even look like she might be mocking any of the Aristocra—but there was a subtle look in her eye that promised this was going to be good. "As the discussions ended and the emissaries returned to their ship, one of them said to the Paataatus delegation—" Wutroow paused and peered at her questis. "—and I quote: 'The next time you see Chiss ships come toward you through those stars, they'll be bringing your utter destruction.' " She looked up. "Do I need to identify the direction that emissary was pointing?"

"Nonsense," the Ufsa bit out. "No diplomat would do anything so foolish."

"Apparently one of them did," Wutroow said. "Had Admiral Ar'alani known about that, of course, she would certainly have chosen a different attack vector. But she didn't know."

"And under those circumstances," Ar'alani added, picking up on Wutroow's opening, "I'm sure you recognize that Captain Thrawn's actions were both necessary and proper."

"Perhaps," the Clarr said. His voice and face still weren't conceding the point, but his earlier confidence had definitely cooled. "Interesting. Thank you for your time, Admiral; Captain. You're dismissed. We'll call you back after we've looked into this matter further."

"Yes, Syndic," Ar'alani said, standing up. "One other thing. I fully believe that this attack is the last demonstration we'll need to launch against the Paataatus. Their diplomats seem fully committed to withdrawing to their borders and leaving the Ascendancy strictly alone. If that makes a difference to your deliberations."

"Thank you," the Clarr said again. "Good day."

"They won't, of course," Wutroow said as the two women retraced their steps down the long corridor. "Call us back, I mean. Once they figure out what happened, the last thing they'll want is to draw more attention to such a blunder."

"Agreed," Ar'alani said. "So is that story actually true?"

"Absolutely." Wutroow smiled. "Bluffing an enemy in combat sometimes works. Bluffing the Aristocra doesn't. No, one of the emissaries was actually stupid enough to stand there and point out our optimal attack vector."

"You got this from someone in your family, I assume?"

"Yes, ma'am," Wutroow confirmed. "I'm sorry, but I can't give you the specifics."

"I wasn't going to ask," Ar'alani assured her. "I assume leaking it to you had to do with some larger stakes of family politics, and not just getting Thrawn off the hook?"

"No, that was just a fortunate side effect." Wutroow gave Ar'alani a sideways look. "I note you didn't credit Thrawn with that prediction of future Paataatus inaction."

Ar'alani felt her nose wrinkle. Normally, she hated the common practice of one officer taking credit for another's achievements or ideas. But in this case . . . "I'll make sure to correct the record in a year or two, assuming the prediction works out," she said. "Today I don't think it would have gone over well."

"But you wanted to get it on the record," Wutroow said, nodding. "And this was your best way of doing that. I guess you never realize how important family connections and pipelines are until you lose them."

"No, you don't," Ar'alani said, feeling an old and distant sense of loss. "So enjoy it while you can."

"What, *me*?" Wutroow gave a small laugh. "I appreciate the compliment, Admiral. But there's no way I'll ever make flag rank."

"You never know, Captain," Ar'alani said. "You really never know."

CHAPTER FOUR

Che'ri came out of Third Sight with slightly bleary eyes, a horrible tiredness, and a massive headache. It felt like an overload spell starting to come on.

She hoped desperately it wasn't an overload spell.

"We're here," someone said.

Che'ri turned her head, careful not to move it too quickly. Senior Captain Thrawn was seated in the command chair, with Mid Captain Samakro on his left and Thalias on his right.

That was new. Most of Che'ri's momishes had walked her to and from the bridge but stayed in the suite while she was on duty. She'd always assumed they simply weren't allowed inside.

Maybe they all could have stayed if they'd wanted to, and just didn't want to. Or maybe Thalias was special because she'd been a sky-walker.

Thrawn and Samakro were looking at a planet centered in the main viewport.

Thalias was looking at Che'ri.

Quickly, Che'ri turned back to her controls, the sudden movement hammering an extra jolt of pain into her head. *Never show weakness,* she'd been warned over and over again. *A sky-walker never shows weakness. She's always ready to continue on, cheerfully and efficiently, making one more journey, and one more after that, until her captain allows her to rest.*

"No energy emissions," the woman at the sensor station called.

"No masses of refined metal, no indications of life activities. Planet seems dead."

"Not surprising, given the environment," Samakro said. "Scratch one more. On to the next system?"

There was a pause. Che'ri kept staring at the controls in front of her, hoping Thrawn would say no.

But she was sure he would say yes. No one had told her what this journey was all about, but they seemed to be looking for something important. A captain like Thrawn wouldn't want to waste any time.

Could Che'ri navigate with an overload spell coming on? She'd never tried before. But she had a job to do, and there was no one else aboard who could do it. If Thrawn said they should go on—

"I think not," Thrawn said. "The ship and warriors could use a few hours' rest."

Che'ri felt tears blurring her eyes. Tears of relief that she could rest. Tears of shame that she was too tired to go on.

Thrawn knew. She could hear it in his voice. He could say everyone else needed rest, but he knew. It was all on her. All on Che'ri. She was the reason they had to stop.

"Helm, bring us into high orbit over the planet," the captain ordered.

"Yes, sir," the man at the console next to Che'ri's said.

She watched his fingers moving on the controls, fascinated despite her aches and blurry vision. She'd played some flying games on her questis, but watching someone doing it for real was a lot more interesting.

"Sensors, extend your search outward during the inbound," Thrawn continued. "Once we're in orbit, refine the search toward the planet."

"Yes, sir," the woman said.

"What are you expecting to find?" Samakro asked.

"Not expecting, Mid Captain," Thrawn corrected. "Merely speculating."

Che'ri frowned. Speculating? About what? She kept listening, hoping Samakro would ask.

But he didn't. "Yes, sir," was all he said. Che'ri heard his footsteps as he walked away.

"Thank you," Thalias said quietly.

Che'ri squeezed her eyes tightly shut against the pain and shame, spilling the tears down her cheeks. Thalias knew, too. Did Samakro know?

Did *everyone* on the ship know?

There was a breath on Che'ri's cheek, warming the tears. "Are you all right?" Thalias asked softly into her ear. "Shall I help you back to the suite?"

"Can I stay here a little longer?" Che'ri asked. "I can't . . . I don't want to be carried."

"Is she all right, Caregiver?" Thrawn asked.

"She will be," Thalias said, pressing her hand against Che'ri's forehead. The cool and the pressure felt good. "Sometimes sky-walkers come out of Third Sight with sensory overload that presents with aches and sparkle-vision. If it goes into a full-on spell, it can take some time to throw it off."

"All the more reason to stop for now," Thrawn said.

"Yes," Thalias said. "At any rate, I'd like to give Che'ri a few minutes here to start her recovery before we walk back to the suite."

A small bit of comfort whispered through the pain. None of Che'ri's other momishes had ever really understood these overload spells. One of them had even gotten angry with her. It was nice to have someone who knew what they were, and what to do about them.

"Take all the time you need," Thrawn said. "I'm not surprised she was affected so strongly, given this system's parameters."

Che'ri frowned, opening her eyes and peering at the planet the *Springhawk* was moving toward. It didn't look any different from any other planet she'd seen on this trip. What was so special about it?

"Not the planet," Thrawn said.

Che'ri jerked, the movement sending another wave of pain through her head and shoulders. The captain's voice had come from right behind her.

Captains didn't usually get close to their sky-walkers. She didn't know if they weren't supposed to, or if they just didn't. But Thrawn was standing right beside Thalias. Almost close enough to touch.

"Look at the tactical display," Thrawn continued, pointing at one of the big screens beside the viewport. "It gives you a wider view of the system as a whole."

Che'ri squinted at the display, trying to sort out all the lines and curves and numbers.

And then she got it, and felt her eyes go wide.

There wasn't just one star out there, like she'd thought. There were *four* of them.

"Quadruple star systems like this are quite rare," Thrawn said. "I imagine navigating into the middle of one takes an extra toll on Third Sight."

"Yes, I imagine it does," Thalias said, shifting hands to bring her other, colder one onto Che'ri's forehead. "Why are we here? I mean *here*?"

"Do you really want to know, Caregiver?" Thrawn asked.

Thalias's hand against Che'ri's forehead suddenly went stiff. "Yes, sir," Thalias said. "I really do."

Thrawn stepped around to Thalias's other side. "A refugee ship was found drifting in one of the Ascendancy's outlying systems," he said, his voice low. Maybe Che'ri wasn't supposed to hear this part? "We're following the likely vector the ship came from in the hope of identifying the people. A question, Lieutenant Commander Azmordi?"

"No, sir," the lieutenant commander said stiffly. "But may I remind the captain that there are certain areas that are to be kept"—squinting past Thalias's hand, Che'ri saw him pointing at her—"within the senior officer corps?"

"Your concern is noted, Lieutenant Commander," Thrawn said. "However, at some point Sky-walker Che'ri and Caregiver Thalias may be required to perform extraordinary tasks. It's important that the team knows what's at stake and is mentally prepared."

Che'ri frowned. *The team.* No one had ever called her part of a team before. She'd never even thought of herself that way. She was the sky-walker, and her caregiver was her momish, and that was all.

Che'ri guided the ship where it needed to go, and the caregiver made her meals and put her to bed at night. They weren't a team.

Were they?

"Yes, sir," Azmordi said. Che'ri had heard enough unhappy officers to know what one sounded like, and this one definitely wasn't happy.

But he didn't keep arguing.

"It occurred to me that the refugees wouldn't want their enemy to know where they were going," Thrawn continued. "I also read from the way the family units had been gathered together on the destroyed ship that the people had a close sense of comradeship. It seemed to me that such people would prefer to travel in groups. Or, if not a group, then at least with a companion ship."

He paused, like he was expecting one of them to say something. Che'ri looked at the four stars again, trying to think through her headache.

And then, suddenly, she had it. "I know!" she said, raising her hand. "The four stars. It's hard to get in here."

"Yes," Thrawn said. "Which means . . . ?"

Che'ri felt her shoulders hunch. She didn't have any idea what it meant.

"Which means it's a perfect place for two ships to rendezvous," Thalias said. "A place where any pursuers would hesitate to look. Do you think we'll find the other ship here?"

"Possibly." Thrawn paused again, and Che'ri had the feeling he was looking at her. "Sky-walker Che'ri, are you ready yet to return to your quarters?"

The moment of excitement disappeared. Che'ri wasn't part of the team anymore, just someone there to move the ship around. "I think so," she said with a sigh.

"Let me help you," Thalias said. She took Che'ri's arm with one hand, and undid the safety straps with the other. "Are you ready to stand up?"

"Yes," Che'ri said. She stood up, stopped as her head spun suddenly with vertigo. The universe settled down, and she nodded.

"Okay," she said, and walked around the chair. With Thalias still holding her arm, she went to the bridge hatchway.

A moment later, they were walking down the corridor. "Are you hungry?" Thalias asked as they reached the door to their suite. "Or would you like a hot bath first?"

"A bath," Che'ri said. "Did you get overload spells like this?"

"Sometimes," Thalias said. "Mostly when I was just starting out, but I had occasional ones right up to the end. Probably none of them was as bad as this one, though." She shook her head. "A four-star system. The worst I ever had was a three-star one. You're pretty amazing, Che'ri."

Che'ri wrinkled her nose. "Not really."

But the words felt good. Captain Thrawn taking the time to talk to her had felt good, too.

A hot bath would feel *really* good.

"Well, you are," Thalias said. "Let me get you settled, and I'll go draw your bath. Would you like your questis while you wait?"

Three hours later, with Che'ri bathed, fed, and finally asleep, Thalias returned to the bridge.

To find that the *Springhawk* was no longer alone. Floating half a kilometer away from the viewport, its outer lights dark, was an alien ship.

Samakro was seated in the command chair, talking quietly with one of the other officers. He spotted Thalias, muttered a final comment, and as the other man headed for one of the consoles he beckoned her over. "How is Che'ri?" he asked.

"Sleeping," Thalias said, stopping beside his chair and gazing out at the alien ship. The blocky shape made it look more like a freighter than a warship, she decided. "Where's Senior Captain Thrawn?"

"He went aboard with a survey team." Samakro shook his head. "Damnedest thing."

"The ship?"

"The captain," Samakro said. "How did he know it would be here?"

Thalias started to remind him of Thrawn's earlier analysis, re-membered in time that Samakro hadn't been there for that. "He has his methods," she said instead. "Where was it?"

"Orbiting on the other side of the planet," Samakro said. "It wasn't until just after you left that it came into sight."

Thalias winced. A dead ship, probably with dead people aboard. Had Thrawn known or suspected when it would come out of hiding? Was that why he'd suddenly wanted her to take Che'ri out of there and get her back to their suite?

Because the helm officer was right. There were definitely some things that should be kept hidden from the sky-walkers.

"So what's *your* story?" Samakro asked.

"Excuse me?" Thalias asked, frowning at him.

"Please," Samakro said scornfully. "A former sky-walker, now working as a caregiver? Doesn't happen anymore. From what I've heard, once sky-walkers are done they want to get as far away from that life as they can."

"It wasn't that bad," Thalias said, only lying a little.

"Right," Samakro said. "*And* Mitth family, *and* aboard Thrawn's ship? If you're really who you claim to be, that's a pretty heaping pile of coincidence."

The memory of her brief conversation with Syndic Thurfian flashed back to mind. Samakro had no idea. A flicker of movement caught her eye: one of the *Springhawk*'s shuttles, detaching from the ship and heading back. "If you have a point, please make it," she said. "The captain's on his way back."

"The Mitth sent you to observe us," Samakro said. "Don't bother denying it—the officer who put you on the *Springhawk* told me that's how you first tried to get aboard, and also that a Mitth syndic showed up at the last minute to give you a push."

Thalias kept her expression wooden. "And?"

"And I've seen the flaming mess observers can make aboard a war-ship," Samakro said. "They get in the way, they never know where to stand or which way to jump, and they introduce way more family politics than is healthy."

"I'm not here to make trouble."

"Doesn't matter," Samakro said. "You just will." He pointed at the ship floating in front of them. "Everyone over there is dead. Everyone on the ship that was attacked at Dioya is dead. Someone made them that way, someone who may be brand new to us. And somewhere along the line, we may have to fight them."

His pointing finger shifted to Thalias. "I don't want to die because people were ignoring their boards and instead looking over their shoulders to see if the Mitth observer was watching them."

"I think that's a sentiment we can all get behind," Thalias said stiffly. "Let's make a deal. *I'll* do everything I can to not make a mess. *You'll* do everything you can to let me know when I'm making one anyway."

"Don't say that if you don't mean it," Samakro warned. "We do have a brig, you know."

"Don't threaten something you can't follow through on, Mid Captain," Thalias said. "Don't forget I'm the only one who can take care of your sky-walker."

"Since when?" Samakro scoffed. "You mix up soup when she gets sick, you cuddle her when she's crying, and you make sure none of us dangerous warrior types scare her."

"Trust me, there's a lot more to it than that," Thalias said, pushing away her reflexive annoyance. If Samakro was trying to goad her into making enough trouble that he had an excuse to lock her up, he would have to try harder than that. "So what do we know about that ship? You said everyone was dead? How?"

Samakro took a deep breath. "All we know so far is that the hyperdrive failed, which is what stranded them here. At least this batch wasn't murdered like the last group—looks like they ran out of air." His lips compressed briefly. "Not the worst way to die, for what it's worth."

"It also means an intact ship and intact bodies," Thalias said.

"Right," Samakro said. "Hopefully, that'll give us what we need to backtrack them the rest of the way to their system."

"Mid Captain Samakro, this is the captain." Thrawn's voice came over the bridge speaker. "Is the examination room prepared?"

Samakro keyed the mic at his chair. "Yes, sir," he confirmed. "We have four tables set up in Ready Room Two, and the medics and equipment are standing by."

"Excellent," Thrawn said. "Join me there, if you would."

"On my way, sir."

He got three steps toward the bridge hatch before Thalias caught up with him. "Where do you think you're going?" Samakro asked, frowning at her.

"Ready Room Two," Thalias said. "Whatever the captain's found, it may impact on where we're going and how Che'ri does her job. I need to know everything so that I can prepare her when the time comes."

"Of course you do," Samakro said sourly. "Fine. Lead the way."

"Right," Thalias said hesitantly. "Ah . . ."

"You don't know where it is, do you?"

Thalias huffed out a breath. "No."

"Didn't think so," Samakro said. "Follow me. And when we get there, stay out of the way. And don't make a mess."

The ready room was smaller than Thalias had expected, and with four tables plus the medical team crammed in the place was already crowded when she and Samakro arrived.

The medics, naturally, quickly moved out of the way to give the *Springhawk*'s first officer some space. Thalias, also naturally, had to work her way through them, avoiding elbows and glowers, until she reached a corner that wasn't being used.

She was still fine-tuning her position when Thrawn and the bodies arrived.

There were four of them, as Thrawn had implied. Three were of the same species: medium height, with pronounced chest and hip bulges, their skin a light pink but with purple splotches around the eyes, all topped by feathery head crests. Their arms and legs were spindly but looked well muscled. They were dressed in clothing that was alien, but nevertheless with a style and detail that gave Thalias the impression of being someone's finery.

The fourth body, in stark contrast, was tall and thin, with enlarged shoulders, elbows, wrists, knees, and ankles. Its skin was a pale gray, and across its temples was a crosshatch of green, red, and blue tattoo scars. It was dressed in a dark-red, totally utilitarian jumpsuit.

"There's nothing like these in our records," Thrawn said, gesturing to the three pink bodies. "But the fourth . . . do you recognize it, Mid Captain?"

"Yes," Samakro said, stepping close and peering at its stony face. "I don't know the species, but those temple scars mark him as a Void Guide."

He looked over at Thalias. "They're one of the groups who hire themselves out as navigators for long-range travel through the Chaos," he added.

"I know," Thalias said. She'd been aboard a warship once that had been escorting a diplomatic mission, and both ships had hired aliens from the Navigators' Guild to help reinforce the carefully designed illusion that the Chiss had no navigators of their own. She and her caregiver had been kept out of sight in their suite, but she'd seen some vid views of the navigator at his job.

She didn't remember that navigator looking anything like this dead Void Guide. But then, the guild was made up of a lot of different groups and species.

"Actually, I'd have been surprised if you *did* know his species," Thrawn commented. "The Navigators' Guild goes to great lengths not to identify the species or the systems of its members. At any rate, his presence is a stroke of luck."

"Why?" Thalias asked.

"Because some of the bridge recordings survived the death of the crew and passengers," Thrawn said. "Naturally, those records are in the inhabitants' language."

"Which I assume we don't know?" Samakro asked.

"Correct," Thrawn said. "The analyzers might be able to do something with it, but without a linguistic basis to start from they're unlikely to make much progress."

"But they also had to talk to their navigator," Thalias said as she suddenly saw where Thrawn was going with this. "And unless he could speak their language, they would have used a trade language."

"Exactly," Thrawn said, inclining his head toward her. "And because the Void Guides' main operational area overlaps with ours, there's a reasonable chance it'll be a language we know."

"You said some of the recordings survived," Samakro said. "Any navigational records among them?"

"An excellent question, Mid Captain," Thrawn said, his voice going grim. "The answer is no. It appears the navigator was the last to die, and erased as many records as he could before the end. The only reason we have the audio recordings is that they were stored in a different location than the others and he apparently missed them."

Thalias stared at the Void Guide body, a creepy feeling seeping through her. "He didn't want anyone to know where they'd come from," she said. "He was working with their enemies."

"Or was working to keep their enemies from backtracking them," Samakro suggested.

"No," Thrawn said. "If that was the situation, the captain would have deleted the records himself. The timestamp indicates that wasn't the case."

He turned back to Samakro. "I'll be here for the next few hours, observing the dissection. I want you to make two copies of the audio records: one for the analyzers and one for my personal examination."

"Yes, sir," Samakro said. "With your permission, I'd like to also make an extra copy for myself. Senior Commander Kharill takes over the watch in half an hour, and I can begin listening to it while you watch things down here."

"Excellent idea, Mid Captain," Thrawn said. "Thank you."

He looked at the Void Guide's body. "He went to some trouble to hide these people and their home from us. Let's see what we can learn of them despite his efforts."

Thalias watched as Thrawn examined the bodies, noting the special attention he gave to their clothing and adornments. But once that part was over, and the medics stepped forward with their surgical equipment, she decided she'd had enough.

The suite was dark and quiet as she slipped inside and locked the hatch behind her. She tiptoed across the dayroom, wondering if a hot bath would feel good or if she was too tired to do anything except curl up in bed—

"Thalias?" a tentative voice came from Che'ri's room.

"I'm here," Thalias called back softly, changing direction toward the half-open hatchway. "Did I wake you?"

"No, I was already awake," Che'ri said.

"Sorry," Thalias said. "Are you hungry? Can I get you something to eat?"

"No." Che'ri hesitated. "I had a nightmare."

"I'm so sorry," she said again, opening the hatch all the way and stepping inside. In the faint glow from the luminous escape pod markers, she saw that Che'ri was sitting up in bed, hunched over with her arms hugging one of her pillows to her chest. So much for that hot bath. "Do you want to talk about it?"

"No, I guess not," Che'ri said. "It's okay."

But she was still clutching that pillow. "Come on," Thalias encouraged as she sat down at the end of the girl's bed. "Tell me yours, and I'll tell you one of mine."

"You had nightmares, too?"

"We all did," Thalias said. "Just like the overload spells. I don't know if those things are part of Third Sight itself or if it's just all the pressure sky-walkers are under. But we all had them." She patted Che'ri's knee through the blanket. "Let me guess. You were lost and everyone was mad at you?"

"Almost," Che'ri said. "I was lost, but they weren't mad. At least they didn't say anything. But they kept looking at me. Just . . . looking."

"Yes, I had that one, too," Thalias said ruefully. "No one would talk to me, and they wouldn't listen. Sometimes they couldn't even hear me."

"I remember thinking it was like being stuck in a big soap bubble," Che'ri said.

Thalias smiled. "That part's from your bath."

"What?"

"Your bath," Thalias repeated. "The soothement bubbles. Your brain picked up on that memory and slapped it into your dream."

"Really? Brains do things like that?"

"All the time," Thalias said. "Yours took the soothement bubbles, added in your fears of getting lost, sprinkled on some of the feeling you get on the bridge that none of the grown-ups are paying any attention to you, then baked all of it inside a dream. Pop it from the oven, and there's your nightmare."

"Oh." Che'ri pondered that a moment. "Doesn't sound so scary that way."

"Nope," Thalias agreed. "Almost silly, in fact, once the lights are back on. Doesn't mean it's not terrifying when you're in the middle of it, but it helps make it better when you can figure out the pieces afterward. It's just your brain and your fears messing with you."

"Okay." Che'ri hugged the pillow a little tighter. "Thalias . . . did you ever get lost?"

Thalias hesitated. How should she answer that? "Not when I was your age," she said. "I'll bet you never got lost, either."

"But you got lost later?"

"I sort of got lost once or twice," Thalias admitted. "But that was when they already knew my Third Sight was fading, and they were running me through tests inside the Ascendancy. They do that on purpose, because they know that if the sky-walker loses the track it won't be dangerous to the ship."

"And then you were done," Che'ri murmured.

"And I thought my life was over." Thalias smiled. "But as you see, it wasn't. Yours won't be, either."

"But if I get us lost . . . ?"

"You won't," Thalias said firmly.

"What if I do?"

"You won't," Thalias said. "Trust me. And trust yourself."

"I don't think I can."

"You have to," Thalias said. "Uncertainty can be the most difficult and frightening of mental states. If you're always wondering which way to go, you might freeze up and not go anywhere. If you're afraid you can't do something, you might not even try."

Che'ri shook her head. "I don't know."

"Well, you don't have to know anything tonight," Thalias said. "All you have to do is lie down and try to get back to sleep. You sure I can't get you something to eat?"

"No, that's okay," Che'ri said. She looked down at the pillow in her arms, then shifted it around behind her. "Maybe I'll draw for a while," she added, settling herself against the pillow and snagging her questis from the bedside table.

"Sounds good," Thalias said. "Do you want me to sit with you?"

"No, that's okay," Che'ri said. "Thanks."

"You're welcome," Thalias said, standing up and backing toward the hatchway. "I'll leave the door open. If you need anything, just call, okay? And try to sleep."

"I will," Che'ri said. "Good night, Thalias."

"Good night, Che'ri."

Thalias waited another hour, just in case Che'ri changed her mind and decided she needed something. By the time she finally turned off her light and settled into bed, Che'ri's own room light was out, and the girl was once again fast asleep.

And of course, because Thalias had talked about them, her own sky-walker nightmares chose that night to come back.

"This just came in, Admiral," Wutroow said, handing over her questis. "Not entirely sure what it means."

Ar'alani ran her eyes over the message: *Rendezvous with me at the following coordinates as soon as possible. Bring only the* Vigilant. *Do not hire a navigator.*

"I checked the coordinates," Wutroow continued. "It's pretty far out. Without a navigator it'll take four or five days to get there."

"Not exactly Thrawn's usual definition of as soon as possible,"

Ar'alani agreed. "All right. I assume you signaled Naporar and asked if they could assign us a temporary sky-walker?"

Wutroow nodded. "I did. And—"

"No, no, let me guess," Ar'alani said. "You got shunted around to at least three different desks until you finally reached someone who said it would be a month before anyone was free?"

"Not exactly," Wutroow said, her voice odd. "I got sent directly to Supreme General Ba'kif." She lifted a finger for emphasis. "Not the general's *office*. The general."

"Ba'kif took your call *personally*?"

"I was rather shocked, too," Wutroow said. "Especially when he said a sky-walker would be waiting for us when we reach Naporar."

"Well, that's one for the archives," Ar'alani said, frowning. "No fuss or anything?"

"Not about the sky-walker," Wutroow said. "But there was one other odd thing. When we see Thrawn, we're supposed to ask about his sky-walker's caregiver. There's apparently some confusion as to who she is and how she got the job."

"Really," Ar'alani said, looking at the questis note again. So whatever Thrawn was doing was important enough that one of the top people on the Council was taking a personal interest, while at the same time there was something going on under the surface involving his sky-walker and her caregiver.

Naturally, Thrawn would be oblivious to both currents. "Very well," she said. "Set course for Naporar; best speed we've got."

"Yes, ma'am," Wutroow said.

"And once we're on the way," Ar'alani added, handing back the questis, "have the weapons crews start full-service scans on their equipment."

"You think there'll be combat at the other end of this trip?"

"Thrawn's there," Ar'alani reminded her. "So, yes, I'd say that's pretty much guaranteed."

CHAPTER FIVE

The *Springhawk* was waiting precisely where Thrawn had said he would be. A quick shuttle ride across, and within an hour of arriving in the system, Ar'alani and Wutroow were sitting in the briefing room with Thrawn and Samakro, reading through Thrawn's data and proposal.

Ar'alani took her time looking through the material. She read it a second time, as she always did such things. Then, just to make sure it really said what she thought it said, she read it a third time.

By the time she lifted her eyes from the questis, she saw that Wutroow and Samakro had made it through, as well. The two officers were gazing at the sections of table in front of them, their expressions a mixture of surprise, disbelief, and apprehension.

She shifted her gaze to the end of the table. Thrawn was waiting patiently, trying to hide his own anxiety. "Well," she said, setting down her questis. "It's inventive, I'll give it that."

Some of Thrawn's anxiety faded away. Apparently, a lot of his concern had been centered on how she would react. "Thank you," he said.

"With all due respect, Senior Captain, I'm not sure that was a compliment," Samakro spoke up. "The plan may be inventive, but I don't think it's physically possible."

"Actually, Mid Captain, I've seen it done," Ar'alani said. "Back at the Academy, Captain Thrawn pulled off this same maneuver." She raised her eyebrows. "On the other hand, that was a patrol ship. This time you're talking about a heavy cruiser. Big difference."

"Not as big as it might seem," Thrawn said. "True, the *Springhawk*'s mass is greater, but its thrusters and maneuvering jets are correspondingly more powerful. With proper care and preparation, I believe it can be done."

"And you're sure this is the right system?"

"The indications are there," Thrawn said. "I won't know for certain until I've examined the mining station."

Ar'alani pursed her lips and picked up her questis again. It certainly wasn't going to be easy. The place Thrawn proposed to infiltrate was what was colloquially known as a *box system*: unusually strong electromagnetic fluxes wrapped around the outer edges, interacting with the solar wind to create even more obstruction to hyperspace travel than usual. Unless a ship was willing to come out of hyperspace outside the cometary belt and spend days or weeks traveling through space-normal to the inner system, there were only a dozen reasonably safe inward pathways.

Even more intimidating was the fact that some cataclysm millennia ago had seeded the inner system and much of the outer system with large meteors, making the entire area a sort of miniature version of the Chaos itself. Taking those additional navigational hazards into account, the number of safe lanes to the inhabited planet dropped to exactly three.

Three routes to one single, isolated planet, unknown to the Ascendancy and apparently unconnected with any known species in the area. A somewhat larger selection of pathways to the outer asteroid belt, which consisted of several tightly packed clusters and a number of possibly abandoned mining space stations.

But while the mining stations might be abandoned, the rest of the system was active enough. Thrawn's brief reconnaissance had picked up a fair amount of travel within the system, mostly between the planet and a handful of colony or manufacturing stations orbiting it. Unfortunately, the *Springhawk* had been too far out to tell whether or not those ships were similar to the destroyed refugee ships whose records Thrawn had now shared with her and Wutroow.

And just to add spice to the whole thing, all three of the entry routes were being patrolled by small warships of a completely different design.

"So you think this is the system the refugee ships came from," she said, looking up at Thrawn again. "You further think they're under blockade by these other ships."

"Less a blockade than an interdiction," Thrawn said. "You can see the patrol ships' configuration is mainly designed to control access to the main planet. The asteroid stations aren't as heavily guarded and are therefore more accessible."

"But they *are* still guarded," Wutroow pointed out. "And I'm only counting three good paths in and out of the system."

"Only if you want the planet," Thrawn said. "If you want the asteroid station I've indicated, there are several other workable vectors."

"At least until the blockaders get a few more ships," Ar'alani said.

"Indeed," Thrawn agreed. "It therefore seems to me that if we want to do this, we have to do it soon."

"How long did you sit out on the edge observing them?" Ar'alani asked.

"Only three days," Samakro said.

"A full three days," Thrawn corrected. "Long enough for me to analyze their patrol pattern and learn how to penetrate it."

"Again, unless they've gotten more ships in the past fifteen hours," Ar'alani said.

Thrawn's lip twitched. "Yes."

For a few moments, the conference room was quiet. Ar'alani gazed at her questis, pretending to study it, weighing the options. For anyone else, she knew, three days wouldn't be nearly enough to analyze an alien patrol pattern, let alone figure out a way through it.

But for Thrawn, three days probably really *was* enough, Samakro's doubts notwithstanding. Ar'alani couldn't have come up with a plan herself this quickly, but she could see that Thrawn's had a good chance of working.

On the other hand, this was hardly going to be a sleepwalk. Thrawn's proposed course should get them in well ahead of any pursuit from the handful of patrol ships watching the outer system, but

if the blockade's commander detached some of his closer-in planetary forces he might catch the two Chiss ships in a pincer. "What
about exit strategy?" she asked. "We'll need one immediately, and
you'll need one eventually."

"There we have two interesting options," Thrawn said. As if,
Ar'alani thought wryly, this whole thing didn't come under the
heading of *interesting*. "The typical box system is bounded for the
most part by external flux patterns interacting with solar wind. These
two points"—he tapped his questis—"mark the outer system's two
gas giant planets."

Ar'alani smiled tightly as she saw it. "Planets which carve out
small holes in the solar wind as they travel along their orbits."

"Holes you can pop in and out of without confusing your hyperdrive or your sky-walker," Wutroow said. "Huh. Hard to hit from the
outside, though, unless you've got really good planetary data."

"But not as difficult going from the inside," Ar'alani said, "since
you know right where the planets and the gaps are." She looked at
Thrawn with sudden realization. "That's how the refugee ships got
out past the patrols, isn't it?"

"That's my assumption," Thrawn said.

"And now, of course, we've also got the planetary data we need,"
Wutroow added. "So we go in through Shadow Number One and exit
through Shadow Number Two?"

"Exactly," Thrawn said. "And the *Springhawk* can subsequently
leave through either. They're close enough together for your pur-
poses, but far enough apart that the blockaders won't be able to sufficiently guard both, if they even wish to do so."

"Unless, as we all keep saying, they've found more ships," Wutroow
pointed out.

Thrawn nodded. "Yes."

"Okay, I'm confused," Wutroow said, frowning at her questis. "You
don't blockade a place unless you want to take it over. I'm sure it's a
great place to live, but why would anyone else want it?"

"Box systems have some advantages," Samakro said. "As we've already noted, they're easy to defend and don't get much random traf-

fic passing through. As such, they're ideal as supply depots, staging areas, and maintenance facilities."

"But easy to defend also means easy to bottle up," Wutroow pointed out.

"Our unknown opponents do display a certain degree of arrogance," Thrawn said. "Something we'll be able to use against them when the time comes." He looked at Ar'alani. "*If* the time comes," he amended. "Admiral?"

Ar'alani pursed her lips. It was a gamble. But then, so was all warfare. "All right, let's do it," she said. "Pick your spot, and we'll rendezvous there." She lifted a finger. "Two things first. Before we head out I want your sky-walker and her caregiver moved to the *Vigilant*. You're going into danger, and I want them safe. You can do a jump-by-jump to get out and then rendezvous with us to get them back."

"I agree that Sky-walker Che'ri should join you," Thrawn said. "But I'll need Thalias to remain with me."

Ar'alani frowned. "Why?"

"The alien clothing and the positioning of the bodies suggests the males hold their females in high esteem," Thrawn explained. "If I have a female with me—"

"A moment, Senior Captain?" Wutroow put in, frowning. "What do you mean, from their clothing and body positions?"

Thrawn shook his head. "I wish I could explain it, Senior Captain," he said. "I can see it. I can understand it. But I can't really put it into words. The point is that if I have a woman with me, I believe any guards we encounter will be less likely to attack before listening to our explanations."

"I thought you said the mining stations were deserted."

"I believe they were," Thrawn said. "But as Admiral Ar'alani pointed out, it's been fifteen hours since our last observation. It's mostly a precaution."

"And you really think a woman can talk them down?" Wutroow persisted. "How?"

"Let's skip the *how* for a moment and focus on the *who*," Ar'alani said. She could sympathize with Wutroow—she'd certainly had her share of trust-me moments with Thrawn—but she also knew there was a point at which he simply couldn't put his analysis into words. "Thalias is a civilian, which limits what you can order her to do."

"I believe she'll be willing to volunteer."

"That's not the point," Ar'alani said. "If you want a woman to accompany you, there are plenty of female officers to choose from."

Thrawn shook his head. "I need the *Springhawk* to be at full combat capability in case something goes wrong. That means every officer and warrior at their posts."

Ar'alani shifted her attention to Samakro. "Mid Captain?" she invited.

"Unfortunately, Senior Captain Thrawn is correct," Samakro said reluctantly. "We're not exactly shorthanded, but we have more than our fair share of inexperienced personnel aboard. If Thalias is willing, she's probably the one who should go."

Ar'alani looked back at Thrawn. "You really think you can prove this is where the refugees came from if you get aboard that station? Even if there are no people or bodies or anything else aboard?"

"Absolutely," Thrawn said. "There'll be designs and patterns that will quickly settle the question."

At which point . . . what? Ar'alani had no idea what Ba'kif's plans were once Thrawn located the origin of the destroyed ship.

But figuring that out was his job, not Ar'alani's. Her job was to work with Thrawn to get the proof Ba'kif needed.

"All right," she said. "But only if Thalias is willing. If not, she stays with the *Vigilant* and you choose someone else."

"Understood," Thrawn said. "Whenever you're ready, Admiral, I have the coordinates for our rendezvous prepared."

The *Springhawk* was ready. Or at least it was as ready as Samakro could make it.

Samakro himself, not so much.

He could appreciate that the Council thought this mission was important. He could also appreciate that Thrawn's plan was probably their best chance of slipping into the alien system and gaining that data without having to engage either the inhabitants or the ships riding herd on them.

That last point was crucial. Ascendancy policy was to do whatever was necessary to avoid preemptive combat against potential adversaries. An incursion into someone else's territory, even just to gather data, drifted perilously close to the line. The faster Ar'alani could get the *Vigilant* in and out, the less chance either Chiss ship would need to fire its weapons.

"*Vigilant*?" Thrawn called.

"We're ready," Ar'alani's voice came back. "Vector locked; maneuvering jets charged. Let me know when to go."

"One moment," Thrawn said, leaning forward a bit in his command chair as he gazed at the tactical display. "I need Blockade Four to move a little farther in its orbit . . . there. Stand by countdown: Three, two, *one*."

There was the subtle shift in the deck vibrations as the *Springhawk* moved forward. Samakro peered up through the bridge canopy, confirming that the *Vigilant* was also in motion and staying in perfect sync with the smaller cruiser.

In perfect sync, and *way* too close for comfort.

Samakro scowled. In theory, the plan was simple: The *Springhawk* would fly alongside the *Vigilant*, staying close to its hull and hiding in the bigger ship's sensor shadow, until they reached the point where the cruiser would slip away and duck inside one of the asteroid clusters. The *Springhawk* would go dark, hopefully undetected, and let the *Vigilant* lead away any pursuit.

In practice, the whole thing was a disaster crouched to spring. Thrawn had opted not to use tie cables to connect the ships, pointing out that a small error in either ship's vector would create a visible ripple that an alert sensor operator might spot. Tractor beams were impractical for the same reason, plus the added disadvantage of generating a possibly detectable energy signature. Connecting the two ships with maglocks, allowing the larger ship to simply carry the smaller one, would show a blatant mass/thrust discrepancy.

So instead Thrawn was going to attempt the kind of close-in flying normally associated with air shows.

The problem being that he was attempting it with a cruiser and a Nightdragon instead of the smaller and far more maneuverable missile boats.

"Pitch shift on one," Thrawn called. "Stand by countdown: Three, two, *one*."

Samakro tensed, waiting for the inevitable collision. To his relief and mild surprise, the inevitable didn't happen. Both bows tilted upward at precisely the same time, and to precisely the same angle, and the ships continued on.

"Blockades One and Two are reacting," came a voice from someone on the *Vigilant*. "Increasing speed and moving onto intercept vectors."

"Time to intercept?" Ar'alani asked.

"Projected intercept . . . three minutes after *Springhawk* disengages."

"Thrawn?" Ar'alani asked.

Thrawn didn't answer. Samakro looked over at the command station, to see his commander working his questis. "I suggest a two percent increase in speed, Admiral," he said.

"Two percent, confirmed," Ar'alani said. "Course changes?"

"The next two can run as scheduled," Thrawn said. "I'll need to recompute the others."

"Understood," Ar'alani said. "Speed increase and starboard turn ready."

"Acknowledged," Thrawn said. "Stand ready speed increase. Three, two, *one*."

There was a slight sensation, as much imagined as felt, as the *Springhawk* increased its speed. "Stand ready starboard turn," Thrawn continued as the two ships settled into their new vectors. "Three, two, *one*."

This turn was larger than the earlier pitch maneuver, shifting them a full seven degrees. Once again, the two ships stayed in perfect formation.

"Get busy on those revisions," Ar'alani warned. "The portside change is scheduled for three minutes from now."

"Acknowledged," Thrawn said, his fingers skipping over his questis. "They'll be ready when we need them."

Samakro peered out through the canopy, feeling sweat gathering beneath his tunic collar. The more course changes they made, the higher the odds that one of the ships would make a mistake and the whole illusion would pop like a bubble.

But Thrawn had insisted on piling complexity onto their incursion, arguing that a steady, straight-in vector might raise suspicions of a second intruder, while multiple course changes should allay any such concerns.

The other option being the conclusion that whoever was in charge of the mission was crazy. That was certainly the one Samakro himself was going with at the moment.

The minutes ticked by. One by one the course shifts were recalculated and factored in. Samakro watched the tactical as the two ships continued inward, listening to the sensor officer's running commentary on the status of the pursuing blockade ships. A third had joined the party now, angling in from a direction that would bring it into clear view of the *Springhawk* nearly a minute before the cruiser was scheduled to break off. Thrawn and Ar'alani discussed the situation, and once again the Chiss ships increased their speed a few percent. Samakro continued to watch and listen, keeping a close eye on the *Springhawk*'s weapon and defense monitors, just in case Thrawn's plan degenerated into a battle.

And then, suddenly, they were there.

"Stand ready to break off," Thrawn said. "Admiral?"

"Standing ready," Ar'alani said. "Blockades One and Two now four and a half minutes from intercept, Blockade Three ninety seconds from visual. We'll continue on for three minutes, then head for Shadow Two and hyperspace. That should give you enough time to settle in."

"Acknowledged," Thrawn said. "We can make do with two minutes if you need to break early."

"I'll keep that in mind," Ar'alani said. "We'll wait for you at the rendezvous. Good luck."

"Helm?" Thrawn called.

"Standing ready, sir," Azmordi confirmed.

"Prepare to veer off," Thrawn said. "Stand ready: Three, two, *one*."

With multiple puffs of compressed gas the *Springhawk* angled to portside, moving away from the *Vigilant* on a vector that would take it across the edge of the nearest asteroid cluster. Samakro held his breath, focusing his attention on the tactical display. If the blockade ships spotted them, the charade would be over.

He twitched reflexively as the *Vigilant*, now pulled ahead of them, put on a sudden burst of speed, shifting its angle as if Ar'alani was trying one last maneuver to try to get to the planet in the distance before her pursuers reached combat range. If she was able to keep the blockaders' attention on her for a few more seconds, they might pull this off. The slowly wobbling asteroid that was their goal loomed ahead of them—

With another blast of cold gas the *Springhawk* braked to a halt beside the asteroid. Another carefully tuned pulse, and the cruiser had matched itself to the asteroid's slow spin. Samakro looked at the tactical, noting that the blockade ships were still fully invested with chasing down the *Vigilant*.

"Full stealth mode," Thrawn ordered.

All around them, the bridge displays and monitor boards winked red and then went dark. "We appear to have arrived undetected," Thrawn added calmly.

Samakro took a deep breath, making one more visual sweep to make sure all nonessential systems had been locked down. "So it would appear," he said, matching his commander's tone. "How long do we wait?"

Thrawn looked past him at the stars now tracking slowly across the sky. "We need to allow the *Vigilant* to escape and the blockade ships to return to their picket positions. A few hours, no more."

Samakro nodded. And then it would be time for Thrawn to slip over to the abandoned mining station floating halfway across the asteroid cluster.

Where they would find out if this whole gamble had been worth the effort.

The *Vigilant*'s sky-walker was named Ab'begh, and she was only eight.

But she had some interesting moldable play figures and some really nice colored graph markers. And she had a *lot* of building snaps. Way more than Che'ri had.

They were starting to play with them when Ab'begh's momish told them to stop.

"It's reading time, girls," the woman said. "Put away the snaps and get your questises. Come, come, come. Toys away; questises out."

"Do we have to?" Ab'begh asked in a whiny voice. "We want to play."

Che'ri made a face. A whiner. Great. She hated being around whiners.

Still, Ab'begh had a point. "We just did some trips," Che'ri spoke up. "We're supposed to get to rest now."

"Oh, fissis," the momish said, wiggling her fingers like she was throwing away Che'ri's words. "You did *two* trips, maybe two hours each. I've seen sky-walkers do ten hours at a stretch and come up smiling and ready for more."

"But—" Ab'begh started.

"Besides, reading *is* resting," the momish said. "Come on, come on—questises and chairs. Now."

Che'ri looked at Ab'begh. If they both insisted, maybe they could talk themselves into at least another few minutes. Che'ri had started a really neat design with her snaps and wanted to finish it before she forgot where all the pieces were supposed to go.

But Ab'begh just sighed and put down her own snaps. She stood up tiredly and went to one of the chairs.

"Che'ri?" the momish said. "You, too."

Che'ri looked at her snaps. This woman wasn't Che'ri's own momish. Maybe she wasn't allowed to tell another momish's sky-walker what she had to do.

But Che'ri had had a couple of momishes like her. Arguing with them hadn't usually gotten her anywhere.

Besides, Ab'begh was looking at Che'ri with pleading in her eyes. Che'ri might get away with defying the momish, only to have that annoyance come back to dump on the little girl after Che'ri was gone. She'd had a couple of momishes like that, too.

Nothing to do but go along with it. Making a face, she went over to where she'd put her things, dug her questis out of her pack, and climbed into the chair next to Ab'begh's.

She would never admit it to Thalias or anyone else, but she hated reading.

"There you go," the momish said. Now that she'd gotten her way, she sounded a little more cheerful. They always did. "Reading is very important, you know. The more you practice, the better you get."

"It's not study time," Ab'begh said. "We don't have to study, do we?"

"It's study time if I say it's study time," the momish said sternly. "Which you know perfectly well. When our ship is on a journey we never know when you'll be called to the bridge, so we have to study when we have the chance." She looked at Che'ri. "But since we have a guest, and her classes won't be the same as yours, no, we're not doing studies. But you still have to read," she added as Ab'begh started to say something. "Whatever you want. Half an hour, and then you can play until dinnertime."

There was a ping from the hatch. "Enter," the momish called.

The hatch slid open, and Admiral Ar'alani stepped into the suite. "Everyone all right?" she asked.

"Do you need Ab'begh?" the momish asked.

"No, it's all right," Ar'alani said, holding up a hand and smiling at Ab'begh as the little girl put down her questis. "I expect the *Vigilant* to stay where we are for the rest of the night. If we have to go anywhere, we can do a short jump-by-jump. So, no, you girls can relax."

She shifted her eyes to Che'ri. "I mostly came by to tell you, Che'ri, that Thrawn and the *Springhawk* have made it to the asteroid where they'll be hiding for the next few hours. They're safe, and it doesn't look like anyone saw them."

"Okay," Che'ri said. She still wasn't fully clear on what all the fancy flying had been about, but she was glad the *Springhawk* was safe. "Thalias is with him, right?"

"Yes, she is," Ar'alani said, her voice sounding a little strange. "But I'm afraid you'll have to sleep here tonight. I'll have an extra bed brought in for you."

"She can sleep in my bed," Ab'begh said, sitting straight up in her chair. "It's big enough."

Che'ri cringed. She'd never ever had to share a bed. And with an eight-year-old? "I'd rather have my own," she said. She looked at Ab'begh's suddenly disappointed expression—"I kick a lot when I sleep," she added.

"Can you put the bed in my room?" Ab'begh asked. "I—" She stopped and looked over at the momish. "I sometimes get scared," she finished in a little voice.

Che'ri winced, feeling guilty. After talking with Thalias about nightmares . . . "That would work," she said. "Sure. We can take some figures with us and play before we go to sleep."

"Caregiver?" Ar'alani asked.

"If it's all right with Ab'begh, it's fine with me." The woman actually smiled. "I remember having sleepovers when I was their age. Pretty sure I can whip up a few snacks for them, and we'll make it an event."

"Sounds reasonable," Ar'alani said. "But." She raised a warning finger. "When your caregiver says it's time for lights-out, girls, it's time for lights-out. If we need you, we don't want you so tired you'll accidentally steer us into a supernova."

"Yes, ma'am, we will," Ab'begh promised, her earlier excitement starting to bubble up again.

"Anything else we can do for you, Admiral?" the momish asked.

"No," Ar'alani said. "I just wanted to let you all know what was happening. Have a good evening—" She gave both girls a pretend frown. "And get some sleep."

The frown disappeared, she smiled again, and left.

"This is going to be fun," Ab'begh said, bouncing a little on her chair. "It'll be fun, right?"

"Sure," Che'ri said.

"We'll make sure of it," the momish promised. "Right now, it's still reading time. Half an hour, and the sooner you start, the sooner you'll be done."

"You want to read a story about tree people?" Ab'begh asked, holding her questis toward Che'ri. "There are lots of good pictures."

Che'ri wrinkled her nose. A picture book? She might not like to read, but she was *way* past picture books. "That's okay," she told the younger girl. "I've got something else I'm supposed to read."

"She said we didn't have to study."

"This isn't studies," Che'ri assured her. "Go on, get busy. I want to get back to those snaps."

"Okay." Settling herself cross-legged in her chair, Ab'begh propped her questis on her knee and started to read.

Che'ri picked up her questis, her eyes straying over to the low table where Ab'begh's colored graph markers were scattered. Her last momish had told her graph markers got all over everything and wouldn't let her have them.

But that was her last momish. Maybe Thalias would let her get some. She'd ask her once they were back on the *Springhawk*. If she could get some graph markers, and some paper, she could do some real artwork.

Looking back at the questis, she punched up the list. Along with the familiar storybooks—some of which she'd read more than once— she spotted a longer one: some stories about Mitth'raw'nuruodo.

She frowned. She'd completely forgotten about the file Thalias had sent her. It was pretty long, and there were bound to be big complicated words.

But with Thrawn and Thalias and the *Springhawk* in danger, maybe reading some of it would help her feel better. Thalias had seemed to think it would, anyway.

And just because she started, it didn't mean she had to read the whole thing.

Settling herself comfortably in the corner of her chair, she braced herself and opened to the first page.

MEMORIES IV

General Ba'kif had told Ziara that she had good instincts. But she quickly learned that *good* unfortunately didn't mean *perfect*.

The first such lesson came very quickly. The weekend after Thrawn was acquitted he called to invite her out, to help him celebrate and as a thank-you for her help. From the enthusiastic way he talked about the evening, she'd envisioned a night of music and food, perhaps a gymnastic or musical performance, and certainly a modicum of drink.

What she got instead—

She looked around her at the quiet patrons and the somber colors, at the neatly arranged hangings, pictures, sculptures, and drapings. "An art gallery," she said, her voice flat. "You brought me to an *art gallery*."

"Of course," he said, giving her a puzzled look. "Where did you think we were going?"

"You said there would be insight, drama, and the excitement of discovery," she reminded him.

"There is." He pointed down a hallway. "The history of the Ascendancy is in these rooms, some of the pieces dating back to Chiss participation in the wars between the Galactic Republic and the Sith Empire."

"I seem to remember that era not being a particularly glowing time for the Ascendancy."

"Agreed," Thrawn said. "But look at how our tactics and strategies have changed since then."

Ziara frowned. "Excuse me?"

"Our tactics and strategies," Thrawn repeated, frowning back.

"Yes, I heard you," Ziara said. "Why are we talking tactics in an art gallery?"

"Because the one is reflected in the other," Thrawn said. "Art mirrors the soul, from which tactics arise. One can see in artwork the strengths and weaknesses of those who created it. In fact, if one has a sufficient variety of art to study, one can extend and extrapolate to the strengths, weaknesses, and tactics of entire cultures."

Abruptly, Ziara realized her mouth was hanging open. "That's . . . very interesting," she managed. Maybe, she thought belatedly, she shouldn't have worked so hard to get him off the hook after all.

"You don't believe me," Thrawn said. "Fine. There are alien artworks two chambers over. You pick whichever culture you want, and I'll show you how to read their tactics."

Ziara had never been in an alien art wing, in this gallery or any other. The closest she'd ever come to non-Chiss artifacts, in fact, was the twisted chunk of debris from a Paataatus warship that was displayed at the Irizi family homestead on Csilla. "Where did all this come from?" she asked, looking at the various flats and sculptures as Thrawn led the way through the entry arch into the hall.

"Most were purchased by various merchants and traders and subsequently donated to the gallery," Thrawn told her. "Some are from species we still have contact with, but the majority are from aliens we encountered during the Sith Wars, before the retreat back to our own borders. Here we go."

He stopped in front of a clear-sided case containing translucent bottles and plates. "Scofti formal tableware, from a governmental regime a hundred years ago," Thrawn identified them. "What do you see?"

Ziara shrugged. "It's pretty enough. Especially those internal color swirls."

"How about durability?" Thrawn asked. "Does it seem sturdy?"

Ziara looked closer. Now that he mentioned it . . . "Unless that material is a lot stronger than it looks, not at all."

"Exactly," Thrawn said. "The Scofti change leaders and governments frequently, often under violence or the threat of violence. Since each new leader typically reorganizes the prefecture's palace, all the way down to the décor and the tableware, the artisans see no point in making anything for them that will last longer than a year. Indeed, since the new master often takes pleasure in publicly destroying the personal items of his or her predecessor, there's a strong incentive to deliberately make everything fragile."

"Really." Ziara eyed him suspiciously. "Is that really true? Or are you just guessing?"

"We've been in marginal contact with them for the past twenty years," Thrawn said, "and our records support that conclusion. But I made that assessment from the gallery's artifacts before I looked up the history."

"Mm." Ziara looked at the items another moment. "Okay. What's next?"

Thrawn looked around the room. "This is an interesting one," he said, pointing toward another display case nearby. "They called themselves the Brodihi."

"*Called*, past tense?" Ziara asked as they walked over to it. "They're all dead?"

"We don't actually know," Thrawn said. "These artifacts were recovered from the wreckage of a downed ship over three hundred years ago. We still don't know who they were, where they came from, or whether they still exist."

Ziara nodded as she did a quick scan of the case's contents. More dinnerware—plates plus elongated flatware, all decorated with angled rainbow-colored stripes—plus a few tools. In the back of the case was a picture of an alien with a long snout and a pair of horns jutting from the top of its head, along with a short description of the creatures and the circumstances of the discovery. "So what can you tell me about them?"

"You'll note the angled color bars on the flatware," Thrawn said. "In order for the lines to match, the knives, forks, and spoons must be angled toward the center of the table and then back toward the edge."

Ziara nodded. "Like a pair of opening bird wings."

"Or . . . ?" Thrawn prompted.

Ziara frowned and took another look at the alien picture. "Or like the shape of their horns."

"That was my conclusion, as well," Thrawn agreed. "Also note that while the spoons and forks will point toward the center of the table, the knives must be pointed backward, toward the edge for the color bars to line up. What does that tell you?"

Ziara studied the display, trying to visualize one of the creatures sitting where she and Thrawn were standing, waiting for food to be put on his plate. "The knives are much better weapons than the spoons and forks," she said slowly. "Positioning the points toward you suggests that you have no animosity or designs against the others at the table."

"Very good," Thrawn said. "Now add to that the fact that if you turn the knives over, the pattern suggests that they point *toward* the center like the other flatware instead of toward the table's edge. What does *that* suggest?"

Ziara smiled. The structure of their own Chiss culture

gave the answer to that one. "That there's a social or political hierarchy involved," she said. "Depending on your rank relative to the others at the table, you turn your knife inward or outward."

"Again, that was my conclusion as well," Thrawn said. "One final thing. Note the length of the flatware, clearly designed to deposit the food several centimeters down the snout instead of at the front."

"Seems odd," Ziara said. "I'd assume most species' taste receptors would be at the front of the mouth, on the tongue or their equivalent."

"That does seem to be the general pattern," Thrawn said. "It makes me think that their outer rim of teeth was their traditional weapon, and the jaws developed so that they could bite into an enemy without tasting his flesh or blood."

Ziara wrinkled her nose. "That's disgusting."

"Agreed," Thrawn said. "But if we should ever meet them, we would have an idea of their likely tactics. Close-in weaponry like teeth and knives should translate into a preference for close-in combat, with long-distance weaponry considered secondary or even dishonorable."

"And a rigid hierarchy with an underlying threat of violence would warn us about with whom and where we negotiate," Ziara said, nodding. "Interesting. Okay. Where to next?"

"You want to see more?" Thrawn asked, frowning a little.

She shrugged. "We've come this far. Might as well make an evening of it."

She quickly came to regret giving him such an open invitation. By the time she called a halt an hour later, her head was spinning with names, images, and tactical inferences. "Okay, this is all very interesting," she said. "But near as I can see, almost all of it is very theoretical. Where we have the aliens' history, you could have looked it up and backfilled your analysis to fit it."

"I've already said I didn't do that."

"But you might have come across something when you were younger and forgotten you'd read it," Ziara pointed out. "That's happened to me. And where we don't have any history, we'll probably never know if you're right or wrong."

"I see," Thrawn said, his voice suddenly subdued. "I'm ... I thought this would be interesting to you. I'm sorry if I wasted your time."

"I didn't say that," Ziara protested, eyeing him as a sudden idea occurred to her. "But I'm a practical person, and when I hear a new theory I like to give it a test."

"Shall we ask the Ascendancy to declare war on someone?"

"I was thinking a little smaller," she said. "Come on."

She headed toward the exit. "Where are we going?" Thrawn asked as he caught up with her.

"My quarters," she said. "I do a little wire sculpting in my spare time to relax. You can study it and see how well you can read my personal strategies and tactics."

Thrawn was silent a couple of steps. "Are you assuming we'll someday be at war with each other?"

"Yes, and sooner than you think," Ziara said with a smile. "Because after you finish, we're going to go downstairs to the dojo and go a couple of rounds."

"I see," Thrawn said. "Stick, or unarmed?"

Ziara gave him the choice. He chose stick.

"Okay," Ziara said, bouncing a few experimental steps on the mat and swinging the two short sticks in her hands to loosen up her wrists. The lightweight face and chest protectors didn't interfere with her movements, and the soft-coat sticks felt sturdy in her hands, with the same weight and balance as actual combat sticks. "And if you've found some recordings of my combat sessions, say so now before I call cheats on you."

"I've never seen you fight," Thrawn assured her. "You may choose when the bout is over."

"Thank you," Ziara said. "And that was your first—*mistake!*" she shouted as she leapt forward. A quick head-ribs-head combo should end the fight before he lost too much of his dignity.

Only it didn't. Thrawn blocked all three attacks, putting his sticks up in the right spots and in the right order. Her ribs-head-elbow-feint-ribs combo didn't get through, either. Neither did her best feint-feint-hip-ribs-head-feint-stomach.

She scowled, taking a step back to regroup and re-assess. Beginner's luck, obviously, but it was starting to become a bit worrisome. So far he was just standing there, casually blocking her attacks but launching none of his own. But that would change soon enough. Time to crank things up a notch, get an attack through, force him to counterattack or at least make him move his damn feet. She leapt forward again, slipping into a feint-rib-feint—

Only this time, on the second feint, he stopped being passive and made his move. Slipping in through the opening created by the feint, he tapped her stick farther out of line, spun in a tight circle within the gap, and brought his own stick to lightly tap the side of her head protector. Even as she tried to bring both sticks back in at him, he spun again and took a long step out of her reach.

She leapt forward, trying to get to him while his back was still turned. But he was faster, turning to face her and again blocking her double attack.

Again she backed off, taking the opportunity to gulp in

a few lungfuls of air. Thrawn didn't follow, but remained where he was.

Clearly, her preferred combat techniques weren't working. Time to switch it up a bit. Just because she liked these tactics best didn't mean she hadn't been taught others. Taking one final breath, she again charged.

Only this time, instead of using the feint-attack combinations, she came straight at him, jabbing forward with both sticks, one aimed at his face the other at his chest. He blocked the first, but the second slammed into his chest protector with a thoroughly satisfying *thud*. She moved forward, cocking her arms to do it again.

Again, Thrawn was faster. He backed up rapidly, putting himself out of range. She took another step forward, jabbing again, and again one of the two attacks got through. One more, she decided, and she would call the match. She stepped forward—

And abruptly found herself in the midst of a flurry of flashing sticks as he leapt to the attack.

This time it was her turn to back up, cursing silently as she blocked and parried and tried to turn the attack against him. But he wasn't giving her any opening. Her feet felt the change in the texture of the mat, warning that she was getting close to the edge.

Thrawn saw it, too. He came to a halt, allowing her to slow her own retreat before she could slam into the wall.

Another mistake. The pause was just long enough for her to take back the initiative, and once again she charged at him.

He backed up slowly, clearly once more on the defensive. But to her chagrin, her attacks were once again going nowhere as he blocked every feint and thrust.

She broke off the attack and stepped back, and for a long moment they stood facing each other. *Before he lost too much of his dignity*, her earlier smug thought rose back to mock her. "Is there any point to continuing?" she asked.

Thrawn shrugged. "Your choice."

For a long moment pride and determination urged her to keep going. Common sense won out. "How?" she asked, lowering her sticks and walking up to him.

"Your sculptures show your fondness for wide-spaced combinations," Thrawn said, lowering his own sticks to his sides. "Particularly three- and four-coil patterns. Your favorite subjects—groundlions, dragonelles, and predator birds—indicate the short attacks, hesitation feints, and aggression. The particular shape of open areas shows how you compose your feints, and the angular style suggests a spinning attack would be unexpected and disconcerting enough to slow your response."

Which, she remembered, had been his first successful attack. "Interesting," Ziara said.

"But what followed was equally instructive," Thrawn continued. He raised his eyebrows slightly in obvious invitation.

Ziara felt a flush of irritation. She was the upperclassman here, not him. If there was anyone who should be reciting lessons and offering analysis, it should be him, not her.

Which was, she instantly realized, about the stupidest thought she'd ever had in her life. Only a fool passed up an opportunity to learn. "I realized you'd figured out my pattern and changed tactics," she said. "And it worked, at least for a couple of attacks. Then you attacked, and after that I was never able to get through again."

"Do you know why?"

Ziara frowned, thinking back over the fight . . . "I went back to my old tactics," she said with a wry smile. "The ones you'd already figured out how to beat."

"Exactly," Thrawn said, smiling back. "A lesson for all of

us. In moments of stress or uncertainty, we tend to fall back on the familiar and comfortable."

"Yes," Ziara murmured, suddenly noticing where she was relative to him. Well within attack range . . . and she'd never explicitly stated the bout was over.

The moment of temptation passed. Just because she hadn't officially stopped it didn't mean it would be fair to unilaterally start it up again. Thrawn had behaved honorably. She could do no less.

"And the care you put into the sculptures shows you have too much honor to play shoddy tricks against a sparring partner," Thrawn added.

Ziara felt her face warm. "You sure of that?"

"Yes."

For a long moment she was again tempted. Then, spinning on her heel, she stalked across the mat and returned her sticks to the weapons rack. "Okay," she said over her shoulder as she started pulling off her sparring armor. "I'm impressed. You really think you can do the same thing with alien cultures and tactics?"

"I do," Thrawn said. "Someday, I hope I'll have the chance to prove it."

CHAPTER SIX

Five hours after the *Springhawk* went into hiding, Thrawn and Thalias strapped themselves into one of the cruiser's shuttles and headed across the asteroid cluster toward the dark space station floating in the distance.

"The journey may be a bit tedious," Thrawn warned as they moved between the floating rocks and dust. "We'll be using the maneuvering jets exclusively in order to avoid any thruster plumes that our adversaries might detect. That makes for a slower trip."

"I understand," Thalias said.

"Still, it gives us a chance to talk in private," Thrawn continued. "How are you finding your job as caregiver?"

"It's challenging," Thalias admitted, a quiet warning bell going off in the back of her mind. Thrawn could have called her into his office at any point since leaving the Ascendancy if he just wanted to talk in private.

Did he know about that last-minute conversation with Thurfian, and the deal the syndic had forced on her? "Che'ri's pretty easy to live with, but there are some things every sky-walker deals with that can be difficult."

"Nightmares?"

"And headaches and occasional mood swings," Thalias said. "Along with just being a nine-year-old."

"Especially one who's vital to the functioning of the ship and knows it?"

"Right—the horror stories of sky-walker arrogance and demands," Thalias said scornfully. "Pure ice-cap legend. I've never met anyone who's actually seen that happen. Every sky-walker I've known has gone the opposite direction."

"Feelings of inadequacy," Thrawn said. "The fear that she won't measure up to what her captain and ship require of her."

Thalias nodded. Like the nightmares, those were feelings she remembered all too well. "Sky-walkers are always worried that they'll get the ship lost or do something else wrong."

"Though the record indicates very few such incidents," Thrawn said. "And most of the affected ships eventually returned safely via jump-by-jump." He paused. "I presume Che'ri isn't facing any challenges that you yourself didn't also have to overcome?"

"No," Thalias said with a quiet sigh. She really hadn't expected Thrawn to let her aboard without checking up on her, but she'd still sort of hoped he'd somehow miss the fact that she'd once been a sky-walker. "Aside from the whole flying-into-possible-danger part."

"Danger is an implicit part of what we do."

"Except that you all volunteered for this life," Thalias said. "We sky-walkers weren't given that choice."

Thrawn was silent a moment. "You're right, of course," he said. "The greater good of the Ascendancy is the rationale. Also the truth, of course. But the fact remains."

"It does," Thalias said. "For what it's worth, I don't think any of us begrudges our service. I mean, aside from the fears and nightmares and all. And the Ascendancy *does* need us."

"Perhaps," Thrawn said.

She frowned at him. "Just perhaps?"

"A conversation for another day," Thrawn said. "Display Four. Do you see it?"

She turned her attention to the control panel in front of them. Display Four . . . that one.

Centered in the display was a small heat source. A heat source coming from an orbital position near the system's inhabited planet.

A heat source the computer calculated was coming directly toward them.

"They've spotted us," she breathed, her heart suddenly thudding in her throat.

"Perhaps," Thrawn said, still sounding thoughtful. "The timing certainly suggests that, as it was only thirty seconds ago that the ship ran its thrusters to this level of power."

"It's coming straight toward us," she said, feeling a sudden surge of claustrophobia in the cockpit's tight grasp. They were in a shuttle, not a combat ship, with no weapons, no defenses, and all the maneuverability of a fen slug. "What do we do?"

"That may depend on who they are, and where they're going," Thrawn said.

Thalias frowned at the display. "What do you mean? They're coming toward us, aren't they?"

"They could also be heading toward the *Springhawk*," Thrawn said. "Or possibly it's merely a scheduled run to the mining station and the timing is purely coincidental. At their distance, and at this point in their path, it's impossible to more precisely define their ultimate endpoint."

"So what do we do?" Thalias asked. "Can we get back to the *Springhawk* in time?"

"Possibly," Thrawn said. "The more immediate question is whether we want to."

"Whether we *want* to?" Thalias repeated, staring at him.

"We came here to find out if this is the origin point of the doomed refugees," Thrawn reminded her. "My intent was to study the mining station, but a direct conversation would be quicker and more informative."

"Only if they don't shoot us on sight."

"They might try," Thrawn said. "Tell me, have you ever fired a charric?"

Thalias swallowed hard. "I practiced with one a few times at the range," she said. "But always on low power, never on high."

"There's not much operational difference between those settings."

Thrawn tapped a few keys on his console. "Well. Unless the ship increases its speed in the next two hours, we should arrive at the station twenty to thirty minutes ahead of it."

"What if it's aiming for the *Springhawk*?" Thalias asked. "Shouldn't we warn them?"

"I'm sure Mid Captain Samakro has already noted them," Thrawn assured her. "Even if they've spotted the *Springhawk*—and there's a good chance they haven't—I think there's a way to make sure our visitors stop by the station first."

"How?"

Thrawn smiled. "We invite them in."

The mining station was equipped with several docking ports, grouped together at various points around its surface. One cluster included two of the so-called "universal ports" that many species in the region had adopted over the centuries to accommodate varying sizes of ships. Thrawn docked the shuttle with one of them, waited until the bioclear system had run the usual toxin/biohazard check on the station's air, then led the way inside.

Thalias had expected the place to smell old and musty, perhaps with the pungent scent of rotted food or—worse—rotted bodies. But while there was a definite hint of staleness, it was hardly overwhelming. Whenever the owners of the station had pulled out, they'd apparently done so in an orderly fashion.

"This is the place," Thrawn said softly, shining his light into alcoves and rooms as they walked down a wide corridor. "This is where they came from."

"The refugee ships?" Thalias asked.

"Yes," Thrawn confirmed. "The style is unmistakable."

"Mm," Thalias said. She'd looked at everything he had, and she didn't have a clue as to what he was picking up on. "What now?"

"We go to the main control center," Thrawn said, picking up his pace. "That's where our visitors are most likely to dock."

"How are we going to find it?"

"We've passed two floor schematics on the walls since we left the shuttle," Thrawn said, frowning slightly at her. "The main command and control centers were obvious."

Thalias made a face. Not just one floor schematic, but two of them?

Okay. So maybe she *hadn't* seen everything he had.

They found the control center exactly where Thrawn had predicted it would be. The controls and consoles were labeled with an unfamiliar script, but everything seemed laid out in a logical pattern. A little trial and error with the controls, and suddenly the room blazed with light.

"That's better," Thalias said, putting away her own light. "What now?"

"This," Thrawn said, throwing a few more switches. "If I've read the console organization correctly, we should now have turned on the station's external lights."

Thalias stared at him. "You—? But that ship will see us."

"I told you I was going to invite them in," Thrawn reminded her. "More important, our lights will hopefully distract them from the *Springhawk,* should its hiding place have been their original destination."

"I see," Thalias said, freshly aware of the charric riding her hip. "You're not expecting to fight them, are you?"

"I'm hoping to avoid that, yes," Thrawn said. "The equipment bay with the largest docking ports is at the portside edge of the station. We'll wait for them there." With a final look around the control center, he headed for a hatch leading in that direction.

Taking a few deep, calming breaths, Thalias followed.

The equipment bay was larger than Thalias had expected, though with the cranes, maneuvering lifters, overhead cables, and lines of tool and part racks there was also less open space than she'd anticipated. She and Thrawn had just settled themselves in front of the main port when there was a wheeze of vented air and the port began to cycle. "Here they come," she muttered, peering past Thrawn's shoulder as he stood in front of her, partially blocking her view. *They hold their females in high esteem,* Thrawn had said of the aliens they were tracking. If he was right, his protective position in front of her would hopefully connect to that cultural bias.

"Yes." Thrawn paused, his head cocked as if listening.

Then, to Thalias's surprise, he slipped around behind her, reversing their original positions so that she was now in front.

"What are you doing?" she demanded, a fresh sense of vulnerability flooding into her. The people about to come in, and whatever weapons they might be carrying—

The hatch dilated, and four creatures emerged.

Medium height, chest and hip bulges, pink skin, feathery head crests. Exactly like the bodies Thrawn had brought aboard the *Springhawk* from the second refugee ship.

He had indeed found them.

For a moment the two groups eyed each other. Then one of the newcomers spoke, his voice gravelly, his words incomprehensible.

"Do you speak Minnisiat?" Thrawn called back in that trade language.

The alien spoke again, still using his own speech. "Do you speak Taarja?" Thrawn asked, switching to that one.

There was a short pause. Then one of the other aliens took a step forward. "I speak this," he said. "What do you do here?"

"We are explorers," Thrawn said. "My name is Thrawn." He nudged Thalias. "Tell them your name."

"I am Thalias," Thalias said, taking the cue and giving only her core name. For whatever reason, Thrawn apparently didn't want to give out their full names.

The alien's eyes widened and bulged a little as he seemed to study her. "You are female?"

"I am," Thalias said.

The alien gave a whinnying sort of snort. "So do you, Thrawn, then hide behind your female?"

"Not at all," Thrawn said. "I'm shielding her with my body from those you sent to shoot us in the back."

Thalias caught her breath. "You're joking, right?" she muttered.

She sensed him shake his head. "I felt the shift in the air as they entered the secondary hatch behind us."

Thalias nodded to herself. Just as he'd quickly absorbed the feel of the *Tomra* all those years ago, he'd now just as quickly grasped the same details of this alien station.

"We plan no violence," the alien spokesman said hastily. "Merely caution. Your arrival was unexpected, and we were concerned for our safety."

"I apologize in turn for our startlement to you," Thrawn said. "We thought this station was abandoned. That is why we came."

The alien gave another whinny, a shorter one this time. "If you sought to build a home here, you chose unwisely. Even now, it may be too late for you to reverse that error."

"We did not come to live," Thrawn said. "As I said, we are explorers. We search the Chaos for artwork of the lost and forgotten."

The mottling pattern of the alien's skin changed. "You search for *artwork*?"

"Artwork reflects the soul of a species," Thrawn said. "We seek to preserve that echo for those unable to preserve it on their own."

One of the other aliens spoke in their language. "He speaks that there is no artwork here," the spokesman translated.

"Perhaps there is more art woven into the design than he realizes," Thrawn said. "But I am puzzled. I see no evidence of catastrophe or destruction. On the contrary, the station appears completely functional. Why did you abandon it?"

"We did not abandon it," the spokesman said, his voice noticeably deeper. "We were sent away by those who seek dominance over Rapacc and the Paccosh."

"Rapacc is your world, then?" Thrawn asked. "And you are the Paccosh?"

"We are," the spokesman said. "At least, for this current moment. The Paccosh may yet cease to exist. The future of each and every Pacc rests in the hands of the Nikardun, and we fear to contemplate it."

"The Nikardun are those who followed us across your system?" Thrawn asked.

Another whinny. "If you believe they merely followed you, your ignorance is indeed deep. Their intent was to capture or destroy you."

Thalias felt a shiver run up her back. As far as she could remember, she'd never heard even a hint of information about a species with that name. Definitely outside the immediate neighborhood, and very likely outside even the wider region the Expansionary Fleet had explored.

And if this was how they introduced themselves—blocking access to whole systems and chasing down and slaughtering anyone who succeeded in leaving—they weren't likely to become friends of the Ascendancy anytime soon.

"Yet they must hold you and your world in loose hands," she pointed out, the angular Taarja words hurting her mouth. Taarja had been her least favorite trade language during her schooling, but the Mitth family insisted that their merit adoptives learn all the region's most common forms of communication. "Otherwise, how are you here speaking with us?"

"You think we traveled here of our own free will?" the spokesman asked, ducking his head just a bit toward her. "You think we ourselves removed the weapons and defenses from the ship we arrived in? Hardly. The Nikardun ships guarding the approaches to Rapacc did not recognize the design of your ship. They thought this station might still have sensors running that may have gleaned important details when your ship passed nearby. We were ordered here to learn if such records were indeed made."

"Were they correct?" Thrawn asked.

"Correct about the sensors?" The spokesman paused, his eyes flicking between them. "Why do you ask? Do you wish the details of your ship to remain secret?"

"It is said there are those who can deduce the origin of a ship from its design and style of flight," Thrawn said. "The unknown leader of these Nikardun may be one such."

"Their leader is hardly unknown," the Pacc said, a hint of disgust in his tone. "General Yiv the Benevolent has personally come to Rapacc to speak his demands to and share his gloatings with our leaders."

"Such actions speak of supreme confidence," Thrawn said. "Will he return soon?"

"I do not know," the Pacc said. "But more Nikardun will surely come, and if we are not compliant with the orders of those currently here it will go badly for us."

And if the Paccosh failed to capture the strangers who'd blown past the sentry ships and sneaked aboard their station, Thalias suspected, things would probably go even worse. "What are you going to do with us?" she asked.

The spokesman turned back to the others, and for a moment they all consulted together. "Well done," Thrawn said quietly.

"What do you mean?" Thalias asked.

"That question was better coming from you than from me," he said. "Their consideration for females may modify their answer and influence their decision in our favor."

"And if it doesn't?"

"Then the charrics," Thrawn said, his voice calm but determined. "You'll deal with those in front of us. I'll do likewise with the ones behind."

Thalias's mouth went suddenly dry. "You mean just shoot them down?"

"We are two," Thrawn said. "They are four, plus however many are currently unseen and unnumbered behind us. If they decide to take us prisoner, our only chance will be immediate and lethal attack."

A cold chill ran up Thalias's back. Getting pulled into a firefight, shooting and being shot at, had been a terrifying prospect. But at least she could have gone into a heated battle with a mostly clear conscience.

What Thrawn was talking about was straight-up, coldhearted murder.

The Paccosh ended their discussion. "We have no orders regarding intruders," the spokesman said. "We were sent only to examine the sensors." The other alien said a few words. "But we presume the Nikardun would have required your capture if they had known you were here."

"Perhaps," Thrawn said. "The more important question is: What do the Paccosh require?"

The spokesman turned to the others. Thalias lifted her hand to her hair, pretending to adjust a few strands, hopefully drawing a bit of extra attention to herself.

"If you allow us to depart, I will make sure the Nikardun do not detect us," Thrawn added into the silence.

"How can you be sure of that?"

"They did not detect our arrival at this place," Thrawn said. "I doubt they will be more attentive now."

"Surely they saw you turn on the station lights."

"Surely you can remotely activate those systems," Thrawn countered.

The spokesman considered, then inclined his head. "Yes. We can." He hissed out a breath. "The commander has decided. You may leave in peace."

Thalias let her own breath out in a silent sigh of relief. "Thank you," she said.

"You have not yet answered my earlier question," Thrawn said. "Are the station's sensors still operating?"

The spokesman whinnied. "In weeks past, the Nikardun ordered us to shut down the station before abandoning it," he said. "With the lives of each and every Pacc lying beneath their sword, we obeyed our orders to the letter. There are no functioning sensors."

"That is well," Thrawn said. "Farewell, then, and may you yet find freedom and peace." Touching Thalias's arm, he nodded back toward the hatchway that would return them to their shuttle.

"Wait."

Thalias turned back. The Pacc who'd done all the non-Taarja speaking earlier, the one she'd tentatively identified as the group's leader, was walking toward them. She started to take a step backward, stopped as Thrawn again touched her arm.

"This is Uingali," the spokesman said as the Pacc stopped in front of Thrawn. "He has something he wishes to give you."

For a moment Uingali stood motionless. Then, with clear reluctance, he lifted both hands in front of him, one hand tugging at the fingers of the other. A moment later he'd slid a double ring off two of the fingers, the twin circlets connected by a short, flexible mesh. Another moment of hesitation, and he held the double ring toward Thrawn. "Uingali foar Marocsaa," he said.

"The double ring is a prized heirloom of the Marocsaa subclan," the spokesman said quietly. "Uingali wishes you to take it and add it to your artwork, that the subclan and the Marocsaa people will not be forgotten."

For the first time since Thalias had met him, Thrawn seemed genuinely surprised. He looked at Uingali, then at the rings, then at Uingali again. Then, he held out his hand, palm upward. "Thank you," he said. "I will guard it in a place of honor."

Uingali lowered his head in a bow as he placed the double ring in Thrawn's hand. He straightened up, turned, and walked back toward the other Paccosh. They turned in unison as he passed them, and all four headed through the hatchway. There was a brush of air behind Thalias, and she jerked as three other Paccosh, apparently Uingali's backup force, walked silently past the two Chiss and joined their comrades. They all disappeared from sight, the hatch closing behind them.

Thalias peered at the double ring in Thrawn's palm. It was made of a silvery metal, with a series of curved arcs embossed on the base. A cluster of what looked like small snakes rose from the center of the arcs, flanked by two much larger snakes that curved up and around, crossing each other once and ending with their heads and open mouths pointed defiantly upward.

She was still studying the rings when the lights around them abruptly went out. "What—? Oh," she added belatedly. "Remote controls."

"Uingali reinforcing the illusion for any Nikardun observers," Thrawn said as he flicked on his own light. "Come."

He turned and strode toward the hatchway.

"We're heading back already?" Thalias asked as she hurried to keep up with him.

"We have everything Supreme General Ba'kif sent us to find," Thrawn said. "The murdered refugees were Paccosh from the Rapacc system, their oppressors are called the Nikardun, and the Nikardun leader is General Yiv the Benevolent." He seemed to consider. "Plus perhaps a few additional facts that Ba'kif wasn't expecting."

"Such as?"

Thrawn was silent for another few steps. "We located the Paccosh partly because the refugees' ship came from this general direction. We also presume that the Nikardun followed them or in some other way anticipated their arrival in the Ascendancy, then ordered the attack on Csilla in order to distract our attention from the Paccosh destruction."

Thalias nodded. "That makes sense."

"But that leads to another question," Thrawn said. "How did the Nikardun know to stage their ambush at that particular spot?"

"Well . . ." Thalias paused, trying to think it through. "We know the two Paccian ships rendezvoused in the four-star system before the one ship headed for the Ascendancy. Maybe the captain decided we were their best shot at getting help, especially with one of the two ships unable to keep going. Don't know how they knew where we were, though."

"Many of the aliens out here know about us, or at least have a general idea where we are," Thrawn said. "Though our reputation often precedes any actual knowledge. You'll note the Paccosh didn't seem to recognize that we were Chiss. But you miss the critical point of my question. The refugee ship left hyperspace much farther out in the system than was necessary. Far enough that they would have needed several hours of space-normal travel before they were even close enough to initiate communication." He paused. "And far enough that while their slaughter was detected, there was no chance that any of the patrol ships could respond in time."

Thalias breathed a curse as it suddenly became clear. "The only way the Nikardun could be waiting for the ship is if the refugees' navigator deliberately brought them out of hyperspace there." She frowned. "They *did* have a navigator, didn't they?"

"I assume so," Thrawn said. "Presumably a Void Guide, like the second ship's. Note also the fact that we found no such body aboard the first ship."

He paused again, clearly expecting Thalias to follow his path of logic. "The Nikardun took him with them?" she offered.

"Indeed," Thrawn said. "Was he dead, or alive?"

Thalias chewed at her lip. How was she supposed to know *that*?

For that matter, why was Thrawn even going through this logic puzzle with her, especially this way? It was like the schoolwork classes she'd had to take as an occasionally reluctant sky-walker, or the same classes she was now having to inflict on an even more reluctant Che'ri.

"The Paccosh aboard the other ship died much later than those who were attacked in the Ascendancy," he prompted.

Thalias nodded as she finally saw where he was going. Especially since the second group had asphyxiated instead of being murdered like the first group. "He was dead," she said. "If he'd been alive, he'd have told the Nikardun where the other ship was and they'd have moved in and slaughtered them, too, instead of letting them die on their own."

"Excellent," Thrawn said. "We also glean the fact that it was the Paccosh, not the Void Guides, who chose the four-star system as their rendezvous."

"Okay," Thalias said, frowning. "How does that help us?"

"It may not," Thrawn conceded. "But sometimes small bits of knowledge return in unexpected ways." He gestured ahead. "At any rate, I believe we've learned all that we're going to here. A stealthy return to the *Springhawk* is now in order, followed by a hopefully unimpeded exit from the system."

"The Nikardun will be watching," Thalias warned.

"Agreed," Thrawn said. "But after the *Vigilant*'s incursion, I expect the Nikardun will have pulled their sentry lines closer into the inner system. Our escape should be straightforward, as should our rendez-vous with the *Vigilant* to retrieve our sky-walker."

"And then back to the Ascendancy?"

Thrawn looked down at the double ring in his hand. "Not right away," he said. "No, I think we'll go to a Navigators' Guild concourse and hire ourselves a navigator."

Thalias frowned. "You already said we'll have Che'ri."

"In case we need her," Thrawn said. "But the Paccosh indicated there may be more Nikardun ships arriving in the near future. There's something I want to do before that happens."

"Ah," Thalias said carefully. Unless the fleet had changed the rules since she was a sky-walker, a captain who wanted to expand the scope of a mission was supposed to first get authorization.

But that really wasn't any of her business. "You're looking for a Void Guide?"

"No," Thrawn said. He fingered the ring one last time, then put it carefully into a pocket. "No, I think there's someone who will be far more useful to us."

MEMORIES V

"Chiss diplomatic cruiser coming in," Pathfinder dispatcher Prack called above the buzz of conversation filling the Navigators' Guild lounge. "Who wants it?"

The conversation broke off like a door had slammed shut over it, and everyone did their best imitation of being somewhere else.

Including Qilori of Uandualon. He sat unmoving on his bench, his shoulders hunched, still gripping the rim handle of his mug. Chiss. Just his pathetic luck to be on duty when a Chiss rolled in.

"Qilori, where are you?" the dispatcher continued. "Come on, Qilori—I know you're here."

"He's over here," someone two tables over called helpfully.

Qilori sent the other navigator a glare. "Yeah, I'm here," he growled.

"Good for you," the dispatcher said. "Grab your headset, sash up, and sashay down. Your turn for the hot box."

"Yeah," Qilori growled again, his cheek winglets snapping flat against the sides of his head with disgust as he stood up and crossed the room to the dispatcher. The other Pathfinders wanted to jeer at his dirt assignment, he knew—he'd certainly done his share of jeering when the situation was flipped.

But none of them dared. Prack wasn't above changing assignments at the last second if someone higher on his gripe list caught his eye. "So where are they going?" he asked.

"Bardram Scoft," the dispatcher said.

"What are they going there for?"

"Don't know; don't care. Board gate five; fifteen minutes." He gave Qilori a smirking smile. "Have fun."

Fifteen minutes later, his travel bag slung over his shoulder, Qilori watched the boarding gate swing open and a couple of black-uniformed blueskins step out. "You our Pathfinder?" one of them asked in the Minnisiat trade language.

At least this bunch weren't expecting everyone else in the Chaos to speak Cheunh. "I am," Qilori said, waving a hand over his ID sash. "I am Qilori of Uandualon. I'm a Class Five—"

"Yes, fine," the blueskin said. "Come on. We're in a hurry."

He turned and strode back through the gate. Qilori followed, silently cursing Prack for dropping this assignment on him.

No one out here liked the Chiss. At least, no one Qilori had ever met who'd worked with them liked them.

It wasn't just that they considered themselves better than everyone else. Most species had *that* delusion, after all. No, it was that the Chiss didn't seem to think there was even anyone else out here for them to feel superior to. They had a strange and infuriating blind spot where the rest of the Chaos was concerned, as if every other species was entirely composed of particularly clever animals or else had been brought into existence solely for the Ascendancy's benefit.

They barely saw anyone. They certainly didn't care about anyone.

The bridge was pretty much the same as on every other Chiss merchant ship and diplomatic cruiser Qilori had seen: small and efficient, with helm, navigation, defense, and comm consoles. The captain was seated in a chair behind the helm and nav consoles, with other Chiss at all but the nav position.

That seat, of course, was Qilori's.

"Pathfinder," the captain said, nodding in greeting. "As soon as you've taken your place, we'll be off."

Qilori's cheek winglets flattened as he sat down and flexed his fingers over the controls.

Right. Have fun.

The trip was uneventful. On the captain's command Qilori put on his sensory-deprivation headset and slipped into his trance, letting the Great Presence whisper into and around and through him.

As usual, the Great Presence was miserly with Its wisdom and insights, making for a somewhat slower trip than Qilori would have liked. Fortunately, the space in this part of the Chaos was relatively smooth, with only a few of the anomalies that made navigators like the Pathfinders necessary for long-range interstellar travel. They reached Bardram Scoft a few minutes ahead of the captain's proposed schedule, and in a whole lot less time than a jump-by-jump trip would have taken. All in all, Qilori decided as he slipped off the headset, he'd earned his pay.

He blinked away the post-trance cobwebs, flexing the stiffness out of his fingers. The planet loomed large in the viewport as the ship settled into orbit. The bridge had mostly emptied out, with only Qilori and a pilot still there. "Where is everyone?" he asked.

"Preparing the ambassador for the welcoming ceremony," the pilot said. "Scoftic culture requires the highest-ranking military officer to accompany the ambassador, and there may be other protocols to be observed."

"*May* be?" Qilori asked, frowning as he scanned the sky. There were a *lot* of ships out there, more than he'd ever seen at a backwater world like this. "I thought you Chiss liked to be prepared for everything ahead of time."

"We do," the pilot said. "The Scoftic government has changed again, and with it the protocols. Our ambassador must relearn them."

"Ah," Qilori said. So that was it. New government, and everyone nearby had sent emissaries to offer their best wishes and size up the newcomer. "I didn't know the old Prefect had been unwell."

"He wasn't," the pilot said. "He was assassinated. What ship is that?"

"What?" Qilori said, his winglets fluttering with surprise. *Assassinated?* "And everyone's okay with that?"

"It's not unheard of among the Scofti," the pilot said calmly. "That ship. What nation does it represent?"

Qilori peered out the viewport, still struggling at the casualness of it all. "I think it's a Lioaoin."

"Is it a new design?"

"I don't know. How should I know?"

"You're a navigator," the Chiss said. "You see many ships, from many nations."

"Yes, but I mostly only see the insides," Qilori said, frowning. "Why the sudden interest?"

"That vessel shows many of the same characteristics as a group of pirate ships that have been attacking freighters at the outer edges of the Chiss Ascendancy."

"Really?" Qilori asked, trying to sound surprised. There were dark rumors among the various navigator groups that the Lioaoin Regime had turned to piracy to prop up their failing economy. Most of the stories came from the Void Guides, who did more work in that particular region, but he'd heard a couple of his fellow Pathfinders talking about it, too.

He couldn't tell the pilot that, of course. The Navigators' Guild rules of confidentiality and neutrality were unbreakable. "Sounds pretty unlikely."

"You don't believe a pirate group would buy their ships from a local manufacturer?"

"Oh," Qilori said, feeling a slight sense of relief. So the Chiss wasn't even thinking that the Lioaoi were officially involved. "No, I see what you mean. I suppose that's possible."

"Yes," the pilot said. "Have you ever traveled to Lioaoin space?"

"Once or twice, yes."

"You could find your way there again?"

"From the Chiss Ascendancy? Of course. I could find my way to any system you wanted. That's what navigators do."

"The Lioaoin Regime will do for now," the pilot said. "Suppose I wanted to approach from a different direction than the Ascendancy? Say, from here at Bardram Scoft?"

"*Are* we heading there?"

The pilot gazed out the viewport for another moment. "Not yet," he said, his voice thoughtful. "Perhaps later. What's your name?"

"Qilori of Uandualon," Qilori said, frowning. Where was the Chiss going with this line of questioning?

"Are you normally to be found at the Navigators' Guild station where we hired you?"

"I move around a lot between the various guild stations," Qilori said. "Obviously. But Concourse Four Forty-Seven is my official base station, yes."

"Good," the Chiss said. "Perhaps we shall work together in the future."

"That would be wonderful," Qilori said, studying the Chiss's profile. Few of them even bothered to learn his name, let alone want to know how to find him. Fewer still would bother to study another species' ship design.

Who *was* this Chiss, anyway?

"And *your* name?" he asked. "In case you specifically ask for me?"

"Junior Commander Thrawn," the Chiss said softly. "And yes. I shall most definitely ask for you."

CHAPTER SEVEN

Qilori had never expected the Chiss named Thrawn to ever blacken his sky again. He'd certainly hoped he wouldn't. But yet here he was, back at Guild Concourse 447, asking specifically for Qilori of Uandualon.

And a senior captain now, to boot. Qilori didn't know a lot about Chiss military ranks and promotion schedules, but he had the distinct impression that Thrawn was younger than most Chiss who'd achieved that rank.

Considering what had happened at Kinoss a few years ago, he supposed he shouldn't be too surprised.

"It's good to see you again, Qilori of Uandualon," Thrawn said as Qilori was ushered onto the bridge.

"Thank you," Qilori said, looking around. He'd never been on a Chiss warship before, and the difference between this and his usual freighter and diplomatic cruiser assignments was like the difference from sweet to sour. Weapons boards, defense boards, status panels, multiple displays, a full complement of black-uniformed blueskins—

"Are you familiar with the Rapacc system?" Thrawn asked.

Qilori jerked his attention back from the lights and displays, fighting to keep his cheek winglets still. *Rapacc.* That was one of the places Yiv the Benevolent had under blockade, wasn't it?

Yes—he was sure of it. Qilori didn't know Yiv's final plan, whether the Benevolent would directly annex the system or leave the Paccosh as tributaries. But either way the Nikardun were certainly already there.

What in the Great Presence's Name did Thrawn want with Rapacc?

"Pathfinder?" Thrawn prompted.

Abruptly, Qilori remembered he'd been asked a question. "Yes, I know the system," he said, again trying to keep his winglets steady. "Difficult to get into. Nothing very interesting once you do."

"You might be surprised," Thrawn said. "At any rate, that's our destination." He gestured to the navigator's station. "At your convenience."

There was nothing for it. Guild rules apart, Qilori could hardly tell Thrawn that the Nikardun would be as happy to cut a Chiss warship to ribbons as they would any other unwelcome intruder. Apart from all the other considerations, a warning like that might prompt Thrawn to wonder how Qilori knew so much about Yiv and the Nikardun, and where he'd learned it.

So Qilori would take the Chiss to Rapacc as ordered. And he would hope to the Great Presence that the system's Nikardun overseer would take the time to pull the valuable and totally innocent Pathfinder out of the wreckage before ordering the ship's final destruction.

He would hope it very, very much.

The bridge was quiet as Samakro came in, with only the command, helm, primary weapons, and primary defense stations occupied. Plus, of course, the alien Pathfinder sitting at the navigation station, and the two charric-armed guards standing on either side of the hatch keeping a watchful eye on him.

Mid Commander Elod'al'vumic was seated in the command chair, her fingers tapping noiselessly and restlessly on the armrest as she gazed through the viewport at the undulating hyperspace sky. She looked up as Samakro came alongside her. "Mid Captain," she greeted him.

"Mid Commander," Samakro greeted her in turn. "Anything to report?"

"The Pathfinder came out of his trance again an hour ago, took a ten-minute break, then went back under his headset," Dalvu said. "He said another three-hour shift should bring us to Rapacc. We took a location reading while we were in space-normal, and it looked like we were in the right position."

"I presume you reported all this to the captain?"

Dalvu's shoulders gave a small twitch. "I sent him the message. Whether or not he noticed is something you'd have to ask him."

Samakro felt his eyes narrow. A disrespectful comment that managed to be not *quite* over the line into something actionable.

Dalvu wasn't the type to come up with such opinions on her own, let alone have the audacity to speak them. Apparently Kharill had been sharing his displeasure regarding the new command structure with his fellow officers. "I believe you'll find Captain Thrawn on top of the situation," he told her. "Hold things as is for another hour, then start bringing the *Springhawk* to combat status. I'll want us at full battle—"

"*Combat* status?" Dalvu cut him off, her eyes going wide. "We're going into combat?"

"I'll want us at full battle stations thirty minutes before we reach Rapacc," Samakro finished.

"But *combat*?"

"Probably," Samakro said. "Why, did you think we had some other reason for going back to Rapacc?"

Dalvu's lips curved in an almost-scowl. "I assumed Captain Thrawn forgot something and we were going back to get it."

Samakro gazed down at her, counting down five seconds of silence. Dalvu's scowl was gone after the first two seconds, and by the fifth she was starting to look distinctly uncomfortable. "I suggest you keep any derogatory thoughts about the captain to yourself," Samakro said quietly. "His mental state is not your concern, nor is his fitness to command, nor is his authority to issue orders aboard this vessel. Is that clear, Mid Commander?"

"Yes, sir," Dalvu said in a more subdued tone. "But . . . are we even authorized to fight these people?"

"We're always authorized to defend ourselves," Samakro reminded her. "And given the blockade ships' reaction on our last incursion, I suspect we won't have to wait very long on that count."

"Yes, sir," Dalvu muttered, lowering her gaze.

Samakro pressed his lips together, his annoyance at her reluctantly fading away. Unfortunately, she had a point. They'd been fine on their last run into the system; but that time they'd had a Nightdragon running backup. Now it was just them. "You weren't aboard the *Springhawk* back when Thrawn was first in command, were you?"

"No, sir," Dalvu said. "But I've heard stories of his . . . reckless-ness."

"Best to take those with a sideways look," Samakro advised. "Just because Thrawn doesn't lay out his tactics in advance for everyone to see doesn't mean he doesn't have them. Whatever he's got planned for today, he'll get us through it."

He took a deep breath and looked again out the viewport. "Trust me."

It was time.

The shimmering disk of the Great Presence loomed large in Qilori's unseeing eyes. The undulating rumble echoed in his unhearing ears. Reaching blindly to the hyperdrive lever at his right, he squeezed off the locking bar and wrapped his fingers around the lever. He waited until the disk filled his vision, then delicately pushed the lever forward. He waited another moment, savoring the experience one final time, then shut down the sound-blocking part of his headset.

The Great Presence vanished as a quiet hum of Chiss voices filled his ears. He pulled off the headset, blinking as his eyes adjusted to the muted bridge light, and peered through the viewport.

They had arrived.

Casually, he looked around him. All the stations were occupied, but none of the Chiss seemed to be watching him. Keeping his movements small, he reached into one of the storage pouches built into his ID sash and keyed his comm. He'd spent the last three rest periods recording a message for the Nikardun ships lurking out there and then figuring out how to tap into the ship's short-range transmitter.

A sharp voice from the Chiss at the sensor station cut through the conversational hum. Qilori ran his eyes quickly over the displays, found the tactical one—

He felt his cheek winglets flutter. Three ships were angling in toward the *Springhawk,* one from starboard, the other two from behind. The markings on the display were all in unreadable Cheunh script, but he knew the ships had to be Nikardun.

His winglets fluttered harder. If the attackers had gotten his message—and if the blockade commander decided a Pathfinder was worth saving—they might go easy on their prey, at least until they'd battered most of the life out of it.

If the commander wasn't feeling so charitable, Qilori had seen his last star-rise.

The deck gave a sudden jolt. Qilori jerked in response, fully expecting to see a flash of laserfire or a wall of flame from a missile blaze through the bridge wall. But nothing. He looked at the tactical again, frowning.

And tensed. The jolt hadn't been a Nikardun attack, but the recoil as a shuttle separated from the *Springhawk*'s flank. Even as he watched, it headed toward the inner system and the planet Rapacc at an incredibly high acceleration.

He clenched his teeth. If Thrawn was hoping whoever was in there would escape, he'd already lost his gamble. The two aft pursuers veered off, accelerating in turn as they chased after the shuttle. Qilori couldn't read the markings on the velocity/intercept curves, but he had no doubt the two Nikardun would catch the craft long before it reached Rapacc or even the relative safety of one of the asteroid clusters. They would catch it, and with a barrage of laserfire or the more delicate twist of a tractor beam they would destroy or capture it.

On the tactical, he saw that the *Springhawk,* its errand apparently fulfilled, was now angling away from the inner system and the fleeing shuttle. Attempting, no doubt, to clear the system's collection of orbiting debris and reach a safe hyperspace jump-off point before its remaining pursuer could get into combat range. Qilori eyed the tactical, noting that the Nikardun had put on a burst of speed of his own.

He frowned. The *remaining* pursuer. The last of three Nikardun ships that had been sitting at the *Springhawk*'s entry point, ready to give battle.

A point that Thrawn had deliberately specified out of the handful of safe vectors available. Was it simply bad luck that had brought them to a spot where three Nikardun had been waiting?

Maybe. Maybe he just didn't know enough about the system.

But in that case, why hadn't he come out of hyperspace much farther out and done at least a quick recon before committing himself and his ship to this vector? At least then he might have found a way or route that would have given his shuttle a better chance of getting somewhere before it was destroyed.

A cold chill ran up his back. No, Thrawn couldn't be that shortsighted. Not the Thrawn whose battle tactics Qilori had had the misfortune to see firsthand.

Which left only one other option. Thrawn had arrived on this particular vector because he *wanted* the Nikardun to attack him.

Qilori looked back and forth among the banks of displays, trying to make sense of it all. Was the *Springhawk* just a feint, a diversion to let the actual intruder slip into the Rapacc system unhindered? Could there be someone out there aiming for the asteroid clusters, maybe, moving stealthily in the hope that with Nikardun attention focused out here they wouldn't be spotted until it was too late?

But he couldn't see anything like that on any of the displays. No other ships, no other vectors, no indication of anything else in the system. Surely the Chiss would have their own vessels marked, even if they were stealthed and undetectable to the Nikardun. Wouldn't they?

The pursuing Nikardun patrol ship put on an additional burst of speed. Qilori watched nervously as it finally reached firing range—

Abruptly, as if Thrawn had just noticed the threat coming up on his starboard side, the *Springhawk* made a sharp turn away from its attacker. The pursuing ship opened fire with its spectrum lasers, and a large piece of debris detached itself from the Chiss ship's flank and fell backward. The *Springhawk* shifted direction, just slightly, the Nikardun adjusting its own vector to match.

And suddenly Qilori realized what was going on. The object falling behind the *Springhawk* wasn't battle debris from the Nikardun attack, as he'd thought. It was, in fact, another of the Chiss ship's shuttles.

And the Nikardun, now blasting toward the *Springhawk* at top speed, was about to run straight into it.

Qilori's first horrible thought was that the shuttle would crash into the oversized bridge viewport that marked all of Yiv's combat ships. But the Nikardun captain spotted the obstacle in time to twist the ship aside.

Unfortunately, there wasn't time to twist it far enough. The shuttle missed the viewport to slam instead into the portside weapons cluster, wrecking that group of lasers and missile launchers and setting the ship spinning.

A second later the starscape outside the *Springhawk*'s viewport spun crazily as the Chiss ship did its own yaw rotation. Qilori gripped his armrests, fighting against vertigo, as the *Springhawk*'s movement brought the stern of the tumbling Nikardun into view. There was a multiple flash of laserfire, and the fiery yellow glow from the Nikardun's thruster nozzles flared once and then faded as the damaged engines behind the nozzles shut down. Qilori held his breath, waiting for the salvo that would blast the helpless ship into dust.

The salvo didn't come. Instead, the *Springhawk* slowed, waiting for the Nikardun's momentum to bring it closer. The Chiss ship moved up and over, settling itself above the Nikardun's dorsal sensor ridge, out of line from the remaining flankside weapons clusters. On the tactical, the green lines of two tractor beams winked into existence, connecting the two ships. The hazy circle of a Crippler net spun out from the *Springhawk*'s hull between the tractor beam projectors and wrapped itself around the Nikardun vessel, sending a high-voltage charge through the hull and eliminating the possibility that the crew might activate a scuttling system.

And as the *Springhawk* turned toward hyperspace, all the pieces finally fell into their pattern.

The escaping shuttle—running on automatic, Qilori realized now—had indeed been a diversion. But not for a second Chiss ship. It was just Thrawn, and he'd brought them to that particular spot because he wanted the Nikardun to chase him. This whole thing had never been about death, destruction, infiltration, or even just delivering Yiv a message. Thrawn had simply dropped by hoping to capture a Nikardun ship.

And he'd done it.

"Pathfinder?" Thrawn's voice came from right behind him.

Qilori jerked. "Yes, Captain?" he managed.

"We'll be traveling to a nearby system to hand off our prize," Thrawn said. Said it so casually, too, as if they'd just picked up an order of groceries from the corner shop. "After that, we'll be returning to Concourse Four Forty-Seven. Will you need rest time before we leave?"

"No, not for a while," Qilori said. Thrawn might not sound anxious to leave this neighborhood behind, but Qilori sure as the Great Presence was.

"Good," Thrawn said. "I trust you found the exercise interesting?"

With an effort, Qilori flattened his winglets against his cheeks. "Yes, Captain," he said. "Very interesting indeed."

It wasn't easy for even a Pathfinder to requisition a ship for his own personal use. But Qilori had been at Concourse 447 long enough to build up a collection of owed favors.

More important, he had a collection of blackmail material on several key people. Between the favors and the threats, he soon found himself speeding away from the station, bound for the Primea system, capital of the Vak Combine.

Thirty-five hours later, he was there.

Primea was in the early stage of a Nikardun conquest, which meant Yiv was still greeting and meeting with planetary leaders, talking about the benefits of joining the Nikardun Destiny, and letting his orbiting warships provide a silent warning of what would happen if they refused. Qilori gave his name and the urgency of his mission to the first gatekeeper, and the second gatekeeper, and the third. Six hours after his arrival, he was finally ushered into Yiv's throne room aboard the Battle Dreadnought *Deathless*.

"Ah—Qilori!" Yiv called, his cheerful booming voice echoing in the oppressive stillness of the throne room. Draped over his shoulders like living epaulets were the fungoid strands of the strange creatures he'd taken on as symbionts. His cleft jaw was open in what passed for a smile with Nikardun, but which Qilori had always thought looked more like a predator preparing to strike.

At least he was in a good mood, Qilori thought with a tinge of relief. The talks with the Vaks must be going well. "Come. Tell me what news you bring from the lips of the Great Presence."

Qilori grimaced as he walked the gauntlet between the two lines of watchful Nikardun soldiers. Yiv was mocking him, of course, as he mocked or dismissed all who didn't believe solely in the godhood of Yiv himself. But right now the Benevolent's famous ego wasn't nearly as concerning as his somewhat less famous temper.

Qilori had never brought Yiv bad news before. He had no idea how such messengers were treated.

"I bring news from Rapacc, your Benevolence," he said, stopping between the last pair of guards in the gauntlet and dropping forward to lie facedown on the cold deck at Yiv's feet. "News, and a warning."

"That news has been delivered," Yiv said, his earlier jovial manner vanishing like morning dew under twin suns. "Do you presume to waste my time with a story I already know?"

"Not at all, your Benevolence," Qilori said, his back itching with the eyes and weapons that were undoubtedly ranged on it. "I expected you would have heard one of your blockade frigates had been captured. What I came here to add to that tale is the name of the being responsible."

"You were the navigator on his ship?"

"Yes, your Benevolence. He asked specifically for me."

For a long moment, Yiv remained silent. Qilori held his position, trying to ignore the creeping sensation rippling through his skin. "Rise, Pathfinder," Yiv said at last. "Rise, and tell me all."

With a sense of relief, Qilori scrambled to his feet. Something tapped his shoulders a short but sharp blow; hastily, he dropped back to his knees. "The Chiss came and hired me—"

"His name, Qilori," Yiv said, his voice soft and deadly. "I already know the ship was Chiss. I want his *name*."

Qilori's winglets fluttered. "Thrawn. Senior Captain Thrawn."

"His *full* name."

The winglets stiffened in panic. "I don't know," he breathed. "I never heard it."

"And you didn't bother to learn it for me?"

"I'm sorry," Qilori said, staring at Yiv's feet, not daring to raise his eyes to that jovial, implacable face. He was going to die today, he knew with a dark sense of his fragile mortality. The Great Presence awaited him.

Would he be absorbed and lost forever? Or would he be deemed worthy to ride the hyperspace ridges, guiding future Pathfinders through the Chaos?

For a long moment the room was silent. "You will meet him again," Yiv said at last. "When you do, you will obtain for me his full name."

"Of course, your Benevolence, of course," Qilori said quickly, fearing the hope singing suddenly through him. Mercy? From Yiv the Benevolent?

No, of course not. Yiv felt no mercy. Qilori was simply a tool that was still worth keeping.

For the moment.

"Return to your station," Yiv said. "Guide your ships. Do your job. Live your pathetic little life. And bring me his name."

"I will," Qilori promised. "While breath remains in me, I will never cease to serve you."

"Exactly," Yiv said, a hint of his usual humor finally peeking through the blackness. "While breath remains in you."

General Ba'kif finished reading through the proposal and looked up from his questis. "You're serious, Junior Commander," he said flatly.

"Quite serious, General," Junior Commander Thrawn confirmed. "I'm convinced the Lioaoin government is connected to the pirates that have hit our shipping off Schesa and Pesfavri over the past few months."

"And you think this Pathfinder knows about it?"

"Qilori," Thrawn said. "Yes, he knows, or at least suspects."

"It would be hard to keep a secret like that from the Navigators' Guild," Ba'kif agreed, again studying the numbers. A jump-by-jump from Lioaoin space to the affected Ascendancy worlds would certainly be safer for those with criminal intent—no need to involve outside witnesses. But such a voyage would take at least three weeks of travel each way. Under the circumstances, it wasn't unreasonable that the pirates might opt for speed and efficiency, relying on guild confidentiality to keep their secret. "You're sure the ships are the same?"

"The designs are different enough to preclude obvious connections," Thrawn said. "But there are notable similarities that go beyond mere functionality."

Ba'kif nodded. He'd had a couple of conversations with Mid Captain Ziara about Thrawn's theories of art and tactics, and they'd reluctantly concluded that neither of them had whatever spark of insight or genius—or insanity—was required to make the connections that Thrawn seemed to intuitively grasp.

But just because they couldn't see it didn't mean he was wrong. "Assume you're right," he said. "Further assume you can prove it. What then?"

A frown creased Thrawn's forehead. "They've attacked ships of the Ascendancy," he said, as if expecting a hidden trap in Ba'kif's words. "We deal out punishment."

"And if the Lioaoi themselves aren't involved?" Ba'kif asked. "What if the pirates merely bought or hired Lioaoin ships?"

"I wasn't suggesting we attack the Lioaoin Regime or worlds," Thrawn said. "Merely the pirates."

"*If* you can distinguish them from the innocents," Ba'kif warned. "We have little data on current Lioaoin ship design. For that matter, the Lioaoi and pirates both could have bought the same style ship from a third party."

"I understand," Thrawn said. "But I believe I'll be able to make it clear which ships are enemies and which are friends."

"I'll settle for which are enemies and which are neutrals," Ba'kif said sourly. "The Ascendancy has barely even acknowledged the existence of others out there, let alone shown any interest in pursuing friendships with any of them."

"Enemies and neutrals, then," Thrawn amended. "If I can't make a clear distinction, I'll take no action."

For a moment Ba'kif eyed him. The man was clever enough, and Ba'kif had seen his strategic and tactical abilities.

The question was whether he had perhaps just a little

too much confidence in himself. If he did, and if that confidence made him overstep the line, some operation in the future could blow up in his face. Possibly the very operation he was now proposing.

But this particular group of pirates was becoming more than just a nuisance. They needed to be dealt with before someone out there got the idea that the Ascendancy could be attacked with impunity. If Thrawn thought he'd found the handle they needed, it was worth giving him a shot. "Very well, Junior Commander," he said. "How many ships will you need?"

"Just two, sir." Thrawn considered. "No. Actually, it would be best if I had three."

The sense of the Great Presence faded, and Qilori removed his headset to find that they'd arrived. The heartworld of the Lioaoin Regime stretched out before them, green and blue and white, encircled by a swarm of freighters, couriers, docking and repair stations, and watchful military patrol ships.

Out of the corner of his eye, he saw Thrawn lean forward. "Well?" Qilori asked carefully.

For a few seconds, Thrawn was silent. Then he nodded. "Yes," he said. "These are the ships."

Qilori winced, his cheek winglets stiffening. "Are you certain?"

"Quite certain," Thrawn said. "The design of the patrol craft are similar enough to those of the pirate ships to leave no doubt."

"I see," Qilori said. He didn't, actually—to him, the patrol ships looked nothing like the ones the Lioaoin corsairs used.

But what he thought didn't matter. Thrawn was convinced, and if he got word back to the Ascendancy, there was likely to be a highly lethal response. And it was just as likely that more than a few Pathfinders would be caught in the middle.

Whether Thrawn could actually get that word to anyone who mattered, of course, was the crucial question. Their freighter was already deep enough into the planet's gravity well that the hyperdrive was useless, and their current course was taking them ever deeper. If Thrawn veered off right now and headed back toward deep space, they might get clear before someone started to wonder why a Chiss freighter had suddenly decided it didn't want to do business with the Lioaoi after all.

But Qilori didn't hold out much hope that Thrawn would be smart enough to simply cut and run.

Again, he was right.

"I need a closer look," Thrawn said, taking the helm controls and angling deeper into the gravity well toward a pair of patrol ships floating beside one of the repair docks. "I suspect the ship inside that station is one of those that recently attacked the Massoss system."

"This is a bad idea," Qilori warned, his winglets pressing tightly against his cheeks. "If the Lioaoin Regime is involved with the pirates, you risk stirring up a massive stinger nest."

"Are you saying the regime *is* involved?" Thrawn asked coolly, turning those glowing red eyes onto Qilori.

Qilori gazed back, cursing himself for saying even that much. The first thing every navigational group learned when it joined the Navigators' Guild was that it was forbidden to speak about one client to another. The most heinous criminal activity needed to be as safe from exposure as the most innocent freighter passage or military exercise.

But right now, breaches of protocol were the least of Qilori's worries. Just before they arrived here, right when his trance was lifting, he'd sensed through the Great Presence that there were fellow Pathfinders nearby. If they were aboard some of the corsairs—and if any of those corsairs were prepped for flight–they could follow Qilori effortlessly through hyperspace no matter how many jinks or re-coursings Thrawn tried.

And none of the corsairs were likely to care if silencing a troublesome Chiss also required the death of an innocent Pathfinder.

"I don't know if the regime is part of it," he said. "Just trust me when I say this isn't a safe place to be."

Thrawn wasn't listening. He was staring out at the ships and docks, his glowing eyes narrowed slightly.

"I mean it," Qilori said, trying one final time. "If they suspect you're hunting pirates–"

"You think they only *suspect*?" Thrawn echoed. He cocked his head. "Yes; point taken. Let's remove any lingering doubts." He keyed the comm–

And suddenly it was as if he'd lost his senses. "Alert!" Thrawn called. "I've found the pirates. Repeat: I've found them. Get out of here and report back!"

Qilori gasped. What in–? "Thrawn–?"

Thrawn keyed off the comm. "There," he said, his voice and expression back to their usual coolness. "Now they know for certain."

"What in the Depths did you do?" Qilori said in a strangled voice. "You've just painted a death mark on us. They'll be coming after us–"

"There they go," Thrawn said, pointing at a spot on the main display.

Qilori looked at the display in time to see a ship flicker and disappear into hyperspace. "My second ship," Thrawn identified. "One of my colleagues is aboard, with one of yours navigating it back to the Ascendancy." He turned the helm yoke over, and the freighter curved smoothly away from the planet. "And now, as you suggest, it's time to leave."

"Yes, let's," Qilori muttered, slumping in his chair as

Thrawn ran the thrusters to full power. The patrol ships were starting to move, and as Qilori looked up at the high-orbit docking bays he saw three corsairs emerge, their own thrusters blazing as they angled toward him and Thrawn, hoping to intercept them before they could escape into hyperspace.

Either Thrawn also saw them or else he'd anticipated the response. He was already on it, shifting the freighter's course onto a vector that would slip it past the potential trap.

But it would do him no good. The corsairs were on the move, and if there were Pathfinders aboard there was nothing Thrawn could do to prevent them from following him back to Chiss space. They would get him, and the oh-so-clever backup ship that had already left, and the Lioaoin ships would continue to attack and plunder everyone in the region.

Maybe the corsairs would try to rescue Qilori and the other Pathfinder before they destroyed the Chiss ships. Probably they wouldn't.

But at this point, all he could do was hope. "Where are we going?" he asked as they approached the edge of the gravity well.

"Kinoss," Thrawn said. "It's the closest system, and there should be fast couriers there who can take our message to Csilla and Naporar."

"Fine," Qilori said, setting his hands on the controls. Maybe one of the two Chiss freighters would at least be able to send a message before the corsairs jammed their transmissions and then destroyed them.

Probably they wouldn't.

The trance this time was one of the hardest Qilori had ever experienced. On top of the usual course intricacies was an overlaid mesh of dark and distracting images, visions of pursuing ships guided by fellow Pathfinders. He nearly lost the path more times than he cared to remember, and twice he was forced to return to space-normal to regain his connection to the Great Presence.

Thrawn said nothing during those retrenchments. Probably dreaming of glory for ending the pirate menace, or assuming the course stutters would throw off any pursuit.

The other Chiss freighter had already arrived when they finally reached the Kinoss system. Qilori could see its thrusters in the distance ahead, driving the vessel toward the planet. Even as Qilori finished rising from his trance Thrawn had taken the controls and turned to follow.

Futility. Even before the thrusters were up to full power, four Lioaoin corsairs winked into view on the aft display.

"Ah," Thrawn said, still with that maddening calm. "Our guests have arrived."

"I'm so surprised," Qilori muttered.

"I doubt that," Thrawn said. "I did some study on the Pathfinders after our first encounter. Your colleagues can track you through hyperspace, can they not?"

Qilori shot him a startled look. That was supposed to be a deep, dark secret. "That—no. Not true."

"I think it is." Thrawn gestured to the aft display. "The Pathfinder style was evident in the last pirate attack. I hoped you and I would arrive at the Lioaoin heartworld before those navigators were returned to their bases."

"You *wanted* them to follow us?"

"Of course," Thrawn said, as if it was obvious. "With any other navigators there would be uncertainty as to their emergence point, if indeed they were able to follow us at all. With Pathfinders aboard, I could be sure the pirates would arrive precisely where I wanted them."

"You mean right on top of us?" Qilori retorted. He looked again at the aft display.

And felt his winglets go rigid. Where there had been four ships behind them, there were now five. The four Lioaoin corsairs he'd already seen . . . and a Chiss warship.

"Mid Captain Ziara, this is Junior Commander Thrawn," Thrawn called toward the comm. "I believe your targets await you."

"Indeed they do, Commander," a soft female voice came back. "I suggest you continue on your present course.

"It should give you the best view of their destruction."

CHAPTER EIGHT

"Interesting," Supreme General Ba'kif commented as he set his questis aside. He'd read the report twice, Ar'alani had noted as she watched his eyes move back and forth across the text, the first time she'd ever seen him do that. Either he'd been trying to glean as much information as he could, or else he was stalling while he tried to figure out what to say and do about it. "You realize, of course, that stealing someone else's ship, under *any* circumstance, is a serious breach of regulations."

"The Nikardun ships attacked us, sir," Thrawn said. "I understood that regulations permit self-defense."

"Absolutely," Ba'kif said. "And if you'd blown the damn thing to dust, no one would have given it a second thought. But *capturing* it?" He shook his head. "And you, Admiral. I know you and Thrawn have a long history, but I'm a little surprised that you agreed to be a part of this."

"Actually, General, I made a point of refreshing my memory on the regulations before I accepted Captain Thrawn's proposal," Ar'alani said, mentally crossing her fingers. "There's nothing that specifically says capturing an attacker's ship is a violation."

"I think you'll find it falls under the general heading of preemptive strikes," Ba'kif said. "Which is definitely how certain of the Aristocra will interpret it once they hear about this. Some of them might even demand the ship be returned."

"Without its crew?" Thrawn said. "That might be a bit awkward."

Ar'alani felt her throat tighten. More than just a *bit* awkward, given that the Nikardun crew was gone because they'd committed mass suicide minutes before the Chiss boarding parties breached the hatches. For a while she'd rather hoped it had at least been a combination of murder and suicide, with perhaps the officers under orders to slaughter their warriors before taking their own lives. That would have indicated that it was only a few of the Nikardun that were that fanatical. But the medic team had concluded that all the deaths had been self-inflicted.

What kind of compulsion and dominance did this Yiv the Benevolent hold over them that they would willingly go to such violent extremes?

"True enough," Ba'kif conceded. "Well. Until the syndics decide to write specifics into the law, I suppose we can treat it as a gray area." He tapped the questis. "In the meantime, what kind of hellish nighthunter nest have you just kicked over?"

"A nighthunter nest that I believe will soon be hunting us," Thrawn said grimly. "They clearly know about the Ascendancy. They also feel confident enough in their own strength to slaughter a refugee ship right on our threshold. And"—he gestured to the questis—"they're already moving into our outer neighborhood."

Ba'kif huffed out a breath, looking back at the questis as if the data on it might suddenly change to something less disquieting. "You're sure they've had contact with the Lioaoin Regime?" he asked. "I looked at all the indicators you marked, and I confess I can't see whatever it is you think you've found."

"It's there, sir," Thrawn said. "It's subtle, but it's there."

"What we *don't* know," Ar'alani put in, "is whether this is evidence that they've been to the Lioaoin heartworld itself or whether they've just picked up some Lioaoi art and artistic influences along the way from someone else."

"That's why we need to go to the heartworld in person," Thrawn said. "I need to examine the local situation, and I can't do that from transmission analysis or even third-person investigator reports."

"You know what the Syndicure will say about anyone going to the Lioaoin Regime," Ba'kif warned. "Especially *you* two."

"That's why we wanted to keep it quiet," Ar'alani said. "And the Expansionary Fleet *does* have a fair degree of flexibility in its duties."

"Which I'm no longer in direct command of," Ba'kif reminded her, glancing with an odd sort of wistfulness around his new Csilla office.

Ar'alani could sympathize. This office was bigger than his old Expansionary Defense Fleet office on Naporar, as befit his newly exalted position as the Ascendancy's top general.

But the office was on Csilla, which meant that it was not only under the planet's frozen surface, but also within downwind spitting distance of the Syndicure and the rest of the Ascendancy's governmental centers.

And just because the Aristocra weren't supposed to interfere with military matters didn't mean they were pleasant to be around.

"But you *are* in overall command of personnel in the fleet," Thrawn pointed out. "A directive from you would surely be acknowledged and carried out."

"The *Springhawk* is undergoing hull repairs, but we could take the *Vigilant*," Ar'alani said. "Thrawn could come aboard as an officer or even just as a passenger and take a quick, unobtrusive look."

Ba'kif snorted. "You know what certain syndics think of your definition of *unobtrusive*." He glanced at his desk monitor and gave a small snort. "And by sheer coincidence—or perhaps not—two of those syndics have just arrived in my inner office."

Ar'alani's first impulse was to urge the general not to let them in. But it would be a useless gesture. Clearly, someone had spotted her and Thrawn coming here; just as clearly, the two syndics weren't going to go away just because the Defense Force's supreme general told them to.

Official policies of separation of duties or not, non-interference or not, the confrontation the syndics were obviously here for was going to happen. Might was well have it out now.

Ba'kif had apparently come to the same conclusion. He tapped a key, and the door slid open. "Welcome, Syndics," he said briskly as the three officers rose to their feet. "How may I serve you?"

Ar'alani turned to face the newcomers. Mitth'urf'ianico, one of the syndics of Thrawn's family, led the way. That was standard procedure whenever the family wanted to deliver a message to the military regarding one of their own without tugging on any of the tangled web of interfamily politics.

Striding along close behind him was Irizi'stal'mustro, one of the syndics of Ar'alani's former family.

She felt her eyes narrow. That was *not* standard procedure. Thurfian might be here to talk about Thrawn on behalf of the Mitth, but she was no longer part of the Irizi family, which meant Zistalmu had no reason to talk about her to Ba'kif.

But there was an even more interesting subtext about this whole thing. Given the intense rivalry between the Irizi and Mitth, two syndics from those families who wanted to see Ba'kif on general military matters would normally have arranged to come one at a time, not together.

Or was that the point? Could Thurfian and Zistalmu have worked up this joint meeting to underscore a high-level opposition to Thrawn's recent activities, a resistance that superseded family politics?

"Good day, General," Zistalmu said, inclining his head to Ba'kif. "Admiral; Senior Captain," he added, making the same gestures to Ar'alani and Thrawn. "Are we interrupting anything important?"

"I was discussing an upcoming mission with two of the Expansionary Fleet's finest officers," Ba'kif said.

"Really," Thurfian said with a feigned enthusiasm that wouldn't fool a child. "Given the presence of Captain Thrawn, may we assume this mission is connected to the report the fleet submitted to the Syndicure three days ago?"

Ar'alani stifled a curse. Normally, reports from the fleet could sit on the syndics' questises for days or weeks without being read by anyone except their aides and the lower-ranking Aristocra. At the moment, that was especially true of any report that didn't connect to the Csilla attack investigation.

Apparently, at least for these two, Thrawn's name garnered the same level of notice.

"We submitted several reports that day," Ba'kif said. "Which one specifically are you referring to?"

"You know perfectly well which one," Zistalmu said, his eyes shifting to Thrawn. "The unauthorized intrusion into an alien system, and the subsequent attack on alien ships in that system."

"First of all, the *Springhawk*'s mission to the Rapacc system was not unauthorized," Ba'kif said. "As you know, there was an attack on the edge of the Dioya system—"

"An attack against *aliens*," Zistalmu cut in. "Meanwhile, the question of the attack on Csilla—an attack launched against actual Chiss citizens—has yet to be resolved."

"I trust you're not suggesting the fleet is incapable of handling more than one investigation at a time," Ba'kif said, putting some stone into his voice.

"Not at all," Zistalmu said. "But if investigation was the goal, I would submit that Captain Thrawn's attack at Rapacc went far beyond his orders and mandate. Yet I see no indication that a tribunal has been seated or even scheduled."

"The *Springhawk* was attacked," Ba'kif said. "Standing orders allow him the right of defense."

"Within very narrow and sharply delineated limits," Thurfian put in. "But that's the past, and a matter for a tribunal. Our major concern is for the future. So I ask again: Does this proposed mission relate to the Rapacc attack?" He threw an accusing look at Thrawn. "Time is not so long, nor memory so short, that we've forgotten his old Lioaoin fiasco."

"I'm hardly likely to forget it, either," Thrawn said quietly.

Quietly, but Ar'alani could hear the hidden embarrassment and ache in his voice. "I trust you aren't here just to scrub at old wounds," she put in, hoping to draw some of Zistalmu's attack in her direction.

It was a waste of effort. Thurfian merely shot her a brief, unreadable look, then returned his attention to his primary target. "As I already stated, we're looking to the future, not the past," he said. "We understand you claim to have found Lioaoin paintings or sculptures or some such on that illegally seized ship. I trust, Supreme General, you're not seriously thinking of letting Captain Thrawn anywhere near the Lioaoin Regime."

"Why not?" Ba'kif asked. "The Lioaoi certainly hold their share of blame for what happened back then."

"So you *are* sending him to the heartworld," Zistalmu said, pouncing on the words like a groundlion. "Are you mad?"

"I believe the Nikardun have moved into the Lioaoin Regime," Thrawn said. "We need to know whether the Lioaoi have been completely subjugated, or whether they still stand against their would-be conquerors."

"We need to know nothing of the kind," Thurfian retorted. "What happens outside our borders is none of our business. As I thought was made clear to you the first time you meddled in that region's affairs."

"And when the Nikardun arrive in the Ascendancy?" Thrawn asked.

"*If* the Nikardun arrive in the Ascendancy," Thurfian shot back.

"Exactly," Zistalmu seconded. "Really, Captain Thrawn. Someone of your vaunted tactical expertise can surely see that if we were such an enticing target, they would have moved against us already. It seems obvious to me that the stories told about us out in the Chaos have warned them away."

"Unless they're waiting until they have enough strength to defeat us," Ba'kif said.

"Fine," Zistalmu said. "Let's look at that possibility, shall we? You claim the Nikardun are subjugating other species and creating an empire. Correct?"

"We've seen evidence of such activity, yes," Ba'kif said.

"And controlling a conquered species requires force and the presence of arms, does it not?"

Ar'alani felt a sour taste in her mouth. She could see where Zistalmu was going with this.

As, too, could Ba'kif. "It may require less than you imagine," the general said. "If the planet is sufficiently subjugated, a few monitoring ships and a small ground contingent could easily suffice."

"Especially if they utilize a system of hostages or extortion," Ar'alani added.

"The point remains that as they move toward us, they continue to bleed ships and troops," Zistalmu said. "So the longer they wait, the less likely they are to be a threat."

Ba'kif shook his head. "It doesn't always work that way."

But it was a losing argument, Ar'alani could see from the expressions on the syndics' faces. It might be a true argument, but it was also a losing one.

"Yet that, too, is a conversation for another day," Thurfian said. "Since Captain Thrawn's ship is still undergoing repairs, and Admiral Ar'alani's is about to leave on a diplomatic mission, it would seem that *nobody* will be traveling to the Lioaoin Regime."

"Excuse me?" Ba'kif said, shooting a look at Ar'alani. "What diplomatic mission is this?"

"The Ascendancy is sending a new ambassador to Urch, the capital of the Urchiv-ki," Thurfian said. "As the *Vigilant* is one of the finest warships in the Expansionary Fleet, and as its commander is one of the fleet's finest officers"—he inclined his head to Ar'alani—"it was decided that ship and commander would play host to Ambassador Boadil'par'gasoi."

"I see," Ba'kif said, his tone going frosty. "And when were we to be informed of this decision?"

"You're being informed now, General," Zistalmu said evenly. "The *Vigilant* will leave in three days."

Ba'kif looked at Ar'alani. "Can you be ready that quickly?"

"We can," Ar'alani said, trying to keep her own irritation out of her voice. The Syndicure was *not* supposed to pull stunts like this.

On the other hand, maybe they'd missed an angle. The *Springhawk*'s repairs were supposed to take another two weeks, and Zistalmu was clearly expecting Thrawn to be out of commission that long. But much of the ship's damage was cosmetic, and as the *Springhawk*'s captain Thrawn could declare the ship ready to fly without those particular repairs being completed. If he did, by the time the *Vigilant* left for Urch he could be nearly ready to pull the *Springhawk* out of bluedock and slip away for a surreptitious visit to the Lioaoin Regime.

"Sadly, though, Sky-walker Ab'begh has been reassigned," Zistalmu continued. "However, as the *Springhawk* won't be going anywhere for at least a couple of weeks, Sky-walker Che'ri and Caregiver Thalias have been transferred to your command."

"As has Captain Thrawn," Thurfian said. "He served under you once, and I'm sure his contributions will be equally welcome this time."

"I imagine he'll welcome the chance to visit Urch," Zistalmu said with a condescending little smile. "I understand their art galleries are the pride of the Urchiv-ki people."

Ar'alani suppressed a sigh. So they hadn't missed a bet after all. "I'm sure he will," she said. "I'll be honored to have him aboard."

With a sudden intake of breath, Che'ri's hands twitched one final time against the controls; and as Thalias looked out the viewport she saw the star-flares disappear into the starry background and the blue-and-white half circle directly ahead.

They'd arrived at Urch.

Thalias scowled at the planet. Big deal.

She stole a look at Thrawn, standing with Ambassador Ilparg behind Ar'alani's command chair. Thrawn himself was unmoving and calm; Ilparg, in contrast, was opening and closing his hands and rocking slightly back and forth on his heels. Clearly anxious to get to his new diplomatic post, and not very patient about the extra time it had taken the *Vigilant* to get here.

Thalias stepped behind Che'ri, rubbing gently against the tenseness of the girl's shoulder muscles and sending a mental glower in the direction of the grouchy ambassador. Che'ri had had to make a small additional curve through the final section of the Chaos leading into the Urch system, and the unexpected detour had made the *Vigilant* several hours late. In Thalias's experience that sort of thing happened quite frequently, and neither Ar'alani nor Thrawn had blamed

Che'ri in the slightest for the delay. Nor would any other reasonable person.

Ilparg, unfortunately, didn't fall into that category. He was clearly used to the more well-defined travel parameters within the Ascendancy and apparently had never understood that the term *the Chaos* wasn't simply someone's random idea of a good name.

That made him an idiot. What made him a contemptible fool was that he hadn't been shy about voicing his opinions and criticisms within Che'ri's hearing. Last night it had taken Thalias two hours of soothing, a good dinner and a hot bath, and every single one of her limited repertoire of lullabies to get Che'ri to sleep.

"And what exactly is the delay now?" Ilparg grumbled.

"We're waiting on the Urchiv-ki controller to give us permission to launch your shuttle," Ar'alani explained.

"Yes, I understand that," Ilparg said testily. "Wouldn't it be best if I was actually *in* the shuttle when that permission comes?"

"Patience, Ambassador," Thrawn said.

Thalias winced. Of all the soothements Thrawn could have offered, *patience* was the one least likely to get him anywhere.

"I have all the patience I need, Senior Captain," Ilparg said acidly, glaring at Thrawn. "What's needed here is results. Action and results. Since they don't seem to have noticed us, a second call would seem to be indicated—"

"There," Thrawn said, pointing at a spot on the aft visual display. "You see it?"

"Yes," Ar'alani said. "You're sure it's Lioaoin?"

Thalias felt her breath catch in her throat. Something was going on out there. She could tell by the expressions on Ar'alani's and Thrawn's faces, and by the matching tautness in their tones. Something was going on, and it wasn't good.

"Not one hundred percent, no," Thrawn said. "Their ship design has changed since we saw it last. But there are enough similarities that I think it probable."

"What are you talking about?" Ilparg demanded. "What do the

Lioaoi have to do with anything? This is Urch"—he shot a look at Che'ri—"unless our navigator has gotten us lost again."

Thalias took a deep breath. Enough was enough. "Excuse me, Ambassador—"

"This is Urch Planetary and Space Control," an alien voice erupted from the bridge speaker, its Taarja mangled almost beyond recognition. "Chiss ship is not permitted to release shuttle. Repeat: Chiss ship will not release shuttle. Ambassador of Chiss not welcome to Urchiv-ki, nor to her planets or space."

"That's impossible," Ilparg sputtered. "A treaty was endorsed—the Syndicure approved it." He drew himself up to his full height. "Admiral Ar'alani, call him back," he ordered. "Tell him you wish to speak with a senior member of the Tower Dimension—"

"Quiet," Ar'alani said, her face turned to the tactical display.

"Kindly do not address me in that—"

"I said quiet," Ar'alani repeated. She hadn't raised her voice, but suddenly an icy chill ran down Thalias's back.

Ilparg clearly felt the threat in her voice, too. He opened his mouth to speak, seemed to think better of it, and fell silent.

"What do you think?" Thrawn asked.

"I count eight ships visible," Ar'alani said. "The Lioaoin, six probable Urchiv . . . and that one."

"The Nikardun frigate," Thrawn said.

"That's what I was thinking," Ar'alani agreed, her voice going a shade darker. "That ridiculously large bridge viewport is a dead giveaway. The question is whether the Urchiv-ki have been completely conquered or if they're still in the same interdiction phase as the Paccosh."

"I'd guess the latter," Thrawn said. "But on a practical level, as long as they're willing to do General Yiv's bidding, their precise status is irrelevant."

"True," Ar'alani said. "Still, if they're planning to destroy us, they're certainly taking their time about it."

"*Destroy* us?" Ilparg gasped.

"There's no real hurry," Thrawn said, ignoring the ambassador's outburst. "We're already too deep in the gravity well for a quick escape, and their net pattern is coming together nicely behind us."

"Personally, I think they're going for a mirror payback," Senior Captain Wutroow put in.

"Interesting thought," Ar'alani said. "Rather ambitious of them."

"What's a mirror payback?" Che'ri whispered, looking up at Thalias.

Thalias shook her head. "I don't know."

"It's a counterthrust by one side that exactly corresponds to an earlier stroke by the other," Thrawn said, looking over at them. "In this case, Captain Wutroow is suggesting the Nikardun hope to capture the *Vigilant* in the same way that we captured one of their patrol ships."

Che'ri's shoulder muscles went rock-hard beneath Thalias's fingers. "No," she breathed. "They . . . no."

"Don't worry, they won't," Ar'alani said. She hesitated a moment, then rose from the command chair and walked over to Che'ri's navigation station. "You had trouble getting into this system, Sky-walker Che'ri," she said in a low voice.

"I'm sorry," Che'ri breathed. "It was just—"

"Yes, yes, I know," Ar'alani said, a distracted sort of soothing drifting across the tightness of her voice. "I'm not blaming you—this part of the Chaos is particularly nasty to navigate. My question is, just how solidly are we blocked in?"

"In other words," Thrawn added, coming up beside Ar'alani, "are there particular exit vectors that would get us out faster and easier than any of the other routes?"

"Just take your time and think, Che'ri," Thalias said. "Being right is better than being fast."

She felt Che'ri take a deep breath, watched the girl's hands move hesitantly across the controls and small displays of her board. "This way," she said, moving her finger to a line about thirty degrees from the *Vigilant*'s current heading.

"That's not the way we came in," Ar'alani said.

"Because we would have had to circle around even more," Che'ri said, some pleading in her voice. "And there were some big asteroids in the way. Ambassador Ilparg was already mad at me for how long it was taking—"

"It's all right, Che'ri, it's all right," Ar'alani said. This time the soothing sounded more genuine. "We just need to get out of here, preferably faster and farther than they can easily follow us. Doesn't matter if it takes us out of the way to get back to the Ascendancy. Helm, do you have the vector?"

"Yes, ma'am," the pilot confirmed.

"Problem," Wutroow said. "We're going to have to angle outward to get to it. If we do that, we'll be moving right into their net."

Ar'alani pursed her lips. "Not necessarily."

"We won't necessarily move into their net?" Wutroow asked, frowning.

"We don't necessarily have to angle outward," Ar'alani corrected. Pulling out her questis, she scribbled briefly on it. "Thrawn?" she asked, handing it to him.

Thrawn peered at the questis. "The *Vigilant* wasn't really designed for this kind of maneuver," he warned as he handed the device to Wutroow. "But I think it can handle the strain."

"What strain?" Ilparg croaked, a layer of suspicion coating the fear in his voice. "What are you proposing?"

"Don't worry about it," Wutroow advised, tapping the questis. Out of the corner of her eye, Thalias saw the image and data appear on one of the helm displays. "Mid Commander Octrimo?"

"I see it, ma'am," the pilot said hesitantly. "Are you sure about this?"

"They want to take the *Vigilant* intact," Ar'alani reminded him. "One way or the other, this guarantees that doesn't happen. Execute."

"Yes, ma'am." Visibly bracing himself, Octrimo keyed his board.

And with a sudden muted roar as the thrusters ran to full power, the *Vigilant* leapt forward.

Aiming straight for the planet in front of them.

Ilparg gave a strange sort of squeal. "Admiral!" he bleated. "What are you *doing*?"

"Course change one," Ar'alani said over the rumble. "Three, two, *one*."

Outside the viewport Urch moved off to the left as the *Vigilant* shifted its vector. At least, Thalias thought dimly through the agonized pounding of blood in her head, they were now headed for the edge of the planet instead of straight toward its center. This way, the resounding crash would take a little longer to happen.

"Urchiv ships moving in pursuit," Wutroow called from the sensor station. "Lioaoin hanging back. Nikardun . . . ramping up power; looks like he's going to try to cut us off."

"Increase speed five percent," Ar'alani ordered. "Course change two: Three, two, *one*."

The planet moved a little more to the side, and now it looked like they were only going to cut through the edge of the atmosphere. Thalias tried to remember if she'd ever heard of a Chiss Nightdragon running at high speed through a planet's atmosphere, but she couldn't.

"Urchiv ships picking up speed," Wutroow announced. "But unless they've got a lot more in reserve, there's no way they can catch us. Ah—they've figured that out. Dropping back."

"Any sign of intercept craft from the surface or behind the disk?" Ar'alani asked.

"Nothing detectable," Wutroow said. "At this point—"

She broke off as the *Vigilant* gave a sudden lurch. "Entering atmosphere, Admiral," Octrimo said. "Cutting deeper; hull temperature starting to rise. No danger yet."

But there would be, Thalias knew. Her physics classes were only a vague memory, but she remembered enough to know there were good reasons why ships didn't move through planetary atmospheres at this speed.

"What about the Nikardun?" Ar'alani asked.

"A little unclear—the turbulence is interfering with the sensors," Wutroow said. "But I think he's falling behind, too."

The buffeting was growing stronger. Thalias knew she should find a seat and strap in, but she could sense Che'ri's fear and didn't want to abandon the girl. She could almost hear the *Vigilant* groaning under the unfamiliar stresses and heat and pressure.

Imagination, of course. But still she could hear the ship's agony . . .

"Last course change," Ar'alani said abruptly into the muted cacophony. "Sky-walker, get ready."

"I am," Che'ri said, her voice trembling.

"Course change: Three, two, *one*."

Octrimo keyed his board, and the *Vigilant* angled away from the planet one final time. The battering began to lessen.

And suddenly the haziness around the stars cleared, and the groaning faded away. They were again in the welcome vacuum of space, driving hard along the vector Che'ri had pointed them to. The seconds ticked by, the *Vigilant* driving ever harder toward the distant stars.

"Clear for hyperspace," Octrimo announced.

"Sky-walker?" Ar'alani called.

"Ready," Che'ri called back. "How far do you want to go?"

"As far as you can take us without stressing yourself," Ar'alani said. "Ready . . . *go*."

The stars flared and then faded into the hyperspace swirl, and they were once again safe.

"You can let go now," Thrawn said.

Thalias blinked, only then realizing that somewhere along the line her grip on Che'ri's shoulders had transferred into a grip on the back of the girl's chair. With an effort, she unlocked her fingers and took a step back. "We did it," she said.

"We did," Thrawn agreed. "We of the fleet like to think of ourselves as heroes. Often, though, the true heroes are those who design and build the warships we take into battle."

"There wasn't supposed to *be* any battle," Ilparg growled. With the danger passed, he was rapidly returning to his normal pomposity. "What was the meaning of all that?"

"The Nikardun are attacking other worlds—" Thrawn began.

"The meaning?" Ar'alani interrupted him. "The meaning, Ambassador, is that this was a trap. Someone wanted to capture a Chiss ship, and they invited you to Urch to make it happen." She smiled, just slightly. "You were the bait."

"I am *not* bait," Ilparg insisted. "Not for anyone. Not for the Urchiv-ki, not for these—what did you call them?"

"Nikardun," Thrawn supplied.

"And not for the Nikardun," Ilparg bit out.

"And the Lioaoi?" Ar'alani asked.

Ilparg frowned at her. "What do the Lioaoi have to do with it?"

"One of their ships was here," Ar'alani said. "And they certainly didn't do or say anything to keep the Urchiv-ki back from us."

"In fact, it looked to me like they were part of the net the Urchiv-ki were setting up behind us," Wutroow added.

"Oh, they were, were they?" Ilparg said, glaring at the rolling hyperspace swirl outside the viewport.

"It certainly looked that way to me," Wutroow said.

"Perhaps we should swing by the Lioaoin heartworld before we return to the Ascendancy," Ar'alani suggested. "Talk to them, maybe ask for an explanation."

Ilparg turned cold eyes to her. "You think we should do that, do you?"

Ar'alani lifted a hand. "I merely offer the suggestion."

"And an excellent suggestion it is," Ilparg said. "Except that I don't intend to ask for an explanation. I intend to *demand* one."

He pointed dramatically toward the hyperspace swirl. "The Lioaoin heartworld, Admiral Ar'alani. At your best possible speed." He held the pose another moment, then gave an equally dramatic turn and stalked off the bridge.

"Interesting," Thrawn murmured. "I assume that was on purpose?"

"You wanted to see the heartworld," Ar'alani said. "Now we're going to."

"Make a note, Senior Captain," Wutroow added. "You can ask and suggest and show why your ideas make sense. But when politicians are involved"—she waved toward the viewport in an imitation of Ilparg's earlier posture—"*that* is how it's done."

CHAPTER NINE

Once again, the star-flares faded and the *Vigilant* was back in space-normal.

"Lioaoin heartworld bearing twenty degrees port, twelve nadir," Octrimo announced from the helm. "Arrived precisely on target, as Chiss sky-walkers always do."

"Acknowledged," Ar'alani said, suppressing a smile at that last, definitely non-standard comment. The entire bridge crew had quietly seethed at Ilparg's disparaging comments about Che'ri's navigation back at Urch—fleet officers and warriors held their sky-walkers dear—but most of them had kept their feelings to themselves. Octrimo, who as helm officer had naturally worked the closest with the girl, had apparently decided to risk a reprimand in order to throw a small dig at the ambassador.

His protective attitude probably wasn't hurt by the fact that his Droc family were strong rivals to Ilparg's own Boadil family.

Not that Ilparg probably noticed the comment. He was standing beside Ar'alani's command chair, his eyes on the distant planet, his mind clearly elsewhere than the *Vigilant*'s bridge.

Ar'alani looked back at the planet and the ships clustered around it, the brief moment of amusement disappearing. Most of the vessels out there were undoubtedly Lioaoin: freighters, patrol ships, two low-orbit bluedock repair stations, possibly a warship or two. The old records suggested there was at least one blackdock in much higher orbit, raising the possibility of another warship in the area, though if it was undergoing repairs it could probably be ignored.

The question was whether there were any Nikardun ships in the mix, there to keep an eye on the locals.

"Sweep complete," Senior Commander Obbic'lia'nuf called from the sensor station. "No matches to the Nikardun ship we saw at Urch."

Which didn't prove anything, Ar'alani knew. Aside from the oversized viewports and the particular placement of the main weapons clusters, none of the Nikardun ships she and Thrawn had run into looked exactly like any of the others. Certainly Yiv didn't seem to go with any kind of standard silhouette.

"Traffic Control is hailing us, Admiral," Wutroow said.

"Never mind them," Ilparg said before Ar'alani could reply. "Get me someone in the Regime Diplomatic Office. If they had anything to do with that Urch business, I want to have it out here and now."

"A moment, Ambassador," Ar'alani said, looking over her shoulder at the bridge hatch. Thrawn was apparently running late. "We're waiting for Senior Captain Thrawn to arrive."

"What do we need him for?"

Because he's the one who can tell us if there are Nikardun ships out there—the obvious reply ran through Ar'alani's mind. *Because he has a feel for tactics that will be crucial if this thing blows up. Because he's got a track record in combat situations that most Chiss commodores and admirals would give their blood firstborn for.*

But she had more tact than Commander Octrimo. She also had none of his family rivalries to deal with. "Because I want him here, and I'm the admiral," she said instead.

Ilparg made a little huffing noise. "Fine," he said. "But he'd better not be long."

The hatch slid open and Thrawn stepped onto the bridge. "My apologies, Admiral," he said as he crossed to Ar'alani and Ilparg. "Apologies, Ambassador. My studies took longer than expected."

"What studies were those, Senior Captain?" Ilparg asked suspiciously.

"Tactical data," Ar'alani put in.

"Tactical data?" Ilparg repeated scornfully. "Is that what the Expansionary Fleet calls art these days?"

Ar'alani clenched her teeth. "The first rule of strategy is to know your enemy, Ambassador," she said. "That includes their battle tactics; but also their history, their philosophy, and, yes, sometimes even their art."

"I accept the first two," Ilparg said, the disdain still in his voice. "The third is of little to no value. However, now that Senior Captain Thrawn has graced us with his presence, perhaps you'd be good enough to contact the diplomatic office as I requested?"

"Certainly, Ambassador," Wutroow said, stepping to Ilparg's side and deftly easing him away from Ar'alani and Thrawn. "We can hail them better from the comm station. This way, please."

"Thank you for trying," Thrawn said softly as he came up beside Ar'alani.

"Don't worry about it," Ar'alani advised. "Sometimes it's good to have your talents underestimated." *Though not when your career is being evaluated,* she added silently to herself. "What did you find?"

"Our Lioaoi art files are extremely limited," Thrawn said. "But they should be adequate to our needs."

"Glad to hear it." Ar'alani waved toward the viewport. "There's your canvas. Paint me something."

For a moment, Thrawn stood silently, his eyes tracking across the scene in front of them. Ar'alani shifted her attention between him and the tactical display, wondering when the Lioaoi were going to make their move. If the Nikardun were here, this group must have heard about the Urch incident by now.

Could the Urchiv-ki have somehow failed to identify the *Vigilant* before it escaped from their encirclement? Impossible. Could they perhaps not have at least one communications triad on the entire Urchiv-ki capital planet capable of transmitting a message this far? Even more unlikely.

So what were the Nikardun waiting for?

Unless the whole thing was just a product of paranoia and imagination. The alien nations out here were always fighting among themselves—Ar'alani knew that all too well. If the Nikardun were just some small-time species the Chiss hadn't run across, and their battles were purely local ones—

"Those nine fighters," Thrawn said, pointing to a group of small ships just coming around the planetary disk. "The craft themselves are a variant of Lioaoin design, but their formation and flight pattern aren't typical."

"Maybe they've updated their tactics since the last time you saw them," Ar'alani suggested.

"No," Thrawn said slowly. "Lioaoi like vertical formations. Their artwork clearly shows that. They would normally put nine ships like that in a three-stack wedge. This formation is planar and far more spread out."

Ar'alani nodded. That was definitely not a stacked-wedge formation. "Looks like it's designed for a pincer maneuver, too."

"Indeed," Thrawn said. "Attack, not defense. Again, contrary to the usual Lioaoin predisposition. But it's not just the formation. The pilots seem . . . hesitant, somehow. As if this formation is new to them."

"Maybe they're fresh recruits."

"All nine of them?" Thrawn shook his head. "No. Those are one-person gunboats. The Lioaoi would never put that many untried pilots alone without a more experienced ship and crew nearby in case of trouble. Certainly not that deep in the gravity well."

"I agree that's how they did things before," Ar'alani said. "But fleets change doctrine all the time. Maybe not this drastically, but they do adjust and adapt to new tech or situations."

"This is Lioaoin Orbital Command," a voice came over the speaker.

Ar'alani blinked. She'd been so focused on the distant ships and Thrawn's analysis that she'd almost forgotten their ostensible purpose for being here.

"This is Ambassador Boadil'par'gasoi of the Chiss Ascendancy," Ilparg replied with all the dignity and arrogance Ar'alani had come to expect from the diplomatic corps in general and Ilparg in particular. "I wish to speak to someone in the diplomatic office concerning the aggressive treatment we received a few days ago at the Urchiv-ki capital of Urch."

"What makes you think the Lioaoin Regime has anything to do with the Urchiv-ki?" the voice came back.

"There was a Lioaoin ship present when the Urchiv-ki attempted to capture our ship," Ilparg said.

Ar'alani hissed out a breath. What the hell did Ilparg think he was doing? Handing over information like that, especially without getting anything in return, was the height of foolishness. "Ambassador—"

"No, let him go," Thrawn said, closing a warning hand over her arm. "Let's see their reaction to who we are."

Ar'alani scowled. Yes, that *would* be Thrawn's plan, giving the Lioaoi a nudge and seeing how they reacted. All well and good, provided the reaction wasn't to throw everything they had at the intruders.

Still, the *Vigilant* was a fully armed Nightdragon, and they weren't yet too deep into the heartworld's gravity well. No matter what the Lioaoi had, Ar'alani had no doubt she could get them out with only minimal damage to her ship. Around the side of one of the bluedocks she saw something move into view . . .

And felt her eyes widen.

"Uh-oh," someone across the bridge breathed.

Ar'alani's hands closed involuntarily into tight fists. It was a warship.

A *huge* warship—*Battle Dreadnought* class at least, half again the *Vigilant*'s size. Its flanks bristled with weapons clusters, angular lines marked sections of heavy armor, tight-spaced patterns of nodes proclaimed the existence of a strong electrostatic barrier.

And the overly large bridge viewport—the arrogantly, invitingly, overly large viewport—marked it as Nikardun.

"Admiral?" Wutroow asked, a hint of urgency in her voice.

Ar'alani eyed the Nikardun warship, noting particularly the vectors and positions of the ships around it, then gave the tactical display a long, careful look. "Hold course," she ordered Octrimo. "They're not making any threatening moves."

"That could change at any minute," Wutroow warned.

"No," Thrawn said. "They could move to attack mode, but it would take more than simply a minute."

"Agreed," Ar'alani said. "At their distance and orientation, any move would be well telegraphed."

Wutroow seemed to brace herself. "Yes, ma'am."

"The diplomatic office has no understanding of that which you speak," a different Lioaoin voice came over the speaker. "But we welcome the friendship and mutual respect of the Chiss Ascendancy. Will you approach, Ambassador, that we may have a conversation? Or shall we send transport for you?"

Ilparg looked back at Ar'alani. "Admiral?" he prompted.

"Well, we're definitely not moving any closer," Ar'alani said. "And under the circumstances, we're not letting you go in, either."

"So we're just leaving?"

"Why not?" Ar'alani said. "We've gotten what we came for."

Ilparg frowned. "What exactly did we get?"

"The presence of a Nikardun ship," Thrawn said.

"Which took no action against us," Ilparg countered.

"And the fact that the Lioaoi don't want to talk about Urch," Ar'alani added.

Ilparg snorted. "I believe that's what's known as negative information."

"It's still information," Ar'alani said. "Regardless, it's all we're going to get. So offer your apologies, say your farewells—feel free to translate that into diplomatic-speak—and we'll be on our way."

"A moment, Admiral," Thrawn said thoughtfully. "With your permission, I'd like to run one additional experiment. Those nine gunboats seem unusually interested in us."

Ar'alani turned her attention back to the group of small fighters they'd noted earlier. Their pincer formation had opened up a little, but otherwise nothing seemed to have changed.

She felt her eyes narrow as she saw what Thrawn was referring to. The formation had opened up because the gunboats had suspended the maneuver they'd been in the middle of and were now drifting, their thrusters quiet, the tidal effects of the planetary gravitational field slowly moving them apart. "At the very least they're interested in being able to swing into action at a moment's notice," she said. "And in any direction."

"Exactly," Thrawn said. "And I see no reason other than the *Vigilant* why they should suddenly be so watchful."

Ar'alani scratched at her cheek. The Nikardun Battle Dreadnought was making no move, but the fighters were in ready position. Someone hedging their bets?

Or was it something more interesting? Was it an indication that there were two different chains of command operating?

Either way, it was worth exploring further. "I trust whatever you have in mind won't involve the discharge of weapons?"

"Not at all," Thrawn assured her. "I'd simply like to tell them I'm here."

"What do you expect that to accomplish?"

"I don't know. That's why it's an experiment."

She gave him her best strained-patience look. But Thrawn's hunches were usually worth chasing down. "Very well. Helm, be ready to turn and get us out of here."

"How quickly?" Octrimo asked.

"Hopefully, not very," Ar'alani said. "It looks like they're trying to play innocent, and it would be nice to leave them thinking we'd bought their act. But I want speed and power in reserve if we need it. Sky-walker Che'ri?"

"I'm ready," Che'ri said. Her voice was shaking a bit, but the words were firm enough.

Ar'alani gestured to Thrawn. "Ready?"

"Yes," he said, taking a step closer to her command chair. "Watch the gunboats."

She nodded and tapped the comm switch. "Go."

"This is Senior Captain Thrawn, Ambassador Ilparg's supervisor,"

Thrawn said. "Thank you for your interest, but the ambassador does not feel prepared at this time for a full diplomatic conversation. The Chiss Ascendancy will be in future communication with you regarding this matter."

The Lioaoin gave some kind of wordy but mostly meaningless reply. But Ar'alani wasn't really listening. Seven of the nine gunboats Thrawn had told her to watch had activated their thrusters at the mention of his name, moving out of formation with their bows swinging toward the *Vigilant*.

But they'd barely begun their maneuver when they abruptly throttled back, holding their new positions for another moment before dropping back into place with the two gunboats that hadn't left their orbits. The whole thing took barely five seconds, with all nine ships back in formation before Thrawn even finished his statement.

The half of her brain that was monitoring the conversation recognized that it was over. She tapped the comm switch again and nodded to Octrimo. "Take us out, helm," she ordered. "Nice and easy and calm. Sky-walker, stand ready."

She turned her attention to the Battle Dreadnought, wondering if its captain would now decide to drop his own innocent act. But the Nikardun continued its leisurely orbit as the *Vigilant* turned and drove back out of the gravity well. Che'ri leaned over her control board, and with a burst of star-flares they were back in the safety of hyperspace.

Wutroow crossed the bridge to Ar'alani's side. "So what exactly did we learn?" she asked.

"You weren't watching the gunboats?" Ar'alani asked.

"You and Thrawn were watching them. I figured someone ought to keep an eye on the Dreadnought."

"Yes. Good thinking." Ar'alani looked up at Thrawn. "Your idea, Senior Captain. Go ahead and lay it out."

"Seven of the nine gunboats reacted to my name by starting to move toward us," Thrawn told Wutroow. "That suggests both that I'm known to the Nikardun, and that there's some kind of standing order regarding me. But a moment later all seven returned to their formation."

"So whoever was commanding the fighters was all set to come charging over and avenge the horrible insult you delivered at Rapacc," Wutroow said slowly. "Only someone higher in the command chain countermanded the order."

"That's how I read it," Ar'alani confirmed. "Which immediately implies in turn what I said earlier. Even under provocation, even with standing orders, they're trying very hard to pretend they're not a threat to us."

"One problem," Wutroow said, lifting a finger. "I thought we decided the gunboats were Lioaoin. Why would they care about Thrawn? I mean, aside from the obvious?"

"Not so obvious anymore," Ar'alani said. "Certainly after all these years, there can't be any standing orders concerning him. At least, not from the Lioaoi."

"I suppose not," Wutroow said. "So . . . ?"

"So we were wrong earlier," Ar'alani said, feeling a sense of looming dread. "We thought the Lioaoi might just be learning new battle tactics. They are, but they're learning them under Nikardun supervision."

"The Lioaoi in the gunboats knew the Nikardun orders concerning me," Thrawn said. "The seven pilots who reacted did so far too quickly for it to be otherwise. Detailed standing orders of that sort aren't typically shared with subjugated peoples. Furthermore, the gunships were armed—their forward swivel lasers were visible, as were their missile ports. We know from the Paccosh that the Nikardun remove the weapons from their conquered peoples."

"Which strongly suggests the Lioaoi aren't Nikardun subjects," Ar'alani said quietly, gazing out at the roiling hyperspace swirl. "They're allies."

For a moment none of them spoke. Then Wutroow huffed out a breath. "Great," she said. "So now what?"

"We need more information," Thrawn said. "Admiral, can you divert the *Vigilant* to Solitair before returning to the Ascendancy?"

"Absolutely not," Ilparg said firmly, striding up to them. "First the Lioaoin Regime; now you want to go to the Garwian Unity? How many ways are you trying to get yourself in trouble?" He turned his glare onto Thrawn. "Never mind *you*. How many ways are you trying to get *me* into trouble? I'm already far removed from my mandate."

"Your position and mandate aren't the issues here, Ambassador," Ar'alani said, studying Thrawn's face. "The *Vigilant* is my ship, and it goes where I order it. If I decide there's data to be gathered, I'm obligated to follow through on it."

"Not if the Syndicure declares your decisions improper," Ilparg warned.

"If that happens, so be it," Ar'alani said. "But even the syndics have only limited authority over a senior fleet officer."

"There should be only minimal trouble for either of you," Thrawn said. "I can take a shuttle in while the *Vigilant* returns to the Ascendancy. That should add only a few hours to your travel time."

"You don't want us to wait?" Ar'alani asked, frowning. "What if the Garwians don't want to talk to you?"

"I believe they will," Thrawn said. "If I may ask a favor, Admiral, I'd like to borrow your office for the next hour or two."

"Of course," Ar'alani said. "Take all the time you need. Caregiver Thalias, bring Sky-walker Che'ri out of Third Sight as soon as it's convenient and safe. She's to then reroute us to the Garwian capital planet of Solitair."

"Yes, Admiral," Thalias said. She hadn't missed a word of the discussion, Ar'alani could see, but she showed no inclination to question the decision. "It'll be a few more minutes before Che'ri can be disturbed."

"At your own timing and judgment, Caregiver," Ar'alani assured her. "Captain Thrawn, my office is yours."

MEMORIES VII

Thrawn shook his head. "Unacceptable," he declared. "Completely unacceptable."

Ziara's years in the Expansionary Defense Fleet had honed her ability to cringe on the inside without letting the accompanying emotion show in her face or stance. Nonetheless, this time it was a very near thing. A junior commander, even one who'd just received impressive accolades, *never* talked to a senior officer that way. It would serve him right if Ba'kif slammed him right down to the floor.

Fortunately for Thrawn, Ba'kif had an above-average patience level. "Do I need to detail for you the protocols on preemptive strikes?" he asked, his voice calm.

"No, sir," Thrawn said. At least, Ziara thought, he got in a *sir* this time. "I simply don't see how it applies in this case. The ships were of Lioaoin design, they were using Lioaoin docking facilities, and they pursued us from the regime heartworld. It seems indisputable that the pirates are, in fact, under direct Lioaoin control and supervision."

"Of course it's disputable," Ba'kif said. "The regime has categorically disputed it."

"They're lying."

"Perhaps," Ba'kif said. "But we have only what we have: circumstantial evidence and an official denial."

"So we allow them to go on their way unscathed?" Thrawn persisted.

"What would you have us do?" Ba'kif asked. "Launch a full-scale war fleet to descend upon the heartworld and destroy every governmental and military installation we can find?"

Thrawn's lips compressed briefly. "It would hardly take an entire fleet," he hedged.

"You're evading the point," Ba'kif said. "Let me make it clearer. Would you destroy property and condemn people to death for the possible actions—the *possible* actions—of their government?"

"And what of *our* people?" Thrawn countered. "We've also suffered losses of property and life."

"Those who inflicted those losses have been killed or punished."

"Those who did the actual deeds, perhaps. Not those who sent them."

"Again, you have no proof."

Thrawn's eyes flicked to Ziara. "Then let me obtain it," he offered. "Let me go to the regime as a merchant or diplomat and find a way into their archives. Official orders, or perhaps a clear line of plunder distribution—"

"Enough," Ba'kif snapped, his patience finally breaking. "Understand this, Commander, and understand it clearly. The Ascendancy does not attack other systems unless we have clear evidence that they attacked us first. We don't attack militarily, diplomatically, subversively, clandestinely, or psychologically. Those who do not attack us will not be attacked by us. Is that clear?"

"Very clear, General," Thrawn said, his voice as stiff as his posture.

"Good," Ba'kif said. He took a deep breath. "Now, the other item I wanted to discuss with the two of you." He glanced at Ziara, then turned back to Thrawn. "For your sterling performance in planning and executing the mission, Junior Commander Thrawn, you are hereby promoted to senior commander."

A touch of surprise crossed Thrawn's expression. "*Two* ranks, sir?"

"Two ranks." Ba'kif gave a little snort. "Yes, I know. But your success against the pirates has you riding high at the moment, and the Ascendancy does cherish its heroes. And, of course, you're Mitth."

Thrawn's face seemed to fall a little. "Yes. Thank you, sir."

Ba'kif inclined his head and turned to Ziara. "And you, Mid Captain Ziara, are also hereby promoted to senior captain."

"Thank you, sir," Ziara said, her chest seeming to close around her heart. Senior captain. One more promotion, and she would reach commodore.

The rank where everything changed.

"Congratulations to you both," Ba'kif said. "You can pick up your new insignia and IDs from the quartermaster. You're dismissed, Thrawn. Ziara, another moment of your time."

He waited in silence until Thrawn had left the room. "Your assessment, Senior Captain?" he asked, nodding toward the closed door.

"He's brilliant, sir," Ziara said. "Excellent strategist and tactician."

"And his political shrewdness?"

"Poor to nonexistent."

"Agreed," Ba'kif said. "He's going to need a steady hand, both to guide him and to prevent him from continually grabbing the wrong end of the fire stick."

Ziara suppressed a wince. "Do I need to guess, sir?"

"Hardly," Ba'kif said, smiling tightly. "I'm putting him aboard with you as your third officer." He glanced at his questis. "Your new ship will be the patrol cruiser *Parala*."

"Yes, sir," Ziara said, feeling herself straighten up a bit more. Patrol cruisers typically traveled far outside the recognized boundaries of the Ascendancy, gathering intel and watching for potential threats. An interesting and highly coveted assignment. "Thank you, sir."

"You've earned it," Ba'kif said. "I know you'll do whatever is necessary for the defense and protection of the Ascendancy." He drew himself up to full attention. "Dismissed, Senior Captain. And good luck."

She'd expected Thrawn to have already left. Instead, she found him waiting for her outside the general's office. "Trouble?" he asked.

"No," she said. "I'm commanding the *Parala*, and you're my new third officer."

Again, a brief look of surprise. "Really?"

"Really," she said, starting down the hallway. "Quartermaster's this way."

He dropped into step beside her. "Congratulations," he said as they walked. "The *Parala*'s reputed to be an excellent ship."

"So I've heard," Ziara said. "Congratulations to you as well, by the way. Two ranks at once is almost unheard of."

"So I've been told," Thrawn said, his voice going distant. "Though of course what's given can also be taken away."

Ziara leaned forward to peer at his face. "Something wrong?"

He looked sideways at her, then turned to face forward again. "The Lioaoin Regime didn't go into piracy simply because they were bored," he said. "They clearly have a serious financial problem."

"You suggesting we take up a collection?"

He shot her another look, this one carrying an edge of annoyance. "They won't try it again with the Ascendancy," he said. "But the problem remains, as does their chosen remedy. Once they've regrouped and replaced the ships you destroyed, they'll be back, attacking merchants from other systems. What happens to those systems?"

Ziara shrugged. "They'll have to deal with the Lioaoi on their own."

"What if they aren't strong enough to do so?" Thrawn persisted. "Are we supposed to just sit back and watch them suffer?"

Ziara looked him straight in the eye. "Yes."

For a moment they locked gazes. Thrawn turned away first. "Because we don't interfere in the affairs of others."

"Would you rather the Ascendancy became guardians for the entire Chaos?" Ziara asked. "Because that's where that path would take us. We would rescue one, then another, then a third, until finally we stood alone as bulwark against a thousand different aggressors. Is that what you think we should do?"

"No, of course not," he said. "But there has to be a middle path."

For a few steps they walked in silence. "If it helps, I understand what you're saying," Ziara said at last. "Tell you what. When you rise to rule the Aristocra and the Ascendancy, I'll help you work out a solution."

Thrawn gave a little snort. "There's no need to be sarcastic."

"Who says that was sarcasm?" Ziara asked. "The Mitth are an important family, and as General Ba'kif said you're riding high in their estimation. The point is that nonintervention is the Ascendancy's protocol at the moment. Unless or until that changes, we accept our orders and fulfill our duties." She caught his arm, bringing him to a sudden stop, and gazed hard into his face. "And that's *all* we do. Understood?"

A small smile touched his lips. "Of course, Senior Captain Ziara."

"And don't worry that your family's influence was what jumped you those ranks," she continued. "Don't deny it—I saw it in your face. I'm sure the Mitth connection didn't hurt, but the Council doesn't do things just because some syndic wants them to. If they did, *I'd* have been jumped *three* ranks."

"And you'd have deserved it," Thrawn said.

Ziara started to smile. The smile faded as she realized he was serious. "Hardly."

"I disagree." Thrawn seemed to consider that. "I *respectfully* disagree," he amended. "You'll certainly make full admiral someday. The Council might as well promote you now and save themselves some time."

"I appreciate your confidence," Ziara said, turning away and starting to walk again. "But I'm content to take the slow, steady route."

Admiral. Actually, the word had a nice ring to it. Provided, of course, that she was as good as Thrawn seemed to think.

And provided that, while he served under her command, he didn't do something to ruin her chances forever.

CHAPTER TEN

The hatch into Admiral Ar'alani's office slid open. Bracing herself, wondering what this sudden summons was all about, Thalias stepped inside. "You wanted to see me, Senior Captain?" she said.

"Yes," Thrawn replied. "Come in, please. I want to show you something."

Thalias took another step forward, hearing the hatch slide closed behind her, and looked around. Given Thrawn's reputation—or perhaps his notoriety—with artwork, she'd expected to find the office filled with holograms of Garwian sculptures and paintings. To her mild surprise, she instead found him surrounded by a three-dimensional map filled with stars and star routes.

"Here's the Ascendancy," he said, waving a finger through a familiar cluster of stars just off center on the map. "Here's the Lioaoin Regime"—he pointed to a much smaller group of stars to the north-zenith of the Ascendancy. "Here's Rapacc—" He shifted the finger a little way east-nadir. "Here's Urch"—a little more east-nadir and a bit to the south. "And here are the Paataatus worlds." He shifted his finger one final time to a spot on the Ascendancy's southeast-zenith border. "What do you see?"

"The first three are north and northeast of us," Thalias said, wondering why he'd brought in the Paataatus. They were far away from all the others he'd mentioned, and besides they'd already been dealt with.

"Indeed," Thrawn said. "Three different nations under Nikardun attack or besiegement, all three on the edges of the Ascendancy."

Thalias wrinkled her nose. They weren't *that* close, really. Certainly not close enough to be a threat.

"So far none of the Nikardun conquests is encroaching directly on the Ascendancy," Thrawn said, as if he'd read her mind and her silent objection. "But the pattern is troubling. If Yiv is targeting us, this is the ideal way for him to begin."

"All right," Thalias said cautiously. "But if he attacks, can't we deal with him like we did the Paataatus?"

"Interesting that you mention the Paataatus," Thrawn said. "Their artwork and entire culture strongly implies that the defeat Admiral Ar'alani delivered to them should have ended any resistance to us for the rest of this generation. Yet reports from Naporar indicate they may be rearming for another attack. I suggest that they, too, may be under Yiv's influence and control."

Thalias looked at the map again. And if that was true, it was no longer just the Nikardun working their way across the Chaos, with the Ascendancy in their path purely by coincidence. If they'd also conquered or suborned the Paataatus, there was a good chance they were deliberately encircling the Chiss. It was as if Yiv was raising the whole of the Chaos against them. "What can we do?"

"As I told the admiral, we need more information," Thrawn said. "I've spent the past hour studying the map, and there are four other nations in particular whose current status I believe may be revealing. I'm hoping I can persuade the Garwians to take me to one of them under a suitable pretext."

"That sounds . . . extremely dangerous," Thalias said.

"Dangerous, perhaps," Thrawn said. "But not extremely so. The Garwians . . . let's just say they owe me for past events."

Thalias made a face. She'd heard a little about those events, and they weren't counted as being among the Ascendancy's finest moments. "Have you cleared this with the admiral?"

"I have." Thrawn smiled faintly. "I can't say she's enthusiastic about the plan, but she's willing to go along with it."

In other words, happy with the plan or not, Ar'alani was willing to stick her neck beneath the blade alongside Thrawn's. "I see. I assume I'm here because you want something from me, too?"

"Very good," Thrawn said. "Yes, I'd like you to accompany me on this expedition."

Thalias had sort of guessed that was where this conversation would eventually end up. Her mind flicked back to her deal with Syndic Thurfian. "As an additional observer, I assume?"

"Yes." He paused. "And as my family hostage."

Thalias felt her eyes go wide. "As your—*what?*"

"My family hostage," Thrawn repeated.

"Which is what?"

Thrawn pursed his lips. "In certain circumstances, the rivalry between Chiss families is strong enough that they agree to exchange hostages. One member from each side is rematched as a merit adoptive, and that person serves under another family member as servant and hostage. Should hostilities break out between the families, the hostages know they will be immediately killed."

Thalias stared at him. "I've never even heard of that."

"Of course not." Thrawn's gave her a small smile. "Because I just made it up."

She shook her head. "All right, I'm lost."

"It's very simple," Thrawn said quietly. "I expect the Nikardun to know a great deal about the Ascendancy and Chiss culture. To defeat an enemy you must know them, and they are clearly expert conquerors." He stopped, an expectant expression on his face.

Thalias made a face. Playing teacher, just as he had on the Paccosh mining station, waiting for her to come up with the right answer.

But at least this time that answer was obvious. "So if they suddenly learn there's something they *don't* know about us, something really important, they might decide they need to rethink their whole strategy?"

"Exactly," Thrawn said. "At best, it may cause Yiv to abandon his plans against us. At worst, it should buy us some time."

He raised his eyebrows. "The question is whether you're willing and able to play such a role."

The obvious answer—*yes*—rose quickly into Thalias's throat. But even as she opened her mouth to say the word, she realized it wasn't nearly that easy.

She had no idea how a hostage spoke and behaved and thought. Probably there would be some hesitation, some low-level but constant fear for her life, possibly a degree of eagerness to please the one who held her life in his hands. Could she pull all of that off in a believable way?

More than that, going with Thrawn would mean leaving Che'ri alone aboard the *Vigilant*. Certainly the girl could handle a trip back to the Ascendancy on her own—it wasn't like Ar'alani couldn't assign one of her officers to take care of their sky-walker for a few days.

But Che'ri had lost so many other caregivers over her time in the fleet. Would she see Thalias's departure as yet another abandonment, no matter how good or necessary the cause? Thalias could explain the situation before she left, but that didn't necessarily mean Che'ri would hear or understand. Where exactly did Thalias's true duty and commitment lie?

She looked at the map, at the clusters of enemy stars closing in around the Ascendancy. Suddenly her own uncertainties, comfort, and self-respect didn't seem nearly so important anymore. As for Che'ri, Thalias could only do her best to explain it to the girl.

"I don't know how to be a hostage," she said, turning back to Thrawn. "But I'm ready to learn."

Thrawn inclined his head to her. "Thank you," he said. Stepping to the desk, he touched a key. "Admiral, this is Thrawn. Caregiver Thalias has agreed to accompany me. Can you inform Sky-walker Che'ri and make arrangements for someone to take over her care when we reach Solitair?"

"I'd like to tell her myself," Thalias put in. "It might be easier coming from me."

"That's reasonable," Ar'alani said. "Do you have someone you'd recommend to take your place?"

Thalias hesitated. Most of her time aboard the *Vigilant* had been spent with Che'ri or on the bridge. Who did she know well enough to entrust with such a responsibility?

Especially since it needed to be someone of stature and respect if the girl wasn't going to see this as Thalias handing her off to the first person she ran into along the corridor.

Really, there was only one person who fit both criteria.

"Yes," she hedged. "May I think about it a little longer?"

"Of course," Ar'alani said. "Che'ri should be finished with this run in half an hour. I want you on the bridge at that time with your recommendation."

"Yes, Admiral."

"I'll see you then. Ar'alani out."

Thrawn keyed off. "Do you know who you'll ask to take care of her?" he asked as Thalias headed toward the hatch.

"Yes," she said over her shoulder. "But I'm not sure the admiral will approve."

The admiral, Ar'alani thought sourly, very much didn't approve.

But she'd agreed that Thalias could choose Che'ri's caregiver, and she was bound by personal honor to follow through on that promise.

Besides which, Thalias's arguments and reasoning made sense.

Che'ri was curled up in one of the oversized chairs, right where Ar'alani had left her, when the signal and Thrawn's instructions finally arrived from the surface. "I'm back," she announced cheerfully as she crossed the suite toward the girl. "Did you get some sleep? Are you hungry?"

"I'm okay," Che'ri said, her voice soft and weary.

Ar'alani frowned, studying the girl's face. When she was Che'ri's age, she remembered a tendency to go all dramatic when she wanted something, or felt she was being treated unfairly, or just felt like getting some attention. But there was something in Che'ri's expression that told her none of those were the case here. "Are you upset that Thalias left you?"

Che'ri's lip twitched, enough to show that Ar'alani had hit the mark. "She said she had to go," she muttered. "She wouldn't tell me why."

Ar'alani nodded. "Yes, that always drove me crazy, too."

Che'ri looked up, frowning. "You were a sky-walker?"

"No, but I was once ten," Ar'alani said. "Grown-ups were always whispering and keeping secrets. I hated that. But sometimes it's necessary."

Che'ri lowered her gaze. "She's going into danger, isn't she? Captain Thrawn's taking her, and they're going into danger."

"Oh, there's danger everywhere," Ar'alani said, trying to sound casual. "It's not a big deal."

It was, she realized too late, the exact wrong thing to say. Suddenly, without warning, Che'ri's eyes welled up with tears, and she buried her face in her hands. "She's going to die," she gasped between sobs that shook her whole body. "She's going to *die*."

"No, no," Ar'alani protested, hurrying forward and dropping to one knee beside the frightened girl. "No, she's going to be fine. Thrawn's there, too, and he won't let anything bad happen to her."

"It's my fault," Che'ri moaned. "It's my fault. I yelled at her. I yelled at her, and now she's going to die!"

"Easy, easy," Ar'alani soothed. "It's okay. When did you yell at her?"

But even as she asked the question, the obvious answer popped into her mind. The long farewell and explanations that had taken place in the privacy of the sky-walker suite. Thalias's manner and posture as she and Thrawn had headed to the shuttle, a manner which Ar'alani noted at the time seemed unusually subdued even given the gravity of the upcoming mission. Che'ri's refusal to come out of her sleeping room when Ar'alani first came to the suite to check on her after the shuttle left.

Ar'alani had put it down to nerves on both sky-walker's and caregiver's parts. Apparently, however, their farewells had been a lot more fiery than she'd realized.

And now the girl had worked through her anger and tumbled off the other direction into fear and depression and guilt. "It's okay,"

Ar'alani said again. "People yell at each other all the time. It doesn't mean they don't care for each other."

"But I told her I hated her," Che'ri sobbed.

"She's not going to die," Ar'alani said firmly, gingerly resting her hand on Che'ri's shoulder. "Saying something doesn't make it happen."

"I didn't mean to yell." Che'ri sniffed, the crying fading a little as she lowered her hands. "I just wanted some graph markers. So I could draw. But she said she didn't have any, and couldn't get any before she left, and I said Ab'begh has them and that she was a terrible momish—" She covered her face again, and the sobbing resumed.

Ar'alani patted her shoulder gently, feeling like a fresh recruit on her first training mission. She would take a battle against multiple enemies any day over trying to soothe a terrified child. "Listen to me," she said, wincing at the command tone of her voice. "Listen to me," she tried again, this time trying for gentleness. "This isn't like books or vids. This is real life. Just because someone goes off on a mission right after they've had a fight doesn't mean they're going to die."

Che'ri didn't answer. But Ar'alani thought she was crying a little less hard.

"Tell you what," she said. "I'll draw you a hot bath—Thalias said you like those—and while you're soaking I'll make whatever you want to eat. How does that sound?"

"Okay," Che'ri said.

"Okay," Ar'alani repeated. "I'll go start the bath while you figure out what you want."

Che'ri nodded. "Admiral Ar'alani . . . Thalias said you've done a lot of things with Captain Thrawn."

"I've had my fair share of experience with him," Ar'alani said, smiling wryly. "And Thalias's right. Being with Thrawn is one of the safest places she can be."

"Can you tell me about some of the stories?" Che'ri asked hesitantly. "She gave me some, but they're all official and stiff and I . . .

don't read very well. Thalias likes to read but I can't . . ." Without warning, the body-racking sobs were back.

Ar'alani closed her eyes and let out a silent sigh. This was going to be a long, long night.

The Garwians had been reasonably quick to allow the shuttle to land. They were equally quick to order it to leave, citing security concerns about an obvious Chiss craft sitting on the ground and promising that the petitioners would be seen quickly.

But as Thalias and Thrawn continued to wait in the security office anteroom, she began to wonder if they had changed their minds. Certainly no one in the Unity seemed eager or even willing to talk to them.

Thrawn had said that the Garwians owed him a favor. But from the way the people bustling around the office seemed to be avoiding eye contact, Thalias was having serious doubts about the depth of any such gratitude.

She was also having second thoughts about the thick, plaster-like makeup Thrawn had decided should be a proper part of her appearance. She understood the logic of making a family hostage's status instantly apparent to passersby, but with much her face seemingly covered by textured ridges and plateaus she could hardly form any expressions at all.

Which, again, might be part of the whole point of such makeup. Hostages as nonentities, or some such. Still, as she sat there in silence and expressionlessness, feeling the extra weight of the plaster pressing down on her neck and shoulders, she couldn't help wondering what the long-term effects of the stuff might be on her skin.

Finally, four hours after their arrival, one of the Garwians finally stopped in front of them. "Second Defense Overlord Frangelic will see you now," he said in Minnisiat. "Follow me, please."

The Garwian seated behind the desk as they were ushered in was younger than Thalias had expected for what sounded like such a prestigious post. He sat motionless and silent as they walked up to the two guest chairs facing the desk and sat down. Looking over Thalias's shoulder, the alien nodded to their guide, and she heard the door shut behind them.

"I see you've risen in your profession, Second Defense Overlord," Thrawn said calmly. "Congratulations."

"As you have likewise, Senior Captain Thrawn," Frangelic said, inclining his head. "And your companion?"

"My hostage," Thrawn corrected.

Frangelic seemed to draw back in his chair. "Since when do the Chiss keep hostages?"

"Since long before we took to the stars," Thrawn said. "It's sometimes invoked as a security matter between families. We rarely speak of it openly to strangers, but since she is here you must be brought into my confidence. I trust you'll keep it a private matter?"

"Of course. Has she a name?"

Thrawn looked at Thalias, as if he was trying to remember it. "Thalias."

"Thalias," Frangelic greeted her gravely. He studied her a moment, his eyes seeming to trace some of the spirals and ridges of the makeup curling around her face, then returned his attention to Thrawn. "Let me be clear from the outset. The Ruleri have met in special session over the past hour, and they have informed me that their feelings are mixed concerning your return to Solitair. They feel your last interaction with the Garwian people . . . the word *betrayal* wasn't actually spoken, but the thoughts and attitudes tended in that direction."

"I remember things differently," Thrawn said. "But that is the past. Right now, both the Ascendancy and the Unity face an uncertain and dangerous future. I bring a proposal that aims to address both problems."

"Interesting." Frangelic eyed him. "Continue."

"I believe we both face a new enemy called the Nikardun," Thrawn said. Keying his questis, he handed it across the desk. "We know of three, possibly four, nations in the region that have either been quietly conquered or are currently under siege."

"We know these nations," Frangelic said, studying the questis. "As well as two others that seem to have drastically changed both their governments and their attitudes toward outsiders."

"So you agree there is a threat?"

"We agree something has changed," Frangelic said. "The Ruleri are divided on whether or not the changes constitute a threat."

"What do *you* think?"

Frangelic hesitated. "I think the situation needs to be studied further," he said. "I assume your proposal is along those lines?"

"It is," Thrawn said. "You see listed there four nations that I believe may hold useful information. Any Nikardun in those areas would be instantly aware of a Chiss presence, which precludes me from investigating in any official manner. My hope therefore is that I can travel unknown and unacknowledged to one of those nations aboard a Garwian ship."

Frangelic's jaws opened wide, briefly revealing rows of sharp teeth before his lips closed over them, hiding them from sight. The Garwian version of a smile, Thalias remembered reading. "I find it hard to believe a Chiss aboard one of our ships could be truly unacknowledged," he said. "However, as it happens, the Ruleri have a diplomatic mission leaving in two days for one of those on your list: the Vak homeworld of Primea."

"That would be perfect," Thrawn said. "Can you get me aboard?"

"I can try." Frangelic's eyes flicked to Thalias. "And your hostage, too, I presume?"

"Of course. Though from this point onward please refer to her only as my companion, especially in public."

"Of course." Frangelic looked back at the questis. "The Ruleri will never let you travel without a security escort," he continued, as if talking to himself. "Unfortunately, none of my subordinates will understand you or your methods." He looked up and gave another smile. "Nor will they remember you the way I do." He hesitated, then pushed the questis back toward Thrawn. "So if you're to go to Primea, then it follows I must, as well. I'll speak to the envoy commanding the mission and make the arrangements."

"Thank you," Thrawn said. "You will need to explain the presence of a Chiss aboard a Garwian mission. I propose you identify me as an interstellar art expert whom your academics invited to participate in order to study Vak artworks."

"Seems a bit far-fetched," Frangelic said doubtfully.

"Not at all," Thrawn said. "There are theories in the academic world that the Vaks and Garwians were in contact twenty to thirty thousand years ago. Finding indications of such contact, perhaps in overlapping artistic styles or subjects, would help confirm those theories, and possibly allow historians to track the path of hyperspace travel through this part of the Chaos."

"Interesting," Frangelic said. "Is any of that real, or did you just make it up?"

"The theories are completely real," Thrawn assured him. "Somewhat obscure, and hotly debated, but someone on Primea will be able to locate records of them if inquiries are made."

"I hope you're right," Frangelic said. "Very well. I'll have my aide find you quarters, then I'll see about getting us passage on the diplomatic ship."

"Thank you," Thrawn said, standing up. "I'll need to send the details to Admiral Ar'alani before she can take the *Vigilant* out of orbit. Oh, and may I also ask you to bring a medium-sized shipping container aboard the ship?"

"A *shipping container*?" Frangelic echoed, his voice suddenly suspicious. "How much are you planning to bring with you?"

"Actually, very little," Thrawn assured him. "The container is for our return."

"Very well," Frangelic said, still sounding suspicious. "Perhaps you will explain further before our departure."

"Or during the voyage," Thrawn said. "We shall see which works best."

"We shall," Frangelic said. "In the meantime, send your message to your admiral. As quickly as possible," he added, his tone going a bit brittle. "The Ruleri are quite capable of ignoring people and things that are distasteful to them, but it wouldn't be wise to test the breaking point of that ability."

"I understand," Thrawn said. "As soon as I have the details of the mission, the *Vigilant* will be gone. In the meantime, companion, come. While I speak with the admiral, you can go to our quarters and prepare our dinner."

MEMORIES VIII

After all her months aboard the *Parala*, Ziara had developed a sensitivity to every nuance and subtle movement of her ship, its engines, and its general feel.

What was happening right now was about as unsubtle as it got.

She was five steps behind Mid Captain Roscu as both she and the first officer closed on the bridge. Roscu got there first and ducked through the hatchway—"Thrawn, what in hell's name are you doing?" she snarled, her voice echoing out into the corridor.

Scowling, Ziara followed her through the hatchway. And so began another wonderful day aboard the *Parala*.

But this time it was instantly clear that it wasn't just Roscu verbally bludgeoning a more junior officer from a rival family. The overnight bridge crew was sitting stiffly at their posts as Thrawn stood behind the sky-walker and pilot, his hands clasped behind his back, the swirl of hyperspace washing around the viewport. A quick visual sweep of the status boards showed that he'd brought the ship's weapons and electrostatic barrier to full readiness, just one step below battle stations.

"I asked you a question, Senior Commander," Roscu bit out as she strode toward him.

"As you were, Mid Captain," Ziara called firmly. "Status, Senior Commander?"

"We've picked up an urgent distress call from the Garwian colony world Stivic," Thrawn said. "Security Officer Frangelic says they're under attack." He half turned to throw a significant look at Ziara. "By pirates."

"You know the protocol," Ziara said as she strode past the glowering Roscu toward Thrawn, her stomach tightening. It was painfully obvious what Thrawn suspected.

And he was probably right. The Garwian worlds were centers of commerce for a number of local species, and Stivic in particular was within easy strike range of the Lioaoin Regime.

She stopped at his side. "You know we can't do this," she said, keeping her voice low. "The protocols forbid intervention."

"I'm hoping direct action won't be necessary."

Ziara looked down at the nine-year-old girl in the skywalker's chair, her hands moving almost of their own accord as she and her Third Sight guided the *Parala* through the twisting pathways of hyperspace. "A bluff?"

"Perhaps not even that much," Thrawn said. "The sudden appearance of a Chiss warship may be enough to frighten them away."

"And if it isn't?"

His lips compressed. "Then we do nothing."

"That's right," Ziara said. She raised her voice. "All crew: Battle stations. Bridge, prepare to exit hyperspace."

Ten seconds later, the sky changed, the star-flares collapsed, and they had arrived.

At the edge of a horrendous battle.

Ziara felt a knot form in the pit of her stomach. Two Garwian patrol ships were standing gamely against three larger attackers, trying to keep them away from the big orbiting merchant-hub station. Nearby, a fourth attacker and a small freighter drifted together, wrapped in a lock-dock, the pirates presumably busily plundering their prey. A handful of other merchant ships were driving frantically for the safety of hyperspace.

"Security Officer Frangelic acknowledges our arrival," the comm officer reported. "He requests assistance."

Ziara sighed. But there was nothing for it. "Do not respond," she ordered. "Repeat: Do not respond."

"A pity," Roscu commented, coming up behind Ziara and Thrawn. "There were a couple of nice cafés on that hub. May I remind the captain that there's no reason for us to be here?"

"So noted," Ziara said. "Run a check on the electrostatic barrier. I want to be ready in case we're attacked."

Roscu was silent a moment, just long enough to show her displeasure and suspicion, just short enough to avoid an insubordination charge. "Yes, Senior Captain," she said. Turning away, she crossed to the defense station.

"She's right," Ziara said. "This is a military situation between two groups of aliens. Happens all the time out here. Nothing for us to get involved with." She nodded toward the viewport. "As for your perceived threat, I'm not sure the attackers have even noticed us."

"They've noticed," Thrawn said. "Two of the three attackers have repositioned to allow for quick disengagement, and the freighter-locked one has begun a slow rotation to align his main batteries with us." He shook his head slowly. "I can beat them, Ziara. I can take all four, right now, without any serious damage to the *Parala*."

"*Serious* is a highly relative term," Ziara pointed out. "Even if you can, we have no justification. Chiss territory hasn't been invaded, and we haven't been attacked."

"If we move closer, we might be."

"Deliberate provocation is also disallowed."

Again, Thrawn shook his head. "I can see it all," he said,

his voice strained. "Their tactics, their patterns, their weaknesses. I could tell you right here, right now, how to beat them."

"Even at four-to-one odds?"

"The odds don't matter," Thrawn said. "I've studied Lioaoin art since our first encounter with the pirates. I know their tactics and their battle patterns. I know how they utilize their weapons and defenses, and how they take advantage of an enemy's mistakes."

He turned, and Ziara was struck by the intensity of his expression. "No damage," he said softly. "No damage."

Ziara turned away from that look to gaze again out the viewport. No damage . . . except the ruin of his career. And hers, if she gave him permission.

People were fighting and dying out there. True, they were aliens, but Chiss merchants had traded with them and found them to be reasonable enough people. Even the Garwians who didn't die today, those in the hub station for instance, would have their lives irrevocably changed. The *Parala* could cut short that destruction, possibly ensure that the Lioaoi would never return.

At the cost of her career.

It still wasn't too late, she knew. If the rest of the bridge crew could be persuaded to keep quiet . . .

But of course they wouldn't. Not with family politics and rivalries coloring everything they did.

Unless there was nothing for them to talk about.

"You say you could tell me how to defeat them," she murmured, still gazing out at the battle. "Could you tell *anyone*?"

Out of the corner of her eye she saw the subtle shift in his stance. "Yes," he said. "May I remind the captain that the ranging lasers haven't been checked recently for calibration."

"I believe you're right," she said. Not that the low-power

ranging lasers, which gathered distance and velocity data during combat, ever went out of calibration in the first place.

"Request permission to go to secondary command and run a check."

Ziara swallowed hard. Her career... "Permission granted," she said. "While you're there, you'd best make sure all other systems are likewise at battle readiness."

"Yes, Captain." With a whisper of displaced air, he turned and headed to the hatchway.

Roscu returned to Ziara's side. "Getting him off the bridge, I hope?" she asked.

"I sent him to check the weapons sensor systems," Ziara said.

Roscu snorted. "And you don't think he'll be tempted to use them? Because I wouldn't put that past him."

"Senior Commander Thrawn understands the protocols."

"Does he?" Roscu countered. "*I* wouldn't have responded to an alien's distress call if *I'd* had deck officer duty. I daresay neither would you, Captain."

"Perhaps not," Ziara said. "On the other hand, if the battle had been over when we arrived, we *are* permitted to render humanitarian aid."

"But the battle *isn't* over." Roscu paused, and Ziara could feel her gaze. "I assume he relinquished his deck officer position when he left the bridge?"

In other words, with Ziara now back in full command, why was the *Parala* still here? "These pirates appear to be part of the same group I engaged last year off Kinoss," she told Roscu. "I want to watch their attack, see if they've come up with any new weapons or tactics we should be aware of."

"But we're not going to intervene?" Roscu pressed.

"Do you feel a need to quote the protocols to me?" Ziara asked mildly.

"No, of course not," Roscu said, her tone more subdued. "My apologies, Captain."

"Captain?" the operations officer called from his station. "I'm getting activity on the ranging lasers."

"It's all right," Ziara said. "I'm having the calibration checked."

"Understood," the officer said, sounding puzzled. "Did you also order the frequencies to be modulated?"

"Modulated how?" Roscu asked, frowning.

"Just modulated," the other said. "No particular pattern I can see."

"He's probably running them through their full range," Ziara said, focusing on the battle. The Garwian patrol ships were moving off their stand-and-fight positions, shifting to a sort of corkscrewing over-under flanking move against the three pirates. The pirates turned in response, pitching up and down to bring their weapons to bear.

Only they turned too far, overcompensating and exposing their ventral sides to the Garwians. The defenders opened fire, quick precise bursts of spectrum laser blasts at the attackers' exposed bellies—

"Multiple hits!" Senior Commander Ocpior snapped from the sensor station. "Pirates' ventral weapons launchers breached. Venting to space—"

And abruptly both of the targeted pirate ships erupted in fiery blasts as their missile banks exploded.

The third attacker, which had been beginning its own turn, jerked violently as it tried to get clear of the high-speed debris. It had managed to avoid the worst of it when one of the Garwian ships swooped inside its defenses and delivered a devastating salvo. The Garwian barely made it clear before its target suffered its own crippling blast.

Roscu muttered something under her breath. "I'll be cursed," she said. "That was . . . how in hell's name did they pull that off?"

"Pirates disengaging," Ocpior reported. "Spinning up their hyperdrives."

"Acknowledged," Ziara said. The three crippled ships were angling toward deep space, trying to get away before the Garwians pressed their attack. The fourth pirate had taken the hint, releasing the freighter it had been looting and similarly running for its life.

That fourth ship made it to the safety of hyperspace. None of its companions did.

Ziara took a deep breath. "And now, I believe, we can leave. Helm, set course back to our patrol circuit."

She turned to Roscu. "I trust you're relieved, Mid Captain Roscu?" she added.

Roscu was still staring out at the remnants of the battle, a disbelieving expression on her face. "Relieved, Captain?" she asked mechanically.

"Those cafés you mentioned," Ziara said. "Looks like they're still in business."

CHAPTER ELEVEN

Thalias had never been on an alien ship before. No real surprise there—most of the travel she'd done outside the Ascendancy had been while she was a sky-walker, and the Syndicure wasn't about to let such a valuable resource stray outside of Chiss control.

But she *had* been on ships that hosted aliens from the Navigators' Guild, usually diplomatic or military vessels that wanted to maintain the illusion that the Chiss had no navigators of their own but also didn't want to be at the mercy of those aliens if quick travel became necessary.

She'd asked one of the senior officers once what would happen if the regular sky-walker had to take over navigation and the alien navigator learned the Ascendancy's secret. The answer had been vague, but there'd been a coldness in the officer's eyes that had kept her from ever asking again.

But just because the aliens couldn't be allowed to see *her* didn't mean she wasn't allowed to see *them*. On most of those trips, the ship's commander was happy to let her watch one of the bridge monitor viewscreens, just to see how other navigators did things.

It was never as exciting as she expected. Mostly the navigators just sat there, sometimes with their eyes closed, sometimes with them wide open, occasionally twitching the controls as something loomed ahead that the ship had to avoid. It was a long time before she realized that her own sky-walker performance was probably just as dull to watch as theirs.

But here, on a Garwian ship, with her identity and former status of no interest to anyone, she might have a chance to actually observe the navigator up close. Maybe see if there was enough left of her Third Sight to sense what he or she was actually doing.

That was fiercely unlikely, of course. In fact, the chances were virtually zero. Third Sight always left a sky-walker by age fourteen or fifteen, and those years were far in Thalias's past.

Still, as far as she knew, no one had ever tried putting a former sky-walker next to a functioning alien navigator. That alone made it worth trying. As Thrawn had once told her, negative information was still information.

The nighttime bridge crew turned out to be even smaller than the equivalent aboard Chiss ships: just three Garwians, plus of course the navigator. One of the Garwians, presumably the officer in charge, looked up as Thalias came through the hatch. "What are you doing here, Chiss?" she challenged.

"I am companion to Artistic Master Svorno," Thalias said, bowing low and keeping her shoulders hunched. She and Thrawn had discussed just how much they wanted to broadcast her supposed hostage identity: too little and the Nikardun might not hear about it, too much and the fact it was allegedly a Chiss cultural secret could start unraveling. Their decision was for her to call herself a companion, but at the same time present the stance and manner of someone whose life was held in another's hands.

A role that was proving disturbingly easy to settle into. "He asked me to note and memorize the artistic tattoos on our navigator's face."

"Your master is ill informed," the Garwian said tartly. "It's the Vector One navigators who have tattoos. We fly today with a Pathfinder."

"They have no tattoos?" Thalias asked, frowning. "Are you certain?"

The officer waved toward the figure in the navigator's seat. "See for yourself."

Hiding a smile, Thalias crossed to the board, focusing on the figure as she stretched out with all her senses. She caught a whiff of something spicy—somehow, none of the material she'd read on

Pathfinders had mentioned they had a distinctive odor—but there was nothing else. She kept at it, coming right up behind him. Still nothing.

Negative information. Still, it had been worth a try. She stepped around the side of the chair, remembering she was supposed to confirm Pathfinders didn't tattoo their faces—

It was all she could do to keep from gasping with surprise and horror. The alien sitting there—the facial contours, the shape of the cheek winglets, the flow pattern of the bristles above his eyes—she'd seen this one before. In fact—

"I told you," the Garwian said, her tone a mix of satisfaction and contempt.

Thalias nodded, searching for her voice as she took one final, painfully careful look. There was no doubt. "You were right," she agreed. She stepped away from the chair and bowed again to the Garwian. "My apologies for the intrusion."

Thrawn was in the study section of their suite when she returned. "We have trouble," she said without preamble.

He set down his questis, his eyes steady on her. "Explain."

"You remember that Pathfinder you hired for the *Springhawk*'s raid on Rapacc?" Thalias asked.

"Of course. Qilori of Uandualon."

"Right," Thalias said. "He's on the bridge right now."

Thrawn raised an eyebrow. "Is he, now."

"That's *all*?" Thalias demanded. "*Is he, now?* Seems to me a situation like this calls for a stronger response than just *is he, now.*"

"What would you suggest we do?" Thrawn asked calmly. "Ask Frangelic to stop the ship so we can get off? Urge him to imprison Qilori the minute we leave hyperspace, possibly resulting in a boycott of the Garwian Unity by the entire Navigators' Guild?"

"No, of course not," Thalias ground out. She hated when people went immediately to worst-case scenarios. "What if he sees us? Or rather, what if he sees *you*? What if the Nikardun are on Primea? Because they're already out for your blood. A casual word or slip of the tongue from Qilori, and we'll be running for our lives."

"Perhaps," Thrawn said, his eyes narrowing in thought. "On the other hand . . ."

"On the other hand *what*?"

"Hardly the right tone for a hostage to take toward her master," Thrawn said.

"I'll keep that in mind. On the other hand *what*?"

"Our goal is to gather information on the Nikardun and their plans," Thrawn said slowly, his eyes still narrowed. "We've stirred them up at Rapacc and Urch. Perhaps it's time now to do the same at Primea."

"That sounds dangerous," Thalias warned. "What if Frangelic doesn't agree?"

"I wasn't planning to tell him."

Thalias felt her lip twist. "That's what I thought."

"Don't worry," Thrawn soothed. "If we do it right, none of it will reflect badly on the Garwians."

"Great," Thalias said heavily. She could appreciate Thrawn's consideration for their hosts.

But to be honest, it wasn't the Garwians she was worried about.

Qilori had always hated foreign receptions. Diplomatic receptions were even worse. The strange voices and sounds, the odd and often disgusting faces and body types, the alien odors—*especially* the alien odors—all of it added up to the waste of an evening, a day, or occasionally an entire excruciating week. All in all, he would much rather have stayed in orbit on the Garwian ship.

But Yiv was here, and he'd ordered Qilori to come down to deliver a firsthand report on the situation in Qilori's part of the Chaos. And so Qilori was here, too, suffering through the alien odors, watching and waiting his turn from a distance as the Benevolent held jovial court in a corner with some alien diplomats. If Yiv finished his debriefing quickly enough, maybe he could talk the Garwian shuttle pilot into running him back to the ship while the rest of the delegation talked or drank themselves stupid or did whatever else they'd come here for.

"Your makeup is untidy," a severe voice came quietly from behind him. "A family hostage needs to maintain proper decorum. Go elsewhere and fix it."

A familiar voice, somehow. Frowning, Qilori turned around.

A pair of Chiss, one male and one female, stood a couple of meters back. The male was tall with a haughty demeanor and full Chiss formalwear robes draped over his shoulders, while the female was shorter, dressed in a far less elaborate outfit, with some kind of thick, textured makeup slathered on her face. Her shoulders were rounded, her eyes lowered, her expression like that of a favored pet who's just been slapped. Qilori watched as she bowed low and slipped away through the crowd of chatting dignitaries.

Qilori looked back at the male, wondering who the female was to him and why she'd reacted so strongly to his rebuke. His face, now in profile, seemed as vaguely familiar as his voice.

He felt his winglets go rigid. The face—the voice—

It was *Thrawn*.

The Chiss turned away, but for those first few seconds Qilori was rooted to the spot. He'd been told there were two Chiss aboard the Garwian ship he'd been hired to navigate, but they were supposed to be some stuffy academic type and his companion or servant or some such.

Only it wasn't. It was Thrawn. Thrawn in civilian garb, running under an assumed name. And that could only mean one thing.

A big, fat bonus.

His first impulse was to head straight over to the Benevolent, cut into whatever conversation he was having, and give him the news. But common sense and caution intervened. Even if Yiv didn't have him whipped for sheer insolence, breaking protocol that way would draw unwelcome attention. Better—and safer—to wait until the Benevolent had a moment free.

And while he waited for that moment . . .

Thrawn was standing by the sweet-sour section of the food array, surveying the different offerings, when Qilori caught up with him. "I'd stay away from the kiki," he warned, pointing to a mix of red, orange, and pale-blue half-moons. "It takes a particular set of digestive juices to handle it properly."

"Interesting," Thrawn said, peering more closely at the bowl. "Odd that our hosts would even include such a specialized dish."

"Maybe," Qilori said. "But you'd be surprised how many people will gladly trade a minute of delectable taste for an hour of gastric discomfort. I believe you were aboard my ship."

"*Your* ship?" Thrawn frowned, and then his expression cleared. "Ah—you mean you were Envoy Proslis's navigator. I'm Artistic Master Svorno, chief curator of the Nunech Art Collection."

"Pleased to meet you," Qilori said, wondering briefly if he should give his own name or instead come up with something fictitious.

Neither, he decided. Even if Thrawn didn't recognize Qilori's face, he might remember his name, and a false name would be too easy to expose. "What brings you to Primea?"

"The hope of finally putting to rest the absurd theory that the Vaks and Garwians had a trade relationship back in the Midorian Era," Thrawn said. "It was proposed eighty years ago by that fool Professor—" He broke off. "But of course, you're not interested in such things."

"I'm afraid history and artistic theory are far above my intelligence," Qilori said politely with a flicker of cynical amusement. Thrawn could change his name and play dress-up all he wanted, but he would never pass himself off as a true academic until he recognized that such people loved to rattle on about their specialties whether their audiences wanted to hear it or not. "But I'm sure the Vak records will have everything you're looking for. Can I offer any introductions?"

"I've already spoken with all those I need to," Thrawn said, craning his neck and looking around. "I'm also familiar with most of the species here. Few of them have art that's worthy of the name." He lifted a finger. "I haven't seen one of those before. You know them?"

Qilori felt his winglets stiffen. Thrawn was pointing straight at Yiv. "I believe they're called Nikardun."

"Really," Thrawn said. "I've heard some vague and ridiculous stories about them. I don't suppose you could get me through that crowd?"

"I might," Qilori said carefully. Was it really going to be this easy? "I believe the Pathfinders have had some dealings with them. If you'd like to wait here, I'll go see if he's amenable to a conversation."

"All right, but be quick," Thrawn said. "I have early-rising meetings and can't remain here much longer."

"Of course." Expecting everyone else to bend their schedules around his. *That* was more like a true senior academic.

Yiv was laughing at some joke when Qilori reached him. The Benevolent's eyes flicked to him, the rippling of his shoulder symbionts warning the newcomer to wait his turn. Qilori took another step forward, waited until Yiv paused for a breath, and cleared his throat. "He's here," he said quietly.

"Who's here?" one of the Vaks chortled, sparking another chorus of laughter. Either Qilori had unwittingly provided an extra punch line to the current joke or else the group was so drunk they were ready to laugh at anything.

But all the humor had vanished from Yiv's face. "*He* is here?" he asked.

Qilori nodded.

Abruptly, Yiv boomed out a laugh, the sudden sound startling all the others to silence. "A moment of leave, my fine friends," he said with a cheerfulness that didn't extend to his eyes. "I must bid you all farewell for a few moments. I suggest you avail yourselves of the lavish dining display provided by our hosts."

Qilori waited until the crowd had cleared out. Then, at Yiv's small gesture, he stepped to the Benevolent's chair. "Thrawn?" Yiv asked, in a tone warning that Qilori had better not have interrupted him for anything less important.

"Yes, your Benevolence," Qilori confirmed. "He's at mid-distance behind me, dressed in Chiss formalwear." He dared a smiling twitch of his winglets. "He's traveling as an art expert under the name Svorno. He's also heard of the Nikardun and would very much like to meet one."

"Would he, now," Yiv said, his symbionts settling into their epaulet pattern. "Let's not disappoint him, then. Please; bring him over."

"Yes, your Benevolence."

Qilori turned and retraced his steps to where Thrawn was waiting. "Come with me," he said. "General Yiv the Benevolence will see you now."

"*General* Yiv," Thrawn said, scowling. "A military type. So. Unlikely to know anything about his species' art, then."

"I really don't know," Qilori said, feeling sudden tension in his winglets. Surely Thrawn wasn't going to back out of the meeting *now*? The consequences of such a blatant snub might be catastrophic, and not just to Thrawn and the Chiss. "But he might. You never know what bits of knowledge military people have tucked away. You should at least take a moment and ask him."

Thrawn considered, then gave a small shrug. "Oh, very well. If only because I can't properly retire to my quarters until my . . . companion . . . returns."

"Yes, that's—I'm sure you'll find the general interesting," Qilori said. *Companion* . . . but hadn't he called the female a hostage before?

But that didn't make any sense. What kind of hostage traveled openly with her captor? For that matter, since when did the Chiss culture deal with hostages? "Come with me."

Yiv was waiting silently as the Pathfinder and Chiss approached, a half smile on his face, an unblinking gaze in his eyes. "Your Benevolence, may I present Artistic Master Svorno of the Chiss Ascendancy. Master Svorno, General Yiv the Benevolent of the Nikardun Destiny."

"General," Thrawn said, inclining his head in greeting. "I understand that you're a military man."

"That's right, Art Master," Yiv said. "I understand that you aren't."

A hint of a smile touched Thrawn's lips. "Indeed," he said. "A shame. Military men are so seldom interested in art." He half turned and pointed to a large decorated cloth hanging from the ceiling to near the floor. "That tapestry over there, for instance. I would wager you haven't even noticed it."

"Of course I have," Yiv said. "It hangs between the hard-drinks table and the private entrance to the premier's office suite."

"Really," Thrawn said, looking back at the tapestry and the unassuming door beside it. "How do you know that's the premier's private door?"

"Because I've been in his office, of course," Yiv said. "He and I have had many long and interesting conversations together. Would you be so good as to fetch me a drink?"

Thrawn half turned in the other direction, where a waiter was just passing by, and deftly plucked one of the sculpted glasses from his tray. "And the premier invited you in by that door?" he asked.

"No, I've always been brought in through the public entrance on the other side," Yiv said. "But I have a skill with architecture, and it was obvious where the door marking the private entrance exited here into the grand assembly chamber."

"I suppose I can understand the premier wanting a quick escape from the tedium of these events." Thrawn sniffed at the drink, then stepped forward and offered it to Yiv. "I trust this will be to your liking."

"I'm certain it will," the Benevolent said. He held the glass up to his left shoulder, watching with casual interest as one of the symbiont's tendrils slipped in and sampled the liquid. "Yes, I imagine the premier might occasionally wish to move back and forth between public and private events. I personally find it more interesting that the passageway between the two rooms is too long."

"What do you mean, too long?"

"Longer than it should be, given the design of the area," Yiv said. "I trust you aren't offended by my little pet?"

"Not at all," Thrawn assured him. "A poison detector, I presume?"

"Poisons and other inconveniences," Yiv said. He pulled the glass away from the tendril, watched a moment as it continued to undulate, then took a sip of the drink. "They're faster and more precise than most inorganic tests for such things. They also provide an interesting topic for conversation when all others lag."

"Interesting that you say *they*." Thrawn said. "I would assume the correct term was *it*."

Yiv chuckled. "You see? Already it offers opportunity for discussion. Why would you guess the premier needs a too-long passageway?"

"I'm sure I don't know," Thrawn said. "Perhaps a hidden door built into the corridor wall leads to additional quarters or a sanctuary. Or perhaps the extra space is for a guard station to prevent others from using the shortcut. Tell me, what do you see in the design of the tapestry?"

"I'm hardly an expert," Yiv protested mildly.

"You asked my thoughts on the premier's private comings and goings," Thrawn reminded him. "It only seems fair for you to indulge me in turn."

Yiv took another sip and studied the cloth. "Symmetrical pattern," he said. "Contrasting colors. Different sets of contrasting colors, becoming brighter and tending toward red and blue as it flows from top to bottom. The fringe on the left-hand edge seems shorter than the corresponding fringe on the right."

"Shorter, and the threads are also slightly thicker than those on the right," Thrawn said.

"Are they? I can't tell from this distance."

"I studied them earlier from a better vantage point."

"Ah," Yiv said. "The hanging itself is clearly old, which probably explains the inexpertise of its design and construction."

"It's certainly old," Thrawn said. "But I would submit that the design irregularities are deliberate. It was clearly created by two different weavers working in both coordination and contrast. That suggests the Vaks honor both aspects, working for unity while at the same time celebrating difference and uniqueness."

"I would say that's a fair assessment," Yiv said. "Interesting. And you determined that solely by studying a single hanging?"

"Hardly," Thrawn said. "There's a great deal of other artwork here. All of it displays and defines the Vaks' cultural ethos. What do *you* see here?"

"I see what all beings see in others," Yiv said. "Opportunity. For you, the opportunity to add to your knowledge of art. For me, the opportunity to make new friends within the churning sea of life that makes up the Chaos."

"And if the Vaks don't wish to be friends to the Nikardun?"

The Benevolent's smile faded. "We would consider such a rejection to be an insult."

"An insult that would need to be avenged?"

"To be dealt with," Yiv corrected. "*Avenged* is far too savage a word. Your observational skills are impressive."

"Some things are obvious," Thrawn said. "The tendrils on your symbiont, for example, with the inside group thinner than those on the outside. I presume from their rhythmic movement that the inner ones sample the air in the same way the outer tendrils sample your food and drink?"

"Indeed," Yiv said, his smile widening even as his eyes went a shade cooler. "Few people have ever grasped that fact and distinction. None have grasped it so quickly."

There was a movement at the edge of Qilori's vision, and he turned to see the Chiss woman slip past him. Thrawn looked over as she walked to his side, peering closely at her face. "Better," he said. "But not perfect. You will rise an hour early tomorrow morning and practice."

She bowed low. "Yes, my lord," she said softly.

"And this is?" Yiv asked, gesturing toward her.

"A person of no consequence," Thrawn said. "Now that she's finally returned, it's time to retire for the night. Thank you for your time, General Yiv. Perhaps we'll have an opportunity to resume this conversation another time."

"Indeed, Artistic Master Svorno," Yiv said, inclining his head. "I'll look forward to it."

He watched in silence as the two Chiss wended their way through the crowd. Then he again beckoned to Qilori. "So that's the one who stole my ship from Rapacc," he said, his voice thoughtful. "Interesting."

"He's more competent than he seems," Qilori said, wincing a little.

The whole conversation had seemed pretty pointless. If Yiv blamed Qilori for wasting his time—

"You think that display showed *incompetence*?" the Benevolent said contemptuously, still watching the Chiss. "You think just because there were no loud voices or discharged weapons that we didn't engage in combat?"

"But—" Qilori looked at Thrawn as he disappeared through an archway.

"Trust me, Pathfinder," Yiv said, his voice dark, his symbionts undulating in quiet agitation. "I understand this person now, and he is every bit as dangerous as you told me. You were wise to bring him to my attention, and then into my presence."

"Thank you, your Benevolence," Qilori said. He still had no idea what had just happened, but if Yiv was pleased he certainly wasn't going to argue the point. "What are you going to do with him?"

Yiv took a sip of his drink. "The choices are three: to take him as he leaves this event, to do so at another time during his stay on Primea, or to do so as the Garwian envoy leaves for his return to Solitair. All three present difficulties and dangers, not the least of which is my reluctance to move overtly against either the Vaks or the Garwians at this point."

"Or the Chiss," Qilori warned.

"The Chiss are irrelevant," Yiv said scornfully. "They only move after they themselves have been attacked."

"The capture or murder of a senior officer might qualify."

"Only if the officer in question is flag rank, commodore or above," Yiv said.

"Really?" Qilori asked, frowning. "I didn't know that."

"I'm not surprised," Yiv said. "It's not a subject they talk of openly."

"Nor presumably do they speak of traveling with hostages," Qilori said. "But so she appears to be."

The Benevolent snorted again. "You're imagining things."

"Am I?" Qilori countered. "I heard him tell her to go fix her makeup, that a family hostage needs to maintain decorum."

Yiv waved a hand. "A transparent bluff, designed to make me think there are things about the Chiss we don't know. It was obviously spoken for your benefit."

"He didn't know I could hear him."

"It was a bluff," Yiv insisted.

But there'd been some hesitation in the Benevolent's voice just then. Thrawn certainly might be playing him, just as he'd said.

But if he wasn't—if the Chiss really did have a hidden hostage culture—there might be other, more crucial things about them that were also unknown. "So what will you do?"

Yiv turned an icy stare toward him. "Have you become my confidant?" he asked. "Or been raised to the rank of tactical commander by the Destiny?"

"I beg your Benevolence's pardon," Qilori said, cringing back. "I only ask because a decision to take him during the Garwians' departure may require some level of awareness or participation on my part."

Yiv eyed him thoughtfully. "A point," he conceded. "Very well, Pathfinder. Unless I decide differently, the plan will be to intercept the Garwian ship on some pretext as it leaves Primea." His eyes locked on Qilori's. "You will make sure they don't escape into hyperspace before my ships engage."

"Yes, my lord," Qilori said, his heart beating painfully. For a Pathfinder to be part of such an operation was a huge violation of every rule and guideline in the Navigators' Guild code. If it ever came to light, not only would he be finished as a Pathfinder, but depending on the operation's outcome he might well find himself in the executioner's chains.

But he had no choice. His ongoing and very private dealings with Yiv had already put him dangerously far over the line. If the Benevolent decided his tame Pathfinder wasn't useful anymore, Qilori would again find himself on the short track to destruction.

And certainly getting Thrawn out of the way would be a good thing. The Nikardun were ultimately unstoppable, and the less death and destruction they left in their wake the better for everyone.

Yes, Qilori decided. Whatever Yiv wanted him to do, he could certainly handle it.

CHAPTER TWELVE

Ar'alani had seldom known General Ba'kif to be angry. At least, she'd seldom known him to be angry with her.

He was more than making up for it now.

"What in *hell's* name were you thinking?" he snapped, glaring as if he was trying to melt her into slag by eyeflame and willpower alone. "Allowing a sky-walker to be separated from her caregiver is bad enough; actually engineering that separation takes matters to an entirely new level of illegality."

"Never mind that," Syndic Zistalmu ground out, doing his best to aid in Ba'kif's fire-starting efforts. In contrast with the general, Ar'alani was quite familiar with Zistalmu's anger. "Those are minor military matters, and they're not why Syndic Thurfian and I are here. What *we* want to know is how you could let Senior Captain Thrawn insert himself—*again*—into Garwian politics."

"Indeed," Thurfian seconded. Unlike the heat radiating from Ar'alani's other two interrogators, his tone and face were the frozen shell of Csilla. "Did the Aristocra somehow fail to make ourselves clear?"

"Captain Thrawn wasn't inserting himself into politics," Ar'alani said, keeping her voice even. She'd never found much credence in the old saying that soft words eroded hard ones, but she certainly didn't want to make Ba'kif or Zistalmu any angrier than they already were.

Especially with Zistalmu a nanosecond away from demanding

that the entire Syndicure convene to consider charges against her. Unlike her first officer, Ar'alani didn't have a conduit into the sort of family intrigues that could provide her with a counterattack or an exit strategy.

"Really," Zistalmu said, his voice heavy with sarcasm. "He travels aboard a Garwian diplomatic ship, in the company of a Garwian envoy, to a world we ourselves have no political ties to; and that has nothing to do with politics? Have the Garwians converted their diplomatic corps into a knitting club?"

"The mission was one of reconnaissance," Ar'alani said. "Captain Thrawn is trying to determine where else the Nikardun may have established themselves—"

"Have these Nikardun attacked the Ascendancy?" Thurfian interrupted. "Have they shown any indication that they *might* attack the Ascendancy?"

"They destroyed a refugee ship within one of our systems."

"So you claim," Zistalmu said. "The Syndicure has yet to see solid evidence that the Nikardun are the ones responsible."

"All of which is irrelevant anyway," Thurfian said. "If there's neither attack nor imminent attack, it's not a military matter but, as Syndic Zistalmu has already stated, a political one." He turned his glare onto Ba'kif. "Unless you're prepared to claim that General Ba'kif personally authorized this mission."

"Not at all," Ar'alani said quickly. This tactic, at least, she knew: Zistalmu throwing his net wide in the hope of sweeping in as many people as he could. She and Thrawn were already tangled in the mesh, and she had no intention of letting Ba'kif be drawn in alongside them. "But as I'm sure you're aware, Syndic, situations sometimes arise where events proceed too quickly for consultation with superiors."

"An interesting assertion," Thurfian said, the temperature in his voice dropping a few more degrees. "Tell me, has Solitair then lost every one of its triads? Has the Ascendancy lost every one of *its* triads? A ship in deep space may have only one-way communication,

but once Thrawn landed on Solitair that excuse disappeared. If he
didn't report to Csilla or Naporar and ask for orders, it was because
he chose not to."

"Or because the Garwians chose not to let him," Ba'kif said. He
was still angry, Ar'alani could tell, but he could see the two syndics
edging their way into military affairs, and he clearly had no intention
of ceding any of that territory. "The Syndicure is right to question
Captain Thrawn's decisions—"

"To *question* them?" Zistalmu bit out.

"—but that discussion can wait until he's returned and able to
properly defend himself," Ba'kif continued. "The immediate issue at
hand is how to extract him safely from his reconnaissance."

"Why should we?" Zistalmu demanded. "His activities are completely unauthorized. He got himself into this. He can get himself
out."

"Are you sure that's what you want, Syndic?" Ba'kif asked.

"Why not?"

"Because it's Thrawn we're talking about," Thurfian said sourly.
"The general is suggesting there may be worse political and diplomatic consequences if we let him have his way than if we just go in
and pluck him out."

"Well, at least he'd no longer be an embarrassment to us," Zistalmu
grumbled.

"Don't be so sure," Thurfian said, his gaze shifting to Ar'alani.
"How exactly would you do it, Admiral?"

"Straightforwardly," Ar'alani said. "I'd take the *Vigilant* to the
Primea system, contact them, and arrange to pick him up. If I leave
immediately, I should be within the time frame he specified."

"And if they refuse to give him up?"

"Why would they?" Ba'kif asked. "We have no quarrel with the
Vaks."

Ar'alani kept her expression steady. That was true . . . unless the
Vaks were already under Nikardun control. In that case, the simple
pickup mission she was pitching could get very ugly very fast.

"Doesn't mean *they* won't have a quarrel with *us*," Zistalmu said.

"Particularly if they see Thrawn as a spy. But never mind them. What if these Nikardun of yours have taken over?"

"We've already seen they aren't yet ready to engage the Ascendancy," Ar'alani reminded him.

Thurfian snorted. "No need to engage us when they could simply vaporize the Garwian ship with Thrawn aboard and claim it was an accident."

"All the more reason for the *Vigilant* to get there before that happens," Ba'kif said grimly. "If you'll excuse us, we need to get this mission under way."

"Of course," Thurfian said. "Just as soon as we resolve the issue of the *Vigilant*'s sky-walker."

Ar'alani grimaced. She'd hoped they'd forgotten about that. "I promised Che'ri's caregiver I'd take care of her," she said. "I see no reason why I can't continue to do that."

"You don't?" Thurfian asked. "The admiral and commander of a Nightdragon man-of-war, and you think you'll have the time to cater to the needs of a child, too?" He shook his head. "No. We need to find a new caregiver before you can leave Csilla."

"I'm afraid that won't be possible," Ba'kif said. "All sky-walkers and caregivers are already committed to other ships."

"Let me propose a solution," Zistalmu offered. "My wife served as a caregiver for two years before we were married. Her record of that time is very clean. Reinstate her, and she and I can travel aboard the *Vigilant* together."

"Thalias chose *me*," Ar'alani said firmly. "As Che'ri's official caregiver, she has final authority to shift that duty while she's aboard my ship."

"But she's not aboard your ship now, is she?" Zistalmu countered.

"She was when she named me as her replacement," Ar'alani said. "I have no intention of giving up that mandate, and you have no authority to take it from me."

"I have every authority—"

"Enough," Ba'kif cut in. "Syndic Zistalmu, how far away is your wife?"

"She can be here in two hours."

"Call her now," Ba'kif ordered. "Admiral, I agree that regulations support your position. But Syndic Thurfian is right to remind us of your other responsibilities. I'm therefore ruling that Syndic Zistal-mu's wife will share caregiver duty with you, and will take the primary position whenever you're otherwise occupied. Any questions?"

Ar'alani suppressed a scowl. The last thing she wanted was a strange woman suddenly entering Che'ri's life—the girl had enough problems socializing with other people as it was without disrupting things further.

And she *absolutely* didn't want a syndic on her bridge, watching her every movement and undoubtedly gathering ammunition to be used against her somewhere down the line. Couldn't Ba'kif see this was yet another attempt by the Syndicure to intrude on the fleet's sphere of authority?

"No questions, General," she said stiffly.

"Good," Ba'kif said. "Thank you for your interest and input, Syndics. Syndic Zistalmu, you and your wife will report to Admiral Ar'alani's shuttle in three hours for immediate transport to the *Vigilant*. Admiral, another moment of your time?"

Ar'alani stayed where she was, her eyes locked on Ba'kif, as Zistalmu and Thurfian walked through the doorway behind her. She waited until the door closed—

"Don't say it," Ba'kif warned before she could speak. "No, it's not ideal. In fact, it's about as far from ideal as it could possibly be."

"Then why did you agree to it?"

"Because I didn't have any choice," Ba'kif said. "Because if I'd tried to keep Zistalmu off the *Vigilant* he'd have tied us up in procedural twist-wire until Thrawn died of old age." He paused. "And because you *don't* have a mandate . . . because Thalias is not, in fact, an official caregiver."

Ar'alani felt her eyes narrow. "What are you talking about?"

"I'm talking about the fact that she sweet-talked her way aboard the *Springhawk*," Ba'kif said. "She's a former sky-walker herself, which made the sweet-talking a little easier, but the fact is that she has no official credentials."

"But she's Mitth," Ar'alani said, trying to sort it through. "Are you telling me that someone with Thurfian's connections and suspicions hasn't figured that out?"

"On the contrary," Ba'kif said darkly. "He apparently showed up at the last minute to help get her aboard in that position."

"Really," Ar'alani said. "What was the cost of that assistance?"

"I don't know," Ba'kif said. "But there *was* a cost, or will be one somewhere down the line. With Thurfian, that's practically guaranteed. My point is that all he had to do was throw that into the conversation, and you'd have been out completely. But he didn't. The question is why?"

"Possibly because he'd prefer having me involved with our skywalker over turning her completely over to the wife of an Irizi syndic."

"Normally, I'd agree with you," Ba'kif said. "But you've surely noticed that despite their families' rivalries, he and Zistalmu have shown remarkable unity in their attempts to get Thrawn out of the fleet, or at least out of any position of influence. I don't think he'd have a problem with Zistalmu's wife being in complete charge."

"And of course, leaving Thrawn abandoned on Primea would be a permanent solution to their perceived problem."

"Exactly," Ba'kif said. "No, I think he didn't denounce you because that would also have gotten Thalias thrown off the *Springhawk* when she returns, and there's something he still wants her to do. Probably something connected to the price of getting her aboard in the first place."

He waved a hand in dismissal. "But that can wait. Right now we need to get Thrawn off Primea before the situation becomes too much to handle."

"I wouldn't worry about Thrawn, sir," Ar'alani said. "He's expecting me, of course; but if I don't show, I'm sure he'll find his own way home."

"Thrawn's not the one I was worried about," Ba'kif said tartly. "It's the Ascendancy that may wind up in a situation we can't get out of."

"Point taken, sir," Ar'alani said, wincing. "I've got Wutroow working on flight prep. We'll be ready to go by the time Zistalmu and his wife arrive."

"Good," Ba'kif said. "And watch him, Ar'alani. Watch him very closely. I know Zistalmu, and he wouldn't voluntarily walk into possible danger unless he thought there was a way to turn that to his and his family's advantage."

"Don't worry, sir," Ar'alani assured him. "Whatever game he's playing, I think he'll find that his cards aren't nearly as good as he thinks they are."

There was a right way to do things, Qilori fumed to himself as he hurried toward the bridge, and there was a wrong way. In this case, the right way was to keep on schedule, do a proper ship prep, and ensure that the captain, the crew, and especially the navigator were moving along at a steady but relaxed pace. The wrong way was exactly the opposite of all those.

That wrong way was what was happening right now.

"Pathfinder?" someone called from down the corridor in front of him. *"Pathfinder!"*

"I'm coming," Qilori called back, cursing under his breath. Yiv's whole plan to eliminate Thrawn hinged on the Garwian ship being exactly where it was supposed to be when it was supposed to be there. Qilori's job was to make that happen from the Garwian end of the ambush.

But even he wasn't good enough to stall an entire day just because the Garwian envoy had suddenly decided to cut short the negotiations and head home early.

Now what was he supposed to do?

The bridge was the typical scene of chaos when he arrived. The captain was barking orders, the officers and crew were scrambling to get their boards up and running. Off in one corner—

Qilori felt his winglets flatten as he headed for the navigator's seat. Off in the corner, the Garwian he'd heard the others refer to only as Officer Frangelic stood silently, watching the commotion like a director overseeing a stage performance.

"*There* you are," the captain growled as Qilori settled himself into his seat. "How soon can you be ready?"

Qilori glanced at the status boards. They were still deep within Primea's gravity well. Several minutes at least to get far enough out that they could access hyperspace, more like a quarter hour if they made a more leisurely departure. If he insisted on an additional status check of the hyperdrive, the engines, and the environmental systems before they left, it would buy him a little more time.

His winglets stiffened in frustration. A little more time, but not nearly enough. If Yiv hadn't spotted the prep work, the Benevolent would have lost all chance to capture or kill Thrawn.

Which was undoubtedly the whole point of the sudden change in schedule. Thrawn, the envoy, Frangelic—maybe all three together— had decided to sneak Thrawn away from Primea before the Benevolent could launch his attack.

And then a movement on the aft display caught Qilori's eye. Yiv's flagship, the *Deathless,* had appeared over the horizon behind them, running a lower orbit and casually gaining on the Garwian ship.

He felt his winglets relax fractionally. So Yiv hadn't been caught napping after all. Perfect. Now Qilori could let the Garwians move out of the gravity well on their own schedule, then make sure he didn't take them into hyperspace until Yiv made his move—

"Officer Frangelic?" the Garwian at the communications station called. "The Vaks send an answer to your query. They've done a complete search of the diplomatic offices and guest quarters, and neither Artistic Master Svorno nor his companion are anywhere to be found."

"Tell them they must be mistaken," Frangelic said tersely. "If they're not here, they *have* to be there."

Qilori's winglets froze in place. *Thrawn wasn't aboard?* No—that couldn't be. He *had* to be here. If he wasn't—

Then Yiv was about to attack a Garwian ship, and almost certainly kill everyone aboard, for nothing.

"The Vaks are very insistent," the comm officer said. "They've searched everywhere the Chiss might be. There's no sign or trail of them."

Qilori stared at the display and the Nikardun Battle Dreadnought coming steadily up into attack range. He needed to get word to Yiv, and he needed to do it fast.

Only he couldn't. With this many Garwians milling around, there was no way he could get to any of the comm panels without being seen. But without comm access, he couldn't talk to the *Deathless*.

Or rather, *he* couldn't talk to the *Deathless*. "Officer Frangelic?" he called, turning toward the officer. "Excuse me, but I remember Artistic Master Svorno talking at length with General Yiv the Benevolent at the reception our first night on Primea. I believe that among other things they discussed Vak art and art displays. Perhaps the Benevolent will have some idea where he might have gone."

"Perhaps," Frangelic said. "Comm, you heard?"

"Yes, Officer Frangelic."

"Signal to General Yiv," Frangelic ordered. "Put the question to him."

Qilori took a deep breath, his winglets finally relaxing. Thrawn might have slipped out of Yiv's immediate trap, but all he'd really done was postpone his fate. Even though the Vaks weren't yet under full Nikardun domination, Yiv had enough forces in the region to quickly isolate Primea and keep the fugitives on the ground. Sooner or later, either he or the Vaks would run them down.

And really, how long could a pair of blueskins hide among a planetful of aliens?

CHAPTER THIRTEEN

Thalias had known from the start that Thrawn's plan was doomed. Their blue skin was nothing like the pale-amber skin and black stub hairs of the indigenous population, to say nothing about the contrast between glowing red Chiss eyes and the Vaks' dull brown. The hooded cloaks that many of the people wore would make things less obvious, but Thalias had no illusions as to how well that would work in the long run. How many of the locals actually used the hoods, she'd argued, instead of letting the sun and breeze wash over their faces?

The answer, it turned out, was pretty nearly all of them.

"You're just lucky it's raining today," she said as she and Thrawn walked along the street, the light drizzle beating gently on the tops of their hoods and dripping off the fronts.

"Not at all," he replied. "Up to now we've always traveled the city in vehicles, where the hoods are unnecessary. But during those trips I observed that most pedestrians used their hoods nearly all the time, protecting against rain but also against sunlight."

"So really the only danger we were in was if today was just cloudy?"

He chuckled. "A point. But even then, wearing hoods would not be so rare as to attract attention."

Thalias peered past the edge of her hood into the diner they were passing. Inside, she noted uneasily, the Vaks had all laid their hoods back. "That's fine out here," she said. "But eventually we're going to have to go inside somewhere. What happens then?"

"Let's find out," Thrawn said. Taking her arm, he steered her toward a door with a faded sign above it. "In here."

"What is it?" Thalias asked, peering at the sign. She'd made an effort to learn the Vak script over the past few days, but she was a long way from being able to read any of it.

"Hopefully, answers," Thrawn said.

And then they were at the door, and Thrawn had pushed it open and ushered Thalias inside. She blinked, ducked her head forward sharply to shake some of the water from her hood onto the mat at their feet, and then looked up.

To find they were in an art gallery.

Thrawn was already walking slowly forward, the back of his hood moving rhythmically as he turned his head back and forth, studying everything around him. Thalias followed more slowly, looking surreptitiously at the handful of Vak patrons wandering among the easels and pedestals or gazing up the wall hangings and paintings. All of them had their own hoods thrown back—would they notice that she and Thrawn were still wearing theirs? More important, would they wonder why?

A harsh voice rattled off some words behind them. Apparently, they would.

"Good afternoon," Thrawn said calmly in Minnisiat, not turning around. "I'm afraid I don't understand your language. Do you speak this one?"

Thalias grimaced. Everyone in the place was now gazing at the visitors. So much for slipping by undetected.

"I speak it," the voice came back. "Who are you? What do you want here?"

"I came to see Vak art, and to thereby understand the Vak people," Thrawn said. "As to who we are—" He paused, slid off his hood, and turned around. "We are friends."

Someone made a strangling sort of sound. Two or three others gave out with startled-sounding words, and Thalias heard a single whispered *Chiss.*

"The Vak have no friends," the first speaker said. "Not now. Not ever."

Thalias turned, also pushing back her hood. The Vak who had spoken—a female, Thalias tentatively identified her from the cut of her loose-fitting tunic-skirt—had a wide sash across her chest adorned with a double row of intricately carved wooden pins. Did such extra adornment mark her as the gallery's curator?

"Surely that is untrue," Thrawn said. "What about Yiv the Benevolent? He claims to be a friend."

"People claim many things," the curator said. "You, too, have now claimed to be friends. Yet I see no evidence of it."

"Do you see evidence with Yiv?"

"Why do you ask?" the curator countered. "Do you seek to sow discord among the Vaks?"

Thrawn shook his head. "I seek information. The leaders of the Vak Combine seem impressed by Yiv. They see his power, and imagine the Nikardun are respected and honored. They believe that joining with them will bring the same respect to the Vaks."

He lifted a hand. "I merely wish to know if the common people believe likewise."

"What do you know about the common people?" the curator scoffed.

"Only a little," Thrawn admitted. "I can see what is woven into your artwork, that the Vaks strive for unity while still determined to honor the individual. That is a good and proper philosophy. But I seek to understand how that affects the lives of the Vak people."

"Then seek elsewhere," the curator said. "This is a place of meditation and appreciation. I will not be drawn into discussions with strangers of things personal to the Vaks."

"I understand, and bow to your wishes," Thrawn said, taking Thalias's arm. "May your future be of sunlight and peace."

A minute later, the two Chiss were back out in the rain. "Whatever you were hoping to accomplish," Thalias said, "I don't think it worked."

"As I said, I hoped to learn more about the Vaks," Thrawn said. "And, perhaps, to make them aware that as they decide their course with the Nikardun, they should also figure the Chiss into their calculations."

Thalias gave a small snort. "Not that the Syndicure is likely to ever lift a finger to help them. I suppose you also realize that if we keep walking around town this way, we might as well call Yiv and announce ourselves?"

"There will likely be a response," Thrawn agreed. "That, too, may work in our favor. If the Nikardun are sufficiently heavy-handed in their search for us, the Vaks may see less friendship and more dominance in their presence on Primea."

"Only if the leaders notice," Thalias said. "I doubt the people who visit art galleries have much say in their nation's affairs."

Thrawn leaned out from under his hood to give her a puzzled look. "You don't see it?"

"See what?"

He turned back under the hood and for a few steps was silent. "You heard me tell the gallery curator that the Vaks seek unity while still honoring the individual. That's true enough. The problem is that their leaders have carried that philosophy too far. They spend so much time listening to all points of view—I believe they refer to them as thought lines—that they have difficulty arriving at decisions."

"You can't mean *all* thought lines," Thalias said. "There must be billions of Vaks. All of them can't be equally important."

"In theory, yes, they are," Thrawn said. "In actual practice, of course, the number must certainly be limited. But it still leaves the Vaks with a longer decision process than that of most species. That hesitation, as they gather and weigh all opinions, makes the leaders appear weak."

"Well, they won't have that problem if they let the Nikardun move in," Thalias said grimly. "The only thought line that'll matter will be Yiv's."

"Indeed," Thrawn agreed. "We'll attempt to pass that message on to a few more citizens before Yiv or Vak security track us down. After that—or sooner, if it seems prudent—we'll retreat to the hideout I set up two days ago and wait for Admiral Ar'alani."

"Someplace nice and quiet and away from the spaceport, I hope," Thalias said. "The first thing Yiv will probably assume is that we'll try to steal a ship."

"Indeed he will," Thrawn agreed.

"So where are we going?"

Thrawn leaned forward, giving her a smile around the edge of his dripping hood. "To the spaceport," he said. "To steal a ship."

Thalias had envisioned either a stealthy creep through the warehouse area that filled the ground outside the spaceport security fence, or else a mad dash across that same obstacle course. Both mental scenarios ran into a blank space as she tried to imagine how they would get past the fence itself.

In the end, it was neither the dash nor the sneak. It was, instead, a box.

Not just any box. A box—a large crate, really—sitting with a dozen others near one of the entrance gates. Thrawn took a careful look around as they reached it, then popped one of the side panels open and ushered Thalias inside.

From the size, she'd recognized that the crate would have enough room to comfortably house both of them. What she hadn't expected was the seats, the supplies of food and water, and even the crude but serviceable, if potentially awkward, bathroom facilities.

"My apologies for the accommodations," Thrawn said as he sealed them in. There was no lamp, but carefully concealed slits on all four walls admitted both air and light. "I wasn't sure how quickly we could get here, or whether we would have to dodge or outwait patrols, so I specified our pickup for the day after tomorrow."

"That's all right," Thalias said, looking around. "It beats being a prisoner on a Nikardun ship."

"Or floating dead in space."

Thalias winced. "Definitely beats that. You think that's what Yiv was planning?"

Thrawn shrugged. "He certainly has an abundance of confidence. That would suggest he'd want to interrogate me before my death. On the other hand, we captured one of his ships, and the Nikardun may have a strict code concerning vengeance. I'd need more information before I could determine that."

"Erring on the side of caution works for me," Thalias said. "How did you find this crate, anyway?"

"I didn't find it, I made it," Thrawn said. "Rather, Defense Overlord Frangelic and I made it. You'll recall I asked him to bring a shipping container aboard with us?"

"Ah," Thalias said, remembering now. "You said we'd be using it on the trip back."

"And so we are," Thrawn said. "He and I put it together on our journey to Primea, and once we'd learned the Vaks' shipping protocols we labeled it for transfer."

"So you've done this sort of thing before?"

Thrawn smiled. "Hardly. But it seemed straightforward enough."

If it works, Thalias thought. "So where are we being shipped to?"

"We're just going inside the fence," Thrawn said. "The ship we're supposed to be delivered to isn't here yet, but once it arrives it'll need to make a fast turnaround. The standard Vak pattern under those conditions is to gather all the cargo containers together near the designated landing area so that the loading can go more quickly."

"Okay," Thalias said, frowning. "So we're going to some alien world?"

"Not at all," Thrawn assured her. "Once we're through security, we'll choose our moment and board one of the sentry fighters lined up just inside the fence. They're designed for long-range patrols, so there should be plenty of room aboard where we can wait for the admiral."

"And then, what, we just fly up and meet her?"

"Basically," Thrawn said. "Though there might be a complication or two along the way."

"Such as if someone else comes aboard and wants to fly it instead of you?"

"If that happens, we'll invite them to leave."

"Whether or not they want to go?"

"Don't worry, we aren't going to hurt anyone," he assured her. "Your restraint in such things speaks well of you."

"I just don't like beating up someone on their own world," Thalias muttered. "Especially given the Ascendancy's whole non-intervention policy."

"That was actually what I was thinking about when I referred to your restraint," Thrawn said. "Regardless, it won't be a problem. I have a small aerosol of tava mist, more than enough to fill a fighter craft's cockpit."

Thalias frowned. "That's the sleepwalking drug?"

It was Thrawn's turn to frown. "Who calls it that?"

"People at my old school," Thalias explained, rolling her eyes at the memory. "A couple of them let off the stuff in class once just to see everyone act like drooling moon-brains. Hours of harmless fun, I guess."

"The effect hardly lasts for hours," Thrawn said. "An hour at the very most. But it *is* harmless."

"Unless you're doing something tricky," Thalias said. "Like, say, flying a sentry fighter?"

"We'll ease them outside and away from the fighter long before they get that far," Thrawn promised. "And I have nostril filters for us so that we won't be affected."

"Handy," Thalias said, eyeing him closely. "Do you normally carry that stuff around with you?"

"It's always worth taking precautions when facing uncertainties," Thrawn said. "I knew we'd need to steal a ship, so I planned accordingly. Don't worry, we'll get through this."

"Okay," Thalias said. Personally, she wasn't feeling all that confident, but she was willing to trust him. "Can I take off this makeup now? This stuff has to weigh half a kilo."

"It's closer to a third, actually," Thrawn corrected. "And no, you'd best let it be. There's always a chance we'll be discovered and you'll need to continue playing your role."

"Fine," Thalias said reluctantly. Actually, aside from the weight, she was starting to get used to the contoured hardshell paste. What she hated most about it was the broader idea it represented, and the role of a nervous hostage she had to play while she was wearing it. "So; another day and a half. I don't suppose you brought a pack of cards."

"Actually, I did," Thrawn said. "But I thought we could talk first."

"About?"

"About why you asked to come aboard the *Springhawk*."

A warning bell went off in the back of Thalias's brain. "I came to take care of Che'ri," she said cautiously.

"That's why you were aboard," Thrawn said. "But it's not why you asked to come. One of my officers informed me that the Mitth sent you to investigate my performance as the *Springhawk*'s commander. Is that true?"

Thalias felt her hand squeeze itself into a fist. "I assume that would be Mid Captain Samakro?"

"Does it make a difference where the information came from?"

"It might," Thalias said. "Did he give a reason for telling you that?"

"Not specifically," Thrawn said. "I believe he's concerned about cohesion in the command structure if family matters interfere."

"That may be what he *says*," Thalias said. "But I'm guessing he's hoping for some of that family interference."

"To what end?"

"To the end of the Mitth deciding they don't want you commanding the *Springhawk* and having the Expansionary Fleet move you somewhere else," Thalias said. "That would open the way for Samakro to take back command."

"Your analysis holds several logical flaws," Thrawn said. "First, the Nine Families don't dictate military assignments. Second, Mid Captain Samakro has no reason to wish command of the *Springhawk*.

With his experience and capabilities, he'll surely be offered a more prestigious ship than a mere heavy cruiser."

"The *Springhawk* is pretty prestigious," Thalias told him. "Maybe more than you realize. But even if it wasn't, the Ufsa family would still want it back. It got taken away from them, and they're notorious for resenting anything they see as a political backslide."

"I see," Thrawn said.

Thalias peered closely at him in the dim light. From the slight frown around his eyes, it was clear that he didn't see at all. "But to answer your question, no, the Mitth didn't send me," she said, picking her words carefully. "In fact, the family fought me the whole way. I was just lucky that I was able to join the ship as a caregiver instead of a family observer."

"Interesting," Thrawn said. "Did they give a reason for not wanting you as an observer?"

"They didn't actually say anything, one way or the other," Thalias said. "They just kept throwing barriers in my way. New forms I suddenly needed to fill out, new people I had to chase down to approve my request, new people on Csilla or Naporar who had to be brought into the loop. That sort of thing."

"Perhaps they didn't think you were qualified to observe," Thrawn suggested. "Or perhaps there was interference from other families."

"If there were other families in the mix, I never saw them," Thalias said sourly. "As for qualifications, I've got the full complement of eyes, ears, and brains. What else do I need?"

"That would be a question for the family," Thrawn said. "But it leads to yet another question. If the family didn't initiate your arrival, it was *your* doing. Why?"

Thalias braced herself. She'd hoped to avoid that question completely, but down deep she'd known it would eventually rise up to slap her in the face.

She'd come up with a couple of plausible-sounding lies, and for a moment she was tempted to use one of them. But sitting here, listening to his measured voice, she knew it would be useless. "It's going to sound stupid," she warned.

"Noted. Continue."

She braced herself. "I just wanted to see you again," she said. "You changed my life, and I . . . I wanted to see you again, that's all."

He frowned at her. "Really. How exactly did I change your life?"

"We met once before," she said, feeling even more ridiculous. Of course he wouldn't remember such a minor interaction. "It was a long time ago, when I was finishing my last trip as a sky-walker."

"Ah, yes," Thrawn said, still frowning. "Aboard the *Tomra*, when I was a cadet."

"That's right," Thalias said, breathing a little easier. So he *did* remember her. That eased at least a little of the awkwardness she was feeling. "Captain Vorlip came in, you talked—"

"And she spun me around to see if I could really feel the ship as I'd claimed."

"Yes," Thalias said. "And you impressed her."

"Did I?"

"Of course," Thalias said. "She told me afterward that—"

"Because she also sent fifty downmarks ahead of me to Taharim."

Thalias felt her eyes widen. "She did *what*? Why?"

"For unauthorized intrusion into the *Tomra*'s command area," Thrawn said. "I was three months working them off."

"But—" Thalias sputtered. "But she was *impressed* by you."

"Perhaps as a person she was impressed," Thrawn said. "Perhaps even as a spacefarer. But as an officer of the Chiss Ascendancy, she had a duty to enforce regulations."

"But it was an honest mistake."

"Intent and motivations are irrelevant," Thrawn said. "Judgment can focus only on actions."

"I suppose," Thalias murmured, her gut twisting inside her. So his memory of her would always be linked to an unpleasant episode in his career. Wonderful.

"How exactly did our meeting change your life?"

Thalias sighed. The last thing she wanted was to keep talking about it. But she'd decided to tell the truth, and there was no way out of it now. "You gave me hope," she said. The words sounded a lot sillier when she said them aloud than they had when they were just bouncing around inside her head. "I mean . . . I was thirteen. I thought my life was over. You told me I'd find a new path, and that I could choose how things worked out."

"Yes," Thrawn said, his voice thoughtful. Not sympathetic, not encouraging, not even really responsive. Just thoughtful.

Thalias had thought about this moment for a long time. She'd wondered what he would say, what *she* would say, and if it would open up new vistas for her life and her future.

And now nothing. He was thoughtful. Just thoughtful.

She closed her eyes, wishing she was anywhere else in the galaxy. She should never, never have started down this path in the first place.

"I had an older sister," Thrawn said, his voice almost too soft for her to hear. "She was five when she disappeared. My parents would never tell me where she went."

Thalias opened her eyes again. He was still sitting there in the gloom, still looking thoughtful.

But now there was something new in his eyes. A distant, well-hidden, but lingering pain. "How old were you?" she asked.

"Three," Thrawn said. "For a long time I assumed she'd died, and that I would never see her again. It wasn't until I reached bridge officer rank that I was finally told about the sky-walkers, and realized what must have happened to her." He gave her a small smile, tinged with the same distant sadness. "And I'll *still* never see her again."

"You might," Thalias said, moved by an obscure desire to comfort him. "There have to be records somewhere."

"I'm sure there are," Thrawn said. "But most sky-walkers want to disappear into obscurity after they finish their service, and the Ascendancy's long had a practice of honoring those wishes." He lifted a hand. "We all have regrets, however, just as we have hopes that will never be fulfilled. The key to a satisfying life is to accept those things that cannot be changed, and make a positive difference with those that can."

"Yes," Thalias said. But just because something couldn't be changed didn't mean a person shouldn't hammer away at it anyway. Secrets could sometimes be brought to light, and even Thrawn could be wrong.

"In the meantime, we have time to rest and think out our future strategy," Thrawn continued, pulling a pack of cards from his pocket. "You can choose the first game."

CHAPTER FOURTEEN

"**A**re you certain," Zistalmu said, "that you know *exactly* what you're supposed to do?"

Ar'alani drew in a deep breath, pulling with it every bit of patience her mind and body could muster. "Yes, Syndic," she said. "I think we've been over it enough times."

"Because I'm serious," he went on, as if he hadn't heard her. Or more likely didn't believe her. "If either the Garwians or the Vaks refuse to give him up, or deny knowing anything about him, we turn the ship around and go home."

"I understand," Ar'alani said.

Which wasn't to say that she agreed with him. Or that she had any intention of following such a ridiculous order.

Defying an Aristocra syndic could mean the end of her career, of course. But she'd put her career on the line so many times before that it was almost becoming routine.

What *wasn't* routine was why Zistalmu and Thurfian both seemed so single-mindedly determined to destroy Thrawn. She'd been mulling over that question since their departure from the Ascendancy, and she was no closer to figuring it out now than she had been then.

Maybe it was time she did something about that.

She looked over at the navigator's station. Che'ri was sitting there, her breathing slow and steady, deep in Third Sight as she guided them toward Primea. Standing beside her was Zistalmu's wife, who'd never offered Ar'alani her proper name but had instead insisted that everyone aboard call her Nana. A rather annoying affectation, in Ar'alani's opinion. Possibly why the woman had only lasted two years as a caregiver.

But right now all that mattered was that for the next minute neither she nor anyone else was in position to listen in.

"A question, Syndic," Ar'alani said as Zistalmu started to turn away. "For my own curiosity."

"Yes?"

She turned her full gaze on him. "Why do you and Syndic Thurfian hate Thrawn so much?"

She'd expected some kind of reaction from him. To her surprise, his expression didn't even twitch. "About time," he said calmly. "I've been expecting you to bring up that topic since we left Csilla."

"Sorry, I've had other things on my mind," Ar'alani said. "May I have an answer?"

"First ask the correct question," Zistalmu said. "We *don't* hate Thrawn. Actually, we both admire his military skill. We resist him because he's a threat to the Ascendancy."

"To the Ascendancy?" Ar'alani countered. "Or to the Irizi family?"

Zistalmu shook his head. "You really don't see it, do you? In that case, there's no point in continuing this conversation."

"Excuse me, Syndic, but there's every reason to continue," Ar'alani said. "You're aboard the *Vigilant,* under my authority, and you're obligated to answer any reasonable question and obey any reasonable order. Unless you plan to invoke official Syndicure secrets—and I *will* follow through on that if you try it—you'll tell me how Thrawn is a threat to the Ascendancy."

Octrimo called a warning from the helm. "Breakout in thirty seconds, Admiral."

"Acknowledged." Ar'alani raised her eyebrows toward Zistalmu. "Talk fast."

"There's no time for a proper explanation," the syndic said. "But really, you don't need one. You've seen enough of Thrawn and his career to understand. If you don't, it's because you choose not to."

Ar'alani shook her head. "Not good enough."

"It's all you're going to get." Zistalmu nodded toward the viewport. "And we're here."

Ar'alani turned to see the hyperspace swirl collapse into star-flares and then into stars. Looming directly ahead was a half-lit planet with dozens of ships of all sizes moving in or out or simply drifting steadily along in their orbits.

"Primea, Admiral," Octrimo announced.

"I read forty-seven visible ships," Senior Commander Biclian added from the sensor station. "Checking configurations for anything that looks Garwian."

"Acknowledged," Ar'alani said. "Senior Captain Wutroow, a signal to the planetary diplomatic office. Identify us, and tell them we're trying to reach Artistic Master Svorno."

"Yes, Admiral," Wutroow said. She leaned over the comm officer's shoulder and began speaking quietly.

"I'm not picking up anything that looks like a Garwian," Biclian reported. "Maybe it's on the other side of the planet."

"Admiral, Primea Central Command acknowledges," Wutroow relayed. "They claim the Garwian diplomatic ship left three days ago with all personnel aboard."

"There you go," Zistalmu said briskly. "Looks like Thrawn managed to extricate himself without any fuss or drama. Now, if we can say our farewells and head back to the Ascendancy—"

"Captain, please ask for clarification," Ar'alani ordered. "I want a list of all the personnel on that ship. I also want copies of all transmissions to and from the Garwian before it left."

"What makes you think they'll have all that available?" Zistalmu demanded. "Or will give it to you if they do?"

"Captain?" Ar'alani prompted.

"Message delivered," Wutroow confirmed. "Waiting for a reply."

"We've got movement," Biclian cut in. "Five small ships breaking orbit toward us, and another eight patrol ships rising from the surface. Make that *nine* from the surface."

"Patrol ships?" Zistalmu asked, clearly confused. "What are they doing?"

"You should read the Defense Force's after-action reports more closely, Syndic," Ar'alani said, eyeing the small ships assembling between the *Vigilant* and the planet below. "Small fighters are a line in the dirt, a warning that the defenders are serious."

"Yes, I understand that part," Zistalmu growled. "I'm wondering why they think fourteen fighters constitutes any kind of threat. Do they expect them to scare us away?"

"Of course not," Ar'alani said. "But a couple of wings of fighters isn't as provocative as a group of full-class warships would be. That makes it easier for both sides to back down if neither really wants a fight. And if the intruder *does* want one, it's not so much of a loss to the defenders if the fighters get blown out of the sky."

"But we're not going to do that, are we?" Zistalmu asked, his voice dark and ominous.

"Not unless we're attacked first," Ar'alani said. "Captain? Any word on my request?"

"Central Command says they don't have that information," Wutroow reported. "They say they have to refer me to the diplomatic service."

"I trust they're doing so?"

"So they say." Wutroow pointed at the tactical. "Looks like they're working into a lens formation."

Ar'alani nodded. Or at least, thirteen of the patrol ships were. The fourteenth was moving forward, ignoring his companions' more cautious stance. "Octrimo, that fighter on the extreme starboard seems to be spoiling for a fight," she said. "Start drifting us toward him. Nice and easy—don't make it obvious."

"You think that's him?" Wutroow asked.

"We'll know in a minute," Ar'alani said, checking the distance. The patrol ship was almost in range now. Another few seconds . . .

Abruptly, a double flare of laserfire blasted from the fighter squarely at the *Vigilant*.

"Hit on starboard ventral weapons cluster," Biclian reported tersely. "Low-power blast, no damage."

"Acknowledged," Ar'alani said.

Zistalmu inhaled sharply. "What are they *doing*? I thought you said they weren't trying to be provocative."

"Targeting sensors have kicked into rapid record mode," Wutroow called.

"Modulated laserfire coming in—" Biclian began.

"Thank you, Senior Commander," Ar'alani cut him off. She'd known what Thrawn was planning as soon as he opened fire on the sensor cluster and had hoped she could slide it past Zistalmu without him noticing.

No such luck. "Modulated how?" the syndic asked. "Admiral? The laser is modulated how?"

"I'm not sure yet, Syndic," Ar'alani hedged. "We'll have to see what the computer makes of it."

"Let me guess," Zistalmu said, eyes narrowed with suspicion. "That's Thrawn, isn't it? And he's somehow adapted the fighter's laser to transmit a message. Is that it?"

Ar'alani mouthed a silent curse. So much for keeping the syndic in the dark long enough to bring Thrawn aboard.

So much, too, for keeping Thrawn's favored method for surreptitious communication secret. Up to now, only she and Thrawn had known how he'd managed his communication with the Garwians during the Lioaoin pirate attack on Stivic all those years ago. He'd obviously planned in advance to pull the same trick here, knowing that Ar'alani would recognize it and be able to extract the message.

What he couldn't have anticipated was Zistalmu inviting himself onto the mission.

The question of Thrawn's possible interference in that particular incident had long since been forgotten. But all it would take was Zistalmu putting the pieces together to drag it back into the light. And with Zistalmu and Thurfian both out for Thrawn's blood, that could be a serious problem.

Right now, Ar'alani had more pressing matters to deal with. Two of the Vak patrol ships had broken out of their lens formation and were pursuing Thrawn's ship. So far they hadn't fired, but someone had clearly figured out that the rogue fighter had been commandeered and was hoping to stop it. Meanwhile, off to portside, two much larger Vak warships had come into view around the planetary rim, moving steadily toward the *Vigilant*.

And then, around the planetary rim to starboard, a much larger ship had appeared.

A Nikardun warship.

"Vak warships moving toward portside flank," Wutroow called. "Close-combat distance in two point three minutes. Patrol ships moving up in defensive lens; combat distance ninety seconds."

"Picture coming through," Biclian reported. "On Sensor Two."

Ar'alani looked at the specified display. The data Thrawn was sending seemed to be a schematic of one of the Vak patrol ships.

She smiled tightly. A schematic, moreover, with all the weapons and targeting sensor systems marked. Everything she would need to take all the fight out of them without loss of life or serious damage to the ships themselves.

"Prepare lasers," she ordered. "Target patrol ships' weapons sensors. Target *very* carefully—I don't want any additional damage."

"Just a moment," Zistalmu cut in. "Are you mad? You can't launch an unprovoked attack."

"It's not unprovoked," Wutroow said. "One of them fired on us, remember?"

"That was Thrawn."

"So you've suggested," Ar'alani said evenly. "Until that's been confirmed, we operate on the assumption that the Vaks have attacked us. Captain Wutroow, pick three of the patrol ships and fire—"

"Belay that order," Zistalmu snapped. "I forbid any action. You will prepare to withdraw—"

"Incoming!" Biclian snapped. "Four heavy cruisers, coming in from hyperspace behind us."

"Acknowledged," Ar'alani said, feeling a sudden sense of unreality as she gazed at the display. They were heavy cruisers, all right, arrayed in a diamond combat formation.

Only they weren't Vak ships, or even Nikardun.

They were Lioaoin.

"Yaw turn—one eighty," she ordered. "Stand by lasers and spheres on new targets."

"Lioaoin flagship is signaling, Admiral," the comm officer called. She touched a switch—

"—to intruder," a Lioaoin voice came over the speaker, its Minnisiat clear and precise. "You are threatening the peace and safety of the Vak Combine. Leave immediately, or be fired upon."

"Admiral—" Zistalmu began.

"Quiet." Ar'alani cut him off as she tapped her comm switch. "This is Admiral Ar'alani aboard the Chiss Expansionary Defense Fleet ship *Vigilant*," she said. "We mean no harm to Primea or the Combine. One of our people has gone missing, and we're here to inquire about his whereabouts."

The words were barely out of her mouth when all four Lioaoi ships opened fire.

"Barriers up!" Wutroow barked. "Target enemy lasers."

"Prepare spheres," Ar'alani added, her brain spinning as she tried to figure out what in hell was going on. What were Lioaoi even doing here at Primea, let alone attacking a Chiss warship on sight?

And then, suddenly, she got it.

Damn the Nikardun, anyway.

"Spheres: Fire when ready," she bit out. "Target all Lioaoin ships; concentrate on weapons clusters."

"Enemy lasers impacting on the hull," Wutroow reported, her voice tight but controlled. "Barriers diffusing about eighty percent. Spheres on their way."

Ar'alani nodded. Enough plasma sphere impacts, enough ion bursts eating into the electronics, and the attackers' ability to continue fighting would be neutralized.

But it would take half a dozen shots to sufficiently disable any one of the ships, and there were four of them for her to deal with. And the *Vigilant* had only a limited number of spheres available.

Unless . . .

"Continue targeting weapons," she ordered, searching the displays. Thrawn's patrol ship . . . there it was, coming up fast. The two Vak fighters that had been in pursuit, she noted, were falling back. Apparently, they didn't want him badly enough to charge into a combat zone.

Perfect.

"Octrimo, what's our best course out of here?" she called.

"Wait," Zistalmu protested. "Now, when we're actually attacked— *now* you want to run?"

"Shut it," Ar'alani said. "Octrimo?"

"Best exit route is portside," Octrimo reported. "But that vector will take us into close-combat range with both Three and Four."

The Lioaoin ship designated as Four, Ar'alani noted, being the one farthest to portside. Time to gamble. "Concentrate sphere fire on Three," she said. "Octrimo, take us out on your vector."

"On *Three*?" Zistalmu put in. "But Four's closer—"

"If I have to tell you again to be quiet, I'll have you removed from the bridge," Ar'alani warned.

Zistalmu sputtered something but fell silent.

The laserfire from the four Lioaoin ships was increasing as the *Vigilant* headed toward the open space to the Lioaoin formation's left. Attackers Three and Four began moving sideways to block the Chiss escape, though Three's efforts were now being slowed by the cascade of plasma spheres hammering into its hull.

But with the flanking fire from One and Two continuing to blast away at the *Vigilant*'s starboard hull, even just a single Lioaoin in front of the *Vigilant* would make escape problematic. Presumably, the Lioaoi and their Nikardun masters knew that and were counting on it.

Unfortunately for them, they'd all forgotten about Thrawn.

The Vak patrol ship shot past the *Vigilant* on full power, ducking through the scattered laserfire from the Lioaoin ships, charging straight toward Attacker Four with lasers blazing. Ar'alani held her breath, waiting for the Lioaoin to respond, wondering if she and Thrawn had read the situation correctly.

They had. For those first crucial seconds the Lioaoin didn't return fire, having apparently been ordered to shoot at the Chiss warship but avoid combat with Nikardun and the local Vak forces. She could envision the frantic calls from the Lioaoi to Primea, the questions running up the chain of command, transferring over to the Nikardun warship, the furious corrections coming from the general in charge, possibly heading directly to the Lioaoi, possibly having to go the reverse path so as not to give the Chiss confirmation that the Nikardun were even involved—

And as the farce finally played itself out, the Lioaoin ships belatedly opened fire.

But it was too late. Thrawn's surgical attack had already destroyed Four's combat ability, tearing into the ship's heavy laser sites and blinding their missile fire-control sensors. For a moment the other three Lioaoi continued to fire, but as the *Vigilant* drove through Four's shadow their weapons went silent lest they hit their comrade. Thrawn's fighter finished its run and turned toward the *Vigilant*—

And jerked suddenly as a final laser shot sliced across its aft thrusters.

"Hit on patrol ship!" Wutroow snapped.

"Tractor beam!" Ar'alani snapped back. "Bring him in."

"On it," Wutroow confirmed. "Tractor engaged . . . locked . . . bringing him in."

"Starboard spheres: One final volley," Ar'alani ordered. "Keep them back."

"Vak warships moving up," Biclian warned.

But it was a waste of effort, and everyone knew it. The *Vigilant* would be far enough out of Primea's gravity well in twenty seconds, and would have Thrawn aboard in thirty. The only ships close enough to stop them were the Lioaoin cruisers, and thanks to her and Thrawn's combined attack they, too, were out of luck. "Sky-walker Che'ri, get ready," she called.

"She's ready," Zistalmu's wife said.

Ar'alani scowled. "Sky-walker Che'ri?" she asked pointedly.

"I'm ready, Admiral," the girl's voice came back. Her confirmation was quieter and maybe a little more tentative than Nana's, but it confirmed to Ar'alani that Che'ri was, indeed, ready.

Ar'alani had had other caregivers insist on speaking for their young charges instead of letting them speak for themselves. She'd never liked it then, either. "Good," she said. "As soon as we confirm Captain Thrawn's aboard, we'll go. Captain Wutroow?"

"Almost there," Wutroow said. There was a small clunking sound as the shrapnel from a pair of disintegrated Lioaoin missiles bounced off the *Vigilant*'s hull near the viewport. One final, desperate, useless attack. "Aboard," Wutroow confirmed. "Crash webbing's deployed . . . confirmed capture . . . outer hatch closing . . . outer hatch sealed."

"All right, Che'ri, we've got him," Ar'alani said. A long road, with a blaze of fire and noise at the end of it. She could only hope Thrawn had found everything he'd come here for. "Take us home."

MEMORIES IX

"How much longer?" Senior Captain Ziara asked.

"Two minutes," the tense reply came from the helm.

Ziara nodded, wincing to herself. Two minutes. Two hours since Thrawn's emergency call, with no communication possible in hyperspace, and now two more minutes. Depending on how deep the excursion liner had been in the planetary gravity well when Thrawn and his newly assigned patrol boat reached it, Ziara and the *Parala* could arrive just in time to join Thrawn in watching helplessly as eight thousand people fell to their blazing deaths in the thick planetary atmosphere. "Tractor beams ready?" she asked.

"Ready and waiting, Captain."

"Standing by for breakout," the pilot announced. "Three, two, *one*." The hyperspace swirl vanished—

And there, ten kilometers ahead, the drama stretched out in front of them.

Ship losses of this sort were rare these days, but no less horrific for all that. The excursion liner, a compact cylinder with a pair of wide D-shaped wings stretching out on opposite sides and housing the more expensive suites, was deep into the roiling upper atmosphere of the triple-ringed gas giant planet it had been cruising past. Already its wake was visible as it plowed through the tenuous gasses, the drag eroding its orbital velocity and threatening it with a death spiral into the crushing depths. A few hundred meters in front of it, trailing a smaller wake, was the *Boco,* straining for all it was worth to stabilize the liner.

Straining, and losing. Even without running the numbers, Ziara could see that the sheer difference in mass between the two ships would make it impossible for the *Boco* to pull the liner free. In fact, even adding the *Parala*'s tractors to the mix might not be enough.

"Senior Captain Ziara," Thrawn's voice came from the bridge speaker. "Thank you for your prompt response. Would you join me off the liner's bow?"

"On our way," Ziara said, gesturing the order to the helm. The sensor display lit up with the relevant numbers . . .

Just as she'd feared. "But it won't do any good," she added quietly. "Even together we can't make this work. Are the passengers off yet?"

"Unfortunately, no," Thrawn said. "By the time the thrusters failed, the liner was already too deep into the radiation and magnetic bands to launch escape pods."

"They're still *aboard*?"

"It's all right," Thrawn said. "The passengers and crew are all gathered in the central cylinder behind adequate shielding."

Ziara hissed between her teeth. That wasn't at all what she'd meant. "Did you get through to anyone else?" she asked, her eyes running down the numbers. Another hour, and even a full Nightdragon wouldn't be able to tow the liner free.

"No one else is coming," Thrawn said. "Please hurry. Time is short."

"Short?" someone muttered. "More like *nonexistent.*"

"Just pull us parallel to him," Ziara said, wondering what Thrawn had in mind.

"In position, Captain," the pilot called.

"Tractors on," the weapons officer added. "Status . . . no good. Liner's still drag—"

An instant later she broke off with a startled gasp as the *Parala* jerked violently. "*Boco*'s dropped its tractors!"

"Increase thrust," Ziara ordered, staring at the display. Not only had the *Boco* disengaged its tractors, but it had veered away from the *Parala* and was making a tight curve back toward the liner.

And as the *Boco* settled into position alongside the liner, its spectrum lasers flashed, blasting into the junction points where the portside luxury wing connected to the central cylinder. "Captain, he's *attacking* them!" the sensor officer yelped.

"Stand fast," Ziara said. "Ready emergency power to the thrusters."

"But Captain—"

"I said stand fast," Ziara snapped. "Don't you see? He's lightening the ship."

The words were barely out of her mouth when the portside wing broke away, the sudden change in the liner's mass again sending a jolt along the tractor beam line and into the *Parala*. The *Boco* was already moving to the liner's other side, blasting away at the connectors of the starboard wing. Ziara watched, bracing herself . . .

The wing snapped away and disappeared into the atmosphere below. "Emergency power!" Ziara ordered. "Get us out of here."

And as the *Parala* vibrated and creaked with the additional stress, the liner finally began to move away from the planet. A moment later there was another, smaller jolt as the *Boca* returned to Ziara's side and added its own tractors and thrusters to the effort. Slowly but steadily, they eased the liner out of the atmosphere and the gravity well.

Fifteen minutes later, the crisis was over.

"Thank you for your assistance, Senior Captain Ziara," Thrawn's voice came as the two ships finally cut back on their thrusters and disengaged their tractors. "Without you, the liner would indeed have been lost."

"Thank you in turn for your quick thinking," Ziara said, eyeing the liner. The ship's beautiful external wings, gone, with their fancy suites and, no doubt, the inhabitants' fancy possessions gone with them. "A word of warning, though. If I were you, I wouldn't expect a lot of thanks from anyone else."

"You've never been to Csilla, have you?" Ziara asked as the shuttle headed down toward the shimmery blue-white surface of the Chiss homeworld.

"No," Thrawn said, gazing out the viewport. "All my training and briefings took place at the Expansionary Fleet complex on Naporar."

Ziara peered at his profile. There was a tightness around his eyes and lips. "You seem worried."

"Worried?"

"The state of seeing large nighthunters lurking in your future," Ziara said. "You know you have nothing to be concerned about, right? The liner owners can squawk all they want, but the fact remains that you saved eight thousand people who otherwise would be compressed mush right now."

"I imagine anything resembling mush would have long since dissipated into tendrils of shredded organic molecules within the atmospheric currents."

"Oh, I like that one," Ziara said. "Okay if I borrow it?"

"You're welcome to it." Thrawn nodded at the planet.

"No, I was just thinking. I've been in trouble before, but I've never been called to such a high-level hearing."

"Because all the other questionable things you did were essentially military," Ziara reminded him. "This one is essentially civilian. More important, it's civilian connected to one of the Nine Families. That puts you on everyone's scanners."

"Yet you suggest I don't need to worry?"

"No, because the passenger list included Aristocra from at least five of the other Nine Families," Ziara said. "When pique comes to poke, five-to-one odds make a pretty decent battle position."

"I hope it won't come to that." Thrawn nodded toward the viewport. "Is that Csaplar?"

Ziara craned her neck. Barely visible in the otherwise featureless surface was what appeared to be a massive city frozen in the ice. "Yes," she confirmed. "Capital of the Chiss Ascendancy, and once the flower-spray of culture and refinement. We'll be landing at the spaceport on the southwest edge and taking a tunnel car westward to fleet headquarters. You won't see that complex from up here, by the way—it's mostly underground."

"Yes, I know," Thrawn said. "You say Csaplar was once a center of culture. Not anymore?"

"Sadly, no," Ziara said. "But it really was marvelous once."

"Odd," Thrawn said, sounding a bit confused. "I would think that a city population of seven million would be more than enough to support both a government *and* the arts."

"One would think so," Ziara agreed, looking casually around the shuttle. Too many people. But there would be plenty of time later to tell him the truth. "But don't worry. I'm sure we'll find *something* down there to do."

The hearing, as Ziara had predicted, was short and perfunctory. The Boadil family, which had owned the doomed liner, had sent a representative who loudly insisted that Thrawn be punished, demoted, or possibly thrown out of the Expansionary Defense Fleet altogether. Three of the five families whose members had been saved from death were also represented, countering that Thrawn deserved promotion, not censure. In the end, it all balanced out, and Thrawn ended up exactly where he'd started.

With one crucial exception. For whatever reason, for whatever obscure political favor someone owed someone else, Thrawn's patrol ship—his very first command—was taken away from him.

"I'm so sorry," Ziara commiserated as she and Thrawn rode their tunnel car back to the city. "I never expected the fleet to do *that*."

"It's all right," Thrawn said. His voice was calm, but Ziara could hear the disappointment beneath it. "Considering how many millions I cost the Boadil, neither of us should be surprised by their vindictiveness."

"*You* didn't cost anyone anything," Ziara ground out. "*You* didn't take the liner too close to that planet. *You* didn't ignore the engineers who warned the electronics were having trouble with the magnetic field twists. *You* didn't push the engines and scramble the thrusters in the first place. If I were the Boadil, I'd be looking to nail the liner's captain to the floor, not you."

Except they wouldn't, she knew, feeling the sharp edge of bitterness. The Boadil were political allies with both the Ufsa and her own Irizi family . . . and the liner's captain had been Ufsa. Thrawn was the only scapegoat available for the mess, and so he'd received the full brunt of Boadil anger and embarrassment.

"Thank you," Thrawn said. "But you don't need to be angry on my behalf. Together we saved eight thousand lives. That's what's important."

Ziara nodded. "Yes. Absolutely."

"So," Thrawn said, his tone businesslike again. "With my command gone, I no longer have convenient passage off Csilla. I presume the fleet will take note of that and find me transport to wherever post they next assign me."

"Hopefully, they won't need to go out of their way on that count," Ziara said. "I've already put in a request for you to be reassigned to the *Parala* as one of my officers. If that's approved, you'll leave with me."

"Thank you," Thrawn said, inclining his head toward her. "I noticed a number of hotels clustered around the space-port. I can find housing there while I await my new orders."

"You could," Ziara said, pursing her lips thoughtfully. The thought that had just occurred to her . . .

The family wouldn't be happy about it, she knew. But right now she didn't really care. Thrawn had been unfairly dumped on, and if she couldn't fix it she could at least show him that he hadn't been abandoned by the entire Ascendancy.

"But I've got a better idea," she said. "We've got at least a few days, more likely a week. Why don't you come to the Irizi homestead with me?"

"To your *homestead*?" Thrawn echoed. "Are strangers even allowed?" A muscle in his cheek twitched. "Especially strangers from rival families?"

"I don't know, and I don't care," Ziara said. "I'm blood, and I'm an honored member of the fleet who just helped save eight thousand lives. I don't know how far all that will take me, but I'd rather like to find out. You game to find out with me?"

"I don't know," Thrawn said hesitantly. "I don't want you to get in trouble on my behalf."

"I'm not worried about it," Ziara said. "Did I mention that my grandfather was an amazingly passionate art collector?"

Thrawn smiled. "If I haven't mentioned it recently, Ziara,

you have a knack for seeking out and exploiting your opponents' weaknesses. Very well. Shall we once again charge headlong into danger?"

"We shall," Ziara said. "Besides, we've just survived an encounter with a malicious gas giant planet. Really, how bad could my family be?"

The area around the Csaplar spaceport was loud and busy, crowded with people, hotels, restaurants, and entertainment of all sorts. The Irizi homestead was about three hundred kilometers to the northeast, on the far side of the city. Ziara got them a two-person express overground tube car and they headed off.

Across the city. Not, as was usually done, around it.

She wasn't supposed to do that, she knew. Thrawn wasn't supposed to know the truth about the Ascendancy's capital city—no one except senior syndics, flag officers, and the Patriarchs of the Nine Families knew the full truth—and there were plenty of tunnel car routes that would avoid the aboveground sections entirely.

But once again, she didn't care. The fleet and Aristocra had treated Thrawn shamefully, and her lingering anger over that had awakened a peculiar but surprisingly delicious sense of defiance.

Besides, she reminded herself as they left the spaceport and headed through the buildings and parks and the maze of other overground tubes, it would be an interesting tactical exercise to see how long it took Thrawn to figure it out.

Not long at all, as it turned out. They'd crossed a little more than a third of the sprawling metropolis, and she was watching his expression closely as he stared out the viewport, when his eyes suddenly narrowed. "Something's wrong," he said.

"What do you mean?" Ziara asked.

"There don't seem to be any people here," Thrawn said. "Not since we left the spaceport area."

"Of course there are," Ziara said, pointing across the way at another tube car paralleling theirs in the distance. "You can see two people right there."

"They're the exceptions," Thrawn said. "The other cars we've seen have been empty."

"Maybe they're just too far away for you to see inside," Ziara said, feeling both guilty and surprised at how much fun this game was. "You can see that the car exteriors tend to be reflective."

"No," Thrawn said. "The empty cars ride higher on their rails than the full ones. We've also passed through three connecting loci, and there were no cars or passengers waiting at any of them."

He turned, fixing her with such an intense look that she reflexively drew back a little. "What's happened to our capital, Ziara?"

"The same thing that happened to the whole planet," Ziara said quietly. "I'm sorry—I shouldn't have done that to you. But you're not supposed to know."

"To know what? That the people of Csilla are gone?"

"Oh, they're not gone," she said. "Well, yes, most of them are, but the big exodus happened over a thousand years ago. What they taught you in school about how changes in the sun's output and the slow freezing of the surface forced the population of Csilla underground is mostly true. What the histories leave out is that the numbers that were moved below were a far cry from the four billion who'd been living here at the time."

"Where did they go?"

"Other planets," Ziara said. "Mostly Rentor, Avidich, and Sarvchi. The Syndicure and fleet headquarters were kept here, along with a lot of the cargo and merchant facilities.

Some of the families moved their homesteads to worlds where they already had strong presences, but most didn't want to leave Csilla entirely."

"They also moved underground?"

"Right," Ziara said. "My family's new homestead—well, new as of a thousand years ago—is in a huge cavern about two kilometers below the surface. Still on our same land, of course. The Irizi are a bit obsessive about territory and history."

"So how many people actually live on Csilla?"

"Sixty or seventy million," Ziara said. "Though all the official records put the number at eight billion." She waved at the city around them. "All the rest of this is just for show."

"For whom?"

"Our visitors," she said. "Our alien trading partners." She felt her throat tighten. "Our enemies."

"So a few continue to live aboveground to create the illusion," Thrawn murmured. "Light and heat are also maintained. Tube cars continue to travel across the remaining cities, pretending to be the traffic of a thriving population." He looked at Ziara. "I presume that on the far side our tube will descend into one of the tunnels?"

She nodded. "There are a few hundred people in Csaplar at any given time. They're rotated out frequently so they don't have to put up with the conditions up here for very long. The rest of the city—the *real* city—is spread out in caverns, mostly concentrated around the Syndicure complex. More illusion for our diplomatic visitors."

"And of course, most civilian visitors and merchants stay close to one of the spaceports," Thrawn said, nodding. "The activity there and around the government complex disguises the emptiness of the rest of the city."

"Right," Ziara said. "Your next question is probably why this is all such a big secret."

"Not at all," Thrawn assured her. "I understand the strategic advantages of maneuvering a potential enemy into wasting a massive amount of force on what's essentially an empty shell." He looked her squarely in the eye. "*My* question is why you've told me all this. Surely I'm not senior enough for that kind of classified information. Especially not after today."

"I told you because you thrive on information," Ziara said. Her anger-driven defiance was starting to fade, leaving a bit of discomfort behind. The law was clear: Officers of Thrawn's current rank weren't supposed to know any of this. "The more you know about a situation, the better you are at coming up with the strategy and tactics necessary to handle it. Anyway, you'll be called in for the top-level briefing soon enough." She felt her lips pucker. "When that happens, try to act surprised."

"I will," he promised. "Speaking of surprises, does your family know you're bringing a guest?"

Ziara shook her head. "No, but it won't be a problem."

Thrawn raised his eyebrows slightly. "You assume."

"Yes," Ziara conceded. "I assume."

CHAPTER FIFTEEN

The law was clear.

The *Vigilant* had been attacked by forces of the Lioaoin Regime. The attackers had identified themselves as such, removing any question as to whether they might be pirates or privateers or some other unofficial and unauthorized group. The Defense Hierarchy Council had certain required responses to such a situation, as did the Aristocra and the Syndicure. The law was clear.

Which wasn't to say that any of those groups was at all enthusiastic about carrying out their duties.

"This," Second Officer Kharill said, "is madness."

Samakro gazed out the viewport at the roiling hyperspace sky. Personally, he couldn't agree more with his subordinate's assessment.

But Kharill *was* his subordinate, and Samakro was the *Springhawk*'s first officer, and part of his duty was to quash talk like that aboard his ship. "The ancient philosophers would agree with you," he said. "On the other hand, most of those same philosophers would say that all war is madness. Take that to its logical extreme, and we're all out of a job."

"Maybe," Kharill said. "I can't say I'd be opposed to a few years of peace."

"That might depend on the underlying cause of that peace," Thrawn said from behind them. "Good morning, gentlemen."

"Good morning, Senior Captain," Samakro said, hastily standing up from the command chair and turning as Thrawn stepped through the hatchway onto the bridge.

To his mild surprise, Thrawn waved him back down. "I'm not taking over your watch, Mid Captain," he said. "I only stopped by to check on our progress."

"We're on schedule, sir," Samakro said, looking over at the navigator's station. Che'ri was sitting upright in her seat, showing none of the subtle signs of sky-walker fatigue that would require a return to space-normal and a rest period.

In contrast Thalias, holding watch behind the girl, was sagging where she stood, apparently right on the edge of falling asleep.

But then, she'd been with Thrawn on the Vak homeworld of Primea, a witness to everything that happened there. That had put her under the spotlight for the same wearying round of Council and Syndicure hearings and interrogations that Thrawn and Ar'alani had endured. Under the circumstances, Samakro was mildly surprised the young woman was on her feet at all.

"Excellent," Thrawn said. Out of the corner of his eye, Samakro saw the other look at Che'ri, make his own visual assessment of her condition, and come to the same conclusion. "You realize, of course, that peace has several different flavors."

"Sir?" Samakro asked, frowning.

"I was returning to the topic raised by Senior Commander Kharill," Thrawn said. "If the Ascendancy was conquered and our cities left in ruins, that would be peace of a sort."

"That wasn't what I was suggesting, sir," Kharill said stiffly.

"I hardly expected that it was," Thrawn assured him. "But that would be a conqueror's concept of peace. A different conqueror might prefer the Chiss to be under his unbreakable control, to obey his orders without question. For him, that would be a version of peace."

"I meant the kind of peace where no one is shooting at anyone else," Kharill said.

"That's the kind most civilized people wish for," Thrawn said. "But how is that to be achieved?"

"I don't know, Captain," Kharill said. "I'm not a philosopher."

For a moment Thrawn eyed him in silence. Then he inclined his head slightly. "Understood. Go check on the plasma sphere supply. I suspect we'll be using them a great deal in the coming hours."

"Yes, sir." With clear relief, Kharill headed across the bridge toward the weapons station.

"He *is* a good officer, sir," Samakro said quietly.

"I know," Thrawn said. "His chief failing is a lack of curiosity."

"I'd have said no imagination."

"All beings possess imagination to varying degrees," Thrawn said. "It can be encouraged and nurtured, or can sometimes shine out in moments of stress. But curiosity is a choice. Some wish to have it. Others don't. How is the peace he wished for to be achieved?"

"Through the mutual respect and goodwill of all beings, of course," Samakro said, daring a small ironic smile.

Thrawn smiled back. "And how is that respect to be achieved?"

Samakro's smile faded. "By proving beyond any doubt that the Ascendancy can and will respond to an attack with overwhelming force."

"Indeed," Thrawn said. "And that's why this mission isn't madness, but instead is vitally necessary."

"Yes, sir," Samakro said. "But I believe Commander Kharill was referring less to the philosophy than to the question of why only our two ships were sent."

"You don't believe the *Springhawk* and *Vigilant* will prove an even match for the Lioaoin heartworld's core defenses?"

Samakro hesitated. "To be honest, sir, no."

"Perhaps a more complete understanding of the situation would help," Thrawn said. "There are four different groups in play, each with their own interests and agenda. First are the Nikardun, who wanted to capture or destroy Admiral Ar'alani at Primea but didn't want the Ascendancy's vengeance to fall on either themselves or the Vak Combine. General Yiv therefore called in a force from the Lioaoin Regime to make the attack and take that risk."

"I thought that connection hadn't been established."

"If not, you need to believe that the Lioaoi traveled all the way to

Primea in order to attack a Chiss warship they couldn't possibly know was coming."

Samakro grimaced. "Yes, I see your point."

"So Yiv has achieved the first of his objectives, though at the risk of sacrificing the strength of his Lioaoin allies," Thrawn said. "The second objective, now that he's turned our anger toward the Lioaoi, is to gauge the Ascendancy's will to deliver a reprisal. That will help him revise his plans if necessary as he looks forward to his ultimate war against us."

"Which means sending only two ships wasn't a good move on the Council's part," Samakro said. "It's going to make us look weak or indecisive."

"Yiv may indeed interpret it that way," Thrawn agreed. "But he could also interpret it as supreme confidence, that two Chiss warships are deemed adequate to deliver the necessary message. Add to that the Lioaoin interest in keeping damage to their regime to a minimum."

"Which we don't care about."

"Perhaps not," Thrawn said. "Still, if we can strike a balance between maximizing our message and minimizing our damage, the Lioaoi may remember that restraint in the future."

"Assuming they don't just turn the ships we don't destroy against us," Samakro warned.

"All the more reason to defeat Yiv and remove his stranglehold on the region as quickly as possible," Thrawn said grimly. "Certainly the Lioaoi wouldn't move against us without Nikardun pressure."

"But the Syndicure must first recognize the threat," Samakro pointed out. Though to be honest, he wasn't fully convinced of it, either. It was a long way from gobbling up whisker cubs like the Lioaoin Regime to tangling with the nighthunter that was the Chiss Ascendancy. "At any rate, meeting both those objectives requires us to do some damage without getting blown out of the sky."

"There's that," Thrawn agreed. "But the admiral believes we can strike the necessary balance."

"A moment," Samakro said, frowning. "Are you saying Admiral

Ar'alani *asked* for only two ships? I thought that was the syndics' decision."

"They were happy enough to go along with it," Thrawn said. "But no, it was the admiral."

"I'm glad *she's* confident," Samakro muttered.

"She is." Thrawn cocked his head. "There's another reason for taking only a small force, though, a tactical reason. What do you think it might be?"

"I have no idea."

"Think," Thrawn urged. "You have the knowledge and vision. Apply them to the problem."

Samakro suppressed a grimace. This was what he got for suggesting Kharill lacked imagination.

Still, it was an intriguing question. Two Chiss ships . . . an unknown number of opponents . . . a tactical reason . . . "It will certainly be easier to evaluate the Lioaoin tactics when they only have two of us to shoot at," he commented, stalling for time while he tried to think. Two Chiss ships . . .

"Exactly," Thrawn said, inclining his head. "Well done, Mid Captain."

Samakro blinked. "That was it?"

"Of course," Thrawn said. "It comes down to minimizing variables. It would be even easier if we'd brought only one ship, but we didn't think the Council would accept that."

"But you say the Syndicure was all for it?"

Thrawn's gaze drifted away. "Some of the syndics were reluctant to launch any attack at all, believing Ar'alani and I deliberately provoked the Primea incident. Others, I'm sure, believe two ships will be enough. Others . . ."

"Others?" Samakro prompted.

Thrawn shrugged. "I suspect a small number are hoping that both Ar'alani and I will be killed in the battle, thereby eliminating any future embarrassment we might bring to the Ascendancy."

Samakro stared at him. "That's . . ."

"Paranoid?" Thrawn offered.

"I was going to say outrageous," Samakro said. "If the fleet has a problem with you or Admiral Ar'alani, the Council can discipline or demote you. It's not the Syndicure's job to meddle in those decisions."

"But it *is* their job to do what's best for the Ascendancy," Thrawn said. "Sometimes obligations and restrictions overlap."

"Well, if they're looking for us to curl up and die for their convenience, they're going to be disappointed," Samakro said firmly. "This is the *Springhawk*. We don't lose battles. Not to anyone. Guaranteed."

"I'll look forward to yet again proving that," Thrawn said. "I'll leave you the bridge now, Mid Captain. Let me know if our skywalker needs a rest break. Otherwise, I'll return before our rendezvous with the *Vigilant*." With a final nod, he turned and retraced his steps to the hatchway.

Samakro stared at the hatch for a long moment after he left, his blood burning inside him. He didn't especially like Thrawn. He certainly didn't like the way he skated to the edge of the line and occasionally blew straight past it. Sometimes he left chaos and messes behind him that other people had to clean up, and Samakro hated that, too.

But he also had no damn interest in the Aristocra, the syndics, or anyone else outside the fleet chain of command interfering with military matters. The *Springhawk* and *Vigilant* would go to the Lioaoin heartworld as ordered, they would deliver the Ascendancy's message, and they would return. *Both* of them.

And with any luck, they would return covered with honor. Because that, too, was how the *Springhawk* did things.

Guaranteed.

The two ships reached the rendezvous system, an easy jump-by-jump from the Lioaoin heartworld. There the commanders and their senior officers met aboard the *Vigilant* for a final briefing and consultation.

Samakro wondered if either Ar'alani or Thrawn would mention

their private goal of delivering the Chiss message with as little damage to the Lioaoi as possible. But neither of them did.

Probably just as well, he decided. This whole thing was tangled enough without dragging in any last-minute complications.

The conference ended, and the *Springhawk*'s officers returned to their ship. Che'ri and the *Vigilant*'s sky-walker were taken off their respective bridges and ensconced in their suites out of immediate harm's way. Ar'alani gave the order, and the ships entered hyperspace for the final jump.

And then they were there.

"Status reports," Thrawn called calmly from his command chair.

"All systems ready," Samakro said, pacing back and forth behind the helm, weapons, defense, and sensor stations. "Counting twelve Lioaoin midsized warships in low orbit. *Vigilant* is moving inward."

"Lieutenant Commander Azmordi, keep us in formation," Thrawn ordered. "Let's see how long it takes them to notice us."

"Four of the warships rising from orbit," Dalvu reported from the sensor station, her fingers tapping at keys. "Make that six . . . no; make it all twelve."

"Not long at all, apparently," Thrawn said conversationally.

"You'd think they had a guilty conscience," Samakro commented, trying to keep his voice steady. Two warships that size would be trivial for the *Vigilant* and *Springhawk* to handle. Four would be reasonable. Six would be a stretch.

Twelve . . .

"They're trying to frighten us away," Thrawn said, as if he'd sensed Samakro's sudden concerns. Or more likely, he'd sensed the entire bridge crew's concerns. "Don't worry, they aren't all coming for us."

"Certainly looks like they are," Dalvu said under her breath.

"Watch your tone, Mid Commander," Samakro admonished her quietly. "The senior captain knows what he's talking about."

"Perhaps you should explain to her why they'll send no more than four ships against us," Thrawn invited.

Samakro frowned, eyeing the ships. What was Thrawn seeing that he wasn't?

He smiled suddenly. It wasn't anything his commander was seeing, but simple tactical logic. "Because the Chiss have a reputation," he said. "The Lioaoin High Command knows all about it, and won't believe the Ascendancy has sent only two ships to slap them down for their attack at Primea. They'll assume we're either a diversion or part of a larger encirclement force. Either way, they'll want to keep the bulk of their force close in for protection."

"Exactly," Thrawn said. "Watch for four of the ships to continue toward us, while the rest deploy in a defensive high-orbit pattern."

A light blinked on the comm console. "Admiral is hailing them," Samakro reported.

Thrawn nodded. "Let's hear what she has to say."

The comm officer touched a switch. "This is Admiral Ar'alani of the Chiss Expansionary Defense Fleet, commanding the *Vigilant*," Ar'alani's clear voice came over the bridge speaker. "Forces of the Lioaoin Regime have knowingly and with prejudice attacked a ship of the Chiss Ascendancy. Have you any explanation to offer before we pass judgment?"

Silence. "I say again," Ar'alani said, then repeated the message.

"The Nikardun are here," Thrawn said quietly.

"I'm not picking up any non-Lioaoin ships," Dalvu said.

"Then they're on the surface, or aboard Lioaoin ships," Thrawn said. "But the regime would certainly attempt to excuse their actions at Primea if they weren't afraid of reprisals from their allies."

Samakro thought back to what Thrawn had said about the Nikardun sacrificing the Lioaoi to keep themselves and the Vaks out of the Chiss target zone. "So the Nikardun just let them walk to the slaughter?" he asked. "Doesn't say much about their value to the Nikardun."

"More likely it indicates the even greater value General Yiv places in the Vak Combine," Thrawn said. "I see we have four ships approaching."

Samakro looked at Dalvu's profile, caught the sour look on her face. Thrawn had called the exact number of the Lioaoin response, and for some reason his casual show of competence annoyed her. "Confirmed, Senior Captain," she said reluctantly.

Thrawn touched a switch on his command chair. "Admiral, I believe our opponents are on their way."

"I concur, Senior Captain," Ar'alani's voice came back. "Ready to deploy probe."

"*Springhawk* stands ready," Thrawn confirmed. "Deploy at will."

Samakro craned his neck to look out the viewport at the *Vigilant*, running in the near distance off the *Springhawk*'s portside bow. There was a flicker of thruster fire, and the probe shot away from the larger ship. "Probe away," he confirmed to Thrawn.

"Acknowledged."

Samakro watched as the object accelerated toward the four Lioaoin ships, which had now positioned themselves in a vertical diamond formation. This whole scenario was, at least on the surface, exactly the same trick Thrawn had used at Rapacc to set up the *Springhawk*'s capture of that Nikardun patrol ship. The probe—really just one of the *Vigilant*'s shuttles—was playing decoy, giving the Lioaoi something to focus on while the real threat lay elsewhere.

At least, that was what Thrawn and Ar'alani hoped they would see. The question now was how much of the Rapacc incident the Nikardun had shared with their allies.

And, even more important, if they'd also shared whatever countermeasures they'd come up with for any future uses of the gambit.

Apparently, the answer to both was yes. "Probe is faltering," Dalvu announced. "*Vigilant* seems to be losing control."

"Comm interference increasing," Samakro confirmed, peering at the comm displays. "Lioaoi are trying to jam *Vigilant*'s control signal. To jam *and* override."

Samakro looked at the tactical. The probe's original vector had been toward the ventral ship in the Lioaoin formation. Now it was wavering back and forth as the *Vigilant* and the Lioaoi fought for control.

The Lioaoi won. With a final skittering surge, the probe settled down on a new vector, one that would take it harmlessly through the center of the Lioaoin formation and from there to disappear into the empty light-years of the Chaos. "At least we know now that they can learn," Samakro commented.

"Indeed," Thrawn agreed. "And as you see, Mid Captain, that can be a good or a bad thing."

"Yes, sir," Samakro said. The probe was nearly to the Lioaoin ships, moving steadily now under the control of its new masters. It entered the open space in the center of the formation—

"Fire," Thrawn said.

At their current distance, Samakro knew, certainly against warships equipped with electrostatic barriers, a spectrum laser attack would be not just futile but laughable. But the warships weren't Thrawn's target. Instead, the *Springhawk*'s lasers flashed a burst of energy into the small, unprotected shuttle.

And as the hull shattered, the four breaching missiles that had been packed aboard shot outward, one toward each of the Lioaoin warships.

The Lioaoi saw the attack coming, of course, and even at so close a range they had enough time to respond. But with a friendly ship directly behind each incoming missile, none of the warships could launch the level of countermeasures necessary to fully neutralize the attack. A few laser shots tentatively lanced out, and one of the missiles was caught and disintegrated. But the blast merely released the warhead's acid globs, leaving the deadly fluid to continue onward toward its target. A second later, as the warships tried in vain to move out of harm's way, the missiles struck.

The actual physical damage was probably minimal. Even the incredibly strong acid that breachers were loaded with could penetrate only so deep into a warship's hull, and the lateral spread of a single missile's worth was only so great. Electronics, sensors, and weapons systems would be damaged, but that damage would be fairly localized.

But the psychological effect more than made up for it. All four Lioaoin ships lurched violently, breaking formation. A second later the moment of instinctive panic seemed to subside, and the captains began systematically rotating away from the Chiss ships, trying to turn their new points of vulnerability out of the reach of enemy lasers.

They had each managed about a forty-degree turn when the *Vigilant*'s lasers flashed out.

And the second shuttle—the dark, silent, cold, all-but-undetectable second shuttle that had been towed invisibly behind the first—shattered and sent its own cargo of breacher missiles into the reeling Lioaoin warships.

"Lioaoin Regime, I'm still waiting for that explanation," Ar'alani's voice came over the speaker. "Perhaps you should start with an apology, and we'll go from there."

"Lioaoin ships falling back," Dalvu reported. "Two other ships rising from defense orbit."

"Admiral?" Thrawn asked.

"Apparently, they're not yet ready to concede," Ar'alani said, her voice icy. "Fine. We're here to deliver a message. Let's deliver it."

"Acknowledged," Thrawn said. "*Springhawk:* Prepare for battle."

There was a soft double-thump from somewhere nearby. Che'ri, sitting in her chair pretending to draw, gave a violent jerk. "What was that?" she whispered.

"It's okay," Thalias said from the couch facing Che'ri's chair, where she'd been pretending to read. "Probably just some stray shrapnel from a missile our lasers destroyed."

"What about the acid?" Che'ri asked, peering at the upper corner of the suite.

"There isn't any," Thalias said, sternly ordering her own heart to calm down. "We're the only ones who use breacher missiles with acid. Everyone else uses explosives. Once our lasers destroy or detonate them, there's nothing that keeps coming toward us." There was another set of thumps, six of them this time. "Except maybe a few small leftover pieces of the missile," she amended.

"What happens if the pieces get through?"

"They won't," Thalias assured her. "The electrostatic barrier can slow them down a little, but more important is that the *Springhawk* has really good, thick armor."

"Okay," Che'ri said. But it was clear from her anxious expression that she wasn't really satisfied. "How come nobody else uses acid?"

"I don't know," Thalias said. "I suppose it's not as impressive as explosives. Probably harder to make the missiles work, too."

"How come *we* do?"

"Because when it works, it works really well," Thalias said, feeling a twinge of sympathy. When she was Che'ri's age, the officers and caregivers would never answer her questions about things like this. Only later had she learned they'd been forbidden to talk to skywalkers about these details.

Probably still were, actually, which meant Thalias would likely get in trouble if anyone found out about this. But she could remember feeling terrified during her ships' battles as she sat alone with her caregiver and wondered what was going on.

Knowing how the ship's weapons worked might not be much comfort. But then again, it might.

"If the missile gets close enough before the enemy's lasers hit it, the acid will keep going as a big glob," she continued. "Pretty hard to shoot down a glob of liquid. Electrostatic barriers can't do much to slow it down, either, so when it hits it starts eating into the metal of the hull."

"So it opens the hull to space?"

"Not unless the hull is very thin or has already been damaged," Thalias said. "But it can destroy any sensors or fire-control systems and corrode any communications links that cross the area. Even better, from our point of view, it blackens the hull metal and creates pits, both of which help the metal underneath absorb the next batch of spectrum laser fire we put there."

"And *that* opens the hull to space?"

"It absolutely can," Thalias said. "It won't wreck the whole ship, of course—you've seen how many emergency bulkheads the *Springhawk* has down the passageways. But it's a warning to the enemy ship that we have the upper hand."

There was another double-clunk, farther away this time. "What happens if one of these pieces hits the viewport?" Che'ri asked.

"Probably nothing," Thalias said. "The point defenses around the bridge are pretty good, and there are blast shields that can be raised if they see something big coming. And the viewport material itself is pretty strong and thick."

"I mean, it's nice being able to see outside when we're flying somewhere," Che'ri mused. "But I always worry that we'll run into something."

"It's a risk," Thalias conceded. "But the viewports aren't just because we like looking at the stars. There are lots of ways that sensors and electronics can be damaged or distracted or confused. The bridge officers need to be able to actually see what's going on out there. There are also a couple of triangulation observation areas where other warriors can help aim and focus our attacks."

"I guess that makes sense." Che'ri peered closely at her. "How come no one's ever told me this before?"

"They're not supposed to," Thalias admitted. "Actually, there are a lot of things they're not supposed to tell sky-walkers."

"Yeah." Che'ri made a face. "They treat me like a—" She broke off.

"Like a child?" Thalias suggested.

"I'm *not* a child," Che'ri flared. "I'm almost ten years old."

Thalias's first reflex was to point out that ten years old was well within the definition of *childhood*. Her second reflex was to try the kind of soothing *there, there* noises that her caregivers had so often given her.

But as she looked into the girl's eyes, into all that fear and uncertainty, she realized neither approach would be any good. The two of them were far more alike than Thalias had realized until now, and for her the only thing that could ease fear was knowledge. "I know," she said, nodding tacit recognition of Che'ri's assessment of herself. "More than that, you've lived through more pressure and stress in the past three years than most Chiss will face in their entire lifetimes."

Che'ri's eyes turned away. "It's okay," she muttered.

"It's okay—and it's going to be okay—because you're strong,"

Thalias said. "You're a sky-walker, and Third Sight seems to come with a special mental toughness."

"I don't know," Che'ri said, her eyes focused on something light-years away that only she could see. "I don't feel very tough."

"Well, you are," Thalias said. "Trust me. And for whatever it's worth, most of the things they don't tell you they also don't tell anyone outside the military. Most of what I just said I had to dig out on my own after I left."

"Did you get in trouble?"

"Not really. I got a few warnings, though." Thalias made a show of wrinkling her nose as if in thought. "Though I suppose I might have gotten some *other* people in trouble."

That got her a small, tentative smile. "Did they deserve it?"

"I like to think the galaxy runs on balance," Thalias said. "Those who deserve trouble get it, and those who don't, don't."

"You really think it works that way?"

Thalias huffed out a sigh. "Not even close," she conceded. "Sadly. You hear that?"

Che'ri looked up, frowning. "No."

"Exactly," Thalias said, feeling a small sense of relief. "There haven't been any more shrapnel thuds. I think the battle is over."

"I hope so," Che'ri said, straining her ears. "I hate battles."

"So does everyone else," Thalias said. "Well. There'll probably be some talking now, and Captain Thrawn will let the Lioaoi know he could have flattened their whole planet if he'd wanted to, and then some more talking. Somewhere along in there we'll be called back to the bridge, and you'll start us on the path for home."

"I hope so," Che'ri said, a shiver running through her.

"Trust me," Thalias said. "So that leaves us only two questions."

Che'ri frowned. "Which ones?"

"What you want for dinner," Thalias said, "and whether you want to eat it now or wait until your first break."

MEMORIES X

Recruitment duty, Aristocra Zistalmu reflected as he awaited his visitor, was among the most tedious of tasks a family member could be assigned. Tedious, and usually frustrating. Most of the time, the recruiter didn't even know why that particular person had been chosen.

In this case, at least, Zistalmu knew exactly why Mitth-'raw'nuru had been chosen. And he wondered if the Irizi family had gone completely mad.

The expected tap came at the door, at precisely the specified time. "Come," Zistalmu called.

The panel slid open. "Senior Commander Mitth'raw-'nuru, reporting as requested," his visitor said formally as he stepped into the room.

"Senior Commander Thrawn," Zistalmu said, nodding and gesturing to the chair in front of him. "I'm Aristocra Irizi'stal'mustro."

"Aristocra Zistalmu," Thrawn said, nodding in return as he lowered himself into the indicated chair. "I was surprised to receive your invitation."

"Yes," Zistalmu said, keeping his voice neutral. "I understand you briefly visited the Irizi family homestead a couple of weeks ago."

"Yes," Thrawn said. "I don't recall seeing you there."

"Sadly, the press of Syndicure business prevented me from being at the event," Zistalmu said. "You've made quite a name for yourself over the past few years."

"Sometimes that name is appended to a curse."

At least he recognized how polarizing his career and he himself were. Zistalmu hadn't been sure the man was even *that* self-aware. "Sometimes people don't appreciate your talents and skills," he said. "I understand you've had some problems with certain members of the Mitth family."

Thrawn's eyes narrowed slightly. "I understood that the family still supports me."

"Perhaps," Zistalmu said, the bitter taste of resentment in his mouth. Why the Irizi family wanted this man was beyond him, and why they'd saddled *him* with the recruitment was even more opaque. But he'd been given the job, and there was nothing he could do but see it through. "I simply note that those who feel your exploits reflect badly on the family aren't reluctant to say so."

"I'm sorry they're displeased," Thrawn said. "At the same time, I have to fulfill my duties to the Expansionary Defense Fleet to the best of my ability."

"I don't disagree," Zistalmu said. "But I've asked you here to assure you that, whether or not the Mitth recognize your dedication, the Irizi family certainly does."

"Thank you," Thrawn said, inclining his head. "Though given the tensions between our two families, I doubt your support will help my position."

"I believe the Irizi family was thinking of helping your position more directly."

A frown creased Thrawn's forehead. "How?"

Mentally, Zistalmu shook his head. In the military realm, Thrawn had demonstrated a fair degree of insight and tactical ability. But in the political realm, he might as well have been dropped straight out of the sky. "I'm suggesting that you detach from the Mitth," he said, "and accept a position instead with the Irizi."

"A position as merit adoptive?"

"Not at all," Zistalmu said, bracing himself. This was the most odious part of the whole offer. "That may be good enough for the Mitth, but not the Irizi. We're prepared to offer you the position of Trial-born."

"That's . . . very interesting," Thrawn said, clearly taken aback. "I . . . that's extremely generous."

"It's no more than you deserve," Zistalmu said. That had caught his attention, all right. A merit adoptive brought in via military service automatically lost the relationship when that service ended. A Trial-born not only kept the connection but if deemed worthy could advance to the status of ranking distant, where his bloodline would thereafter be incorporated into the family's. "And of course, coming in at that status means you wouldn't ever need to go through the Trials themselves. Your exemplary service has apparently been deemed an adequate substitute."

"I'm both honored and humbled," Thrawn said. "I'm not certain how my detachment from the Mitth would benefit the Irizi."

"It would serve in many ways," Zistalmu said. "Our overall presence in the military—well, that's a political matter. Nothing you need concern yourself with. Let's just say that we can always use another distinguished high-ranking military officer, and the Irizi believe you're the best choice."

"I see," Thrawn said, nodding slowly, his forehead creased in thought.

Zistalmu held his breath. If this worked—if Thrawn accepted the offer—then it would be finished. The Irizi would have him, and the Mitth wouldn't.

Whether the Irizi would someday regret that was of course another question. But that was their problem. All Zistalmu needed to focus on was how a successful recruitment here and now—whether he agreed with it or not—would raise his own name and prestige within the family.

"I appreciate your interest," Thrawn said. "But I can't make a decision without further thought."

"Think as long as you wish," Zistalmu said, keeping his face neutral, struggling to balance the mix of annoyance, regret, and relief. Was Thrawn really such a fool that he couldn't see how immensely valuable this move would be? "Just bear in mind that if you delay too long, some other up-and-coming officer might catch the family's eye instead."

"I understand," Thrawn said. "Thank you for your time, and for your offer." He stood to go, then paused. "Your comment about distinguished high-ranking officers. It occurs to me that you already have one such in your family: Senior Captain Ziara."

"Yes, we do," Zistalmu said ruefully. "But not, I'm afraid, for much longer."

"Senior Captain Irizi'ar'alani," Supreme Admiral Ja'fosk intoned. "Stand forth."

This was it. Bracing herself, trying to keep her breathing steady, Ziara stepped forward into the center of the flood-lit circle facing Ja'fosk and the other two senior officers.

"State your name," Ja'fosk said in that same death-knell tone.

"Senior Captain Irizi'ar'alani," Ziara said. Was he trying to be intimidating, she wondered, or was that merely a side effect of his ultra-formal voice?

"That person no longer exists," Ja'fosk said. "That name no longer exists. You are no longer of Irizi. You are no longer of any family."

Ziara held his gaze, a knot in her stomach. She'd known this moment was coming for the past week, and had anticipated it for much longer. But even with all that mental preparation, it was an unexpectedly emotional moment. Unlike many Irizi, she'd been born into the family, with no merit challenges, rematches, or Trials to pass. She was a full-blood daughter, with all the privileges and honor that position bestowed.

But not anymore.

"The Ascendancy is your family," Ja'fosk continued. "The Ascendancy is your home. The Ascendancy is your future.

"The Ascendancy is your life."

Ziara had heard those words many times over the past week as she practiced for the ceremony. But not until this moment, hearing them spoken in Ja'fosk's stentorian voice, did they seem real. *The Ascendancy is your life.*

But really, hadn't it always been so? Once she made the decision to join the Defense Force, hadn't she effectively surrendered her future to the greater good of her people?

And having offered her life, was it such a loss to offer also her ties to her family?

"Senior Captain Irizi'ar'alani is no more," Ja'fosk said. He reached to the table behind him and picked up a flat box. "In her place"—he held the box toward her—"now stands Commodore Ar'alani."

Bracing herself, Ziara stepped forward and took the box. Through the transparent lid she saw that it was her new commodore's uniform, blazing white instead of the black one she'd worn throughout her entire career. The insignia pins were already in place on the collar, and where the Irizi family shoulder patch would have been was the multi-circle symbol of the Chiss Ascendancy.

"Do you accept this uniform and this new life?" Ja'fosk asked.

Ziara took a deep breath. No; not Ziara. Not anymore. "I do," Ar'alani said.

Ja'fosk bowed his head . . . and as he did so, Ar'alani thought she detected a small, slightly bittersweet smile.

Remembering, perhaps, when he himself had stood in her place. And had lost his own family.

Ar'alani's promotion celebration party was winding down, and the crowds of well-wishers had dwindled to a lingering few, when Thrawn finally made his appearance.

"Congratulations, Commodore," he said, inclining his head to her. "You'll remember I said you'd be here one day."

"Actually, as I recall, you suggested I'd someday make admiral," Ar'alani reminded him. "I still have a ways to go."

"You'll make it," Thrawn said. "I understand you've been assigned the *Destrama* and Picket Force Six."

"I have," Ar'alani confirmed. "I've also requested that you be made my first officer."

"Really," Thrawn said, clearly surprised. "I thought your babysitting duties had ended."

"You think you were aboard the *Parala* because General Ba'kif wanted me to look after you?"

"I think it was more a matter of wanting you to make sure I didn't go off the edge." Thrawn paused. "Again."

"There may have been a bit of that," Ar'alani conceded. "But that's not really relevant. I asked for you because you're a good officer." She smiled faintly. "I also suspect there'll be a promotion for you somewhere along the way."

"Thank you," Thrawn said. "I'll try not to make you regret your decision." He hesitated. "I'm in need of advice, Commodore, if you have a moment to spare."

"For you, what moments I can't spare I'll make," she said, glancing past his shoulder. None of the other guests were close enough to hear. "And when it's just the two of us, it can just be Thrawn and Ar'alani."

He gave a sort of hesitant smile. "Thank you. That's . . . I'm honored."

She smiled back. "So. What do you need?"

"I was recently approached by one of the Irizi," he said, lowering his voice a little. "He said that some of the Mitth are unhappy with me, and may try to have me released."

Ar'alani's first instinct was to deflect the conversation elsewhere. Family politics were always a touchy subject.

But she didn't *have* any family politics. Not anymore. "What was his name?"

"Aristocra Irizi'stal'mustro."

Ar'alani nodded. "Zistalmu. Never met him, but I know of him. Let me guess: He thought you should request to join the Irizi instead?"

"Actually, his tone and phrasings suggested that the rematching was already a given," Thrawn said. "There was certainly no mention of interviews or other barriers to my acceptance. He also suggested I would be a Trial-born instead of a merit adoptive."

"Interesting," Ar'alani said. "You say all this was suggested, but not stated outright?"

"There wasn't any formal invitation, if that's what you mean."

"It is." Ar'alani pursed her lips, her gaze drifting around the room. The two Irizi who'd been here earlier were long gone, with only a few of the minor families still represented. "Okay, here's the relevant history. The Irizi have always been strong supporters of the military, particularly the Defense Force. They like having family in the upper ranks—feel it buys them additional prestige, which is of course one of the currencies among the Aristocra."

"Prestige is a currency?"

"Of a sort," Ar'alani said. "There are a whole lot of things that factor into a family's position and power. Some of them are financial or historical; others are more nebulous, like prestige and reputation."

"I see," Thrawn said, though Ar'alani was pretty sure from his expression that he didn't. "What does this have to do with the Mitth and me?"

"The Mitth are overall in a stronger position than the Irizi, at least at the moment," Ar'alani said. "Over the past few years, the Mitth have also tried to cut into the Irizi military strength by recruiting promising cadets and officers."

"Such as me?"

"Very likely," Ar'alani said. "It was clear all the way back at the Academy that you had a strong career ahead of you. The point is that, perhaps a bit belatedly, the Irizi have recognized your potential and are hoping to steal you from the Mitth."

"Do you think he was right about the Mitth wanting to rematch me?"

Ar'alani shook her head. "Impossible to say. I don't have a feel for Mitth politics and structure the way I do with the Irizi. I'd guess that if you can avoid doing anything . . . controversial . . . in the future, you should be all right. Merit adoptives are always on probation until they've proved themselves. But once they do, and once they've passed the Trials, they'll hold a much more secure status. And of course, if and when you're elevated to ranking distant, you'll be largely untouchable."

"I see," Thrawn said. "Yet if the Irizi are more military-minded, would they perhaps not be a better family for me?"

Ar'alani hesitated. *No family. No family.* "In all honesty, I've never been comfortable with the way the Irizi dominate Defense Force personnel. I know we're supposed to ignore family identity as we serve, but we've all seen rivalries bleed over into conversation and even duty assignments."

"So you'd recommend I stay with the Mitth?"

"That's a decision you have to make for yourself," Ar'alani said. "Being blood of the Irizi was very good for my career, and the family's done the same for many others. But what was good for me may not be good for you."

"I understand," Thrawn said. "Thank you. I owe you a debt."

"You're welcome." Ar'alani dared a smile. "And not just one, you know. I like to think I contributed my small bit to keeping you in the academy over that cheating charge."

"Your contribution was far larger than you perhaps remember," Thrawn assured her. "And your assistance has hardly been limited to the distant past. I never properly thanked you for your support in the aftermath of the Stivic incident."

"My support was completely unnecessary," Ar'alani said, looking him squarely in the eye. "The Garwians have stated on the record that it was Security Officer Frangelic who spotted the weakness of the pirates' tactics and found a way to exploit it. From the way they were raving about him, he's probably been promoted by now."

"And he richly deserves whatever accolades he's received."

"Agreed." Ar'alani cocked her head. "Just out of curiosity, I looked into it afterward, and I couldn't find an obvious way to tie a comm into a ranging laser."

"There isn't," Thrawn said. "But there's a spot where a questis can be linked for data downloading and analysis."

"And connectors like that can usually run either direction," Ar'alani said, nodding. "So you tied your questis into the laser's frequency-modulation option and used voice-to-script?"

"Just script," Thrawn said. "If there was an inquiry afterward, having a voice recording would narrow the search a bit too much."

Ar'alani nodded again. "The Garwians owe you. I hope they realize that."

"I didn't do it for their gratitude," Thrawn said, sounding a bit surprised that Ar'alani would even think of it in those terms. "I did it for the good of their people, and for all who would otherwise have faced those same attackers."

"A high-minded goal," Ar'alani said. "I wish the Ascendancy appreciated it more."

Thrawn smiled. "Nor did I do it for our gratitude."

"Indeed." Again, Ar'alani looked over his shoulder. Still six people lingering, but they were engrossed in conversation with one another and would never miss her. "Tell you what. Let's go someplace a little quieter, and you can buy me a celebratory drink."

She touched his arm. "And while we drink," she said, "you can tell me all the other goals you have that the Ascendancy will pretend not to be grateful for."

CHAPTER SIXTEEN

The bluedock foreman shook his head as he ran to the end of the listing. "I don't know what it is with you folk," he said. "This is the second time in two months. Do you *deliberately* run into the middle of your battles?"

"Of course not," Samakro said stiffly. "It's hardly the *Springhawk*'s fault if the Council and Aristocra keep sending us out into the Chaos to fight people."

"It's hardly their fault if you don't win the battles faster, either," the foreman countered, half turning to peer out the viewport at the *Springhawk* floating nearby, silhouetted against the blue-white disk of the frozen Csilla surface filling half the sky.

"We won it fast enough," Samakro assured him. "And let's not get overly dramatic, shall we? There's not *that* much damage."

"You don't think so?" the foreman said sourly. "Well, I suppose that's why *you're* out there running into missile salvos and *I'm* in here putting your ship back together." He lifted a finger. "Sensor nodes needing replacement: seven. Hull plates needing replacement: eighty-two. Spectrum lasers needing repair or refurbishment: five. And what's this nonsense about adding an extra tank of plasma sphere fluid?"

"We use a lot of plasma spheres."

"And where exactly does Senior Captain Thrawn suggest I put it?" the foreman retorted. "His quarters? *Your* quarters?"

"I have no idea," Samakro said. "That's why you're in here performing maintenance miracles and we're out there making people regret tangling with the Chiss Ascendancy."

"This would *take* a miracle," the foreman grumbled, looking at the questis again. Still, he seemed pleased by Samakro's small compliment. "The least he could do is come ask for these miracles in person."

"He's in consultation with General Ba'kif right now."

The foreman sniffed. "No doubt planning his next foray into trouble. Fine. I'll get started on the rest of this, and see if I can find enough space somewhere for this impossible plasma tank he wants."

"If anyone can do it, you can," Samakro assured him. "What kind of time frame are we looking at?"

"At least six weeks, maybe seven," the foreman said. "If I get a rush order from Ba'kif or Supreme Admiral Ja'fosk, I can maybe slice a week off that."

"Well, go ahead and get started, and I'll see about getting you that rush order," Samakro said. "Thank you."

"Thank me by *not* wrecking your ship next time."

"What, and make the Council wonder if they still need people like you?" Samakro asked blandly.

"I'd love to see the Council try their hand at this job," the foreman said. "The Ascendancy would never fly again. Go on, get out of here—I've got work to do."

Fifteen minutes later, Samakro was on a shuttle heading for the surface.

A hard knot in his stomach.

Do you deliberately run into the middle of your battles? the foreman had asked. Samakro had waved off the sarcasm . . . but in the core of his heart he wasn't nearly that certain. There'd been at least two times during the Lioaoin skirmish, maybe three, when Thrawn had taken the *Springhawk* far deeper into the enemy fire zone than he'd had to. Nearly all of the damage the foreman had groused about had come from those particular sorties.

Had Thrawn been trying to glean additional information on the new Lioaoin tactics, as he'd claimed? Or was it possible he was starting to lose the judgment and tactical insight that had raised his name to such prominence?

Thrawn had implied he'd initiated his current meeting with Ba'kif. But maybe it was the other way around. Maybe Ba'kif had noticed the same troubling subtext in the after-action reports and was having some of the same doubts as Samakro. Maybe he'd called Thrawn in to find out what was going on.

And if the general decided Thrawn was no longer capable of commanding the *Springhawk* . . .

Samakro took a deep breath. *Stop it,* he ordered himself. Even if Thrawn was relieved of command, that didn't necessarily mean Samakro would be restored to it. The *Springhawk* still had an important name, and the Ufsa family wasn't the only one who would love to have one of their own in charge.

Still, it was an interesting thought.

"An interesting thought," General Ba'kif said, pursing his lips. "The question is whether that thought is dangerously inspired or merely criminally insane."

"I don't see why either adjective has to be attached, sir," Thrawn said, his voice carrying his usual mix of respect and confidence. "The small scout ship I'm proposing—"

"You *don't*?" Ba'kif interrupted.

"No, sir," Thrawn said calmly. "A scout ship could easily slip the three of us past any sentries or watchers General Yiv might have placed along the way. The data we collect would not only give us a better idea of how large this so-named Nikardun Destiny is, but also offer hints as to how solidly those behind Yiv's battle line are being held and controlled."

"To what end?"

"There are several possibilities," Thrawn said. "We might be able to foment revolt among some of them—"

"Preemptive action," Ba'kif interrupted again. "Never get past the Syndicure."

"—or possibly lease bases or supply depots from them—"

"More preemptive action."

"—or, if there are unconquered peoples scattered among them, we might learn how they were able to resist the Nikardun."

Ba'kif frowned thoughtfully. That last could indeed be quite instructive. Even better, a straightforward data-gathering mission wouldn't generate nearly as much outrage among the Aristocra as Thrawn's other suggestions.

But even there, the whole thing was swimming in risk and uncertainty. "Independence and resistance are a difficult combination to maintain," he pointed out. "Any halfway-competent conqueror would never permit it."

"Unless Yiv isn't aware of the situation," Thrawn said. "In fact, as you suggest, that's probably the only way such a situation *could* continue."

"So independence, resistance, and vacuum-tight secrecy," Ba'kif said. "The odds against these theoretical allies existing are getting rather tall. Do you need anything else from them? Proficiency in small arms, maybe?"

"No, nothing else," Thrawn said. Either he hadn't noticed Ba'kif's sarcasm or had chosen to ignore it. "We can find a way to work with whatever other skills they might possess. The primary focus now has to be on finding them."

"*If* they exist."

"If they exist," Thrawn conceded. "At any rate, I've already spoken to Caregiver Thalias and Sky-walker Che'ri, and both have indicated willingness to go with me."

"You spoke of confidential matters to unauthorized personnel?" Ba'kif asked, hearing his tone go ominous.

"Sky-walkers and their caregivers know many things even senior officers sometimes don't," Thrawn said. "That said, no, I offered no restricted information. I merely posed the question of whether they would accompany me on a long-distance journey of unspecified destination and purpose."

For a few seconds Ba'kif gazed at him, weighing the options, considering the possibilities, assessing the risks. Nothing about this mad scheme exactly filled him with confidence.

But if the information Thrawn and Ar'alani had brought back about the quiet infiltration of the Nikardun was even halfway accurate, *something* had to be done. And the quicker, the better.

"There are members of the Syndicure who consider you an ungimbaled laser," he said, pushing the questis back toward Thrawn. "There are times I'm inclined to agree with them."

"The Nikardun are a serious threat, General," Thrawn said quietly. "Possibly the most serious the Ascendancy has faced in recent history. General Yiv is competent and charismatic, with the ability to both conquer and enlist those in his path."

"And if we find these potential allies you're hoping for? How do you propose an alliance to a Syndicure that has refused all such entanglements for centuries?"

"Let's first find them," Thrawn said. "We'll deal with the Aristocra if and when we have to."

Ba'kif sighed. *Ungimbaled laser* . . . "You're sure you won't be missed?"

Thrawn nodded. "Mid Captain Samakro is overseeing the *Springhawk*'s repairs. It requires enough work to keep it in bluedock for at least six weeks."

"How did you arrange that much damage?" Ba'kif held up a hand. "Never mind. All right, I'll have a scout ship assigned to you and get it prepped. But not a word to either Thalias or Che'ri about your actual mission until you're under way. Understood?"

"Understood."

"One final consideration, then," Ba'kif said, putting the full weight of his long career into his voice. "You're not only putting yourself at risk, but also risking the lives of the two women, one of them an immensely valuable sky-walker. If the whole thing goes crash-dive, are you prepared to have their deaths on your conscience?"

"I'm aware of the danger," Thrawn said. "I would never want the weight of such memories and regrets. But I'm more prepared to see their deaths through my action than I am to put the entire Ascendancy at the same risk through my inaction."

Ba'kif nodded. He'd thought Thrawn's answer would be something like that. And unfortunately, he had to agree with him. "The ship will be ready by the time you've collected your fellow travelers and your supplies," he said. "Your orders will be cut but sealed. No one will know about your mission but me."

"Thank you, sir," Thrawn said, standing up. "Thank you, too, for not adding the extra burden of a reminder that your career is also on the line."

"You worry about your sky-walker and the Ascendancy," Ba'kif growled. "*I'll* worry about my career. Now get out of here. And may warrior's fortune smile on your efforts."

"I wonder what they're talking about," Che'ri murmured, looking up from her questis and the picture she'd been drawing. She craned her neck toward General Ba'kif's closed office door, halfway down the busy corridor, as if moving her head a couple of centimeters closer would magically give her the ability to see or hear through it.

"I don't know," Thalias said, resisting the impulse to remind the girl that she'd made that same half-question comment twice already, and that the answer wasn't going to change until Thrawn came through the doorway.

But the topic of the unheard conversation wasn't hard to guess. Thrawn's vague question about whether she and Che'ri would be willing to go with him on a special mission would have been intriguing enough even if it hadn't immediately been followed by this meeting with Ba'kif. But it *had* been followed by the meeting, and the only reasonable conclusion was that the two of them were discussing the details of that mission.

"They're coming," Che'ri said suddenly.

Thalias looked at the still-unopened door, feeling a touch of bittersweet memory. Back when she was Che'ri's age, she'd been able to do that same trick, using Third Sight to know a couple of seconds in advance when something was about to happen. Most people—at least those who knew what sky-walkers were—took the whole thing in stride. But there'd been a few others who'd never gotten used to it. Freaking them out was half the fun of doing the trick.

The door opened, and Thrawn emerged. Ba'kif followed, but stopped in the doorway, and for a moment the two men held a final bit of inaudible conversation. Thrawn nodded at last and started down the corridor toward Thalias and Che'ri—

"Good afternoon, Caregiver Thalias."

Thalias turned. Syndic Thurfian was standing there, smiling the smile she'd seen on him way too many times. The look was never a genuinely friendly one, and it was nearly always the prelude to bad news. "Good afternoon, Syndic," she replied. "What can I do for you?"

"I wonder if you'd be good enough to come to my office for a few minutes," Thurfian said. "There's a matter I'd like to discuss with you."

Thalias felt her stomach tightening. *No—not now.* Of all the times he could have chosen. "I'm sorry, but my commander is on his way," she said, keeping her tone neutral as she nodded back toward Thrawn. "I'm certain he has some official duty for us."

"*I'm* quite certain he hasn't," Thurfian said, still smiling. "Apparently you've forgotten that your ship has gone into bluedock for some fairly extensive repairs. Unless General Ba'kif has dug up a spare ship, Senior Captain Thrawn can't possibly need you."

"You might be surprised at Captain Thrawn's ingenuity," Thalias said, feeling sweat gathering under her collar. It was now, all right. The worst possible time, and so of course he'd chosen it. "At any rate, I'm under his command, not yours."

"Well, let's ask him, then, shall we?" Thurfian shifted his gaze over Thalias's shoulder. "Senior Captain Thrawn," he said, his voice holding the same false cheer as his smile. "I need to borrow your caregiver for an hour or so. Surely you have no objection?"

"None at all," Thrawn said, his eyes flicking briefly to Thalias. "I presume you won't also need Che'ri?"

A hint of a frown touched Thurfian's face. "No, I just need Thalias. Why would I need Che'ri?"

"I don't know," Thrawn said. "That's why I asked. I'm glad you don't need her, as she's fallen slightly behind in her studies. I expect the *Springhawk*'s repair schedule will give her time to catch up."

Thurfian's frown disappeared. "Ah. Of course."

"I should be there to help her," Thalias said doggedly, trying to think. If she couldn't find a way out of this—

"This won't take long," Thurfian promised. "Until later, Captain Thrawn."

"Until later," Thrawn answered.

The Syndicure complex was about a hundred kilometers from fleet headquarters, a short twenty-minute trip by tunnel car. Neither Thalias nor Thurfian spoke during the journey, mindful of the half dozen other officers and Aristocra in the car who might overhear any conversation.

They were nearly to the end of their journey when Thalias finally came up with a plan.

Not a good plan. Probably even a desperate one. But it was all she had.

It took two minutes in the privacy of the restroom for her to set things in motion. Two minutes of time, and way more courage than she thought she possessed. But then it was done, and she was committed, and she could only hope she hadn't brought complete ruin upon herself.

They arrived and, still in silence, Thurfian walked her down the corridors of Ascendancy power to his office.

"All right, I'm here," she said as Thurfian ushered her into his office and motioned her to a chair. "What's this all about?"

"Oh, please," Thurfian protested mildly. Closing the door, he circled behind her and sat down at his desk. "Don't pretend you don't know what this is about. You promised me a report. It's time to deliver."

He activated a questis and pushed it across the desk to her. "Tell me everything you know, everything you've learned—*everything*—about Senior Captain Thrawn."

For a long minute the young woman just sat there, her face rigid, her body unnaturally still. Seeking, no doubt, a way out of the trap.

The trap she'd stepped into of her own free will, of course. It was either that promise, or Thurfian would have turned around, walked back into the personnel office, and canceled her appointment as the *Springhawk*'s sky-walker's caregiver. With a threat like that hanging over her, she'd had no choice but to agree.

But it hadn't been willingly. Not by a long shot. Even now, as he looked at her expression and body stance, it was clear she was hoping to get out of the deal.

Too bad. Her hopes didn't matter, nor did her reticence. All that mattered was that Thrawn was up to something new, and Thurfian was getting tired of his antics. He needed a lever he could use against the maverick, and Thalias's detailed knowledge of Thrawn's other recent activities was that lever. "Come, come—we haven't got all day," he said into the taut silence. "The sooner you finish, the sooner you can go back to fawning over your big hero."

"I assumed this would wait until the entire campaign was over," Thalias said, making no move toward the questis.

"I never gave you any sort of timetable," Thurfian reminded her. "The deal was very clear: I would get you aboard the *Springhawk*, and you would be my spy."

Thalias flinched visibly at the word. Thurfian didn't care about that, either. "Everything you need to know about Senior Captain Thrawn is in the official records," she said. "Once you've read them, I can answer any other questions you have."

"I *have* read them," Thurfian countered. "And you're stalling."

"Not stalling," Thalias said, standing up. "It just so happens I have an appointment elsewhere. If you'll excuse me—"

"Sit down," Thurfian said, putting all the coldness of Csilla's surface into his voice. "You don't wish to talk about Thrawn? Very well. Let's talk about your family."

"Don't you mean *our* family?"

"I mean your original family," Thurfian said. "The family who bore you, and who held your allegiance before you were taken away from them to become a sky-walker."

Thalias paused, standing halfway between her chair and the door, a whole play of emotions skittering across her face. She had no memory of those years, Thurfian knew, which made this the ideal additional lever to use against her. "What about them?" she asked at last.

Thurfian hid a smile. She was trying to sound calm and uninterested, but the tight muscles in her throat and cheeks gave away her sudden interest and uncertainty. "I thought you might like to hear about their current situation," he said. "And how you could perhaps help them." He paused, waiting for her to respond.

But she remained silent. A cool character, for sure, who wouldn't be easily swayed. But Thurfian had had plenty of experience manipulating such people.

"They're not in great shape, you see," he went on. "The family has always been poor, but the recent shift in the prices of certain minerals has pressed particularly hard on them. The Mitth family has many resources, some of which could be turned in their direction."

"I don't even remember them."

"Of course not," Thurfian said. "You were far too young when you were taken. But does that really matter? They're your people. Your blood."

"The Mitth are my people now."

"Perhaps." Thurfian gave a little shrug. "Perhaps not."

Thalias's eyes narrowed. "What's that supposed to mean? I'm a full member of the Mitth."

"Hardly," Thurfian said. "You're a merit adoptive, and a relatively new one at that. You have a long path ahead of you before your position is anything other than precarious."

Thalias looked down at the questis. "Are you suggesting that my position with the Mitth depends on my betrayal of Thrawn?"

"Betrayal? Of course not," Thurfian said, putting some righteous indignation into his voice. "Thrawn is a member of our family"—*at least for the moment,* he reminded himself silently—"and talking about him hardly qualifies as betrayal. On the contrary, not reporting any questionable activities is where betrayal would lie."

"Then let's make this simple," Thalias said. "I've never seen him do anything questionable, illegal, or unethical. I've certainly never seen him do anything against the Mitth. Good enough?"

Thurfian gave a theatrical sigh. "You disappoint me, Thalias. I'd hoped you had a future with the Mitth. But if we can't even trust you to help us keep watch on a potential danger to the family, I can't see how we can keep you with us. But that's your decision. I can keep watch on Thrawn myself."

He raised his eyebrows slightly. "Starting with whatever he's up to right now. I noticed he was talking with General Ba'kif again, so that's probably the best place to start. Perhaps I'll take an hour or two to look into that before I begin your rematching procedure."

Thalias tried to hide her reaction. But it was no use. His offhanded threat to rematch her back to her old family had done the trick. He would give her the next hour to consider what life without the Mitth would be like, and then he would start the procedure.

Abruptly, she pulled out her own questis and peered at it. "All right," she said. "You win."

Again, Thurfian hid his smile of triumph. Really, sometimes it was just too easy. "Excellent," he said, gesturing her back to the chair. "Though as I think further, I wonder if it would be better to head back first for our talk with General Ba'kif. You can begin your report along the way."

"You're right, we're leaving," Thalias agreed. "But not to fleet HQ." She held up her questis. "You're to take me instead to the Mitth homestead."

Thurfian's sense of triumph vanished. "What?" he asked carefully.

"You said it yourself," she said. "I don't have a stable position with the family. So I've made arrangements to remedy that."

"How?" he asked, his blood suddenly running cold. If she denounced his interest in Thrawn to the wrong people . . .

No, that couldn't be it. She couldn't possibly know enough about the labyrinthian web woven around the upper ranks of the family. "If you think there's anyone higher than me you can appeal to—"

"I'm not going to appeal," she said. "I'm going to take the Trials."

He stared at her. "The *Trials*?"

"Merit adoptives can ask at any time to take the Trials," Thalias said. "If they succeed, they become Trial-born."

"Kindly do not lecture me on my own family's policies," Thurfian said stiffly. "And that's only *if* they succeed. If they don't, they lose even merit adoptive status."

"I'm aware of that," Thalias said. There was a slight tremor in her voice, but her jaw was firmly set. "But you were going to throw me out of the family anyway." She lifted the questis again. "I've petitioned the Office of the Patriarch, and the petition's been accepted."

"Fine," Thurfian said between clenched teeth. Curse this woman, anyway. "I'll give you the instructions on how to get to the homestead—"

"The Patriarch's Office has requested that you accompany me."

Thurfian hissed out a curse. The final spiral to his plans. She'd outmaneuvered him completely.

She . . . or Thrawn.

Could he have anticipated this confrontation? Certainly Thalias couldn't have come up with such a dangerous scheme on her own. And if it was Thrawn, how had he persuaded her to risk her entire future with the Mitth for him?

Just one more reason this man needed to be taken down.

"Of course," he said, standing up. "I wouldn't miss it for all the riches in the Ascendancy."

Che'ri had never been good at reading adult faces. But even so, she had no trouble seeing that Thrawn was surprised and concerned as he put away his questis. "Is something wrong?" she asked anxiously.

He hesitated a moment before answering. "It appears Caregiver Thalias won't be joining us," he said.

"Oh," Che'ri said, looking past him at the little ship he'd brought them to. The last of the crates of supplies were just being taken aboard by the dockworkers, and he'd said they'd be leaving as soon as Thalias arrived.

Only now they weren't? "So what are we doing?"

Thrawn turned to gaze at the ship. "This mission is vitally important, Che'ri," he said quietly. "Thalias didn't say much—I gather she wasn't free to talk openly—but it was clear she would be occupied for at least the next few days."

"So we're not going?" Che'ri asked, still struggling to read his expression.

"That depends on you." He turned to look at her. "Are you willing to go with me, just the two of us, into the depths of the Chaos?"

For a moment Che'ri's mouth and tongue and brain seemed frozen. A sky-walker never went anywhere without a shipful of people around her. That was the first rule and promise she'd been given when she first began her training. Girls like her were too rare to risk to anything less than a full warship or diplomatic cruiser. What Thrawn was asking was never done. Ever.

But he'd said it was important. Could it be important enough to break all the regular rules? "Can we do that?" she asked hesitantly.

He shrugged, a small smile touching his lips. "Physically and tactically, of course," he said. "I can fly, you can navigate, and the ship itself is well enough armed to get us out of any trouble we're likely to find ourselves in."

"I meant are we going to get in trouble."

"You, no," he said. "Sky-walkers are effectively untouchable by any punishment. You might get a scolding, but that would be all." He paused. "If it makes a difference, Thalias didn't suggest that we wait for her, or that we abandon the mission completely."

"If I don't go, what happens?"

"Then I abandon the mission," Thrawn said. "What would take days under the control of a sky-walker would require weeks or months of jump-by-jump travel. I can't afford months." His lips compressed. "Neither, I fear, can the Ascendancy."

This game, at least, Che'ri knew way too well. An adult would make vague threats or vaguer promises, with big stuff happening either way if she didn't run for the extra hour or skip one of her rest days or do whatever it was they wanted.

But as she gazed at Thrawn's face, she had the eerie sense that he wasn't playing the game. In fact, she wasn't sure he even knew *how* to play it.

And if Thalias really was expecting her to go . . .

"Okay," she said. "Can you—? Never mind."

"What?"

"I just wondered if you could get me some more colored graph markers, that's all," Che'ri said, feeling her face warming with embarrassment. Of all the stupid things to ask for—

"As a matter of fact," Thrawn said, "there are two new boxes already aboard. *And* four binders of art sheets to draw on."

Che'ri blinked. "Oh," she said. "I'm—thank you."

"You're welcome." Thrawn gestured toward the ship. "Shall we go?"

"You're troubled," Thrawn said into the silence of the scout ship's bridge.

Che'ri didn't answer, her eyes focused on the brilliant stars blazing through the canopy, her mind churning with the sheer *wrongness* of this.

Sky-walkers didn't fly alone. Ever. She'd always had a momish along, someone to take care of her and make her meals and comfort her when she woke from a nightmare. Always.

Thalias wasn't here. Che'ri had hoped she would rush in at the last moment and demand that Thrawn take her with them.

But the hatch had been sealed, and the controller had given permission to launch, and Thrawn had taken them out of the cold blue of Csilla's atmosphere into the colder black of space.

Just the two of them. No officers. No warriors.

No momish.

Che'ri hadn't always gotten along with her caregivers. Some of them she'd really, really disliked. Now she was wishing even one of the rotten ones was here.

"They've never understood you, have they?" Thrawn said into her silence.

Che'ri made a face. Like he would know anything about that.

"You want more than what you've been given," he continued. "You don't know what you'll do when you're no longer a sky-walker, and it troubles you."

"I know what happens," Che'ri scoffed. "They told me. I get adopted by a family."

"That's what you'll *be*," Thrawn said. "That's not what you'll *do*. You'd like to fly, wouldn't you?"

Che'ri frowned. "How did you know that?"

"The pictures you've been drawing with the markers your caregiver gave you," Thrawn said. "You like drawing birds and flashflies."

"They're pretty," Che'ri said stiffly. "Lots of kids draw flashflies."

"You also draw landscapes and seascapes as seen from above," Thrawn continued calmly. "Not many your age do that."

"I'm a sky-walker," Che'ri muttered. Thalias had no business showing Thrawn her pictures. "I see things from the sky all the time."

"Actually, you don't." Thrawn paused and touched a key on his control board.

And suddenly all the lights and keys on his board went out and the board in front of Che'ri lit up.

She jerked back. What in the name—?

"There are two handgrips in front of you," Thrawn said. "Take one in each hand."

"What?" Che'ri asked, staring numbly at the handgrips and glowing lights.

"I'm going to teach you how to fly," Thrawn told her. "This is your first lesson."

"You don't understand," Che'ri said, hearing the fear and pleading in her voice. "I have nightmares about this."

"Nightmares about flying?"

"About falling," Che'ri said, her heart thudding. "Falling, being blown around by wind, drowning—"

"Can you swim?"

"No," Che'ri said. "Maybe a little."

"Exactly," Thrawn said. "It's fear that's driving those nightmares. Fear and helplessness."

A touch of annoyance rose above the bubbling panic. First Thalias, and now Thrawn. Did *everyone* think they knew more about her nightmares than she did?

"You feel helpless in the water, so you dream of drowning. You feel helpless in the air, so you dream of falling." He pointed to the handgrips. "Let's take some of that helplessness away."

Che'ri looked at him. He wasn't joking, she realized. He was deadly serious. She looked back at the handgrips, trying to decide what to do.

"Take them."

Abruptly, she realized something else. He wasn't ordering. He was offering.

And she really *had* always wanted to fly.

Setting her jaw, choking back the fear, she reached out and gingerly closed her hands around the grips.

"Good," Thrawn said. "Move the right one to your left, just a bit."

"To portside," Che'ri corrected. She knew that one, anyway.

"To portside," Thrawn agreed with a smile. "See how the positions of the stars changed?"

Che'ri nodded. Their ship had turned a little to the left, the same way she'd moved the handgrip. "Yes."

"The display just above it—there—shows the precise angle of your turn. Now move the same lever forward a bit."

This time, the changing stars showed the ship's nose had dropped a little. "Aren't we getting off course?"

"It'll be easy enough to get back," Thrawn assured her. "Now, the left-hand grip controls the thrusters. Right now it's set at its most delicate level, so that a small movement translates to a small increase or decrease in thrust. Rotating the grip will change that; we won't bother with that right now. Ease it forward—just a little—and note how our speed changes on that display—that one right there."

By the time they finished the lesson, half an hour later, Che'ri's head was spinning. But it was a strangely exciting kind of spin. She hardly noticed any strain over the next few hours as she used Third Sight to guide the ship toward the edge of the Chaos.

When she was done navigating for the day, after they ate dinner together, she asked if he would give her another lesson.

And that night, for the first time she could remember, she had a dream about flying that wasn't a nightmare.

CHAPTER SEVENTEEN

Thrawn had told Che'ri that there was an arc of systems a short distance into the Lesser Space regions outside the Chaos that should be promising. So far, though, the arc had turned out to be a bust.

One of the worlds had looked interesting, but aside from a local patrol force it didn't seem to have any military presence at all. The next three worlds were only sparsely settled, though one of them was at least civilized enough to have a long-range triad transmitter.

But the fifth world . . .

"What are those?" Che'ri asked, staring at the small objects flitting back and forth across the long-range sensor display. They looked like shuttles or missiles or fighter craft, but they seemed hardly big enough for even a pilot, let alone a passenger or two.

"I believe those are robotic combat craft," Thrawn said, his eyes narrowed in concentration as he gazed at the display. "Powered and operated by artificial intelligences called droids."

"They run their warships with *machines*?"

"Some of them, yes," Thrawn said. "Indeed, if the reports are true, one side of the massive war taking place in Lesser Space is largely being waged by such droids."

Che'ri thought about that. "Seems kind of stupid," she said. "What if someone gets into the controls and turns them off? Or gets into the factory and changes all the programming?"

"Or if their intended programming leaves errors and blind spots that can be exploited," Thrawn said. "The desire to minimize warrior deaths is futile if the war is then lost. Increase the focus on Sensor Four, please."

Che'ri nodded and keyed the correct control, a small part of her brain noting with satisfaction how comfortable she'd become in the cockpit over the past few days. Thrawn had turned out to be a much better teacher than she'd expected.

Or maybe she was just a really good learner.

"What do you see there?" Thrawn asked.

Che'ri frowned. There was something weird in the center of the display she'd just adjusted: perfectly round and giving off a strong but alien energy signature. "I don't know," she said. "I've never seen anything like that before."

"I have," Thrawn said thoughtfully. "But the energy shield I saw was aboard a ship. This one appears to be protecting a building."

"It's a *shield*?" Che'ri asked. Now that he mentioned it, it *was* shaped like the shields of the old-time warriors she'd seen pictures of. "Is that like our electrostatic barriers?"

"Same protective function, but much stronger and more versatile," Thrawn said. "The Ascendancy would benefit greatly from that technology."

Che'ri looked sideways at him. He wasn't thinking of trying to go down there, was he? Not with all those robot things buzzing around.

He seemed to sense her look and her sudden fears. "Don't worry, we're not going to charge in on our own," he assured her. "Though with a full complement of decoys aboard, getting through their sentry screen would be trivial. Still, an aerial force implies a similar ground force, and you and I are hardly equipped to deal with that degree of opposition."

"Okay," Che'ri said cautiously. He still had that intense look in his eyes. "So . . . what are we doing?"

"Our mission has always been to find allies," Thrawn said, reaching forward and manipulating one of the sensor controls. "But perhaps we don't need an entire army of them."

"How many people do we need?"

He pointed at one of the other displays. "Let's start with one."

Che'ri blinked in surprise. Centered in the display was another ship, about the same size as theirs. It was floating all dark and silent and low-power, and was clearly watching the same buzzing robot ships she and Thrawn were. "Who's that?"

"No idea," Thrawn said. "But the appearance and energy profile don't match any of the other ships we've seen since leaving the Chaos."

"Doesn't look like the robot ships, either," Che'ri offered.

"Excellent observation," Thrawn said, and Che'ri felt her face warm with satisfaction at the compliment. "It's possible the pilot is scouting for the opposite side of the war. If so, we may have found an ally—there!"

Che'ri stiffened. The other ship's energy profile had suddenly changed. Even as she opened her mouth to ask what was going on, the ship rotated a few degrees, and with a flicker it disappeared into hyperspace.

"Quickly, now," Thrawn said, and Che'ri's board went dark as he took control. "Get ready for Third Sight."

"We're going after it?"

"Actually, I'm hoping to get ahead of it," Thrawn said, running power to the thrusters and hyperdrive. "The first world we visited was the most populous and therefore the most likely place from which to send a message or to rendezvous with allies."

"Wouldn't one of the more empty worlds be better for that?"

"In theory, yes," Thrawn said. "But a scout would want to avoid drawing any more attention than necessary. The fewer the inhabitants, the more scrutiny is automatically attached to strangers."

"Okay," Che'ri said, making a face as she activated the navigator board. By the time they were ready, the other ship would have a good ten-minute lead on them. How did Thrawn think she could get ahead of it?

"It'll be all right if we arrive second," Thrawn said. "But even with their lead, I have no doubt we'll arrive first. A ship that size is unlikely to have a hyperdrive and navigational system equal to a Chiss ship and a Chiss sky-walker."

Che'ri hunched her shoulders once as she got a grip on the controls. Darn right. They were Chiss, and they were *not* going to lose a race. Not to *anyone*. "I'm ready," she said. "Tell me when."

Che'ri's first thought when she came out of her Third Sight trance was that she'd lost. The other ship was nowhere to be seen: not approaching the planet, not in orbit around it. She sighed, pressing her hand to her throbbing head. She'd tried so hard, but—

"There," Thrawn said.

Che'ri felt her eyes widen, her headache instantly forgotten. He was right. The ship they'd seen watching the robot craft had just emerged from hyperspace. "What do we do now?"

"Let's see if they're interested in talking." He keyed the comm. "Unidentified ship, this is Senior Captain Mitth'raw'nuruodo of the Chiss Ascendancy," he said in Minnisiat. "Can you understand me?"

Silence. Thrawn repeated the greeting in Taarja, then in Meese Caulf, then Sy Bisti. Che'ri was trying to remember if there were any more trade languages she'd ever heard of when there was an answering ping from the comm. "Hello, Senior Captain Mitth'raw'nuruodo," a woman's voice came in Meese Caulf. "What can I do for you?"

"It is considered courteous for one party of a conversation to offer his or her name to the other," Thrawn said.

"You think we're going to have a conversation?"

"We seem to be doing so," Thrawn pointed out.

There was a short pause. The other ship, Che'ri noted, was heading toward the planet, without any hint that the pilot might be interested in a closer look at the Chiss visitor. "Call me Duja," the woman said. "My turn. Does the Chiss Ascendancy favor the Republic or the Separatists?"

"Neither," Thrawn said. "We take no side in this war of yours."

"Then I see no reason to talk to you. No offense," Duja said. "You haven't seen a Nubian ship land lately, have you?"

"What does it look like?"

"Shiny silvery metal," Duja said. "Smooth curves, no angles, twin engine pods."

"We have not seen it."

"Conversation over, then," Duja said. "Nice talking to you." There was another ping as she shut off the connection.

Che'ri looked at Thrawn, expecting him to call Duja back and try to persuade her, maybe offer to work together. But to her surprise, he merely closed down the comm. "You're just letting her go?" she asked.

"She's not a warrior," Thrawn said, his voice thoughtful. "A scout, perhaps a spy, clearly someone with training. But not a warrior."

"How do you know she's had training?"

"Her ship is armed," he said, "and as we spoke she rotated slightly so the weapons could be more quickly brought to bear if necessary."

"Oh," Che'ri said. She hadn't seen any of that. "What do we do?"

"We wait," he said. "As I said, she's a scout or a spy. Sooner or later, a warrior will come."

The warrior Che'ri and Thrawn were waiting for, it seemed, was in no great hurry.

Thrawn and Che'ri had been waiting three days when the silvery ship Duja had talked about appeared. It disappeared into the trees a fair distance from a settlement built in and around a group of black stone or wooden spires. A few hours later, Duja's ship rose from the forest and headed away, pursued briefly and uselessly by a couple of the planet's patrol ships. Che'ri waited for the Nubian to follow it, but the big silver ship remained hidden.

And then, again, nothing. Thrawn spent the days studying all the information he could find on the planet—which Che'ri learned was named *Batuu*—and giving Che'ri more piloting exercises with the control board in simulator mode. Che'ri, for her part, ran the exercises over and over, and over and over again. Thrawn hadn't actually said so, but she had a strong suspicion that when the expected war-

rior arrived Thrawn would be leaving the scout ship in her hands.
When that happened, she was determined not to let him down.

And then, even as Che'ri was privately about to give up hope, he
was there.

"Unidentified ship, this is General Anakin Skywalker of the Galactic
Republic," the pilot said over the scout ship's speaker, the Meese
Caulf words a little mangled but mostly correct. "You are intruding
on Republic equipment and interfering with a Republic mission. I
order you to pull back and identify yourself."

"I greet you," Thrawn said in turn. "Did you give your name as
General *Skywalker*?"

"I did. Why, have you heard of me?"

Thrawn caught Che'ri's eye as he touched the MUTE button. "Interesting coincidence," he commented.

Che'ri nodded. The pilot had spoken the word as if it was his
name, but probably he'd just messed up the language.

Thrawn unmuted the comm. "No, not at all," he said. "I was merely
surprised. Let me assure you I mean no harm to you or your equipment. I merely wished a closer look at this interesting device."

"Glad to hear it," the pilot said. "You've had your look. Pull back as
ordered."

Thrawn pursed his lips thoughtfully. Then, very deliberately, he
eased the ship back from the ring they'd moved up to examine. "May
I ask what brings a Republic envoy to this part of space?" he asked.

"May I ask what business it is of yours?" the pilot countered. "You
can be on your way at any time."

"On my way?"

"To continue your travels. To go wherever you were going before
you stopped to look at my hyperdrive ring."

Again, Thrawn touched MUTE. "Opinion?"

Che'ri blinked. He was asking her opinion on this? *Her* opinion?
"I don't know anything about things like this."

"You're a Chiss," Thrawn reminded her. "As such, you have instincts and judgment, perhaps more than you know. Do you think he'll make a good ally?"

Che'ri crinkled her nose. She'd never met this person. She'd barely even heard him speak.

Yet she could sense confidence in him, and strength, and commitment. "Yes," she said. "I do."

Thrawn nodded and unmuted the comm. "Yes, I could continue on my way," he said. "But it might be more useful for me to assist you in your quest."

"I already told you I was on a Republic mission. It's not a quest."

"Yes, I recall your words," Thrawn said. "But I find it hard to believe that a Republic at war would send a lone man in a lone fighter craft on a mission. I find it more likely that you travel on a personal quest."

"I'm on a mission," the pilot insisted. "Directly ordered here by Supreme Chancellor Palpatine himself. And I don't have time for this."

"Agreed," Thrawn said. "Perhaps it would be best if I were to simply show you the location of the ship you seek."

There was a short pause. "Explain," the pilot said quietly.

"I know where the Nubian ship landed," Thrawn told him. "I know the pilot is missing."

"So you intercepted a private transmission?"

"I have my own sources of information. Like you, I seek information, on that and other matters. Also like you I'm alone, without the resources to successfully investigate. Perhaps in alliance we may find the answers both of us seek."

"Interesting offer. You say it's just the two of us?"

"Yes," Thrawn said. He glanced at Che'ri. "Plus my pilot and your droid, of course."

"You didn't mention your pilot."

"Neither did you mention your droid. Since neither will be joining us in our investigation, I didn't think they entered into the discussion."

"Artoo usually comes with me on missions."

"Indeed?" Thrawn said, cocking an eyebrow. "Interesting. I was unaware that navigational machines had other uses. Do we have an alliance?"

The pilot hesitated. Che'ri motioned, and Thrawn touched MUTE. "The pilot of the other ship is missing?"

"I don't know for certain," Thrawn said. "But the lack of activity suggests that may be the case." He shrugged slightly. "Besides, General Skywalker clearly cares about him or her. Raising the level of urgency should help him make up his mind."

"So what answers are *you* looking for?" Skywalker said.

Thrawn touched the key. "I wish to more fully understand this conflict in which you're embroiled. I wish answers of right and wrong, of order and chaos, of strength and weakness, of purpose and reaction." Again, Thrawn looked at Che'ri; and then, suddenly, he straightened up a bit in his seat. "You asked my identity. I am now prepared to give it. I am Commander Mitth'raw'nuruodo, officer of the Expansionary Defense Fleet, servant of the Chiss Ascendancy. On behalf of my people, I ask your assistance in learning of this war before it sweeps its disaster over our own worlds."

Che'ri frowned. *Commander?* She thought he was a senior captain. Had he been demoted?

Probably not. More likely he was just downplaying his rank for some reason, maybe so General Skywalker wouldn't feel threatened by Thrawn's more extensive military experience. Certainly Skywalker sounded a lot younger than Thrawn.

"I see," Skywalker said. "Very well. On behalf of Chancellor Palpatine and the Galactic Republic, I accept your offer."

"Excellent," Thrawn said. "Perhaps you will begin by telling me the true story of your quest."

"I thought you already knew. You know about Padmé's ship."

"The Nubian?" Thrawn shrugged. "The design and power system were unlike anything else I've seen in this region. Your craft displays similar characteristics. It was logical that one visiting stranger was seeking the other."

"Ah. You're right, the Nubian is one of ours. It carried a Republic ambassador who came here to collect information from an informant. When she failed to contact us, I was sent to look for her."

Che'ri frowned. Was Duja the informant Skywalker was talking about? In that case, shouldn't they tell him that she'd already left Batuu?

"I see," Thrawn said. "Was this informant trustworthy?"

"Yes."

"You are certain of that?"

"The ambassador was."

"Then betrayal is unlikely. Has the informant contacted you?"

"No."

"In that case, the most likely scenarios are accident or capture. We need to travel to the surface to determine which it was."

"That's where I was heading when you barged in," Skywalker said. "You said you knew where her ship was?"

"I can send you the location," Thrawn told him. "But it might be more convenient for you to first come aboard. I have a two-passenger shuttle in which we can travel together."

"Thanks, but I'll take my own ship in. Like I said, we might need Artoo down there."

"Very well," Thrawn said. "I'll lead the way."

"Fine. Whenever you're ready."

"I'll make preparations at once," Thrawn said. "One additional thought. Chiss names are difficult for many species to properly pronounce. I suggest you address me by my core name: *Thrawn*."

"That's all right, Mitth'raw'nuruodo. I think I can handle it."

"Mitth'raw'nuruodo."

"That's what I said: Mitth'raw'nuruodo."

"It's pronounced *Mitth'raw'nuruodo*."

"Yes. Mitth'raw'nuruodo."

"Mitth'raw'nuruodo."

It was all Che'ri could do to not break out in giggles. She could hear the difference as well as Thrawn could. But Skywalker clearly didn't get it.

But at least he wasn't stubborn enough to keep kicking at the wall. "Fine," he growled. *"Thrawn."*

"Thank you. It will make things easier. My shuttle is prepared. Let us depart."

He keyed off the comm and began to unstrap. "You'll be all right here alone?" he asked, looking closely at Che'ri.

She swallowed hard. Did she have a choice?

Actually, yes, she realized suddenly, she did. Clearly, Thrawn was willing to back out of the agreement he'd just made if Che'ri asked him to stay with her.

But they'd come out here looking for allies against the Nikardun. Skywalker might be their best hope of that.

She squared her shoulders. "I'm fine," she said. "Tell me what to do."

"Go back to the system with the energy shield," he said. "Stay well clear of the robot ships. When I signal, you're to come down to the place with the energy shield, using decoys to keep the robots away from your course."

"Okay," Che'ri said. She'd only used the decoys in simulations, but it had looked pretty easy. "How many should I use?"

"As many as you need," he said. "In fact, you might as well use them all. If this works as I hope it will, we'll be heading straight back to the Ascendancy, without any need to face other potential threats."

"All right." She took a deep breath. "Are you going to be all right?"

"Of course," he said, smiling confidently. "I'll be armed, and I have every confidence that General Skywalker will be a powerful ally." He looked out the canopy. "But I believe I'll also put on my combat uniform. Just in case."

CHAPTER EIGHTEEN

Even in one of the extra-fast express tunnel cars reserved for Nine Families use, the trip to the Mitth homestead took nearly four hours. During that time Thalias and Thurfian spoke only once, midway through the trip, when Thurfian asked if she wanted anything to eat. She didn't, not because she wasn't a little hungry, but because she didn't want to feel obligated to him. The rest of the trip was made in silence.

Thalias had never been to the vast cavern that housed the Mitth family's Csilla homestead. But she'd seen pictures, and looked at maps, and as they approached the final checkpoint she was fully prepared to look upon the ancestral site of her adoptive family.

She was wrong. Completely and thoroughly wrong.

The cavern was larger than she'd expected. *Way* larger. Large enough that there were actual clouds drifting across the sky, a panoramic blue she would have been prepared to swear was an actual sky above an actual planetary surface. Peeking out from behind the clouds was the blazing disk of a sun she would also have sworn was real. On both sides of the tunnel car tracks were stream-fed lakes, the one on the right big enough that the light wind rustling through the orchards and gardens was able to churn up small waves across its surface.

A dozen buildings clustered around the lakes or nestled under the forest that stretched off past the lake to the left. Some of the structures were clearly equipment sheds, others seemed to be homes, the latter large enough to each house two or three families in comfort. In the distance near the cavern's far end was a range of mountains shrouded in mist. Whether they were built into the wall or were free-standing, she couldn't tell.

And in the center of the cavern, rising majestically from the grass-land and garden arcs surrounding it, was a mansion.

It was huge, eight floors at least, with side wings that stretched out a couple hundred meters. It looked vaguely like one of the old for-tresses that had been common in the days before the Chiss learned to travel the stars, but the design was somewhat more modern and lacked the bristling weapons clusters that had made those ancient structures so intimidating. The exterior was all patterned stone, glass, and burnished steel, with small angled observation turrets at the cor-ners and an asymmetric tessellated roof that gleamed in the artificial sunlight.

"I assume this is the first time you've been here?" Thurfian asked.

Thalias found her voice. "Yes," she said. "All my other dealings with the family were at their compound on Avidich. The pictures don't do this place justice."

"Of course not," Thurfian said. "Fully accurate, fine-grain pictures might contain clues to the homestead's precise location. We certainly can't have *that*."

"I thought this was the Mitth family's old land."

"It is," Thurfian said. "But that land covers over six thousand square kilometers and includes many other caverns like this one, all of which have tube car access. Trust me: No one arrives at the Mitth home-stead without Mitth family permission. This is your last chance to change your mind about the Trials."

Thalias braced herself. "I'm ready."

"Maybe. We'll find out, won't we?"

The car came to a stop a hundred meters from the front of the house, beside a large mosaic design set into the ground. "Your first Trial," Thurfian said as the canopy slid back. "Find your path. If you succeed, you'll be invited inside. If you fail, get back in the car and you'll be taken back to the spaceport." He climbed out, walking along the edge of the mosaic, and headed toward the mansion.

Gingerly, Thalias stepped out of the car, frowning at the mosaic. It seemed familiar . . .

And then she got it. The whole thing was a stylized map of the Ascendancy.

Find your path, Thurfian had said. Did that mean she was supposed to trace out her hopes for the future?

No, of course not, she realized suddenly. The whole existence of this homestead was a grand gesture to Mitth family history. She wasn't supposed to trace out her future; she was supposed to trace out the path that had brought her here.

She took a deep breath. She barely remembered her life before the sky-walker corps, but she knew she'd been born on Colonial Station Camco. That was . . . there. Walking gingerly across the map, making sure she didn't touch any other planets along the way, she stepped onto the Camco mark.

For a moment nothing happened. She was wondering if she needed to lean over and touch it with her hand when the area around the planet lit up briefly with a green glow.

She huffed out a relieved breath as the glow faded away. Okay. From there she'd traveled to the Expansionary Fleet complex on Naporar, where she'd received her sky-walker training. Again being careful not to touch any of the other planets, she walked over to Naporar and stood on it. Again, she was rewarded by a green glow. Next . . .

She froze. Next had been a series of voyages outside the Ascendancy in her role as a sky-walker, guiding military and diplomatic ships to alien worlds and nations.

Only none of those worlds were on the map. Should she go to whichever Chiss system had been closest to those?

No, that couldn't be right. The mosaic was a flat projection of a three-dimensional region of space, and there was no way to know from here which Chiss planet was closest to a given alien nation. But then what was she supposed to do?

She looked up at the house. History . . . but the history of the *Ascendancy*.

She looked back at the map. The last trip she'd taken as a skywalker, the one where she'd met Thrawn, had been from Rentor to Naporar. She crossed to Rentor and gingerly stepped on it.

To her relief, the mosaic again glowed green around her feet. She crossed to Naporar, and was again rewarded.

All right. Next had been a trip to Avidich to meet with the Mitth Aristocra who'd brought her into the family. Then off to Jamiron for her formal schooling . . .

There were three more worlds after that, and each green glow brought back memories of sights and sounds and aromas she'd almost forgotten. By the time she stepped on Csilla, it was almost as if she'd actually revisited those places.

The ground again glowed green. "Welcome, Mitth'ali'astov," a disembodied voice rose from the mosaic. "Proceed to the ancient home to begin your next Trial."

Thalias took a deep breath. "I obey," she said. Walking across the mosaic, her mind still swirling with memories, she stepped onto the soft swish grass and headed toward the house.

There were a *lot* of Trials.

The first four or five were relatively easy: written tests involving general knowledge, logic, problem solving, and Ascendancy history. It was like being in school again, and while Thalias had only been a fair student she'd always loved learning. She breezed through them with relative ease, wondering if the rest of the Trials would be as straightforward.

They weren't.

Next came a test to see if she could cross a three-meter-wide water channel without getting wet, using only boards that were two and a half meters long each. After that she had to climb a smooth-barked tree to reach a sight line that would reveal the answer to an ancient

Mitth riddle. Another family riddle required her to find a subtle pattern in the flower arcs surrounding the mansion.

More than once, as she worked through the puzzles, she wondered if these Trials had been devised since the homestead was moved under the Csilla surface or if they predated that time. If it was the latter, it meant everything that had once been up there had been duplicated in meticulous detail.

Somehow, that degree of commitment didn't surprise her.

She'd assumed the Trials would end with the setting of the cavern's artificial sun. Again, she was wrong. A short six-hour sleep interval, and it was back to another battery of written tests and a couple more outdoor logic problems.

During the entire time, from the moment Thurfian left her at the mosaic map, she hadn't seen another living being. All her instructions had come via the same disembodied voice she'd heard when she'd first arrived, while her meals and room were waiting when she arrived at the designated places.

Finally, two hours past her small noontime meal, she was sent on the final Trial: to climb to the top of the mountain she'd seen rising up behind the mansion.

At first it didn't look too challenging. There was a clearly marked trail, the initial slope was only a few degrees, and the frequent clumps and lines of trees promised lots of shade against the blazing sunlight. Making a private bet with herself that she would be back down in time for an early dinner, she started up.

The nice shallow slope didn't last much past the first line of trees. Fortunately, as the mountain steepened, the path switched to an almost horizontal switchback-type arrangement that would angle her along the side of the mountain instead of straight up it.

A less rigorous climb, but now also considerably longer. Mentally revising her estimate as to how long this would take, she kept going.

She'd been on the path for perhaps an hour, and had made the third switchback turn, when she began seeing tall spikes sticking out of the ground beside the path. There were six in the first group, one of them about a meter tall and five centimeters in diameter, the other five half or a third that height and proportionally thinner. Thalias studied them as she walked past, wondering if this was the lead-in to another puzzle. The taller spike seemed to have a textured or carved surface, and for a moment she considered leaving the path for a closer look.

But while her orders hadn't said she couldn't look at the spikes, they hadn't specifically said she could, either. At this late stage in the Trials, she decided, it would be best to err on the side of caution.

Unless this was supposed to be a test of initiative?

Thalias scowled. Mind games inside mind games.

Still, she could see through the trees that there were more groups of spikes upslope of her current position. She'd keep going and watch for some pattern that would hopefully indicate how exactly she was supposed to jump on this one.

She'd assumed the cluster she'd seen through the tree would be the next one. To her mild surprise, she found a trail of much shorter spikes laid out along the path immediately after the first group. Some of the spikes seemed to be alone, while others formed small groups. Usually there was a slightly taller spike at the center, though none of these had the height or elaborate texturing of the first one she'd encountered. Frowning at each spike as she passed, looking for the still-elusive pattern she knew had to be there, she continued.

Two switchbacks later, the spike clusters suddenly reappeared with a vengeance. Another tall spike, even longer and more elaborately carved than the first one, was set back fifteen meters from the path on a small hummock. Nestled around it were at least fifty other spikes, again of varying heights, again with no pattern of size or positioning she could see.

From that point on the spikes never went away. Tall ones, short ones, occasional huge ones—they were all over the place, set back from the path or running right up beside it.

Two more switchbacks, she decided as she once again changed direction. Two more switchbacks, and if she hadn't found a pattern by then she would head over for a closer look.

"Impressive, aren't they?"

Thalias jerked, nearly twisting her ankle as she spun around toward the voice. Set back ten meters from the latest curve in the path, beneath the gently waving branches of a group of trees, was a carved wooden bench. Seated at one end was an old man, his skin pale with age, his eyes unusually bright as he peered out of the shadows. His hands were folded together in front of him, resting on the top of a walking stick that was as elaborately carved as any of the spikes Thalias had seen. "Yes, they are," she replied, her heart beating a little faster. The first person she'd seen since Thurfian disappeared . . .

He might have been reading her mind. "No, I'm not part of the Trials," he said with an amused and rather conspiratorial smile. "They don't know I'm even up here. Probably tearing their hair out looking for me. But I wanted to speak with you in private, and this seemed the best way to do it."

"I've been here for two days," Thalias reminded him, trying to get a clear view through the dappling of light through the tree leaves. She'd seen that face somewhere before.

"Oh, I know," he said. "I've been watching you. But while it may have looked like you were alone, you never were. Not until they sent you up here." He waved a hand around him. "Besides, there's such a rich sense of Mitth history on this mountain. Makes it the best place to discuss the future of our family." His waving hand stopped at the group of spikes Thalias had just been studying and extended a finger to point at the largest one. "What do you think?"

"I—don't know," Thalias stalled. He looked *so* familiar. "It's impressive enough. But I don't—"

"*Impressive?*" The old man gave a snort. "Hardly. He was a grandstander who always put his own glory above the family. At some point, you see, bringing in Trial-borns and turning them into cousins becomes less about the family's needs and more about impressing those who are dazzled by mere numbers."

"Yes, of course," Thalias said, an electric jolt running through her as she realized what she was looking at. Someone of Mitth blood— a syndic, Councilor, or some other upper-level Aristocra—was memorialized here. The large spike, surrounded by the memorials of those he'd brought into the Mitth from other families.

And with a second jolt she finally recognized the old man facing her. "You're Mitth'oor'akiord," she breathed. "You're the *Patriarch*."

"Very good," Thooraki said. "You paid attention to the row of sim-ulatings along the grand hallway. Impressive." He shrugged. "Sadly, that level of observation skill has nothing to do with the Trials, or you'd have just earned yourself extra points."

"Thank you, Your Venerante," Thalias said. "But honestly, I don't think you're the type to be dazzled by mere numbers."

"Very good, my dear Thalias," the Patriarch said, his smile broad-ening. "Indeed not. I search for quality and cleverness." He cocked his head slightly. "Speaking of which, I was called away as you were starting the water-channel challenge and haven't had a chance to re-view the recordings. Would you be so good as to enlighten me as to your solution?"

"It wasn't that hard," Thalias said. "The channel's only about a meter deep, so I took two boards, placed their ends together in the middle of the channel, then pushed one board to the opposite side and lowered the other to my side. With the two of them angled up against the channel's edges, I laid another board horizontally across them."

"I don't believe that would quite clear the water," the Patriarch pointed out.

"No, Your Venerante, it didn't," Thalias agreed. "So I added two more angled boards, these set into the center of the horizontal, and placed one final horizontal across them."

"Very nice," the Patriarch said. "I remember one Trial-born who began as you did, but then simply laid more boards across the first horizontal until the stack was above the water level."

Thalias felt her lip twitch. Focused on angles and engineering, that solution hadn't even occurred to her.

"Equally effective, but not nearly as elegant," the Patriarch added. "I've always liked elegance, and your records during your sky-walker years suggested you were of that frame of mind. Indeed, that was why I made the decision to bring you in."

"*You* brought me into the Mitth? You yourself?"

"Why not?" he said. "Watching over the family also means watching for those who will make the family stronger."

"I'm honored," Thalias said, feeling a sudden stifling sense of her own shortcomings and inadequacies. "I can only hope I'll someday be able to live up to your trust in me."

"*Someday?*" He gave another snort. "Really, child. You've already repaid my trust many times over. Even now you stand guard between my greatest achievement and those determined to destroy him."

"I don't understand—" She broke off. "You mean . . . *Thrawn*?"

The Patriarch nodded. "Another whom I personally chose to join us."

"Really," Thalias said, frowning. "I thought it was General Ba'kif who pointed the Mitth to him."

"And who do you think pointed Ba'kif?" the Patriarch countered. "Oh, yes. Labaki—that was his name back then—Labaki and I have known each other for a long time. I'm the one who told him about Thrawn and encouraged him to point that fool Thurfian toward him."

He sighed. "I saw greatness in him, Thalias," he said, his eyes and voice going distant. "Greatness, and skill, and loyalty. He will be my crowning, the memorial staff that will someday stand close beside my own." He tapped his walking stick as his gaze clouded over. "*If* he survives."

"I've seen him in battle, Your Venerante," Thalias assured him. "He'll survive."

"You think I fear his loss in war?" The Patriarch shook his head. "No. Barring something unforeseen or uncontrollable, he'll never taste more than temporary defeat. No, Thalias, the threat to him comes from within the Ascendancy. Possibly from within the family itself." He beckoned to her. "Come. Sit beside me, if you would. I fear I have but little time left."

Carefully, uncertainly, Thalias walked across the grass and eased herself onto the bench beside him. "What can I do for you?" she asked.

"You're doing it," he assured her. "You're listening to me, as few others in the family do anymore. More important, you're watching over Thrawn, working with him as an unflinching ally and assistant. Guarding him against his enemies."

He waved out over the mountain. "The transfer of leadership from one Patriarch to the next is designed to run smoothly. Usually it does. But sometimes it belies that promise. Even as we speak, there are several who are preparing their challenges and arguments, maneuvering for the moment when my walking stick is handed over to the historians and carvers for the version that will stand in the soil of the homestead. Some of those see Thrawn as an asset to the Mitth. Others see nothing but threat and danger." He shook his head. "If one of the latter ascends to the Patriarch's Seat . . ." He left the sentence unfinished.

"I don't understand that," Thalias said. "He's a magnificent warrior. How can they see danger in him?"

"The danger is that he'll overreach himself, or take the Mitth into some adventure that leaves us politically vulnerable. Should that happen, our rivals will surely take advantage of our momentary weakness. These particular contenders for the Patriarch's Seat would prefer to trade any potential glory Thrawn might bring to the family for the assurance that he won't bring an equal degree of infamy."

Thalias nodded. "Seeking a steady path without risks."

"Which is foolish," the Patriarch said, his mouth twisting with contempt. "The cautious path merely guarantees a slow slide to irrelevance. The Mitth must take risks—calculated and well planned, but risks nonetheless—if we're to maintain our position among the Ruling Families."

For a moment the only sound was the rustling of the wind through the trees. "What can we do?" Thalias asked at last.

"I honestly don't know," the Patriarch conceded. "I've done all I can. Even as my life stretches toward its conclusion, so my power and authority wane." He smiled sadly. "Don't look at me that way, child. This is as it should be, and as it must. The reins of command must be neatly gathered so as to be handed over to my successor without any sort of delay or uncertainty, lest the other families leap in to exploit such confusion to our detriment."

"I understand," Thalias said, shivering. She'd seen how politics colored relationships even among the professional warriors of the fleet's warships. It must be far more virulent in the Syndicure. "Tell me how to protect him."

"He has friends," the Patriarch said. "Allies. He may not know how to gather them to his side when necessary. That will be your task." He shook his head. "I knew from the start that politics wasn't his strength. But I never realized just how blind he was to those shifting winds."

"I'll do my best," Thalias said. "Assuming I'm still in the Mitth at day's end."

"Still in the *family*?" the Patriarch echoed, frowning at her. "What are you talking about, child? Of course you're in the family. Your travel through the Trials may not have shown brilliance, but it was more than adequate. You're officially a Trial-born now, Thalias, only one step from advancement to ranking distant."

"Thank you," Thalias said, bowing her head to him as a flood of relief washed through her.

"But only if you aren't reported as apparently having fallen off the mountain," the Patriarch said, some of his earlier humor peeking through the darkness of his warnings. "You'd best continue to the top. Study the staffs as you climb. Note the pattern and flow of family history. Meditate on the lives and triumphs of the Mitth."

"And on their occasional failures?"

The Patriarch nodded, the humor fading again. "Especially their failures," he said quietly. "Note closely the gaps in the memorial record, the asymmetries where a syndic's or Aristocra's efforts have been cut off. Failure can be a harsh but capable teacher."

"But only when those who observe it learn from it."

"Indeed." The Patriarch reached over and squeezed her hand. "Thank you for speaking with me, Thalias, Trial-born of the Mitth. And watch over your commander. I cannot help but feel that he holds the key to the Ascendancy's future, whether that future be triumph or ultimate destruction."

"I'll watch over him," Thalias promised. "To my own life or death, I'll watch over him."

The sun had long since set, but there was still a glow in the western sky when Thalias finally emerged from the path. Thurfian had clearly been watching, and as she walked toward the mansion he appeared through the door and motioned her toward a tunnel car waiting by the mosaic map.

"Change of plans," he called as she came within earshot. "I'm needed back at the Syndicure, and the Patriarch said I should take you with me."

"Is there trouble?" Thalias asked.

"None that I'm aware of," Thurfian said. "But Admiral Ar'alani sent a message asking that you be returned to the *Vigilant* as soon as possible." He gave her a suspicious look. "I also note that while I was conveniently distracted, Thrawn managed to slip away."

"That was certainly not my intent," Thalias said, knowing full well that she wasn't fooling him in the slightest. "But since you bring up the Trials, when will I know if I passed them?"

"You think too much like a schoolgirl," Thurfian said sourly. "The Trials aren't an essay to be graded and returned after class." His lip twisted. "*Yes*, you passed. You're now a Trial-born of the Mitth. Congratulations. Get in."

"Thank you," Thalias murmured.

She sat sideways in her seat as they headed out, watching the mansion, the mountain, and the homestead fading in the distance behind them, until the tunnel wall abruptly blocked it from her sight. She'd never dreamed she would actually meet the Patriarch of her adoptive family, let alone have a long and serious conversation with him. She would hold that meeting, and her promises to him, locked away in her heart.

And even as a new chapter of her life was beginning, so now did an era in the Mitth family's life draw to a close.

MEMORIES XI

Once, it was said, the March of Silence in Convocate Hall had been used by leaders of the Ruling Families to arrange for their enemies' censure, imprisonment, or execution. Its construction and acoustics were such that a conversation could realistically hold no more than four or five people without those on the outside edge being unable to hear what was being said in the center.

But that had been thousands of years ago. Now, with the enlightenment that came from political maturity, the March had become a gathering place for Speakers and syndics who wished to discuss political matters without one of them having to show the weakness inherent in meeting in another's office.

As Councilor Thurfian watched Councilor Zistalmu approaching from the other end of the March, he wondered if the Irizi would appreciate the irony of the proposal he was about to lay out.

Zistalmu's path was by necessity somewhat meandering as he carefully skirted the other conversational groups at distances calculated to avoid unintentional eavesdropping. Finally, he reached Thurfian and stepped up beside him. "Aristocra Thurfian," he said, nodding.

"Aristocra Zistalmu," Thurfian returned the greeting.

"Let me get straight to the point. I understand the Irizi have approached Senior Commander Mitth'raw'nuru about detaching from the Mitth and joining your family."

A flicker of surprise and suspicion touched Zistalmu's usually unreadable expression. "I was under the impression such offers were confidential until and unless they were finalized."

"It was a chance overhearing," Thurfian said. "I also understand that he declined your offer."

"Not officially," Zistalmu hedged. "The offer remains open."

"No, he's declined it," Thurfian said. "You've seen Thrawn's record. He doesn't hesitate when he sees a tactical advantage. If he hasn't accepted by now, the answer is no."

"Perhaps." Zistalmu eyed him. "I presume you didn't invite me here simply to gloat at our failed attempt."

"Not at all," Thurfian said. "I invited you here to see if you had any interest in bringing him down."

The unreadable expression held firm this time. But Thurfian could tell it was a near thing. "I don't understand."

"It's simple enough," Thurfian said. Zistalmu could cause immense trouble for him, he knew, if he repeated any of this to one of the Mitth Councilors or syndics. But Thurfian had a good feel for Zistalmu's goals and politics, and he was pretty sure that wouldn't happen. "I've seen Thrawn's record, too. He has the potential to do great things in the service of the fleet. He also has an equal potential of bringing ruin to the Mitth, and possibly to the entire Ascendancy."

Zistalmu favored him with a mocking smile "Bringing ruin to the Mitth doesn't sound so bad." The smile faded. "But the Ascendancy is another matter."

"Then you agree with me?"

"I don't know how you made that jump from a simple

comment in favor of the Ascendancy," Zistalmu said. "But if we're being honest . . . yes, I see the same potential for both glory and disaster."

"Though the rest of the Irizi apparently don't."

Zistalmu waved a hand. "The recruitment offer was their attempt to steal Thrawn away from the Mitth. I doubt any of them bothered to look deep enough into his record to see what you and I are seeing. So what exactly are you proposing?"

"At this point, nothing but watchfulness," Thurfian said, feeling a slight lessening of his tension. "That should be easy to do, given that our two families have already assigned us to watch over military matters. We simply continue that procedure, only with an eye toward coordinating our response if we see something dangerous in the works."

"Won't be easy," Zistalmu cautioned, his eyes narrowed in thought. "For whatever reason, he seems to have made staunch allies of General Ba'kif and Commodore Ar'alani. Those are powerful and influential people."

"I agree," Thurfian said. "Ba'kif's probably untouchable, but Ar'alani was once Irizi. She might still be amenable to pressure."

"I doubt it," Zistalmu said sourly. "I've talked with her once or twice since her promotion, and she's very intent on upholding her new nonfamily status."

"Then we focus on Thrawn," Thurfian said. "And, perhaps, some of his less highly placed allies."

"You'd know more about that than I would," Zistalmu said. "Very well. We'll watch, and wait, and see." He looked around. "And of course, we'll speak of this to no one."

"Absolutely," Thurfian said. "Thank you, Aristocra. Hopefully, we'll never be called upon to act. But if we are . . . ?"

"Then we act." Zistalmu gestured around the corridor. "I trust you noted the irony of our discussion, given the March of Silence's reputed history."

"I did," Thurfian said. "We'll speak again, Aristocra."

"Indeed we will." With a nod, Zistalmu turned and walked away in the direction of his office.

And as Thurfian turned in the other direction, a belated thought occurred to him. The March's history spoke of some of the Aristocra being dealt with for crimes occasionally as dark as treason. The question was whether Thrawn would be the object of any such future charge, or whether it would be Thurfian and Zistalmu.

Only time would tell.

CHAPTER NINETEEN

Thrawn and Che'ri were gone for nearly five weeks, and with each day that passed Thalias felt her soul die a little more. She should have been out there with them, she knew, facing the same dangers they were facing. The fact that her Trials gambit had thrown Thurfian off the scent didn't really count as being useful to their mission.

The Patriarch's command to watch over Thrawn just added that much extra knife twist to her sense of guilt.

She therefore felt a huge sense of relief when Ar'alani finally called to inform her that the scout ship had entered the Csilla system, that it was staying away from the capital itself for the moment, and that a shuttle was on its way to bring Thalias to the *Vigilant*.

It turned out that the travelers' quiet and unannounced return was only the first of the surprises.

"This could change everything," Ar'alani said.

Thalias nodded, thoughts and possibilities spinning through her mind as she gazed at her questis and the details of the Republic energy shield Thrawn and Che'ri had brought back with them. In a quiet spot in the back of her mind, she found extra amazement in the fact that Thrawn and Ar'alani trusted her enough to share their secret.

But then, Che'ri knew everything, too, and sky-walkers and their caregivers spent a lot of time together. The two officers had probably decided that Thalias might as well hear the whole story up front rather than getting it in dribs and drabs from a nine-year-old.

"This is light-years beyond the electrostatic barriers we've been using," Ar'alani continued. "We're going to have to rethink our tactics, our fleet array, the whole balance of power. Everything."

"But our advantage is only temporary," Thrawn warned. "Even if we can reverse-engineer the one we brought back—"

"We can," Ar'alani said. "We will."

"Even if we can," Thrawn continued, "no technology remains exclusive for long. Once it's known to exist, others will develop their own version. Or will simply steal it."

"Not from us," Ar'alani said, her lip twisting. "But getting one from the Republic should be easy enough." She tapped the questis thoughtfully. "The real question is why Yiv hasn't gotten something like this already. You said there was some group of aliens involved with the Separatists, didn't you?"

"Yes, but there's no reason to think they're necessarily associated with the Nikardun," Thrawn pointed out. "Even if they are, they may have the same concerns we do. If they show the Chaos that such a shield exists, the Ascendancy and everyone else will soon have one."

"So they're thinking to use it as a surprise somewhere down the line?"

"As are we," Thrawn said. "But unlike them, we can't afford to wait. We have to use it *now*, and against Yiv, before he knows we have it."

"Though he may already know," Ar'alani warned. "It sounds like you and this General Skywalker made quite a loud mess out there." She shook her head. "*Skywalker*. Bizarre coincidence."

"I understand it's not that uncommon name in parts of Lesser Space," Thrawn said. "But you're absolutely correct. There's no way the incidents on Batuu and Mokivj can be kept quiet for long."

Thalias winced. Running battles, interrogations, wholescale destruction on a planetary scale. *Incidents.*

"Fine," Ar'alani said, setting the questis aside. "You obviously have a plan. Let's hear it."

Thrawn paused, as if gathering his thoughts, and Thalias took the moment to give Che'ri a surreptitious look. The girl had first greeted her with hugs and tears, some of joy and some of simple released tension. In that respect, she was very much the little girl who'd left the Ascendancy on this adventure.

But as Thalias looked at her now, she could see that the journey had added more than a few weeks' worth of age to her. Not in the sense of aging, exactly, with the extra stress or weight that might have been laid on her from weeks of danger or fear or exhaustion. Instead, it was as if a fresh layer of maturity and confidence had settled across the child's face.

"First of all, we know Yiv isn't ready to take on the Ascendancy," Thrawn said. "That much was clear after our first visit to the Lioaoin heartworld. Surrounded by his allies, facing an enemy he very much wanted to capture or kill—"

"You?" Ar'alani suggested.

"Me," Thrawn confirmed. "He nevertheless withheld his fire and let us leave in peace."

"It could simply have been a matter of time and place," Ar'alani said. "But let's assume you're right. Continue."

"We also know that Yiv is still working on bringing the Vaks under his control," Thrawn said. "That caution is evidenced by the fact that, again with Vak forces presumably available to him, he instead brought in Lioaoin warships to handle the fighting when you came to extract Thalias and me from Primea."

"I agree," Ar'alani said. "And given your reading of the Vak passion for exploring all thought lines, it may be proving harder than he expected to get the entire leadership, let alone the entire planet, to follow him."

"Exactly," Thrawn said. "And therein lies our opportunity. If we can draw some of the Vaks to our side and show the rest that Yiv's intentions aren't to build them up in prestige but merely to use them to fight and die in his battles, we may drive a wedge between them. If that doesn't halt his plan completely, it should at least buy us enough time to convince the Syndicure that the Nikardun are a threat that needs to be dealt with."

"Excuse me," Che'ri spoke up hesitantly, half lifting a hand.

Thrawn and Ar'alani looked at her. "Yes?" Thrawn invited.

"What if he just leaves Primea and goes somewhere else?" the girl asked. "There are a lot of other aliens in the area."

"He could do that, yes," Thrawn said. "But he's put a lot of time and effort into winning over the Vaks. I don't think he'll give up without serious persuasion."

"It's not just the Vaks themselves, either," Ar'alani added. "Primea is a center of diplomacy and trade for that entire region, a place where people from all those other alien species you mentioned come to talk and do business. If Yiv can get the Vak leaders to endorse him, or at least let him hang around and meet visitors, he'll have vectors into all those other nations."

"We've already seen that he likes a mixture of conquest by force and conquest by persuasion," Thrawn said. "Even his title, General Yiv the Benevolent, tries to have it both ways. No, I think that if we try to move him off Primea he'll choose to stand and fight."

"Or bring the fight to us," Ar'alani warned. "Even if it's not his preferred timing, he might decide he needs to hit the Ascendancy."

"He won't do it directly," Thrawn said. "He's more likely to send the Paataatus against us again."

"And that's better *how*?"

"Better for him because he doesn't waste his own forces," Thrawn said. "Better for us because we already know how to beat them."

"Well, *you* know how to beat them," Ar'alani muttered. "Sometimes I'm not so sure about anyone else."

"We can beat them," Thrawn assured her. "But no, the crucial battle will be at Primea. If we can demonstrate Yiv's weakness and his treachery in front of the Vaks, they may reconsider their choice of allies."

"Sounds like a long shot," Ar'alani said. "But barring any kind of direct intervention, I think it's all we've got. So how do we do that?"

Thrawn seemed to brace himself. "We invite the Vaks to help us."

And as he laid out his plan, Thalias discovered that he had one more surprise left to offer.

"You disapprove," Thrawn said.

Ar'alani eyed him, her head still spinning from the idea he'd presented to her and the two younger women. "Of course I disapprove," she said. "The whole thing is totally illegal in at least three directions. Not to mention insane."

"Agreed," Thrawn said. "The question is, are you willing to go through with it?"

"Do I have a choice?"

"Of course," Thrawn said. "If you don't want to be part of this, say so now, and we'll do it alone."

"How?" Ar'alani retorted. "If Yiv behaves the way you expect, the three of you will end up alone against his entire Primea force."

"The Vaks will come to our aid."

"*If* the message gets to them and they don't decide to ignore it."

"There are clearly thought lines of distrust toward Yiv," Thrawn said. "The message will offer another thought line, one I hope their culture will require them to at least consider. And if I've read Yiv correctly, he should soon find himself in deeper trouble than he expects."

"*If* you've read him correctly," Ar'alani said, leaning on the critical word. "Come on, Thrawn, this is crazy. Even for you."

"Do you see an alternative?" Thrawn countered. "We can't just sit back and let the Nikardun close in around us, gathering allies and biding their time until the Chaos closes around us and we stand alone against them. Yiv has to be stopped, and this is the best time and place to make our move."

"Again, what if you're wrong?" Ar'alani asked. "What if everything you're reading in Yiv and the Vaks is wrong? You've been wrong before, you know."

It wasn't the most diplomatic thing she could have said, she realized, and instantly regretted it as a flicker of old pain crossed his face. "I'm sorry," she apologized.

"No, you're right," he said. "My failure with the Garwians . . . but this is different. This is war, not politics."

"Which are just two sides of the same coin," Ar'alani said. "You've never understood that or been able to deal with it."

"I know," Thrawn said. "That's why we need to flip this particular coin over to the war side."

Ar'alani sighed. He'd been wrong once—spectacularly wrong—and it had cost him. But it was no use arguing about it.

Besides, he was right. Yiv and the Nikardun had to be challenged, and doing so in a system the enemy wanted to hold on to was their best chance. "I'm not sure the techs are entirely finished with the Vak fighter we brought back from Primea, but Ba'kif can probably talk Ja'fosk into letting us return it. You're sure Che'ri can fly it?"

"Absolutely," Thrawn said. "She proved quite adept at flying our scout ship, and the fighter has similar parameters. I'll just need to relabel some of the controls and run her through an exercise or two and she'll be ready."

"I assume you aren't going to let Ba'kif or Ja'fosk in on that part of the plan?"

"I'm not *that* crazy," Thrawn said with a small smile.

"But they're going to find out eventually," Ar'alani said. "Have you thought about what they'll do to you afterward?"

A muscle in Thrawn's throat tightened. "If we've eliminated Yiv as a threat, it doesn't matter what they do to me." He cocked his head. "*My* real concern is you. What they're going to do to you when it all comes out."

"I'm an admiral," Ar'alani reminded him. "Not nearly so easy to get rid of."

"They'll still try."

"Only if we fail. If we succeed—" She shrugged. "But the future's out of our hands. Let's go with the present. So. First job: Retrieve the Vak fighter from the techs and get it prepped to fly. Second job: Teach Che'ri how to fly it. Third job: Get started on the customized freighter you want. Fourth job: Work out the message you want delivered to the Vaks. Fifth job: Get the Republic shield ready to go for our surprise attack. Sixth job: Get my fleet ready to go."

"That one may be seventh," Thrawn interjected. "Sixth job is probably to get Ba'kif and Ja'fosk to sign off on this."

"I was thinking of waiting on that until after Che'ri and Thalias have left," Ar'alani said. "That's not going to be a pleasant conversation, and it'll be safer if it's too late to call the fighter back. Eighth job—" She braced herself. "Spin it all up, and turn it loose."

"And hope that my assessment of General Yiv is correct."

"Right," Ar'alani said. "Let's *really* hope that."

"They're calling us," Che'ri announced. "That light, right there."

"I see it," Thalias said, her head pounding with a tension that had nothing to do with the extra weight of the hard-crust makeup once again creating the hostage-marking ridges and shallow plateaus across her face. With both the Nikardun and the Vaks here, the entire Primea system was enemy territory.

And she and Che'ri were all alone in the middle of it.

She looked at the girl, leaning forward a little over the fighter's control board, her eyes narrowed with concentration. At least half of her expression was covered by the same makeup that Thalias was wearing, but there didn't seem to be any tension there. Was she feeling any of the qualms Thalias was? "You're awfully calm," she said.

"Aren't I supposed to be?" Che'ri asked, throwing a puzzled look at Thalias. "It's all under control, right?"

"Well . . . sure, I suppose so," Thalias said. "I just . . ."

"You trust him, don't you?" Che'ri pressed.

"Yes, I guess so."

"Because we've both seen him do some amazing stuff," Che'ri went on, still frowning. "Getting that shield generator, getting you off Primea, battles and other stuff. You've seen all that, too, right?"

"Right," Thalias said. "Only this time . . ."

"There's no difference, really," Che'ri said. "It's all under control."

"Of course there's a difference." Thalias said. "All the other times, Thrawn was here with us. If something went wrong, he could adapt or come up with a new plan." She waved a hand around the cramped command deck. "Here . . . Che'ri, we're on our own."

"But he gave us our instructions," Che'ri said. "We know what we're supposed to do."

"I know that," Thalias said. "I'm just saying it's not the same."

"Oh," Che'ri said, the part of her face that Thalias could see suddenly clearing. "It's not that you don't trust Thrawn. You don't trust *yourself*."

"Of course not," Thalias said, hearing the edge of bitterness in her voice. She'd been aware of that nebulous feeling ever since Thrawn first proposed this plan. But up to now she'd never dared to even think those words. Now, with them out in the open, she felt a sudden weight of fear and doubt and inadequacy. "Why should I? What have I ever done to make him—to make *anyone*—think I could be trusted with something this big?"

"Well, you're *here*," Che'ri said. "That must mean he trusts you."

"I asked for a *reason*."

"We don't always get reasons," Che'ri said earnestly. "Whatever he sees in you, it was all he needed. He trusts you." She paused. "So do I, if that helps any."

Thalias took a deep breath, gazing at Che'ri's eyes. The enhanced maturity she'd seen in the girl back aboard the *Vigilant* was still there, and for a moment Thalias noted the irony of a nine-year-old comforting an adult. "You know, when I was your age I remember being terrified of my future," she said. "It was all so big and unknown, and I had no idea what my place in it would be."

"I used to feel that way, too," Che'ri said. "Not so much anymore."

"Which all by itself is crazy," Thalias said. "The future you're facing—for that matter, the future you and I are facing just today—is way less secure than anything I could have dreamed of."

"You just said it," Che'ri said. "Dreams. I never knew what to dream. I mean, I was just a sky-walker. I didn't know if there was anything else I could ever do."

She gestured at the control board in front of her. "But then Thrawn taught me how to fly. In just a couple of weeks he taught me how to *fly*." She smiled, her whole face beaming with happiness and accomplishment. "If I can do that, I can do anything. Do you get it now?"

"Yes," Thalias said. "And I'm happy for you." She took another deep breath, willing the tension away. An accomplished warrior like Thrawn; an accomplished pilot like Che'ri. With them trusting her, how could this go wrong? "You said the Vaks had hailed us. Do we need to send a message back?"

"Whenever you're ready," Che'ri said, pointing to the mic. "Got your speech ready?"

"I've got *Thrawn's* speech ready," Thalias said, forcing a small smile. "Good enough?"

"Good enough." Che'ri touched a switch. "You're on."

Thalias braced herself. This was it. "Greetings to the people of Primea," she called in Minnisiat. "I am Thalias, companion to Senior Captain Thrawn of the Chiss Ascendancy. In his escape from your world some time ago, he inadvertently took this fighter craft with him. It has been repaired, and my pilot and I are here to return it."

"You have stolen from the Vak Combine," a harsh voice came in the same language. "What makes you think you won't be punished for your crime?"

"I would beg the Combine to accept my visit and the spacecraft's return as a gesture of goodwill," Thalias said. "I'm certain that I can explain from Thrawn's thought line the reasons behind his actions."

There was a pause. "There is never a valid reason for theft," the Vak said. But to Thalias's ears he sounded a little uncertain.

Exactly as Thrawn had predicted he would be. "I would again beg your indulgence," she said. "I bring a written explanation and an overture of peace and reconciliation from the senior captain. Will you permit me to land and bring it to your military leader?"

Another pause. "You may land," the Vak said. "I've activated a navigational beacon to guide you."

"Che'ri?" Thalias murmured.

The girl nodded. "Got it. Shifting course now."

"Thank you," Thalias said. "I will bring the document with me. I was ordered to place it directly into the hand of your military leader. I beg you to permit me to fulfill my duty."

"Land first," the Vak said. "Once we've examined the craft and assessed any damage, we shall see about your document."

"Thank you," Thalias said. "We shall look forward to seeing you soon."

There was a click as the Vak closed off the transmission. "So far, so good," Thalias said, trying to sound casual.

"It'll work," Che'ri assured her as the fighter angled down toward the lights of a city far below. "Thrawn's got this. *We've* got this."

Thalias nodded. She still wasn't sure about herself, but she was confident in Thrawn's skills.

Because, really, when had he ever been wrong?

MEMORIES XII

It was a high honor, Ar'alani had been assured, when an alien government invited a Chiss military officer to travel to their world. The fact that Security Chief Frangelic had specifically said the Ruleri would be present had added an even deeper layer to the honor.

And so, as she and Thrawn left their shuttle and walked to the cluster of waiting Garwians, she tried very hard not to be overwhelmed by the mix of a hundred strange odors swirling around her like a morning fog. It was thick enough, and intense enough, that she nearly turned around and headed back to the shuttle and the olfactory security of the *Destrama*.

To her surprise, though, by the time the greeting ceremony was over and she and Thrawn were ushered to a waiting ground car her nose and lungs were already starting to adapt. As they drove across the city toward the planetary security center the smells receded even more, and by the time the car stopped and Frangelic ushered them out onto the street the aroma had become neutral, even edging toward something pleasant.

Though it was possible that the mixture had simply changed along the way. Certainly the large circular courtyard stretched out before them, crowded with pedestrians, had many spots where wisps of smoke marked open-fire cooking, and she'd always liked such aromas.

"This can't be the security center," she commented as Frangelic closed the car door behind them.

"The center is there," he said, pointing to a whitestone building on the far side of the courtyard. "But as you can see, vehicles would have difficulty maneuvering through the weekend Creators' Market."

"Could we not have flown?" Thrawn asked.

"We could have," Frangelic agreed. "But the Creators' Market is one of the finest representations of Garwian culture, and I'd hoped to share it with you."

Thrawn looked at Ar'alani. "Commodore?"

Ar'alani shrugged, sniffing as a shift in the breeze brought another flavor of smoke. Holiday open-fire banquets had been one of her favorite family meals when she was growing up. "Why not?" she said. "Lead on, Security Chief."

"Thank you. This way."

Frangelic set off toward the edge of the courtyard. It was crowded with people, as Ar'alani had already noted, but those on the edges quickly spotted the alien faces and moved out of their path. Some of them bowed toward Frangelic as the newcomers approached, and Ar'alani's first thought was that the gesture was one of subservience or even fear at the sight of his uniform. But Frangelic invariably bowed back, and she eventually concluded the gesture was simply a form of respect between citizens.

"You can see that the booths are laid out in concentric circles," Frangelic said as they approached the outer group. "The ones on the outside are reserved for those who require more space for their wares and equipment, while the smaller ones toward the center are for those with more compact displays."

"You said *creators*," Thrawn said. "What do they create?"

"Anything you want," Frangelic said. "There's a man here who makes unique kitchen utensils for people whose passion is cooking. Over there is a woman who creates historical costumes for remembrance parties. You can smell the aromas of cooking fires for those who wish a particular food preparation or a unique layering of spice or sauce."

"Seems rather inefficient," Ar'alani said.

"Oh, we have the same mass-produced items as all other worlds for everyday use," Frangelic assured her. "These are for those who want the unusual and unique. If you can define or describe what you want, someone here will make it for you. Here, or in thousands of other Creators' Markets across the Unity."

"You spoke of remembrance parties," Thrawn said. "What are those?"

"Ah," Frangelic said, shifting direction. "That is, I believe, a cultural aspect in which the Unity stands alone among all other peoples. Those who attend such parties wear elaborate outfits utilizing features from clothing throughout Garwian history, woven and melded together in subtle and unique ways. The goal of each participant is to create the most beautiful and most intricate melding, while at the same time detecting and identifying the features in the other attendees' garb. Let me show you."

He led the way to a long table and a woman working an old-looking sewing machine. On either side of her were neat stacks of cloth, thread, and sewing implements, while racks behind her held dozens of samples of cloth, leather, silk, and some materials Ar'alani couldn't identify.

"This is Dame Mimott, one of our master designers," Frangelic said, nodding a greeting to her. "Dame Mimott, our guests would like to hear about your work."

The woman regarded Ar'alani and Thrawn in a way that Ar'alani couldn't help but identify as suspicion. "You're not by chance attending the Kimbples' party next Mid Spring, are you?" she asked.

"Really, Mimott," Frangelic said, a hint of scolding in his tone. "You're not suggesting our honored guests would *cheat,* are you?"

For a moment, the woman just stared at him. Then her jaw cracked open in a smile. "Your honored guests, certainly not," she said. "*You,* on the other hand . . ." She cocked her head to the side, her fingertips touching her cheek.

"I assure you, Mimott, if I should by chance be invited to the Kimbples' party, I will graciously decline." He pointed two fingers at the cloth she was working on. "Perhaps you will explain to us your artistry."

"Gladly." The woman spread out the cloth. "This cloth is of course modern, but is of the same design and texture as that used in the Twelfth Era. The stitching style is from the Fourteenth, the particular dye coloring was first used in the Seventeenth, and the edging style from the Eighteenth." She touched the machine. "The machine itself is a refurbished antique from the Fifteenth."

"All this for a single garment?" Ar'alani asked.

"All this for just the underlayer," Mimott corrected with another smile. "There will also be two outer layers, plus a shoulder wrap, gloves, and a hat."

"And all for a single party," Frangelic said. "Though the clothing that's most successful in puzzling the partygoers is put on display to be admired by the entire city."

"If an outfit is designed properly, it can also be easily transformed into other formalwear," Mimott added. "Sometimes even into everyday clothing. Have you other questions?"

"No," Ar'alani said. "Thank you for showing us your work. It's most impressive."

"I am honored," Mimott said. "May your day be warmed with sunshine."

Frangelic gestured, and they moved off. "What do you think?" he asked.

"Beautiful work," Ar'alani said. "My aunt enjoyed occasional sewing projects when I was growing up, but nothing this elaborate."

"We pride ourselves on our craftsmanship," Frangelic said. "But I see time is growing short. Perhaps later I can show you more of the artisans." He picked up his pace, the crowd again opening to let them through.

Thrawn moved close to Ar'alani's side. "Is there a problem?" he asked quietly.

"A problem?" She shook her head. "No. It's just . . . I've never seen aliens as people before. Not like Chiss are people. I've always thought of them as something lesser, something closer perhaps to highly intelligent animals. Some friendly, some harmless, some dangerous." She eyed him. "I suppose you've always seen them for what they are?"

"You mean as people?" Thrawn shook his head. "Not really. I see the people, certainly. But their personhood is seldom at the top of my thoughts."

"Then how *do* you see them?"

His eyes swept the crowd, and Ar'alani thought she could see a hint of both thoughtfulness and sadness in his face. "As possible allies. Possible enemies.

"Assets."

The group was nearly to the Solitair planetary security center when the racket of emergency alarms suddenly filled the air over the Creators' Market. "What is it?" Ar'alani shouted over the noise.

"Solitair is under attack!" Frangelic snapped, breaking into a dead run. "Hurry!"

The alarms had been silenced by the time the three of

them reached the underground situation room beneath the building. "Security Chief Frangelic, reporting for orders," Frangelic called as they hurried toward a small group of Garwians standing in front of a large display wall. The three Ruleri, Ar'alani noted, were also present, conversing together off to one side beside another, smaller set of displays. The screens were of course labeled with Garwian script, which made them unreadable to her.

But there was no mistaking the reason for the alarm. The main viewscreen showed two Lioaoin ships coming in toward the planet. Even as Ar'alani watched, they reached firing range and the nearest of Solitair's orbiting defense platforms opened up with lasers and missiles.

"Security Chief," one of the officers greeted Frangelic tensely as Ar'alani and the others came up to them. Up close, she now recognized him as a general who'd been at one of their earlier meetings, though she couldn't recall his name. "Commodore Ar'alani; Senior Commander Thrawn." He gestured to the displays. "As you can see, the quiet talks we'd envisioned between our two peoples have been violently interrupted."

"Indeed," Frangelic said grimly.

"We were afraid this would happen," the general continued. "With our forces off defending our five outer worlds, the Lioaoi have chosen this moment for a surprise attack. You helped us once, Commodore Ar'alani. Can you also assist us in repulsing this new aggression?"

Ar'alani shook her head, feeling a sense of helplessness. The woman up there in the Creators' Market, diligently sewing her historical clothing . . . "I'm sorry, General, but we can't," she said. "By all standard protocol, we shouldn't even be in your situation room."

"You are our guests, and such guests must be protected," the general said. "If the invaders break through, you could be in the same danger as our own helpless citizens."

"There's little likelihood of that," Thrawn assured him. "Your defense platforms should be more than adequate to protect you from two warships."

"What if there are more lying in wait?" Frangelic countered. "Anything you can tell us about our attackers could spell the difference between survival and utter destruction. Please."

For a moment, Thrawn watched the displays in silence. Ar'alani could see his eyes flicking back and forth: observing, assessing, calculating. If there was something else there, some weakness the Garwians could exploit, he would find it.

"Well?" the general prompted.

"I see two additional weaknesses," Thrawn said. "But Commodore Ar'alani is right. This is something the Ascendancy must stand back from."

"You helped us once," Frangelic said. "Is not the situation here even more dire?"

Thrawn looked at Ar'alani. Back at the general. "The Lioaoi have certain tactical blind spots," he said. "The first—"

"Just a minute," Ar'alani interrupted him. The Garwian officers—all of them—were staring at Thrawn. None were watching the monitors. None were directing their defenses.

But then, why would they? The Lioaoin ships were standing well back from the defense platform, not moving forward, their effort apparently being put into defending themselves against the Garwian barrage.

"Please," Frangelic said, shifting his attention to Ar'alani. "Please don't stand in the way of Garwian survival."

"Is that what I'm doing?" Ar'alani asked. Pulling out her comm, she keyed for the *Destrama*.

Silence. Not just no answer. Silence.

And now all the Garwian officers were looking at *her*.

"Commander Thrawn, please contact the *Destrama*," she said. "There seems to be a problem with my comm."

"Is there," Thrawn said, his voice and face gone suddenly hard. He'd heard the silence from her comm, too. "General, kindly lift your jamming."

"There's no jamming," Frangelic said quickly. "At our depth—"

"Kindly lift your jamming," Thrawn repeated.

Neither his voice nor his face had changed. Even so, a sudden shiver ran up Ar'alani's back. Silently, the general turned and made a gesture to one of the officers at the consoles. The other touched a pair of switches—

"—asking for terms for the Lioaoin Regime's surrender," a taut voice came over Ar'alani's comm. "The Garwians are ignoring them. Commodore, can you hear me?"

"Yes, Commander," Ar'alani said. "I can now, anyway. Stand by for orders."

She muted the comm. "Nice," she said to the general, putting as much frost into her voice as she could. "You claim you're being raided by pirates and maneuver us into bending our protocols to assist. Then, once the Lioaoi have lost a critical number of ships, you launch an assault against—what? An old rival? A new competitor for trade or manufacturing contracts?"

"You speak as if the Lioaoi were innocents," the general said loftily. "Not at all. You recall me speaking earlier of our five outer worlds? Once there were six." His mouth opened in a grin. "Now there will be six again."

"Or possibly seven?" Ar'alani asked.

"Possibly," the general agreed. "There is one of theirs we're most interested in."

He looked at Thrawn. "More insights into our enemies' weaknesses would have been useful. But no matter. Your earlier assistance in that regard was sufficient and much appreciated."

Thrawn held his gaze another moment. Then, deliberately, he turned to Ar'alani. "Commodore, request permission to order the *Destrama* to open fire on the Garwian defense platforms."

An uncomfortable stir ran through the aliens. "A tempting suggestion, Commander," Ar'alani said. "But I'm afraid the protocols forbid such an action. Fully justified though it would be."

"General, the Lioaoi are breaking off," someone called.

"Recalled to defend their worlds, no doubt," the general said. "A futile gesture, but at least there will be no doubt as to which of us won this day." He cocked his head at Ar'alani. "I presume you'll wish to depart as soon as possible?"

"Oh, we'll depart, all right," Ar'alani said. "And you'd best hope with all your strength that we never come back. Because if we do ... let's just say that Captain Thrawn's insights regarding tactical blind spots aren't limited to those of the Lioaoi."

She took a step forward and had the minor and pointless satisfaction of seeing the general take a hasty step backward. "Remember that. *All* of you."

CHAPTER TWENTY

There were ten guards waiting when Thalias and Che'ri emerged from the fighter. "I greet the warriors of the Vak Combine," Thalias called, giving their uniforms a quick once-over. They were of a similar pattern to the uniforms she'd seen at the diplomatic reception she and Thrawn had attended, but these were of a simpler and more utilitarian nature. Not a formal welcome, then, but a serious military situation. "I bring apologies from Senior Captain Thrawn, and offer recompense for his actions."

"You said you had a message," one of the soldiers said. "Let me have it."

"I was instructed to put it directly into the hands of the Combine's military leader," Thalias said. "I'm happy to wait on that arrival, or to travel wherever he or she would like to meet."

"No doubt you are," the soldier said. "But I will take it." He held out his hand, all five claws pointed upward. "Now."

Thalias hesitated. But there was nothing she could do. Anyway, Thrawn had warned her this would probably happen. Pulling out the envelope, she handed it to him. "I presume your leaders will wish to question us about the circumstances that led to this unfortunate occurrence," she said as he slid it into a side pocket of his jacket. "I'm at their total disposal and convenience."

"That won't be necessary," the soldier said. "We have a navigator and ship waiting to take you back to the Chiss Ascendancy. He arrives now."

Thalias frowned. "*No* one wants to talk to us?"

The soldier didn't answer. Instead, he gave an open-hand salute, gestured to his companions, and the whole group of them marched off the landing platform and disappeared through one of the doors.

"Are we still on the plan?" Che'ri asked.

Thalias hesitated. They were, but there were certain parts that Thrawn and Ar'alani had elected to keep from the younger girl. "We'll find out," she said evasively.

"Ah—Thalias of the Chiss Ascendancy," a cheerful voice said from behind them.

Thalias turned, feeling her stomach knot up as she saw the familiar creature walking toward them, a broad smile on his face. "You won't remember me," he said, "but we met—"

"You're Qilori of Uandualon," she interrupted. "You were with General Yiv at the reception."

"Ah—you *do* remember," Qilori said. "Excellent. Come with me—the shuttle to our transport is right down here."

A few minutes later they were in the shuttle's passenger compartment, heading through the thinning atmosphere toward the rows of ships in Primea orbit. "It's a busy place, Primea," Qilori commented, peering out the window. "I'm just as glad I never have to take control of a ship until we're well out of the gravity well and ready for hyperspace. You must have had an interesting time getting through it all."

"Che'ri did," Thalias said, looking around the otherwise empty compartment. "She's the pilot. Where are the other passengers?"

"Oh, they're already aboard the transport," Qilori said. "You were a late addition, courtesy of the Combine government. They must be pleased to have their fighter back."

"It was never our intention to keep it," Thalias said. "Which one's our transport?"

"You'll see it in a minute," Qilori said. "It's . . . there it is, just coming into view."

"Thalias?" Che'ri asked, her voice uncertain. "That doesn't look like a transport to me."

"If by *transport* you mean something to get you from here to there, of course it's a transport," Qilori said. "If you mean *civilian transport,* though, I'm afraid that's not what we're doing today."

He pointed out the viewport. "That, my noble Chiss hostages, is the *Deathless,* a Battle Dreadnought and the flagship of General Yiv the Benevolent of the Nikardun Destiny."

Thalias looked at him, mentally measuring the distance between them. They were both strapped in, but if she got free quickly enough . . .

"Please don't," Qilori said. "The Benevolent would very much like you to be in undamaged condition when he hands you over to Thrawn."

"He's going to give us back to Thrawn?" Che'ri asked hopefully.

"Of course," Qilori said. "He'll message Thrawn, Thrawn will come, they'll meet right on the bridge of that warship, and Yiv will hand you over to him.

"And then, of course, Yiv will kill him."

Treason.

That was really the only word for it, Thurfian thought bitterly as he hurried toward the Convocate Hall for the Syndicure's emergency meeting. *Treason.*

And after all the precautions he'd taken—the meetings and comparing of notes with Zistalmu, the careful reading of every scrap of data from every one of Thrawn's missions and activities—after all that he'd still been taken completely by surprise.

He'd often watched as the arrogant warrior skated up to the line and occasionally stepped over it. But nothing had prepared him to watch Thrawn take a flying leap over that line.

They had him. This time, by every evil of the Chaos, they had him.

But at what cost? What terrible, terrible cost?

The Convocate Hall was packed when Thurfian arrived, and as he headed toward the Mitth section he did a quick head count. The Speakers of all Nine Families were present, as were most of the upper-level syndics. A dozen other lesser families were represented, mostly those with close ties to one of the Nine or aspirations to someday join them in Ascendancy rule. The room buzzed with quiet conversation as those who'd only heard part of the situation were filled in by the others.

Seated at the witness table, a pocket of silence amid the verbal storm, were Supreme General Ba'kif, Supreme Admiral Ja'fosk, Admiral Ar'alani, and Thrawn.

Thurfian had just taken his chair when Ja'fosk rose to his feet.

Instantly the rumble vanished. "Speakers and Syndics of the Ascendancy," Ja'fosk said, throwing a quick, appraising look around the chamber. "I've received a transmission from General Yiv of the Nikardun Destiny." He lifted his questis. "Quote:

" 'I have in my possession the two family hostages of Senior Captain Thrawn, whom he sent to Primea with an offer to the Vak Combine of union and treachery against the peaceful peoples of the Nikardun Destiny. If he wishes the females to be released unharmed, he will travel alone to the attached coordinates in an unarmed freighter with the equivalent of two hundred thousand Univers.' " Ja'fosk lowered the questis. "The coordinates given indicate a high orbit over Primea."

The usual protocol was for one of the Speakers to offer the first response or ask the first question. But Thurfian wasn't much interested in protocol at the moment. More than that, he needed to make sure the entire chamber had the full horrifying situation. "Leaving aside for the moment the question of why Yiv thinks the Chiss have such a thing as family hostages," he said, rising to his feet, "I'd like to know who these two women are." He raised his eyebrows. "Or *are* they both women, or is one a young girl?"

"One of them is a woman," Ja'fosk said, his voice under careful control. "Her name is Mitth'ali'astov. The other is indeed a girl, Che'ri." A muscle in his cheek twitched. "One of our sky-walkers."

A ripple of disbelief and outrage ran through the assembled Aristocra. Apparently, most of them *hadn't* heard the whole story. "I assume Yiv is unaware of her status?" Thurfian asked.

"We believe so," Ja'fosk said. "There's certainly no indication that he even knows about the sky-walker program, let alone has any details."

"I assume there's also no indication that he doesn't," the Plikh Speaker put in harshly. "I would like to know exactly how Senior Captain Thrawn made such a blunder as to put one of our sky-walkers in enemy hands."

"The Nikardun aren't our enemies," Ja'fosk reminded her. "As to Captain Thrawn's reasoning in this matter . . ." He looked down at Thrawn.

"I certainly never intended either of them to be put at risk," Thrawn said. "Their mission was to return the Vak fighter I had borrowed and to bring a warning to the Primea leadership of Yiv's activities among other species in the region. Thalias was supposed to deliver the message, then take a passenger transport to Navigator Concourse Four Forty-Seven, where they would be brought back to the Ascendancy."

"And why was a sky-walker even aboard?"

"Che'ri could pilot the fighter. Thalias could not."

Thurfian felt his lip twist. *Liar.* Thrawn clearly knew or at least suspected what Yiv would do if Thalias and Che'ri came within reach. This whole thing smacked of a back-door approach to getting the Syndicure to order a retaliatory strike.

And if the mood in the chamber was any indication, he was going to get it. If there was one resource the Ascendancy guarded with insane jealousy, it was their sky-walkers.

"This conversation is not over," the Irizi Speaker warned. "We'll want the details of this situation—*all* the details—at some point in the future. If blunders or outright deception are found, the Syndicure will mete out the appropriate consequences."

"Understood," Ja'fosk said. "For now, though, speed is of the essence. We must use whatever means necessary to retrieve the two women."

"I assume," Zistalmu spoke up harshly, "that means a military strike."

"Against those who, as Supreme Admiral Ja'fosk has already admitted, aren't our enemies," Thurfian added.

"They've taken a sky-walker," Thrawn said. "I believe that act in and of itself constitutes an attack on the Ascendancy."

"Even when they're unaware of their crime?"

"They've taken a sky-walker," Thrawn repeated.

Thurfian caught Zistalmu's eye across the chamber, saw his same cynicism reflected in the Irizi's expression. Yes, this had been prearranged, all right. Ja'fosk and Ba'kif might not have known the whole plan going in, but Thrawn and Ar'alani most certainly had.

There would be a reckoning for this down the line, Thurfian promised himself. But for now, that would have to wait. Yiv had a skywalker, and it was abundantly clear that the Aristocra would turn the Chaos upside down if necessary to get her back.

Still, if they were lucky—if they were *very* lucky—Thrawn might finally have outsmarted himself. In which case, Thurfian would happily and with full sincerity join into the Mitth family's eulogy for its fallen hero.

"I think the thing I'll miss most about Thrawn," Yiv commented casually from his bridge command chair, "is the way he always seemed able to read his opponent and plan accordingly. It forced one to keep alert and to learn to anticipate in turn."

Thalias kept silent, focusing instead on the task of not scratching her arms despite the itchy feel of the shapeless robes the Nikardun had given her and Che'ri to wear. She suspected they were prisoner suits, and that they were deliberately designed to be uncomfortable, but she would be damned if she would give Yiv the satisfaction.

"This canister, for instance," Yiv continued, pulling out the small, flat canister that had been concealed inside Thalias's belt buckle. "Hard to tell without opening it, but deep-spectral analysis suggests it's some kind of soporific. Possibly a lethal one?"

"It's not lethal," Thalias said. "It's a sleepwalking drug called tava.

It's the drug my master used on the crew of the Vak fighter when he commandeered it."

"And you just *happened* to have another batch with you?"

"He likes to have backup plans," she said. "I think he put the canister in my belt so he would have extra if he needed it."

"You didn't know it was there?"

Thalias hunched her shoulders. "No. But would it have mattered if I did? As long as we remain family hostages, our master owns us. Heart, soul, and life. He can do what he wishes with all three."

"I would call that barbarous," Yiv said, the strange tendrils on his shoulders waving a little harder than usual, "if that wasn't basically the same arrangement I demand of my own conquered peoples. Perhaps he and I are even more alike than I thought. Did he tell you what the message was that he had you deliver?"

Thalias shook her head. "No."

"It was quite interesting," Yiv said, setting the tava canister on the arm of his chair and pulling out the envelope Thalias had given the Vak soldier at the landing platform. "He's offering an alliance with the Chiss Ascendancy in return for permission to come to Primea and challenge me." He gave a snort and set the envelope beside the canister. "Also excruciatingly naïve. Does he really think the Vaks could make a decision like that without studying every aspect and every nuance?"

"My master is very good at reading cultures," Thalias said.

"Really," Yiv said. "When you return to Csilla, you must look up the story of his dealings with the Garwians and Lioaoi. The *real* story, not the version available to the public."

"Why?" Thalias asked. "What's different about it?"

"Oh, far be it from me to ruin the surprise," Yiv said cheerfully. "But I've had the full truth from the Lioaoi. Let's just say that your master isn't nearly as good as he thinks." He considered. "Not that it matters in this case, because no one in the Combine will ever read his offer. The letter the Vaks actually received was merely an apology and an earnest hope that this won't sour the Combine's view of the Chiss. Content that, I daresay, they won't need to endlessly debate."

Thalias looked at Che'ri. The girl was trying to keep up a good front, but Thalias could see that Yiv's one–two punch with the tava canister and his substitute note had left her shaken.

Yiv had spotted it, too. "I seem to have upset your fellow hostage," he said with feigned concern. "Or perhaps she's simply not as good at hiding her feelings as you are."

"We're hostages," Thalias said. "Our feelings also lie at the mercy of our master and his family."

"No doubt she would learn with age and practice," Yiv said. "Well, perhaps your next master will continue her training. Would you care to retire to a resting area for a bit? I'll want you here with me when Thrawn arrives—I'm sure he'll want to see you—but that will be several more hours."

"Or several more days," Thalias said. "Primea is a long way from the Ascendancy via jump-by-jump travel."

"Not a problem," Yiv said with another broad smile. "He'll certainly wish to hire a navigator for such an important meeting. And that navigator—*my* navigator—is likely even now coming aboard his freighter. A few hours, maybe less, and it will all be over."

"I'm glad you were available for this journey," Thrawn said, handing Qilori a steaming mug.

"As am I," Qilori said, sniffing approvingly. Galara tealeaf, his favorite drink. "I'd just returned to the concourse and was looking over the list of possible jobs when your message came through."

"I'm glad you were willing to wait for my arrival."

"I was happy to do so," Qilori said. "For one thing, voyages with you are never boring. For another—" He hefted his mug.

"The tealeaf?"

"Yes," Qilori said. "Very few Pathfinder employers remember their navigator's preferences. A large number don't even bother to learn our names."

"It seemed appropriate," Thrawn said. "Since this will likely be our last voyage together."

"Really?" Qilori asked, frowning at the Chiss over the edge of the mug. "How so?"

"I'm going to Primea to ransom my two hostages from General Yiv," Thrawn said. "I don't expect the exchange to end well."

"Oh," Qilori said, trying for the right mix of surprise and concern. "Surely you're not expecting treachery? Yiv the Benevolent has always struck me as upright and honorable in his dealings with others. At least when the other party has also been honorable. You aren't planning any tricks, are you?"

"He wanted me to come alone in an unarmed freighter." Thrawn waved a hand around them. "Do you see anyone else? Or any weapons?"

"Well, certainly not from *here*," Qilori said with a shrug. Though considering that he'd given the freighter's hull a thorough visual inspection before coming aboard, and had spent his last rest period surreptitiously checking for weapons controls, he was considerably more certain than his offhanded comment made it look.

Still, there was something odd about the freighter's shape, something that had caught his attention as he'd spiraled around it earlier. It was nothing hugely out of the ordinary for this class of ship, and he couldn't even codify what it was that was different. Yet hours later, it was still nagging at him.

"You can therefore affirm that I've followed his instructions," Thrawn said.

"In which case you should have nothing to fear," Qilori said.

"Perhaps," Thrawn said. "Are you ready for the final segment?"

"I am," Qilori said, taking one last sip of his tealeaf and setting the mug aside. Thrawn was right: It *would* be their last voyage together. Qilori would have to thank the Benevolent later for letting him be present to watch the arrogant, Pathfinder-murdering Chiss die. "Another half hour, and we'll be there."

"Good," Thrawn said, settling himself in his chair. "Let's make an end of it, Qilori of Uandualon. One way, or another."

CHAPTER TWENTY-ONE

nsight. In the end, Ar'alani mused, that was what it came down to. Analysis followed, then extrapolation and countermove. Those were what made a successful military campaign. But it all started with insight.

And if the insight was in error, the rest collapsed like an ice bridge over a bonfire.

Thrawn claimed to understand Yiv. He claimed to understand the Vaks.

But he'd also thought he understood the Lioaoi and the Garwians. His failure there had stirred up old animosities and political conflicts, had gotten a bunch of aliens killed, and had put the Ascendancy in the middle with dirt on its hands. If he was wrong this time, there would be more deaths.

Only this time, many of the dead would be Chiss.

There was a movement to her left, and she looked up to see Wutroow come to a stop beside the command chair. "Breakout in five minutes," the *Vigilant*'s first officer reported. "All systems and stations report ready."

"Thank you, Senior Captain," Ar'alani said. "Anything else?"

Wutroow pursed her lips. "I trust you realize, Admiral, that we're walking on splintered eggs here. We only have Senior Captain Thrawn's assumption that the Vaks haven't completely gone over to the Nikardun side. If they have, we're going to end up fighting both of them. And unless the Vaks attack us directly, we have no authorization whatsoever to fire on them."

"It gets worse," Ar'alani warned, thinking back to the Lioaoi fighters she and Thrawn had seen at the Lioaoin heartworld. "If the Vaks have joined Yiv, there may already be Nikardun crews aboard Vak warships. We won't know for sure who's who until they open fire."

"And until then, they can maneuver all they want, play blocker for Nikardun ships, or even range their weapons against us," Wutroow said darkly. "Until they actually fire, we can't legally do anything."

"Well, maybe we'll get lucky and the Vaks will declare war as soon as they see us coming for them," Ar'alani said. "That would make things easier."

"Yes, ma'am." Wutroow hesitated. "This Republic energy shield Thrawn brought back from the edge of the Chaos. How good is it, really?"

"I don't know," Ar'alani admitted. "I was there for some of the tests when they were figuring out how to wire it to Chiss power systems, and it looked pretty impressive. But how strong it is, and how long it'll last under sustained fire—" She shook her head. "No idea. I suppose we'll find out."

"I suppose we will." Wutroow huffed out a breath. "With your permission, Admiral, I think I'll run the weapons crews through one final system check. I assume you've made arrangements to get sky-walker Ab'begh off the bridge as soon as we arrive at Primea?"

"I've assigned two warriors to take her back to the suite," Ar'alani said. "They'll stay there with her and her caregiver until the battle's over."

"Good idea," Wutroow said. "Thrawn losing his sky-walker was bad enough. If we got boarded and lost ours, too, we'd never hear the end of it."

Ar'alani had to smile. "And if *that's* the only thing you have to worry about today, Senior Captain, your life must be going remarkably well."

"Thank you, Admiral," Wutroow said innocently. "I do my best. With your permission, I'll get started on that weapons check."

With a final urging from the Great Presence, and a final twitch of Qilori's fingers, they arrived.

"Well," Thrawn commented as Qilori pulled off his sensory-deprivation headset. "I see General Yiv has one final surprise for us."

Qilori blinked moisture back into his eyes. Standing thirty kilometers off the freighter's bow was a formation of four massive Battle Dreadnoughts. "Why, did he say he was going to come unarmed, too?" he asked, trying to keep the sudden nervousness out of his voice. That was a *lot* of military hardware out there, a good half of the force the Nikardun had in this region.

He'd assumed Yiv would be content to just bring the *Deathless* to the rendezvous. Apparently, the Benevolent had decided to err on the side of caution.

"No, of course I assumed he would bring extra ships," Thrawn said. "I was referring to the fact that these aren't the coordinates he sent in his message."

"They're *not*?" Qilori asked, feigning surprise. These were the coordinates Yiv had given to *him*, but of course Thrawn wasn't supposed to know that. "I don't understand. These are the ones you downloaded into the ship's computer before we left the concourse."

"Then someone switched them after I handed them to the dispatcher." Thrawn pointed to the left, where the planet Primea was a small dot in the distance. "We were supposed to come out in a high planetary orbit. Apparently, the general wanted to carry out our transaction in a less conspicuous part of the system."

He reached to the control board and keyed the comm. "General Yiv, this is Senior Captain Thrawn. I trust my companions are undamaged?"

The comm display lit up. Yiv was seated in his command chair, his shoulder symbionts waving their usual unnerving rhythm. Kneeling on the deck in front of him were his two prisoners. One of them was the female whom Qilori had seen at the Primea diplomatic reception where Thrawn and Yiv had first met, the female he'd heard Thrawn refer to as a family hostage. The other was much younger, possibly not even in her teens, both of them wearing the same grotesque makeup. Whatever this hostage thing was the Chiss were running, it apparently started very young. "See for yourself the shape of your *hostages*, Captain," Yiv said, leaning on the word as he waved a casual hand over them. "You have the ransom?"

"I do," Thrawn said. "The money is in an equipment pod, ready to send to your ship whenever my companions are in a shuttle. The two craft will cross the void together, of course."

"I'm afraid you misunderstand, Captain," Yiv said, and Qilori shivered at the smug malice in his tone. "The money isn't the ransom. *You* are the ransom."

"I see," Thrawn said calmly. If he was surprised by the sudden treachery, it didn't show in his face or voice. "Do you plan to shoot me down from there?"

"You stole one of my ships and killed one of my crews," Yiv said, the smugness gone. "For that you've automatically earned death at my hand. I'd prefer to bring you aboard the *Deathless* so I can watch you die, but if you insist I can certainly do it from here."

"I do not so insist," Thrawn assured him. "I merely wish to ascertain the parameters of our altered agreement. Do I assume that since the location for our meeting was changed, all the rest of the original provisions are no longer in force?"

"Probably," Yiv said, the smugness back. With the death sentence now pronounced with the proper harshness, the Benevolent was settling back to enjoy watching his enemy squirm. "Are there any provisions in particular you'd like to revisit?"

"Let me first commend you for your insight in moving the meeting to this spot," Thrawn said. "I presume you felt Primea orbit would be too public a venue? Especially since you don't want the Vaks to see how much military force you have in the area?"

"That would hardly be a surprise," Yiv assured him. "They've seen these ships, and more. It's amazing how the presence of Battle Dreadnoughts can smooth out a round of negotiations."

"Perhaps in general," Thrawn said. "Perhaps not with a people like the Vaks. You were also wise enough to stay within the Primea system instead of moving us elsewhere. This way, you can calculate and execute a jump journey over to the planet within a relatively few minutes."

"I don't anticipate any reason to hurry over there," Yiv said. A hint of caution had crept into his voice, Qilori noted with some trepidation of his own. If there was anyone who should be worried about his situation, it was Thrawn. Why was he instead making casual conversation on irrelevant subjects? "Are you expecting the Combine leadership to suddenly need a conversation with me?"

"Not necessarily," Thrawn said. "You asked which part of our agreement I wanted to revisit."

"And?"

"Just one provision," Thrawn said. "The part about me coming to Primea alone."

The hyperspace swirl became star-flares, then stars, and the *Springhawk* had arrived.

"Dalvu: Sensor scan," Samakro ordered, doing a quick visual check of his own. There was a *lot* of traffic out there, ships of all sizes and styles moving in or out or just orbiting Primea while they awaited their turn. Not surprising for a center of commerce and diplomatic contact, but it was going to make drawing out the enemy that much harder.

Or perhaps even impossible if Thrawn's analysis of Nikardun ship parameters proved inadequate to the job. If the task force couldn't pick Yiv's ships out of the swarm, the mission would be over before it even started.

Leaving Thrawn to face Yiv alone.

"*Vigilant* has arrived, Mid Captain," Dalvu announced.

"Acknowledged," Samakro said, peering out at the Nightdragon that had just appeared in the distance in front of the *Springhawk*. As he watched, the rest of Ar'alani's force popped in from hyperspace, the cruisers, destroyers, and missile boats moving quickly into screening formation around her as they arrived. "Kharill, do we have her signal yet?"

"Coming online now, sir," Kharill confirmed. "Open communication to Primea and all the rest of the force." There was a double-click—

"Primea Central Command, this is Admiral Ar'alani of the Chiss Expansionary Defense Fleet," Ar'alani identified herself. "May I assume you received the message from my colleague, Senior Captain Thrawn?"

"This is Command," an official-sounding voice came back promptly. "We did."

"And have you considered it?"

"We have," the Vak said. "We wait upon your confirmation of the identities and locations of Nikardun vessels."

"Acknowledged," Ar'alani said. "Our officers are gathering that data now."

"Dalvu?" Samakro prompted. "Seconds count."

"But so does neatness," Kharill added.

"Agreed," Samakro said, fighting back his impatience. The orbiting Nikardun ships were undoubtedly even now reporting to Yiv that a Chiss fleet had arrived and were requesting orders. The longer the sensor analysis took, the more likely Yiv would order an attack and the Nikardun would get in the first shot.

Normally, that would be a good thing, the excuse the Chiss needed to shoot back. In this case, though, that kind of political spit-splitting would be less than useless.

But they had to be careful. Letting a Nikardun slip unidentified beneath their sensor threshold would be bad enough. Inadvertently targeting an innocent ship would be worse. The seconds ticked by . . .

"Got them, sir," Dalvu said with clear satisfaction. "I make it thirty-two ships, ranging in size from destroyers to missile boats."

"Got the *Vigilant*'s list," the comm officer put in. "Also *Grayshrike*'s and *Whisperbird*'s analyses."

"All four match," Dalvu announced. "Repeat: full confirmation ID on thirty-two enemy ships. Deployment pattern . . . well, well." She touched a key, and the tagged Nikardun ships came up on the tactical.

"Would you look at that?" Kharill said with feigned surprise. "I'd say that's a blockade formation."

"So it is," Samakro agreed. Deployed that way, probably, in order to keep anyone from wandering out of the regular traffic flow and accidentally blundering into Yiv's confrontation with Thrawn, wherever it was Yiv had moved it.

But of course, the Vaks wouldn't know that was the reason.

"*Vigilant*'s sending the profile to Primea Command," Kharill reported.

"Good," Samakro said. "Let's see if they come to the correct conclusion."

"They'd better hurry," Kharill warned. "Yiv can't possibly be hoping to bully a system like this without a lot more firepower close at hand. I'd prefer we have the chance to take out his bumpers before his bruisers get here."

"Admiral Ar'alani, this is Command," the Vak voice came back. "Do I assume from the pattern that we are the object of a Nikardun blockade?"

"I would say so, Command, yes," Ar'alani confirmed. "Will you hold your defense ships back while we clear it out?"

"That question was also asked by Captain Thrawn," Command said. "The answer is now decided. We will hold back."

"Thank you," Ar'alani said. "Task force, you have your targets. Engage at will."

"You heard the admiral," Samakro ordered, tapping ID locks onto the two closest Nikardun ships. "We'll start with these two. Azmordi, get us moving—flank speed."

"No," Yiv said, his eyes focused slightly off to the side. The smugness had vanished completely from his voice, replaced by utter disbelief and a growing anger, his symbionts' tendrils waving restlessly. "It's not possible. You're simply not important enough for the Chiss to send a war fleet to rescue you."

"You assume this display of Chiss power is because of me," Thrawn said. "It's far more likely the Vak Combine itself called for Ascendancy aid."

"Absurdity begets absurdity," Yiv scoffed. "The fools would never make a decision like that. They aren't even close to having all the thought lines they need, let alone to having considered all of them."

"You misunderstand them, General," Thrawn said. "That will prove your undoing. Would you like to know what was in the message I sent them?"

"I *know* what was in the message," Yiv retorted. "I took it from your hostage."

"And substituted something far more innocuous," Thrawn said. "Of course you did. What you failed to realize was that I left another message in the fighter's computer. Would you like to hear what it said?"

Yiv's attention jerked back to the comm from whatever he was looking at, a terrible fire blazing in his eyes. "Tell me," he invited softly.

" 'To Primea Command, this is Senior Captain Thrawn,' " Thrawn said. " 'My companion Thalias has delivered a message to your representative, a copy of which is reproduced below. If it's the same message as you've already received, then all is well, and you may consider my offer at your leisure.

" 'However, if you did *not*, in fact, receive this same message from my companion's hand, we may conclude that some of your officers and troops have conspired with General Yiv to withhold my message from you. If that is the case, I urge you to consider my offer with all necessary speed. To aid in your decision, I also include data from other systems that have had dealings with the Nikardun, as well as information about a ship full of refugees he murdered. I or my representatives will journey to Primea in the near future to discuss the matter with you.' "

Thrawn stopped, and for a long moment Yiv just gazed at him in silence. "Absurdity," he said at last. "The Vaks won't move this quickly. They can't. They consider all thought lines. *All* thought lines."

Thrawn shook his head. "No. What they consider—"

"Curse!" Yiv cut him off, his gaze snapping back and forth to unseen displays around him. "No! They can't be. The Vaks—" He snarled something else, and suddenly the image blanked.

"What's going on?" Qilori asked, his cheek winglets quivering. Three minutes ago, the Benevolent had had everything completely under control. What in the Depths was happening out there?

"I assume Admiral Ar'alani has finished her negotiations," Thrawn said, his voice glacially calm, "and that the Vaks have given permission for her to fire on the Nikardun blockade ships."

"The blockade ships? But—" Qilori strangled off the reflexive protest. Of course a mere Pathfinder hireling wouldn't know that Yiv's current plans for Primea didn't include a blockade. "There's a *blockade*?"

"Presumably merely to prevent anyone from blundering into our conversation," Thrawn said, a little too drily. "But of course the Vaks don't know that. They see only that by imposing his will on Primea's commerce, Yiv has denied them important thought lines."

He turned to Qilori, an odd and discomfiting intensity in those glowing red eyes. "Tell me, Pathfinder. Do you think Yiv will meekly stand by and watch his Primea fleet be destroyed?"

"I don't know," Qilori said helplessly. What was he supposed to say? "I suppose it depends on whether he can afford to lose the ships."

"You offer the wrong question," Thrawn said. "Of course he can afford to lose the ships. The true question is whether he can allow the Vaks to see him bow to Chiss will and cower before Chiss might."

"Surely all the ships at Primea are smaller vessels," Qilori said. "It's no disgrace to lose small warships to large ones."

"It is if there are larger ships available and their commander refuses to risk them."

"Maybe the Vaks don't know he has bigger ships."

"Of course they do," Thrawn chided. "He just said that they did."

Qilori silently cursed at himself. It had been a stupid, stupid thing to say. "I just meant—"

"But these are just worksheet details," Thrawn interrupted. "The answer is, no, he can't afford for Primea to see his weakness." He nodded toward the viewport. "As you see."

"As I *see*?" Qilori repeated, following Thrawn's gaze. The four Nikardun Battle Dreadnoughts arrayed against them . . .

Had become just one. The *Deathless* was still there, its awesome weaponry still turned toward Thrawn's freighter. But the other three Battle Dreadnoughts were gone.

"That should make the battle a bit more of a challenge," Thrawn commented, touching the comm switch. "Provided Admiral Ar'alani hasn't made too much of a mess of the Nikardun blockade ships. General, are you still there?"

"I'm here, Thrawn." Abruptly, the display lit up again with Yiv's face.

Only this wasn't the cheerful, persuasive, charming friend-of-all-peoples face the Benevolent liked to show his would-be conquests. It wasn't even the quietly menacing face that Qilori had seen on far too many occasions, a face that never failed to send palpitations through his cheek winglets even when the threat wasn't directed at him.

This face was something new. This face was pure hatred.

"Your people will die for this," the Nikardun ground out. "Not just you. Not just your pitiable fleet. *All* the Chiss. The Ascendancy will die, shredded like grain, ground down like stone, burned like withered grass. Every last cub will die . . . and you will die here and now, with the certain knowledge that you and you alone were the root and cause of their destruction."

"All because I cost you your foothold on Primea?" Thrawn asked, his voice and face as calm as Yiv's were malevolent. "Come now, General. You merely need to step away and start over." His face hardened. "But I suggest you choose a different part of the Chaos for your next attempt. This region will no longer accept your smiles and promises."

"How little you know, Chiss."

"Then enlighten me," Thrawn invited. "Tell me who you serve, or who follows in your wake. If there's more to know than just the Nikardun, I'm more than willing to listen."

Yiv's mouth opened in a smile that was just as bitterly angry as his glare had been. "Then you'll forever wonder as I send you to your grave." Deliberately, he looked down at the two females kneeling in front of him. "But before you leave this life, I'll show you exactly what I have planned for your entire species."

The *Springhawk* had just sent its third Nikardun patrol boat into shredded oblivion when the three Battle Dreadnoughts suddenly flashed into view.

"And the bruisers have arrived," Kharill announced calmly. "Nice microjump, or whatever they did."

"Looked like an in-system jump," Azmordi said from the helm. "Shorter and easier than even a micro."

"Also doesn't leave enough backtrail to show where it came from," Dalvu added grimly. "If they came from Yiv, we still don't know where he is."

Which meant they couldn't go to Thrawn's aid if he needed them, Samakro knew. Thrawn's life was in his own hands now. If he'd miscalculated any aspect of the plan—if he stumbled on any of the steps—he would likely die out there. So would a lot of Chiss.

And the *Springhawk* would be in need of a new captain.

Stop it! Samakro ordered himself. Thrawn was his commander, the rightful master of this ship, and Samakro's job was to do his duty to Ar'alani and the Ascendancy and to return the *Springhawk* to its master in the best shape he could.

Which was suddenly a more challenging proposition than it had been thirty seconds ago. "Orders, Admiral?" he called.

"We split them up," Ar'alani said. "*Grayshrike, Whisperbird, Stingfly*: Take the one to starboard. I'll take the one to portside. *Springhawk*, you move on the middle one. Don't fully engage, just keep it occupied. Everyone else, watch your backs and continue your attrition of the patrol craft."

"Acknowledged," Samakro said. So the *Springhawk*, all alone against a Battle Dreadnought? Terrific.

"At least she's not expecting us to destroy it outright," Kharill said drily. "I don't suppose you have any idea how we keep something that size occupied?"

Samakro smiled. "As a matter of fact," he said. "I do."

CHAPTER TWENTY-TWO

But before you leave this life, Yiv had said in a voice that had sent a fresh shiver through Che'ri's skin, *I'll show you exactly what I have planned for your entire species.*

He was taking about her, she knew. Her and Thalias. Thrawn had promised that no harm would come to either of them, and Che'ri had held on to that hope through this whole thing.

But now doubt was beginning to chew away at the edges of that hope. Thrawn still sounded confident . . . but he was out there, all alone, and Che'ri and Thalias were in here, surrounded by Nikardun.

And yet, somehow, it felt like Thrawn was still in control. Admiral Ar'alani and a fleet of Chiss warships were at the planet, and they'd done something that had made Yiv so angry or frightened that he'd sent his other three big ships over there to stop them. That had to be part of the plan, didn't it?

She stole a sideways look up at Yiv, wincing. She'd been wrong. He wasn't frightened, not at all. He was just angry. Angry, hate-filled, and confident.

The other Nikardun on the bridge were talking together in a language Che'ri didn't understand. Carefully, trying not to attract Yiv's attention, she leaned a little closer to Thalias. "Do you know what they're saying?" she whispered.

Thalias shook her head. "It's their own language," she whispered back. "It's only when they talk to us or Thrawn that they use Minnisiat or—"

Abruptly, someone gave a wordless scream.

Che'ri flinched back, her heart seizing up. The scream had come from behind her, from Yiv himself. He'd heard her talking to Thalias, and now he was going to hurt her. Another wordless scream, and out of the corner of her eye she saw his hand jab out over her head at one of the other Nikardun. The other gave a nervous-sounding answer and touched a switch on his control board—

"Nikardun Battle Dreadnought, this is the Chiss Expansionary Defense Fleet warship *Springhawk*," a calm Chiss voice came over the speaker in Minnisiat.

Che'ri frowned. Was that Mid Captain Samakro? Why was he talking to one of the Nikardun ships?

"I feel you should know that we're Senior Captain Thrawn's personal ship," Samakro continued. "As such, it's only sporting for me to offer you the chance to surrender before we destroy you."

Yiv gave out another scream and again jabbed a finger. The same Nikardun gave a jerky nod and hastily shut off the transmission.

Jerky. Hasty. Like he was scared?

Carefully, she looked back at Thalias. The older woman was keeping perfectly still, but there was a tiny smile playing at the corner of her mouth. Che'ri frowned.

And then, she got it. The Nikardun on the *Deathless*'s bridge were scared, all right. But they weren't scared of Thrawn. They were scared of their own leader. Whatever Samakro had been trying to do with that transmission, he'd made Yiv even more furious than he'd been before.

Which might not be a good thing, Che'ri realized with a fresh shiver. The stories about Thrawn talked about times when he'd deliberately made an enemy angry in order to keep him from thinking straight. But in this case, Yiv had her and Thalias as hostages, and he'd already threatened to hurt them. Making him angry might just make him hurt them sooner.

"That's good advice, General," Thrawn's voice said over the speaker. "Be advised that if you continue along your current path I'm fully prepared to destroy you."

"Your freighter against a Battle Dreadnought?" Yiv said contemptuously. "Your foolishness is matched only by your arrogance. Both will light your way to destruction. Whatever you do now, you die. You and all the Chiss will die."

"Then make an end of it," Thrawn invited. "Come and take me."

Che'ri could feel her breath coming in quick, shallow gulps. Again, she could sense that this was all part of Thrawn's plan. Again, she had no idea what it might be.

But again, Thalias was smiling.

Again, Qilori hadn't the slightest idea what Thrawn was doing. But the small smile on the Chiss's face chilled him straight to the bone.

He was up to something. Sitting out here, making no move to either advance or retreat, inviting Yiv to come and get him . . . but there wasn't any possible end to this gambit except Thrawn's utter destruction.

And then, suddenly, he got it.

Yiv was focused on Thrawn. Completely and obsessively on Thrawn. Nothing would distract him from that focus.

Which left the *Deathless* completely open to an attack from the rear.

Qilori felt his winglets quivering. He'd never anticipated he might need to communicate surreptitiously with the Benevolent on this trip, and so had never set up a tap into the freighter's comm system. How could he warn him that Thrawn was goading him from here to keep him from anticipating the attack that would come from a completely unexpected direction?

"Pathfinder Qilori."

Qilori jerked. "Yes?"

"You seem upset," Thrawn said. "You're possibly thinking I have another force prepared, waiting for the proper time to launch its attack?"

Qilori's winglets flattened. How in the Depths did he *do* that? "I have no idea one way or the other," he said diplomatically.

"But you know how it could be done, don't you?" Thrawn persisted. "Even given the altered coordinates that you substituted for the ones in Yiv's original message."

"I don't—" He broke off as Thrawn turned those glowing red eyes on him. "It's not my concern."

"Come now, Pathfinder, don't be so modest," Thrawn said. "You and I understand, even if many of Yiv's victims don't. For a long time he's been using the Pathfinders' ability to locate each other through hyperspace to coordinate his attacks."

"No, of course not," Qilori protested reflexively. "Direct cooperation with a military force would be a blatant violation of Navigators' Guild rules."

"And would likely lead the guild to eject the Pathfinders from its organization?"

Qilori swallowed hard. "It could happen," he admitted.

"Not just *could*," Thrawn said. "You'd prefer, then, that I keep that knowledge to myself?"

Qilori glared at him. "Of course," he ground out. "What's your price?"

Thrawn turned back to the viewport. "The price," he said, "is for you to forget everything you see from this point on."

"Fine," Qilori said.

It was a simple enough promise, he told himself. Yiv would probably also want him to forget today's events, and he had a long history of obeying the Benevolent's orders.

"And as to your earlier fear," Thrawn continued, "there's no need for me to launch any attack. The battle for the Vak Combine is taking place over Primea, and has left Yiv with only two options. One: He can stay here and attempt to destroy me, thus giving the impression that he's hiding from the battle. Two: He can leave to bolster his forces, and thus appear that he's running from me." He gestured toward the *Deathless*. "Even now he attempts to decide which of those scenarios will damage his reputation less."

"It will be interesting to see which way he goes," Qilori muttered.

And really, there would be no question of Thrawn keeping that potentially devastating knowledge about the Pathfinders to himself. Not once he was dead.

Another barrage of spectrum laser fire blasted across the *Springhawk*'s hull, knocking out three more sections of the electrostatic barrier and gouging a couple of fresh grooves in the metal. At least, Samakro thought distantly as he shouted orders, Ar'alani couldn't claim he hadn't obeyed his orders.

The *Springhawk* was keeping the Battle Dreadnought busy, all right.

"Watch it, *Springhawk*, you've got two gunboats angling in from ventral portside," one of the other Chiss ships snapped in warning.

"On it," Kharill said, and there was a double-thud as a pair of plasma spheres blasted off toward the attacking gunboats.

"Keep us rolling," Samakro said, looking at the tactical. The two Nikardun were trying to veer out of the paths of the plasma spheres.

But it was too late. Both gunboats flared as the spheres hit them, spraying hot, ionized gas across their sensors and external control lines and sending high-voltage spikes into the deeper parts beneath the hull metal. There were multiple flickers as power systems overloaded or got shunted, and a second later both Nikardun were coasting along, temporarily dead.

"Azmordi, swing us around," he ordered the helm. "Get us behind them. Use them as shields."

"For whatever that'll buy us," Kharill warned quietly.

Samakro grimaced. It wouldn't buy them much, unfortunately. He'd tried dodging, running, feinting, and straight-up toe-to-toe slugging, and while he was wearing down the Nikardun Dreadnought the *Springhawk* was wearing down even faster. Even frequent sniping sorties by some of the other Chiss hadn't been enough to deflect the Nikardun captain from his single-minded pursuit.

Yiv didn't just want Thrawn dead. He apparently wanted everything even associated with him to also be destroyed.

Two more salvos skated across the *Springhawk*'s hull before

Azmordi got them into the protected zone behind the two disabled gunboats. "Okay, we've got a little breathing space," Kharill said. "Any thoughts as to what to do with it?"

Samakro considered. They were still a good distance from the Battle Dreadnought, which was why they hadn't been completely destroyed yet. But the vector they were currently on was taking them closer to their attacker than they'd been so far.

That wouldn't be a particularly good thing once their Nikardun traveling companions got their systems back online. But for the moment . . .

He glanced at the tactical, did a quick distance calculation. Marginal, but it might just work. "How many breachers do we have left?" he asked, looking past the edge of the disabled ships at the Dreadnought and its mockingly big bridge viewport.

"Three," Kharill said.

"Prep them," Samakro ordered. "We'll give it a few more seconds, get as close as we dare, then blast all three straight at the Dreadnought's viewport."

"Yes, sir," Kharill said, a little uncertainly. "You *do* realize we've already tried that, right?"

"From considerably farther away," Samakro reminded him. "If we get close enough, the Dreadnought can blast them whenever it wants to and the acid still won't have time to dissipate before it reaches the viewport."

"Worth a try," Kharill agreed. "Okay; breachers prepped. Call it."

Samakro counted out the seconds to himself, trying to gauge the right time to fire. Too soon and they'd be wasting their last breachers in a useless attempt; too late, and they would risk the two gunboats beside them waking up and adding their own bit of catastrophe into the *Springhawk*'s current mix. "Stand by to fire: Three, two, *one*."

With a soft triple-jolt, the three breacher missiles blasted away, skimming past the gunboats on their way to the Battle Dreadnought.

They'd barely cleared the gunboats' hulls when six spectrum lasers lashed out from the Dreadnought, catching the breachers and blowing them to shreds.

Sooner than Samakro had hoped. But with breachers, destruction of the missiles themselves wasn't the last word. The released masses of acid were still in motion, the tendrils still twisting and spinning as their initial momentum continued to carry them toward their target. Unless the Dreadnought could get out of the way—and the acid was already too close for that—it was going to get hit. Samakro held his breath . . .

And then, almost at the last moment, one of the Nikardun patrol craft shot in from the side, braking hard to put itself directly in the path of the three incoming acid globs.

"It's not big enough," Kharill muttered hopefully. "It can't block all three of them." The words were barely out of his mouth when the Dreadnought again opened fire.

Only this time, the target was the Nikardun patrol craft in front of it. Even as Samakro felt his mouth drop open in disbelief the ship exploded, scattering debris in all directions.

And the debris cloud, unfortunately, *was* big enough to block all three acid globs.

"Curse it," Kharill bit out. "These guys are crazy."

"*Springhawk,* what's your status?" Ar'alani's voice came over the speaker.

"We're still here, Admiral," Samakro said. "But we wouldn't turn down any timely aid you wanted to offer."

"Timely aid it is," Ar'alani said grimly. "I was hoping we wouldn't have to go with this, but so be it. Do you remember the maneuver Thrawn used against the Paataatus when he first took command of the *Springhawk*?"

Samakro looked up at Kharill, found the other staring back with a sour expression. They both remembered, all right. "Yes, ma'am," Samakro said. "When?"

"Hold behind the gunboats you flickered another few seconds, then come out and angle toward low orbit. I'll tell you when to go dark."

"Acknowledged," Samakro said, wondering what this was supposed to accomplish. The Battle Dreadnought had already shown it was willing to go anywhere and through anyone—including its own people—in order to keep pressure on the *Springhawk*. "Azmordi, get ready . . . go." With a wrenching twist, the *Springhawk* pitched away from the gunboats and blasted across the battlefield toward the planet below. "Stand by to go dark." He counted out three seconds—

"Go," Ar'alani ordered.

"Acknowledged," Samakro said. Across the bridge, his officers shut off their systems, their boards going dark, dim emergency lighting coming on.

And with that, the *Springhawk* had become nearly as helpless as it was possible for a warship to be.

Though for the moment, at least, their imminent destruction would be postponed a bit. The firing lines from the Battle Dreadnought were currently blocked by a running battle between two of the Chiss missile boats and a Nikardun destroyer. Another few seconds, though, and the *Springhawk*'s vector would take it into the clear. "Captain?" Kharill prompted.

"I don't know," Samakro said. "Let's see what the admiral has in mind."

They didn't have long to wait. "Vak patrol boat, we have a ship with critical life-support failure," Ar'alani called. "None of our ships are close enough to offer assistance. Can any of your ships render aid?"

"Chiss warship, we are not combatants," a Vak voice came back. "We cannot interfere in your war."

Samakro felt his lip twist. *Your war?* The Chiss were trying to defend the Vak homeworld, for hell's sake. How was that *your war*?

"I know, and I accept that," Ar'alani said, apparently not wanting to get into the politics of the situation. "But under the circumstances surely you can offer humanitarian aid?"

"We will," the Vak said reluctantly. "Nikardun warships, two patrol ships are moving to render humanitarian aid. Do not fire upon them. Repeat, do not fire upon them."

"I confirm that, Nikardun commander," Ar'alani added. "The Vak ships are not entering combat, but only rendering humanitarian aid. Do not, repeat, do *not* fire on them."

Ahead, just off the *Springhawk*'s starboard bow, two Vak patrol ships were on the move, heading toward the supposedly crippled ship. "So do we continue to play dead?" Kharill asked. "Somehow, I can't see the Nikardun standing off and courteously letting us recover before trying to stomp us again."

"I assume Ar'alani's got a plan—"

An instant later the sky lit up as one of the two Vak ships disintegrated in a blaze of Nikardun laserfire. "Nikardun!" Ar'alani snapped again. "Do not attack! Do not attack!"

She might as well have saved her breath. There was a second laser barrage, and the other patrol ship was gone as well. "Nikardun, those were not combatants," Ar'alani ground out.

"Maybe they weren't before," Kharill said, an odd tone to his voice. "But I do believe they are now."

Samakro frowned. He was right. All around them, the Vak patrol ships that had been studiously staying away from the combat zone were suddenly on the move. In groups of three and four they were converging on the Battle Dreadnought, their missiles blazing toward the huge ship, their lasers flashing against its electrostatic barriers and digging into its hull.

"Lesson for today," Kharill continued. "Don't get so focused on one enemy that you end up making another one. Ready to come back to life?"

"Let's not," Samakro said. "Ar'alani said we were teetering on the edge of disaster. It wouldn't look very good if we suddenly showed we weren't."

"Yes, I doubt the Vaks would be happy to know they were betrayed by one side and manipulated by the other," Kharill agreed. "Then . . . ?"

"We sit back," Samakro said. "Try to avoid any obvious attacks.

"And watch the show."

"What is his plan?" Yiv shouted, leaning over to slap Thalias across the back of her head. "*What is his plan?*"

"I don't know," Thalias said.

"He brings in Chiss warships to attack me," Yiv snarled as if she hadn't spoken. "He goads the Vaks into conspiring with them against me. What is his purpose? What is his goal?"

He reached down and dug his fingers into her hair, twisting her head around to face him. "What is his *plan*?"

"I don't—" Thalias winced back as his hand slapped at her face, managing to turn just far enough to take the blow on her ear instead of her cheek. The concussion sent a spear of pain and dizziness through her whole head.

"There's no need for that, General," Thrawn's calm voice said over the bridge speaker. "My plan is to put you in a box. And so you are."

"I can destroy you whenever I choose," Yiv bit out.

"Once you've moved within weapons range," Thrawn amended. "A position I'll note you don't seem that eager to achieve."

"Would you like to see your death coming more quickly?" Yiv retorted. "Helm: Increase speed."

"I thought you wanted to bring me aboard the *Deathless* so that you could kill me yourself."

"You invited me yourself to come get you," Yiv said. "Make up your mind."

"It doesn't matter," Thrawn said. "It's already too late. You've spent too long here for the Vaks and your own people not to conclude you don't wish to join the battle over Primea. Leaving now will be interpreted as an attempt to escape from me. Either way, your reputation is permanently damaged."

"Only if there are any witnesses left to tell a tale other than my own," Yiv said.

"Interestingly enough, I've had that same thought," Thrawn said. "You have only one move left, only one way to salvage your name and position. You'll come within tractor beam range and bring my ship aboard. I'll disembark, you'll transfer my companions aboard, and they'll leave in peace."

Yiv gave a contemptuous snort. "A long way to go, Chiss, just to take me where I planned to go in the first place. As I think about it, perhaps it would be just as satisfying to destroy you where you sit."

"And what of my companions?"

"I told you I'd use them to show what I intended for the entire Chiss species," Yiv said. "You're right, it would be more impressive if you were aboard to watch their dismemberment instead of watching from your freighter."

Che'ri gave a little whimper. *It's all right,* Thalias thought urgently in her direction. *It's all right. Just hold on a little longer.*

"Very well, General," Thrawn said calmly. "If you've chosen to face me, so be it. I await your tractor beam."

For a moment, Yiv remained silent. Testing Thrawn's words for flaws or betrayal, no doubt.

But he wouldn't find any, Thalias knew. More important, Thrawn had twisted the situation to where Yiv was angry and frustrated, and where revenge was the most important thing on his mind. The chance to bring Thrawn aboard alive and personally kill him would drive away any other considerations.

Yiv barked a command. On the main display a hazy blue line appeared, connecting the images of the *Deathless* and Thrawn's freighter. Some numbers shifted, and the freighter began moving forward.

And it was time.

Thalias looked sideways, catching Che'ri's eye. "Hostages no more," she murmured. Turning back forward, watching the freighter moving toward the Nikardun warship, she reached her hands to her face and dug her fingers beneath the edges of her hostage makeup.

For a moment, the thick material resisted. Thalias kept at it, shifting her grip to use her fingernails as claws, noting out of the corner of her eye that Che'ri was doing likewise. Abruptly, the hard crust gave way, breaking and shredding into tiny pieces and leaving throbbing weals on the skin behind.

And with a brief rush of cool and moisture, the compressed tava mist that had been concealed inside the ridges and plateaus blasted into the air.

Thalias's first impulse was to hold her breath. But that didn't really do any good. The mist seeped instantly into her nostrils, the initial honey-scent quickly changing to something more like burnt sugar as the drug began to play with her senses. As the aroma changed again, this time to that of fresh leather, she could hear the sudden flurry of conversation around her growing slower, the pitch of the alien voices going deeper. The bridge itself began darkening even as, paradoxically, the indicator lights and the stars outside the viewport seemed to grow brighter.

And she could feel her mind fading.

It wasn't like the way it felt to fall asleep, with stray thoughts and memories drifting across as she slipped into darkness. This was quicker and more complete, dulling her reason and her self-awareness even as it clouded over her thoughts. And yet, through it all, she was able to hold on to enough to see that it was all working exactly the way Thrawn had said it would.

The bridge was big, and the amount of mist the techs had been able to pack inside the makeup was limited. But even a small amount of the sleepwalking drug was enough to cause confusion and disorientation, and that was all Thrawn needed. As the mist settled around the bridge crew, Thalias saw—both on the displays and through the viewport—that Thrawn's freighter was twisting around, breaking itself free of the tractor beam. A second later the freighter leapt forward, driving at full acceleration straight toward the *Deathless*'s bridge.

The Nikardun were hardly helpless, of course. Even as Thrawn sped toward them Yiv gave a slightly slurred order, and the Battle Dreadnought's spectrum lasers blasted outward toward this threat suddenly bearing down on them. Their aim was tentative, and many of the shots flashed harmlessly into space. However, the *Deathless*'s bridge defenses were strong and the Nikardun only slightly impaired, and many of the shots hit straight and true.

But a barrage that would have quickly demolished an electrostatic barrier and the unlucky ship behind it simply scattered off the Republic energy shield Thrawn and Che'ri had brought back from Mokivj. The freighter came closer . . . closer . . . the defensive laserfire intensified . . .

And then, at what seemed like the last second, the mad rush fal-tered as the freighter slowed slightly. An instant after that the whole Dreadnought shook as the freighter crashed squarely into the over-sized viewport, crushing the forward consoles and scattering those members of the crew from its path. Through Thalias's dreamy disori-entation she felt the sudden outflow of air through the shattered viewport, then felt the flow cut off as the customized freighter nose Thrawn had installed settled precisely into the opening, sealing off the bridge from the vacuum beyond.

Che'ri said something that sounded strangely urgent. Thalias looked over, discovering to her surprise that the girl was half stand-ing up and hanging on to Yiv's right arm, dragging down the weapon he had clutched in that hand. Yiv was trying to pull free, while at the same time cuffing Che'ri around the head and shoulders. A moment of thought convinced Thalias that he shouldn't be doing that, and she got her own arms wrapped around the arm he was hitting the girl with. She had a vague sense that there was something else she was supposed to do, but she couldn't remember what it was.

And then, suddenly, Thrawn was there, plucking Yiv's gun from his hand and wrapping a breather mask around Thalias's face. "Are you all right?" he asked, his voice distorted by his own mask.

"Um-mm," Thalias said brightly as Yiv made a sort of halfhearted lunge. Thrawn evaded the attack easily, sending the Nikardun to land heavily on all fours on the deck. Thrawn gave him a hefty squirt from a tava canister of his own, setting Yiv's shoulder symbionts into a frenzied wriggle, then turned to Che'ri. By the time he'd asked her the same question he'd asked Thalias and had the girl's breather mask in place, Thalias's head was starting to clear. "Data library?" Thrawn asked as he pulled Yiv's arms behind him and fastened the wrists together.

"I think it's that console over there," Thalias said, marveling at how quickly and thoroughly her mind had recovered from the gas. "He also keeps a kind of questis in a compartment in the left armrest of his chair."

"Excellent," Thrawn said. "You get his questis. I'll get Yiv aboard the freighter, then see what I can copy before the rest of the crew breaks through the bridge door."

"We're not going to destroy his ship?"

"I never intended to destroy his ship," Thrawn said. Reaching down, he took hold of one of Yiv's arms and levered the unconscious Nikardun up off the deck. "All I need to do is destroy *him*."

"What about them?" Thalias persisted, pointing to the Nikardun crew members twitching or muttering on the deck. "Once you pull the freighter out of the viewport, won't they all die?"

Thrawn's face hardened. "As Yiv has already said," he reminded her quietly. "No witnesses."

MEMORIES XIII

It was, Ar'alani knew, necessary that she and Thrawn have a talk about what had happened at Solitair. But she managed to find enough excuses to put it off until they were nearly home.

Finally, she couldn't delay it any further.

"I should have seen it," Thrawn said, his eyes fixed on an otherwise unremarkable corner of Ar'alani's office. "I should have seen the signs."

"No," Ar'alani said. "*I* should have. But not you."

"Because you're more experienced?"

"Because you don't understand politics," Ar'alani said. "Politics, vying for position, feuds, grudges, ledger balancing—they're all things you've never gotten a solid grip on."

"But why not?" Thrawn asked. "I don't disagree; but it's all strategy and tactics. Just a different form of warfare. Why can't I read it?"

"Because the techniques of warfare are relatively straightforward," Ar'alani said. "You identify the objective, you gather allies and resources, you devise a strategy, and you defeat the enemy. But in politics, allies and goals are constantly shifting. Unless you can anticipate those changes, you can't prepare for them."

"Alliances can shift in warfare, too."

"But it takes time to move ships and armies around and reconfigure battle lines," Ar'alani said. "You have that time to adapt to the new landscape. In politics, it's all done with words and bits of writing. Half an hour of conversation—less than that if there are bribes involved—and everything has changed."

"I see." Thrawn took a long breath. "Then I need to study this form of combat. Study it, and master it."

"That would be helpful," Ar'alani said.

Only he never would master it, she knew. Just as some were tone-deaf to music, Thrawn was tone-deaf to the nuances and intricate self-serving dances that made up the world of politics.

She could only hope that he and his overseers would be astute enough to keep him in the military arena. There, and only there, would he be of genuine and lasting value to the Ascendancy.

Thurfian had had to swallow a lot of bitter quaffs during his years of dealing with Ascendancy politics. But this quaff was absolutely the worst of all.

"A Trial-born," he said to the man facing him from the comm display. "After the fiasco with the Lioaoi and Garwians, you're making him a *Trial-born*?"

"We have no choice," Speaker Thistrian said heavily. "The Irizi are making serious overtures to him."

"They already tried that," Thurfian said. "He turned them down."

"Never officially," the Speaker said. "And that offer was just to make him a Trial-born. Now I understand they're preparing to offer him ranking distant."

Thurfian felt his eyes widen. "A *ranking distant*? That's absurd."

"Maybe so. Maybe not. And even Thrawn isn't blind enough to miss the political advantages that would give him. All we can do is hope that he'd prefer Trial-born of the Mitth to ranking distant of the Irizi."

"They're bluffing," Thurfian insisted. "They're trying to maneuver us into drawing him in and tying him closer to the family. The closer in he is, the bigger the political fall-out when he makes his next big mistake."

"Maybe he won't."

"Won't make a mistake?" Thurfian snorted. "You don't believe that any more than I do. The man's a menace. Give him enough lead time, and he'll burn himself down. And maybe the Mitth along with him."

"Or maybe he'll do something that raises the Ascendancy to heights it's never before achieved."

Thurfian stared at him. "You're joking, right? To heights it's never *achieved*?"

"It could happen," the Speaker said ruefully. "And if it does, we can't afford to risk that glory shining on the Irizi instead of us."

"With all due respect, Speaker, there won't *be* any glory," Thurfian said. "Certainly the Council isn't looking at all this with starry eyes. They've already demoted him back to mid commander."

"But they've also given him another ship," Thistrian said.

For the second time in less than a minute, Thurfian felt his eyes widen. "They've *what*?"

"A full-rank heavy cruiser this time, too, the *Springhawk*," the Speaker confirmed. "On top of that, there's talk of also giving him his own combat group, Picket Force Two."

Thurfian stared at the Speaker, a chill running through him. "Who's doing this?" he asked, his throat tight. "Someone's burning serious political capital here. Who?"

"I don't know," the Speaker said heavily. "On the fleet side, best guess is that it's General Ba'kif or possibly Admiral Ja'fosk. On the Mitth side—" He shook his head. "It has to be someone close to the Patriarch."

"Could it be the Patriarch himself?"

"I would hesitate to put that name to it," the Speaker said. "But I also wouldn't dismiss that thought out of hand. Certainly Thrawn's life and career have been charmed from the very beginning."

"It's still madness," Thurfian said. "His failures and embarrassments still outweigh his successes."

"I would tend to agree," the Speaker said. "But there's madness, and then there's madness. I looked into Picket Two's current assignment, and it turns out they're working a patrol zone a fair distance past the Ascendancy's east-zenith edge. That would put him far away from the center of Ascendancy politics."

Thurfian ran that over in his mind. Given Thrawn's political ineptness, that wouldn't be the worst assignment they could give him. "It's also on the far side of the Ascendancy from the Lioaoi and Garwians."

"Another plus, in my estimation," the Speaker said. "Mostly what's out there are small nations, single-system groups, empty space, and pirates."

"Great," Thurfian said sourly. "More pirates."

"But on that side of the Ascendancy, the only nations large enough to support a pirate group are the Paataatus," the Speaker pointed out. "That means less potential for political entanglements if he goes hunting. Besides, he's already demonstrated he can beat the frost out of the Paataatus if he needs to, and they know it."

"I suppose," Thurfian said. "The Council could still have sent him out there without giving him a ship."

"Perhaps," the Speaker said. "Still, the *Springhawk's* hardly a major prize. There's no glory to be had there, just the pressures and responsibilities of command. All things considered, it could have been worse."

"Really?" Thurfian countered. Commander of a cruiser and Trial-born of the Mitth. If it could have been worse, he could hardly see how.

But it wasn't over. Not nearly. If Thrawn rebuffed the Irizi again—and if Speaker Thistrian was right that that was a pretty foregone conclusion—it would put Aristocra Zistalmu even more solidly on Thurfian's side. Together, they would continue their efforts to derail Thrawn's career before he did something the Ascendancy might never recover from.

And while they were only two right now, Thurfian had no doubt that more Aristocra would join them in the days and years ahead. If there was one love they all shared, above and beyond all the family politics and squabbling, it was love of the Ascendancy.

"Look at the bright side, Thurfian," the Speaker said into his thoughts. "Whatever Thrawn does next, at least it'll be entertaining to watch."

"I'm sure it will," Thurfian said grimly. "I just hope we all live through it."

CHAPTER TWENTY-THREE

"They're not happy with you, you know," Thalias warned as she set the plate of warmed yapel triangles in front of Che'ri. It was dinnertime, which was supposed to mean a proper balanced meal, but Che'ri had wanted yapels and Thalias had decided that one meal of junk food wouldn't kill her. Heaven knew the girl had earned some indulgence. "I talked to Admiral Ar'alani before she went into the hearing. She said some of the Aristocra want to bring charges against you for putting a sky-walker at risk."

"I know," Thrawn said. "But that sentiment won't go anywhere. As I already told them, I sent you and Che'ri to Primea to return the Vak fighter and deliver a message, fully expecting that you would return to Csilla on the next available transport. It was Yiv's decision that put you at risk."

Thalias nodded. That was true enough, as far as it went.

But at this point it almost didn't matter. The Aristocra could be as furious as they wanted, but the outpouring of gratitude from the Vaks had pulled the momentum from the hope they could mete out any real punishment.

That, and the fact that Thrawn had delivered Yiv alive for interrogation. Thalias had no idea what the Council and Aristocra had learned from him and from the datafiles they'd pulled from the *Deathless*, but Yiv had struck Thalias as the sort who loved to put his own brilliance on display, even if the only person allowed to see and appreciate that brilliance was himself. She had no doubt that the records of his self-indulgence included his precise plans for the Ascendancy.

"At least you're getting better at politics," she said. "Between the Aristocra and the Vaks, you're learning how to play the game."

Thrawn shook his head. "Hardly. Ar'alani and General Ba'kif are handling the dealings with the Aristocra. As to the Vaks, that was never strictly about politics."

"I still don't understand that part," Che'ri said around a mouthful of food. "Everyone said they want to see all sides of things. But then they just took our side and attacked the Nikardun when we asked them to."

"Actually, the solution also came from the admiral," Thrawn said. "At the last moment, she saw something that I hadn't."

Thalias sat up a little straighter. "You missed something?"

"I miss many things," he said. "And I *did* have part of it, of course. The Vaks want to see all the various points of view—all the different thought lines—just as everyone says. But those thought lines aren't given equal weight."

Thalias thought back to the artwork she and Thrawn had seen in the Primea art gallery. "But you said their artwork showed the whole thought line thing," she objected.

"True," Thrawn said. "But if all lines were given equal weight, their art would be a scribble of confusion, with no direction or focus."

"So they decide which thought lines they like best?" Che'ri asked.

"Which ones they like, but more important which ones they trust. There's really nothing surprising about that. No matter what people might say, they always make value judgments of the information and opinions they receive. They couldn't function otherwise."

"I see," Che'ri said, brightening. "When you showed them that Yiv had stolen your message to them—that he lied—he stopped being someone they could trust."

"Exactly," Thrawn said. "Even worse from his point of view, as soon as that happened everything else he'd said became suspect."

"So all his promises and negotiations went straight out the vent," Thalias said.

"Correct," Thrawn said.

"So what was it Admiral Ar'alani saw?" Thalias asked.

"She'd been looking into Vak history, and saw something odd," Thrawn said. "For all the contempt their neighbors heaped on them over the years, on the grounds that they can't make a decision, all of those neighbors have been very careful in their confrontations to never kill a Vak in combat."

Thalias glanced at Che'ri, saw her own surprise reflected in the girl's face. "Really?"

"Really," Thrawn said. "Because they knew the same thing Ar'alani realized. The Vaks value everyone's thought lines . . . but when someone is killed, their thought lines are gone forever. That robs the whole of the Combine of information, and threatens the culture."

"So an attack on any individual is an attack on the whole society," Thalias said, nodding.

"Exactly," Thrawn said. "Whether or not Yiv realized that, the commander of the Battle Dreadnought who'd been tasked with destroying the *Springhawk* apparently didn't care about such subtleties. Ar'alani was able to lure him into firing on a pair of noncombatant Vak ships, killing their crews and awakening that cultural fury. At that point, all the rest of the thought lines suddenly faded away, with only one remaining."

"The one where they join together to protect their world and their people," Thalias murmured.

"And with the battle coordination plan I'd already given them, there was no fumbling or false starts. They and Ar'alani's warships quickly and efficiency joined forces against the Nikardun."

"And she got all that just from reading history?" Che'ri asked.

"That, and the way she looks at the universe," Thrawn said with an oddly sad smile. "Where I see non-Chiss as assets, she sees them as people."

Thalias looked over at Che'ri. A lot of people saw sky-walkers as just assets, too. "Makes her a good commander."

"Indeed it does," Thrawn said. "Certainly a better commander than I."

"Maybe, maybe not," Thalias said. "Different doesn't necessarily mean better or worse. Different just means *different*."

"It was your battle plan, right?" Che'ri put in. "She got them on our side, but it was both of you together who won the fight."

"Along with the warriors of her attack fleet," Thrawn said. "Her officers follow her with confidence, even eagerness. Mine follow me because they're good Chiss warriors."

"So change," Thalias suggested. "Learn how she does it."

"I'm not certain I can."

"I wasn't sure I could fly," Che'ri said. "You taught me how."

"And you've been teaching me how to observe and think," Thalias added. "As to confidence, if you think Che'ri and I put our heads into Yiv's trap just because we're good Chiss warriors, you really don't understand people. Or at least not us."

"And may it be a long time before either of you are forced into such trust again," Thrawn said. "The Ascendancy owes you greatly, Skywalker Che'ri and Thalias, Trial-born of the Mitth."

"You're *Trial-born*?" Che'ri said, smiling with delight. "Wow! That's great!"

"Thank you," Thalias said, blinking at Thrawn. "I didn't know they'd announced that yet."

"A blazing-star hero of the Mitth?" Thrawn smiled. "Trust me. If they could have announced you as a ranking distant, they would have. But that time will come."

"Maybe," Thalias said.

"Sure it will," Che'ri said. "We're heroes. Captain Thrawn just said so."

"You are indeed." Thrawn stood up. "And now I need to get back to the bluedock. The *Springhawk*'s going to need extensive repairs, and I'm told the foreman would like me there in person to hear his report."

"Thank you for coming by," Thalias said. "Che'ri and I wanted to hear how it had all ended, but no one had time to talk to us."

"You're welcome," Thrawn said. "I hope you'll be able to join us aboard the *Springhawk* again in the near future."

"If we have anything to say about it, we will," Thalias promised.

Though that assumed, of course, that she would be allowed to continue as Che'ri's caregiver. Right now, that was anything but certain.

"Then take care," he said. Nodding to each of them, he turned and walked through the hatchway.

Thalias watched him go, the Patriarch's words echoing through her mind. *And watch over your commander. I cannot help but feel that he holds the key to the Ascendancy's future, whether that future be triumph or ultimate destruction.*

"Thalias?"

Thalias turned back to see Che'ri frowning at a yapel she'd picked up. "Yes?"

Che'ri eyed the snack another moment, then set it back down on the plate. "I'm finished with these," she said. "Can I have some *real* food now?"

"You certainly may," Thalias said, smiling. "What exactly would you like?"

The trance abruptly ended, and with a start Qilori found himself wrenched from the Great Presence.

He blinked open his eyes. He was still on the bridge of his current ship, nestled into a configured navigator's seat.

But the lights and displays that should have shown position and status were blank. Somehow, the power to the flight and navigation systems had been shut down.

And as he pulled off his headset, he saw to his surprise that the bridge was deserted. "Hello?" he called tentatively.

No answer. "Hello?" he repeated, staring out the viewport as he fumbled for his straps. The ship was floating dead in space, squarely in the middle of nowhere, with no nearby stars or planets that he could see. What in the Depths had happened? "Is anyone there?"

"Greetings, Qilori of Uandualon," a cultured voice came from the bridge speaker. "Forgive the interruption in our journey, but I wished to speak to you in private."

"Of course," Qilori managed, his winglets fluttering harder than they had since Thrawn's grand confrontation with the Benevolent two months ago. "Yes. I—may I ask your name?"

"You may not," the voice said calmly. "Tell me about Yiv the Benevolent."

Qilori felt his winglets twitch. He'd thought—he'd hoped—all of that was finally past him. Clearly, it wasn't. "I . . . don't know what you mean."

"He disappeared," the voice said. "One rumor says he was killed in action. Another says he defected to the Chiss or someone else. Another says he deserted his forces and went to live in quiet luxury in the far reaches of the Chaos. What do *you* say?"

Qilori pressed his winglets against his cheeks, trying to get them to stop moving. Thrawn had warned that any word from him on the subject of Yiv's fate would end with Qilori being thrown out of the Pathfinders and the Pathfinders being thrown out of the Navigators' Guild. "I . . . don't . . ."

"Do you see where you are?" the voice interrupted. "We're between star systems, light-years from anywhere. If you were to step outside now, your body would float forever in the void, with no one ever knowing what became of you. Would you prefer that to answering my question?"

"No," Qilori whispered. "Yiv was . . . captured. He was taken by the Chiss. By Senior Captain Thrawn."

"And the Nikardun Destiny?"

Qilori waved a hand helplessly. "Yiv *was* the Nikardun Destiny," he said. "He was the undisputed leader. When he vanished . . . there was no one else who could take his place. No one who could continue the relationships he'd built with alien governments. The uncertainty over what had happened to him—that all by itself froze everyone's plans and thoughts. And when the Vaks started describing to everyone in the region how his ships had fired on them . . ." He shook his head. "It all just fell apart. Some of his chiefs are still talking about restarting their road of conquest, but no one believes it anymore. Even if they try, they'll just end up fighting among themselves."

"And Yiv's map to that road of conquest?"

Qilori sighed. "The Chiss got Yiv. They probably got the map and all the rest, too."

For a moment the voice was silent. "You had a bright future ahead of you. Do you wish that to resume?"

"I already told you the Nikardun are gone."

There was a small snort. "The Nikardun were fools. Heavy-handed, destructive fools. Useful in their way, but we always knew they would break like an ocean wave if they ever encountered too firm a sea stack."

"You were the Benevolent's master then?" Qilori asked.

An instant later he regretted his impulsiveness. It was clear he was here to answer questions, not ask them. The deep, cold emptiness of space . . .

"Do you assume, then, that there can be only one military mind that sees the Chiss as the prime obstacle to dominion over the Chaos?" the voice came. To Qilori's relief, there seemed to be more grim amusement than anger in the tone. "No, Qilori of Uandualon. Had we been guiding Yiv's efforts, instead of merely watching them, he would have been far more successful."

"Of course," Qilori said, ducking his head. "I apologize for any offense."

"None is taken. At any rate, the frontal attack has failed, as many of us predicted it would. Clearly, something more subtle will be necessary."

Qilori pricked up his ears. "You're going against the Chiss?"

"Do you disapprove?"

"Not at all," Qilori assured him. "They've taken my life from me. If your offer of a bright future includes revenge on the Chiss, you can count me in."

"Excellent."

Abruptly, the displays and controls came back to life. Qilori took a deep breath, watching as the self-checks cleared, watching as the location display calibrated itself. His earlier assessment had been correct: They were very much in the middle of nowhere.